BLACK SUNDAY

DO NOT BEGIN IT
UNLESS YOU ARE PREPARED TO FINISH IT
IN ONE SITTING!

"Super-suspense! Perfect compulsive page-turnability . . .
The first 50 pages or so make up the finest beginning to
a thriller I've ever read."

—Washington Post

"Breathtaking . . . the awful timeliness of the novel's
plot . . . technology that even Frederick Forsyth would
be proud of . . . all forces converge with an apocalyptic
bang . . . It's that kind of thriller."

—The New York Times

"Arabs, Israelis, a blimp and the Super Bowl—all stirred
into an explosive mixture. A very exciting thriller."

—John Godey, author of
The Taking of Pelham
One Two Three

BLACK SUNDAY

DO NOT BEGIN IT
UNLESS YOU ARE PREPARED TO FINISH IT
IN ONE SITTING!

BLACK SUNDAY

DO NOT BEGIN IT
UNLESS YOU ARE PREPARED TO FINISH IT
IN ONE SITTING!

"Could it really happen? This is the question you continually ask as you tiptoe through this thriller, often straining to keep from peeking ahead."
—Chicago Daily News

"Action-packed, crisp, fast-paced, timely . . . Quite simply a first-class plot told in a first-class fashion."
—Associated Press

"A spellbinder . . . The race to save the Super Bowl is hair-raising, one that will keep you rooted to the chair."
—Hartford Courant

"A thriller of genuine excitement."
—Boston Globe

COULD IT REALLY HAPPEN?

BLACK SUNDAY
IS THE BEST NEW THRILLER OF THE YEAR

PARAMOUNT PICTURES
presents

A ROBERT EVANS
Production

A JOHN FRANKENHEIMER
Film

Starring
ROBERT SHAW
BRUCE DERN
MARTHE KELLER

BLACK SUNDAY

Co-Starring
FRITZ WEAVER
and
BEKIM FEHMIU

Music Scored by
JOHN WILLIAMS

Director of Photography
JOHN A. ALONZO, A.S.C.

Executive Producer
ROBERT L. ROSEN

Based on the Novel by
THOMAS HARRIS

Screenplay by
**ERNEST LEHMAN
KENNETH ROSS**
and
IVAN MOFFAT

Produced by
ROBERT EVANS

Directed by
JOHN FRANKENHEIMER

Services by
Connaught Productions

In Color Panavision®
A PARAMOUNT PICTURE

BLACK SUNDAY

by THOMAS HARRIS

BANTAM BOOKS

TORONTO · NEW YORK · LONDON

To Mary Ellen

*This low-priced Bantam Book
has been completely reset in a type face
designed for easy reading, and was printed
from new plates. It contains the complete
text of the original hard-cover edition.*
NOT ONE WORD HAS BEEN OMITTED.

BLACK SUNDAY

*A Bantam Book / published by arrangement with
G. P. Putnam's Sons*

PRINTING HISTORY

Putnam edition / January 1975

2nd printing ...	January 1975	4th printing ...	February 1975
3rd printing ...	February 1975	5th printing	April 1975

Book-of-the-Month Club selection / March 1975

An excerpt appeared in the August 1975 issue of
COSMOPOLITAN

Bantam edition / March 1976

2nd printing	March 1976	4th printing	May 1976
3rd printing	April 1976	5th printing	May 1976
	6th printing	February 1977	

ISBN 0-553-10940-5

Published simultaneously in the United States and Canada

PRINTED IN THE UNITED STATES OF AMERICA

CHAPTER 1

NIGHT FELL as the airport taxi rattled along the six miles of coastal road into Beirut. From the back seat, Dahlia Iyad watched the Mediterranean surf fade from white to gray in the last light. She was thinking about the American. She would have to answer many questions about him.

The taxi turned onto the Rue Verdun and threaded its way into the heart of the city, the Sabra district, filled with many of the refugees from Palestine. The driver needed no instructions. He scanned his rear-view mirror closely, then turned off his lights and pulled into a small courtyard near the Rue Jeb el-Nakhel. The courtyard was pitch dark. Dahlia could hear distant traffic sounds and the ticking of the motor as it cooled. A minute passed.

The taxi rocked as the four doors were snatched open and a powerful flashlight blinded the driver. Dahlia could smell the oil on the pistol held an inch from her eye.

The man with the flashlight came to the rear door of the taxi, and the pistol was withdrawn.

"Djinniy," she said softly.

"Get out and follow me." He ran the Arabic words together in the accent of the Jabal.

A hard tribunal waited for Dahlia Iyad in the quiet room in Beirut. Hafez Najeer, head of Al Fatah's elite Jihaz al-Rasd (RASD) field intelligence unit, sat at a desk leaning his head back against the wall. He was a tall man with a small head. His subordinates secretly called him "The Praying Mantis." To hold his full attention was to feel sick and frightened.

Najeer was the commander of Black September. He did not believe in the concept of a "Middle East situation." The restoration of Palestine to the Arabs would not have elated him. He believed in holocaust, the fire that purifies. So did Dahlia Iyad.

And so did the other two men in the room: Abu Ali, who controlled the Black September assassination squads in Italy and France, and Muhammad Fasil, ordnance expert and architect of the attack on the Olympic Village at Munich. Both were members of RASD, the brains of Black September. Their position was not acknowledged by the larger Palestinian guerrilla movement, for Black September lives within Al Fatah as desire lives in the body.

It was these three men who decided that Black September would strike within the United States. More than fifty plans had been conceived and discarded. Meanwhile, U.S. munitions continued to pour onto the Israeli docks at Haifa.

Suddenly a solution had come, and now, if Najeer gave his final approval, the mission would be in the hands of this young woman.

She tossed her djellaba on a chair and faced them. "Good evening, Comrades."

"Welcome, Comrade Dahlia," Najeer said. He had not risen when she entered the room. Nor had the other two. Her appearance had changed during her year in the United States. She was chic in her pants suit and a little disarming.

"The American is ready," she said. "I am satisfied that he will go through with it. He lives for it."

"How stable is he?" Najeer seemed to be staring into her skull.

"Stable enough. I support him. He depends on me."

"I understand that from your reports, but code is clumsy. There are questions. Ali?"

Abu Ali looked at Dahlia carefully. She remembered him from his psychology lectures at the American University of Beirut.

"The American always appears rational?" he asked.

"Yes."

"But you believe him to be insane?"

"Sanity and apparent rationality are not the same, Comrade."

"Is his dependency on you increasing? Does he have periods of hostility toward you?"

"Sometimes he is hostile, but not as often now."

"Is he impotent?"

"He says he was impotent from the time of his release in North Vietnam until two months ago." Dahlia watched Ali. With his small, neat gestures and his moist eyes, he reminded her of a civet cat.

"Do you take credit for overcoming his impotence?"

"It is not a matter of credit, Comrade. It is a matter of control. My body is useful in maintaining that control. If a gun worked better, I would use a gun."

Najeer nodded approval. He knew she was telling the truth. Dahlia had helped train the three Japanese terrorists who struck at Lod Airport in Tel Aviv, slaying at random. Originally there had been four Japanese terrorists. One lost his nerve in training, and, with the other three watching, Dahlia blew his head off with a Schmeisser machine pistol.

"How can you be sure he will not have an attack of conscience and turn you in to the Americans?" Ali persisted.

"What would they get if he did?" Dahlia said. "I am a small catch. They would get the explosives, but the Americans have plenty of *plastique* already, as we have good reason to know." This was intended for Najeer, and she saw him look up at her sharply.

Israeli terrorists almost invariably used American C-4 plastic explosive. Najeer remembered carrying his brother's body out of a shattered apartment in Bhandoum, then going back inside to look for the legs.

"The American turned to us because he needed explosives. You know that, Comrade," Dahlia said. "He will continue to need me for other things. We do not offend his politics, because he has none. Neither does the term 'conscience' apply to him in the usual sense. He will not turn me in."

"Let's look at him again," Najeer said. "Comrade Dahlia, you have studied this man in one setting. Let me show him to you in quite different circumstances. Ali?"

Abu Ali set a 16-millimeter movie projector on the desk and switched out the lights. "We got this quite recently from a source in North Vietnam, Comrade Dahlia. It was shown once on American television, but that was before you were stationed in the House of War. I doubt that you have seen it."

The numbered film leader blurred on the wall and distorted sound came from the speaker. As the film picked up speed, the sound tightened into the anthem of the Democratic Republic of Vietnam, and the square of light on the wall became a whitewashed room. Seated on the floor were two dozen American prisoners of war. A cut to a lectern with a microphone clamped to it. A tall, gaunt man approached the lectern, walking slowly. He wore the baggy uniform of a POW, socks and thong sandals. One of his hands remained in the folds of his jacket, the other was placed flat on his thigh as he bowed to the officials at the front of the room. He turned to the microphone and spoke slowly.

"I am Michael J. Lander, Lieutenant Commander, U.S. Navy, captured February 10, 1967, while fire-bombing a civilian hospital near Ninh Binh . . . near Ninh Binh. Though the evidence of my war crimes is unmistakable, the Democratic Republic of Vietnam has not done to me punishment, but showed me the suffering which resulted from American war crimes

like those of my own and others . . . and others. I am
sorry for what I have done. I am sorry we killed
children. I call upon the American people to stop this
war. The Democratic Republic of Vietnam holds
no . . . holds no animosity toward the American people. It is the warmongers in power. I remain ashamed
of what I have done."

The camera panned over the other prisoners, sitting like an attentive class, their faces carefully blank.
The film ended with the anthem.

"Clumsy enough," said Ali, whose English was
almost flawless. "The hand must have been tied to his
side." He had watched Dahlia closely during the film.
Her eyes had widened for a second at the close-up of
the gaunt face. Otherwise she remained impassive.

"Firebombing a hospital," Ali mused. "He has
experience in this sort of thing, then."

"He was captured flying a rescue helicopter. He
was trying to retrieve the crew of a downed Phantom,"
Dahlia said. "You have seen my report."

"I have seen what he told you," Najeer said.

"He tells me the truth. He is beyond lying," she
said. "I have lived with him for two months. I know."

"It's a small point, anyway," Ali said. "There are
other things about him of much more interest."

During the next half-hour, Ali questioned her
about the most intimate details of the American's
behavior. When he had finished, it seemed to Dahlia
that there was a smell in the room. Real or imagined,
it took her back to the Palestinian refugee camp at
Tyre when she was eight years old, folding the wet
bedroll where her mother and the man who brought
food had groaned together in the dark.

Fasil took over the questioning. He had the blunt,
capable hands of a technician, and there were calluses
on the tips of his fingers. He sat forward in his chair,
his small satchel on the floor beside him.

"Has the American handled explosives?"

"Only packaged military ordnance. But he has
planned carefully and in minute detail. His plan appears
reasonable," Dahlia answered.

"It appears reasonable to *you*, Comrade. Perhaps because you are so intimately involved with it. We will see how reasonable it is."

She wished for the American then, wished these men could hear his slow voice as, step by step, he reduced his terrible project into a series of clearly defined problems, each with a solution.

She took a deep breath and began to talk about the technical problems involved in killing 80,000 people all at once, including the new President of the United States, with an entire nation watching.

"The limitation is weight," Dahlia said. "We are restricted to 600 kilos of *plastique*. Give me a cigarette please, and a pen and paper."

Bending over the desk, she drew a curve that resembled a cross section of a bowl. Inside it and slightly above, she drew another, smaller curve of the same parameter.

"This is the target," she said, indicating the larger curve. Her pen moved to the smaller curve. "The principle of the shaped charge, it—"

"Yes, yes," Fasil snapped. "Like a great Claymore mine. Simple. The density of the crowd?"

"Seated shoulder to shoulder, entirely exposed at this angle from the pelvis up. I need to know if the *plastique*—"

"Comrade Najeer will tell you what you need to know," Fasil said loftily.

Dahlia continued unfazed. "I need to know if the explosive Comrade Najeer may choose to give me is prepackaged antipersonnel *plastique* with steel balls, such as a Claymore contains. The weight requested is of *plastique* only. The containers and this type of shrapnel would not be of use."

"Why?"

"Weight, of course." She was tired of Fasil.

"And if you have no shrapnel? What then, Comrade? If you are counting on concussion, allow me to inform you—"

"Allow me to inform *you*, Comrade. I need your help and I will have it. I do not pretend to your expertise. We are not contending, you and I. Jealousy has no place in the Revolution."

"Tell her what she wants to know." Najeer's voice was hard.

Instantly Fasil said, "The *plastique* is not packaged with shrapnel. What will you use?"

"The outside of the shaped charge will be covered with layers of .177 caliber rifle darts. The American believes they will disperse over 150 degrees vertically through a horizontal arc of 260 degrees. It works out to an average of 3.5 projectiles per person in the kill zone."

Fasil's eyes widened. He had seen an American Claymore mine, no bigger than a schoolbook, blast a bloody path through a column of advancing troops and mow down the grass in a swath around them. What she proposed would be like a thousand Claymores going off at once.

"Detonation?"

"Electric blasting cap fired by a 12-volt system already in the craft. There is an identical backup system with separate battery. Also a fuse."

"That's all," the technician said. "I am finished."

Dahlia looked at him. He was smiling—whether from satisfaction or fear of Hafez Najeer, she could not tell. She wondered if Fasil knew the larger curve represented Tulane Stadium, where on January 12 the first 21 minutes of the Super Bowl game would be played.

Dahlia waited for an hour in a room down the hall. When she was summoned back to Najeer's office, she found the Black September commander alone. Now she would know.

The room was dark except for the area lit by a reading lamp. Najeer, leaning back against the wall, wore a hood of shadow. His hands were in the light and they toyed with a black commando knife. When he spoke, his voice was very soft.

"Do it, Dahlia. Kill as many as you can."

Abruptly he leaned into the light and smiled as

though relieved, his teeth bright in his dark face. He seemed almost jovial as he opened the technician's case and withdrew a small statue. It was a figure of the Madonna, like the ones in the windows of religious articles stores, the painting bright and hurriedly executed. "Examine it," he said.

She turned the figure in her hands. It weighed about a half-kilo and did not feel like plaster. A faint ridge ran around the sides of the figure as though it had been pressed in a mold rather than cast. Across the bottom were the words "Made in Taiwan."

"*Plastique*," Najeer said. "Similar to the American C-4 but made farther east. It has some advantages over C-4. It's more powerful for one thing, at some small cost to its stability, and it is very malleable when heated above 50 degrees centigrade.

"Twelve hundred of these will arrive in New York two weeks from tomorrow aboard the freighter *Leticia*. The manifest will show they were transshipped from Taiwan. The importer, Muzi, will claim them on the dock. Afterward you will make sure of his silence."

Najeer rose and stretched. "You have done well, Comrade Dahlia, and you have come a long way. You will rest now with me."

Najeer had a sparsely furnished apartment on an upper floor of 18 Rue Verdun, similar to the quarters Fasil and Ali had on other floors of the building.

Dahlia sat on the side of Najeer's bed with a small tape recorder in her lap. He had ordered her to make a tape for use on Radio Beirut after the strike was made. She was naked, and Najeer, watching her from the couch, saw her become visibly aroused as she talked into the microphone.

"Citizens of America," she said, "today the Palestinian freedom fighters have struck a great blow in the heart of your country. This horror was visited upon you by the merchants of death in your own land, who supply the butchers of Israel. Your leaders have been deaf to the cries of the homeless. Your leaders have ignored the ravages by the Jews in Palestine and have committed their own crimes in Southeast Asia. Guns, warplanes, and hundreds of millions of dollars have flowed from your country to the hands of warmongers while millions of your own people starve. The people will not be denied.

"Hear this, people of America. We want to be your brothers. It is you who must overthrow the filth that rules you. Henceforth, for every Arab that dies by an Israeli hand, an American will die by Arab hands. Every Moslem holy place, every Christian holy place destroyed by Jewish gangsters will be avenged with the destruction of a property in America."

Dahlia's face was flushed and her nipples were erect as she continued. "We hope this cruelty will go no further. The choice is yours. We hope never to begin another year with bloodshed and suffering. Salaam aleikum."

Najeer was standing before her, and she reached for him as his bathrobe fell to the floor.

Two miles from the room where Dahlia and Najeer were locked together in the tangled sheets, a small Israeli missile launch sliced quietly up the Mediterranean.

The launch hove to 1,000 meters south of the Grotte aux Pigeons, and a raft was slipped over the side. Twelve armed men climbed down into it. They wore business suits and neckties tailored by Russians, Arabs, and Frenchmen. All wore crepe-soled shoes and none carried any identification. Their faces were hard. It was not their first visit to Lebanon.

The water was smoky gray under the quarter moon, and the sea was riffled by a warm off-shore breeze. Eight of the men paddled, stretching to make the longest strokes possible as they covered the 400 meters to the sandy beach of the Rue Verdun. It was 4:11 A.M., 23 minutes before sunrise and 17 minutes before the first blue glaze of day would spread over the city. Silently they pulled the raft up on the sand, covered it with a sand-colored canvas, and walked quickly up the beach to the Rue Ramlet el-Baida, where four men and four cars awaited them, sil-houetted against the glow from the tourist hotels to the north.

They were only a few yards from the cars when a brown-and-white Land Rover braked loudly 30 yards up the Rue Ramlet, its headlights on the little convoy. Two men in tan uniforms leaped from the truck, their guns leveled.

"Stand still. Identify yourselves."

There was a sound like popping corn, and dust flew from the Lebanese officers' uniforms as they collapsed in the road, riddled by 9-mm bullets from the raiders' silenced Parabellums.

A third officer, at the wheel of the truck, tried to drive away. A bullet shattered the windshield and his forehead. The truck careened into a palm tree at the roadside, and the policeman was thrown forward onto the horn. Two men ran to the truck and pulled the dead man off the horn, but lights were going on in some of the beachfront apartments.

A window opened, and there was an angry shout in Arabic. "What is that hellish racket? Someone call the police."

The leader of the raid, standing by the truck, shouted back in hoarse and drunken Arabic, "Where is Fatima? We'll leave if she doesn't get down here soon."

"You drunken bastards get away from here or I'll call the police myself."

"Aleikum salaam, neighbor. I'm going," the drunken voice from the street replied. The light in the apartment went out.

In less than two minutes the sea closed over the truck and the bodies it contained.

Two of the cars went south on the Rue Ramlet, while the other two turned onto the Corniche Ras Beyrouth for two blocks, then turned north again on the Rue Verdun. . . .

Number 18 Rue Verdun was guarded round the clock. One sentry was stationed in the foyer, and another armed with a machine gun watched from the roof of the building across the street. Now the rooftop sentry lay in a curious attitude behind his gun, his throat smiling wetly in the moonlight. The sentry from the foyer lay outside the door where he had gone to investigate a drunken lullaby.

Najeer had fallen asleep when Dahlia gently pulled free from him and walked into the bathroom. She stood under the shower for a long time, enjoying the stinging spray. Najeer was not an exceptional lover. She smiled as she soaped herself. She was thinking about the American, and she did not hear the footsteps in the hall.

Najeer half-started from the bed as the door to his apartment smashed open and a flashlight blinded him.

"Comrade Najeer!" the man said urgently.

"Aiwa."

The machine gun flickered, and blood exploded from Najeer as the bullets slammed him back into the wall. The killer swept everything from the top of Najeer's desk into a bag as an explosion in another part of the building shook the room.

The naked girl in the bathroom doorway seemed frozen in horror. The killer pointed his machine gun at her wet breast. His finger tightened on the trigger. It was a beautiful breast. The muzzle of the machine gun wavered.

"Put on some clothes, you Arab slut," he said, and backed out of the room.

The explosion two floors below, which tore out the wall of Abu Ali's apartment, killed Ali and his wife instantly. The raiders, coughing in the dust, had started for the stairs, when a thin man in pajamas came out of the apartment at the end of the hall, trying to cock a submachine gun. He was still trying when a hail of bullets tore through him, blowing shreds of his pajamas into his flesh and across the hall.

The raiders scrambled to the street and their cars were roaring southward toward the sea as the first police sirens sounded.

Dahlia, wearing Najeer's bathrobe and clutching

her purse, was on the street in seconds, mingling with the crowd that had poured out of the buildings on the block. She was trying desperately to think, when she felt a hard hand grip her arm. It was Muhammad Fasil. A bullet had cut a bloody stripe across his cheek. He wrapped his tie around his hand and held it to the wound.

"Najeer?" he asked.

"Dead."

"Ali, too, I think. His window blew out just as I turned the corner. I shot at them from the car, but— listen to me carefully. Najeer has given the order. Your mission must be completed. The explosives are not affected, they will arrive on schedule. Automatic weapons also—your Schmeisser and an AK-47, packed separately with bicycle parts."

Dahlia looked at him with smoke-reddened eyes. "They will pay," she said. "They will pay 10,000 to one."

Fasil took her to a safe house in the Sabra to wait through the day. After dark he took her to the airport in his rattletrap Citroën. Her borrowed dress was two sizes too large, but she was too tired to care.

At 10:30 P.M., the Pan Am 707 roared out over the Mediterranean, and, before the Arabian lights faded off the starboard wing, Dahlia fell into an exhausted sleep.

CHAPTER 2

AT THAT MOMENT, Michael Lander was doing the only thing he loved. He was flying the Aldrich blimp, hovering 800 feet above the Orange Bowl in Miami, providing a steady platform for the television crew in the gondola behind him. Below, in the packed stadium, the world-champion Miami Dolphins were pounding the Pittsburgh Steelers.

The roar of the crowd nearly drowned out the crackling radio above Lander's head. On hot days above a stadium, he felt that he could smell the crowd, and the blimp seemed suspended on a powerful rising current of mindless screaming and body heat. That current felt dirty to Lander. He preferred the trips between the towns. The blimp was clean and quiet then.

Only occasionally did Lander glance down at the field. He watched the rim of the stadium and the line-of-sight he had established between the top of a flag-pole and the horizon to maintain exactly 800 feet of altitude.

Lander was an exceptional pilot in a difficult field. A dirigible is not easy to fly. Its almost neutral buoyancy and vast surface leave it at the mercy of the wind unless it is skillfully handled. Lander had a sailor's instinct for the wind, and he had the gift the best dirigible pilots have—anticipation. A dirigible's movements are cyclical, and Lander stayed two moves ahead, holding the great gray whale into the breeze as a fish points upstream, burrowing the nose slightly into the gusts and raising it in lulls, shading half the end zone with its shadow. During intervals in the action on the field, many of the spectators looked up at it and some of them waved. Such bulk, such great length suspended in the clear air fascinated them.

Lander had an autopilot in his head. While it dictated the constant, minute adjustments that held the blimp steady, he thought about Dahlia. The patch of down in the small of her back and how it felt beneath his hand. The sharpness of her teeth. The taste of honey and salt.

He looked at his watch. Dahlia should be an hour out of Beirut now, coming back.

Lander could think comfortably about two things: Dahlia and flying.

His scarred left hand gently pushed forward the throttle and propeller pitch controls, and he rolled back the big elevator wheel beside his seat. The great airship rose quickly as Lander spoke into the microphone.

"Nora One Zero, clearing stadium for a 1,200-foot go-around."

"Roger, Nora One Zero," the Miami tower replied cheerily.

Air controllers and tower radio operators always liked to talk to the blimp, and many had a joke ready when they knew it was coming. People felt friendly toward it as they do toward a panda. For millions of Americans who saw it at sporting events and fairs, the blimp was an enormous, amiable, and slow-moving friend in the sky. Blimp metaphors are almost invariably "elephant" or "whale." No one ever says "bomb."

At last the game was over and the blimp's 225-foot shadow flicked over the miles of cars streaming away from the stadium. The television cameraman and his assistant had secured their equipment and were eating sandwiches. Lander had worked with them often.

The lowering sun laid a streak of red-gold fire across Biscayne Bay as the blimp hung over the water. Then Lander turned northward and cruised 50 yards off Miami Beach, while the TV crew and the flight engineer fixed their binoculars on the girls in their bikinis. Some of the bathers waved.

"Hey, Mike, does Aldrich make rubbers?" Pearson the cameraman was yelling around a mouthful of sandwich.

"Yeah," Lander said over his shoulder. "Rubbers, tires, de-icers, windshield wiper blades, bathtub toys, children's balloons, and body bags."

"You get free rubbers with this job?"

"You bet. I've got one on now."

"What's a body bag?"

"It's a big rubber bag. One size fits all," Lander said. "They're dark inside. Uncle Sam uses them for rubbers. You see some of them, you know he's been fooling around." It would not be hard to push the button on Pearson; it would not be hard to push the button on any of them.

The blimp did not fly often in the winter. Its winter quarters were near Miami, the great hangar dwarfing the rest of the buildings beside the airfield. Each spring it worked northward at 35 to 60 knots, depending on the wind, dropping in at state fairs and baseball games. The Aldrich company provided Lander with an apartment near the Miami airfield in winter, but on this day, as soon as the great airship was secured, he caught the National flight to Newark and went to his home near the blimp's northern base at Lakehurst, New Jersey.

When Lander's wife deserted him, she left him the house. Tonight the lights burned late in the garage-workshop, as Lander worked and waited for Dahlia. He was stirring a can of epoxy resin on his workbench, its strong odor filling the garage. On the floor behind him was a curious object 18 feet long. It was a plug mold that Lander had made from the hull of a small sailboat. He had inverted the hull and split it along the keel. The halves were 18 inches apart and were joined by a broad common bow. Viewed from above, the mold looked like a great streamlined horseshoe. Building the mold had taken weeks of off-duty time. Now it was slick with grease and ready.

Lander, whistling quietly, applied layers of fiberglass cloth and resin to the mold, feathering the edges precisely. When the fiberglass shell cured and he popped it off the mold, he would have a light, sleek nacelle that would fit neatly under the gondola of the Aldrich blimp. The opening in the center would accommodate the blimp's single landing wheel and its transponder antenna. The load-bearing frame that would be enclosed by the nacelle was hanging from a nail on the garage wall. It was very light and very strong, with twin keels of Reynolds 5130 chromemoly tubing and ribs of the same material.

Lander had converted the double garage into a workshop while he was married, and he had built much of his furniture there in the years before he went to Vietnam. The things his wife had not wanted to take were still stored above the rafters—a highchair, a folding camp table, wicker yard furniture. The fluorescent light was harsh, and Lander wore a baseball cap as he worked around the mold, whistling softly.

He paused once, thinking, thinking. Then he went on smoothing the surface, raising his feet carefully as he walked to avoid tearing the newspapers spread on the floor.

Shortly after 4 A.M. the telephone rang. Lander picked up the garage extension.

"Michael?" The British clip in her speech always surprised him, and he imagined the telephone buried in her dark hair.

"Who else?"

"Grandma is fine. I'm at the airport and I'll be along later. Don't wait up."

"What—"

"Michael, I can't wait to see you." The line went dead.

It was almost sunrise when Dahlia turned into the

driveway at Lander's house. The windows were dark. She was apprehensive, but not so much as before their first meeting—then she had felt that she was in the room with a snake she could not see. After she came to live with him, she separated the deadly part of Michael Lander from the rest of him. When she was with him now, she felt that they were both in a room with the snake, and she could tell where it was, and whether it was sleeping.

She made more noise than necessary coming into the house and sang his name softly against the stillness as she came up the stairs. She did not want to startle him. The bedroom was pitch dark.

From the doorway she could see the glow of his cigarette, like a tiny red eye.

"Hello," she said.

"Come here."

She walked through the darkness toward the glow. Her foot touched the shotgun, safely on the floor beside the bed. It was all right. The snake was asleep.

Lander was dreaming about the whales, and he was reluctant to come out of sleep. In his dream the great shadow of the Navy dirigible moved over the ice below him as he flew through the endless day. It was 1956 and he was going over the Pole.

The whales were basking in the Arctic sun, and they did not see the dirigible until it was almost over them. Then they sounded, their flukes rising under a chandelier of spray as they slid beneath a blue ice ledge under the Arctic Sea. Looking down from the gondola, Lander still could see the whales suspended there beneath the ledge. In a cool blue place where there was no noise.

Then he was over the Pole and the magnetic compass was going wild. Solar activity interfered with the omni, and, with Fletcher at the elevator wheel, he steered by the sun as the flag on its weighted spear fluttered down to the ice.

"The compass," he said, walking in his house. "The compass."

"The omni beam from Spitsbergen, Michael," Dahlia said, her hand on his cheek. "I have your breakfast."

She knew the dream. She hoped he would dream often of the whales. He was easier then.

Lander was facing a hard day, and she could not be with him. She opened the curtains and sunlight brightened the room.

"I wish you didn't have to go."

"I'll tell you again," Lander said. "If you have a pilot's ticket they watch you really close. If I don't check in, they'll send some VA caseworker out here with a questionnaire. He's got a form. It goes like this—'A. Note the condition of the grounds. B. Does the subject seem dejected?' Like that. It goes on forever."

"You can manage that."

"One call to the FAA, one little half-assed hint that I might be shaky and that's it. They'll ground me. What if a caseworker looks in the garage?" He drank his orange juice. "Besides, I want to see the clerks one more time."

Dahlia was standing by the window, the sun warm on her cheek and neck. "How do you feel?"

"You mean am I crazy today? No, as a matter of fact I'm not."

"I didn't mean that."

"Shit you didn't. I'll just go into a little office with one of them and we'll close the door and he'll tell me the new things the government is going to do for me." Something lunged behind Lander's eyes.

"All right, are you crazy today? Are you going to spoil it? Are you going to grab a VA clerk and kill him and let the others hold you down? Then you can sit in a cell and sing and masturbate. 'God Bless America and Nixon.' "

She had used two triggers at once. She had tried them separately before, and now she watched to see how they worked together.

Lander's memory was intense. Recollections while awake could make him wince. Asleep, they sometimes made him scream.

Masturbation: The North Vietnamese guard catching him at it in his cell and making him do it in front of the others.

"God Bless America and Nixon": The hand-lettered sign the Air Force officer held up to the window of the C-141 at Clark Air Force Base in the Philippines when the prisoners were coming home. Lander, sitting across the aisle, had read it backwards with the sun shining through the paper.

Now his eyes were hooded as he looked at Dahlia. His mouth opened slightly and his face was slack. This was the dangerous time. It hung in slow seconds while the motes swarmed in the sunlight, swarmed around Dahlia and the short, ugly shotgun by the bed.

"You don't have to get them one at a time, Michael," she said softly. "And you don't have to do the other for yourself. I want to do it for you. I love to do it."

She was telling the truth. Lander could always tell. His eyes opened wide again, and in a moment he could no longer hear his heart.

Windowless corridors. Michael Lander walking through the dead air of the government office building, down the long floors where the buffer had swung from side to side in shining arcs. Guards in the blue uniform of the General Services Administration checking packages. Lander had no packages.

The receptionist was reading a novel entitled *A Nurse to Marry.*

"My name is Michael Lander."

"Did you take a number?"

"No."

"Take a number," the receptionist said.

He picked up a numbered disc from a tray at the side of the desk.

"What is your number?"

"Thirty-six."

"What is your name?"

"Michael Lander."

"Disability?"

"No. I'm supposed to check in today." He handed her the letter from the Veterans Administration.

"Take a seat, please." She turned to the microphone beside her. "Seventeen."

Seventeen, a seedy young man in a vinyl jacket, brushed past Lander and disappeared into the warren behind the secretary.

About half the fifty seats in the waiting room were filled. Most of the men were young, former Spec 4's, who looked as slovenly in civilian clothes as they had in uniform. Lander could imagine them playing the pinball machine in a bus terminal in their wrinkled Class A's.

In front of Lander sat a man with a shiny scar above his temple. He had tried to comb his hair over it. At two-minute intervals he took a handkerchief from his pocket and blew his nose. He had a handkerchief in every pocket.

The man beside Lander sat very still, his hands gripping his thighs. Only his eyes moved. They never rested, tracking each person who walked through the room. Often he had to strain to turn his eyes far enough, because he would not turn his head.

In a small office in the maze behind the receptionist, Harold Pugh was waiting for Lander. Pugh was a GS-12 and rising. He thought of his assignment to the special POW section as "a feather in my cap."

A considerable amount of literature came with Pugh's new job. Among the reams of advisories was one from the Air Force surgeon general's national consultant on psychiatry. The advisory said, "It is not possible for a man exposed to severe degrees of abuse, isolation, and deprivation not to develop depression born out of extreme rage repressed over a long period of time. It is simply a question of when and how the depressive reaction will surface and manifest itself."

Pugh meant to read the advisories as soon as he could find the time. The military record on Pugh's desk was impressive. Waiting for Lander, he glanced through it again.

Lander, Michael J. 0214278603. Korea 1951, Naval OCS. Very high marks. Lighter-than-air training at Lakehurst, N.J., 1954. Exceptional rating. Commendation for research in aircraft icing. Navy polar expedition 1956. Shifted to Administration when the Navy phased out its blimp program in 1964. Volunteered for helicopters 1964. Vietnam. Two tours. Shot down near Dong Hoi February 10, 1967. Six years a prisoner of war.

Pugh thought it peculiar that an officer with Lander's record should resign his commission. Something was not quite right there. Pugh remembered the closed hearings after the POW's came home. Perhaps it would be better not to ask Lander why he resigned.

He looked at his watch. Three-forty. Fellow was late. He pushed a button on his desk telephone and the receptionist answered.

"Is Mr. Lander here yet?"

"Who, Mr. Pugh?"

Pugh wondered if she was making a deliberate rhyme with name. "Lander. Lander. He's one of the specials. Your instructions are to send him right in when he comes."

"Yes, Mr. Pugh. I will."

The receptionist returned to her novel. At 3:50, needing a bookmark, she picked up Lander's letter. The name caught her eye.

"Thirty-six. Thirty-six." She rang Pugh's office. "Mr. Lander is here now."

Pugh was mildly surprised at Lander's appearance. Lander was sharp in his civilian flight captain's uniform. He moved briskly and his gaze was direct. Pugh had pictured himself dealing with hollow-eyed men.

Pugh's appearance did not surprise Lander. He had hated clerks all his life.

"You're looking well, Captain. You've bounced back nicely, I'd say."

"Nicely."

"Good to be back with the family, I'm sure."

Lander smiled. His eyes were not involved in the smile. "The family is fine, I understand."

"They're not with you? I believe you're married, it says here, let's see, yes. Two children?"

"Yes, I have two children. I'm divorced."

"I'm sorry. My predecessor on your case, Gorman, left very few notes, I'm afraid." Gorman had been promoted for incompetence.

Lander was watching Pugh steadily, a faint smile on his lips.

"When were you divorced, Captain Lander? I have to bring this up-to-date." Pugh was like a domestic cow grazing placidly near the edge of the swamp, not sensing what was downwind in the black shade watching him.

Suddenly Lander was talking about the things he could never think about. Never think about.

"The first time she filed was two months before my release. While the Paris talks were stalled on the point of elections, I believe. But she didn't go through with it then. She moved out a year after I got back. Please don't feel badly, Pugh, the government did everything it could."

"I'm sure, but it must—"

"A naval officer came around several times after I was captured and had tea with Margaret and counseled her. There is a standard procedure for preparing POW wives, as I'm sure you know."

"I suppose that sometimes—"

"He explained to her that there is an increased incidence of homosexuality and impotence among released POW's. So she would know what to expect, you understand." Lander wanted to stop. He must stop.

"It's better to let—"

"He told her that the life expectancy of a released POW is about half the average." Lander was wearing a wide smile now.

"Surely, Captain, there must have been some other factors."

"Oh sure, she was already getting some dick on the side, if that's what you mean." Lander laughed, the old spike through him, the pressure building behind his eyes. *You don't have to get them one at a time, Michael. Sit in a cell and sing and masturbate.*

Lander closed his eyes so that he could not see the pulse in Pugh's throat.

Pugh's reflex was to laugh with Lander, to ingratiate himself. But he was offended in a Baptist sort of way by glib, cheap references to sex. He stopped the laugh in time. That action saved his life.

Pugh picked up the file again. "Did you receive counseling about it?"

Lander was easier now. "Oh yes. A psychiatrist at St. Alban's Naval Hospital discussed it with me. He was drinking a Yoo-Hoo."

"If you feel the need of further counseling I can arrange it."

Lander winked. "Look, Mr. Pugh. You're a man of the world and so am I. These things happen. What I want to see you about is some compensation for the old flipper here." He held up his disfigured hand.

Now Pugh was on familiar ground. He pulled Lander's Form 214 from the file. "Since you obviously are not disabled, we'll have to find a way, but"—he winked at Lander—"we'll take care of you."

It was 4:30 P.M. and the evening rush had begun when Lander came out of the Veterans Administration building into the soiled Manhattan afternoon. The sweat was cold on his back as he stood on the steps and watched the garment district crowds funnel toward the 23rd Street subway station. He could not go in there with them and be jammed in the train.

Many of the VA personnel were taking an early slide from their jobs. A stream of them fanned the doors of the building and jostled him back against the wall. He wanted to fight. Margaret came over him in a rush, and he could smell her and feel her. Talking

about it over a plywood desk. He had to think about
something. The teapot whistle. Not that, for God's
sake. Now he had a cold ache in his colon and he
reached for a Lomotil tablet. Too late for Lomotil.
He would have to find a restroom. Quick. Now he
walked back to the waiting room, the dead air like
cobwebs on his face. He was pale and sweat stood
out on his forehead as he entered the small restroom.
The single stall was occupied and another man was
waiting outside it. Lander turned and walked back
through the waiting room. Spastic colon, his medical
profile said. No medication prescribed. He had found
Lomotil for himself.

Why didn't I take some before?

The man with the moving eyes tracked Lander as
far as he could without turning his head. The pain in
Lander's bowels was coming in waves now, making
goosebumps on his arms, and he was gagging.

The fat janitor fumbled through his keys and let
Lander into the employee's washroom. Waiting outside, the janitor could not hear the unpleasant sounds.
At last, Lander turned his face up to the Celotex ceiling. Retching had made his eyes water and the tears
ran down his face.

*For a second he was squatting beside the path
with the guards watching on the forced march to
Hanoi.*

It was the same, the same. The teapot whistle
came.

"Cocksuckers," Lander croaked. "Cocksuckers."
He wiped his face with his ugly hand.

Dahlia, who had had a busy day with Lander's
credit cards, was on the platform when he got off the
commuter train. She saw him ease down off the step
and knew he was trying not to joggle his insides.

She filled a paper cup with water from the foun-
tain and took a small bottle from her purse. The water
turned milky as she poured in the paregoric.

He did not see her until she was beside him, offer-
ing the cup.

It tasted like bitter licorice and left a faint numbness in his lips and tongue. Before they reached the car, the opium was soothing the ache and in five minutes it was gone. When they reached the house, he fell into bed and slept for three hours.

Lander woke confused and unnaturally alert. His defenses were working, and his mind recoiled from painful images with the speed of a pinball. His thoughts rolled over the safe, painted images between the buzzers and the bells. He had not blown it today, he could rest on that.

The teapot—his neck tightened. He seemed to itch somewhere between his shoulders and his cortex in a place he could not reach. His feet would not keep still.

The house was completely dark, its ghosts just beyond the firelight of his will. Then, from the bed, he saw a flickering light coming up the stairs. Dahlia was carrying a candle, her shadow huge on the wall. She wore a dark floor-length robe that covered her completely and her bare feet made no sound. Now she was standing by him, the candlelight a pinpoint in her great, dark eyes. She held out her hand.

"Come, Michael. Come with me."

Slowly backing down the dark hall, she led him, looking into his face. Her black hair down over her shoulders. Backing, feet peeping white from under the hem. Back to what had been the playroom, empty these seven months. Now in the candlelight Lander could see that a huge bed waited at the end of the room and heavy drapes covered the walls. Incense touched his face and the small blue flame of a spirit lamp flickered on a table near the bed. It was no longer the room where Margaret had—no, no, no.

Dahlia put her candle beside the lamp and with a feather touch removed Lander's pajama top. She undid the drawstring and knelt to slip the trousers off his feet, her hair brushing against his thigh. "You were so strong today." She gently pressed him back upon the bed. The silk beneath him was cool and the air was a cool ache upon his genitals.

He lay watching her as she lit two tapers in holders on the walls. She passed him the slender hash pipe and stood at the foot of the bed, the candle shadows moving behind her.

Lander felt that he was falling into those bottomless eyes. He remembered as a child lying in the grass on clear summer nights, looking into heavens suddenly dimensional and deep. Looking up until there was no up and he was falling out into the stars.

Dahlia dropped her robe and stood before him.

The sight of her pierced him as it had the first time, and his breath caught in his throat. Dahlia's breasts were large, and their curves were not the curves of a vessel but of a dome, and she had a cleavage even when they were unconfined. Her nipples darkened as they came erect. She was opulent, but not forbidden, her curves and hollows lapped by candlelight.

Lander felt a sweet shock as she turned to take the vessel of sweet oil from above the spirit lamp and the light played over her. Kneeling astride him, she rubbed the warm oil on his chest and belly, her breasts swaying slightly as she worked.

As she leaned forward, her belly rounded slightly and receded again into the dark triangle.

It grew thick and soft and springy up her belly, a black explosion radiating tufts as though it tried to climb. He felt it touch his navel and, looking down, he saw suspended in the whorls like pearls in the candlelight, the first drops of her essence.

It would bathe him he knew, and be warm on his scrotum and it would taste like bananas and salt.

Dahlia took a mouthful of the warm, sweet oil and held him in it, nodding gently, deeply to the rhythm of his blood, her hair spilling warm over him.

And all the while her eyes, wide-set as a puma's and full of the moon, never left his face.

CHAPTER 3

A SOUND LIKE a slow roll of thunder shivered the air in the bedroom and the candle flames quivered, but Dahlia and Lander, fixed in each other, did not notice it. It was a common sound—the late jet shuttle from New York to Washington. The Boeing 727 was 6,000 feet above Lakehurst and climbing.

Tonight it carried the hunter. He was a broad-shouldered man in a tan suit, and he was seated on the aisle just behind the wing. The stewardess was collecting fares. He handed her a new $50 bill. She frowned at it. "Don't you have anything smaller?"

"For two fares," he said, indicating the big man asleep beside him. "For his and mine." He had an accent the stewardess could not place. She decided he was German or Dutch. She was wrong.

He was Major David Kabakov of the Mossad Aliyah Beth, the Israeli Secret Service, and he was hoping the three men seated across the aisle behind him had smaller bills with which to pay their fare. Otherwise the stewardess might remember them. He should have tended to it in Tel Aviv, he thought. The connection at Kennedy Airport had been too close to permit getting change. It was a small error, but it annoyed him. Major Kabakov had lived to be thirty-seven because he did not make many errors.

Beside him, Sgt. Robert Moshevsky was snoring softly, his head back. On the long flight from Tel Aviv, neither Kabakov nor Moshevsky had given any sign of recognition to the three men behind them, though they had known them for years. The three were burly men with weathered faces, and they wore quiet, baggy suits. They were what the Mossad called a "tactical incursion team." In America they would be called a hit squad.

In the three days since he had killed Hafez Najeer in Beirut, Kabakov had had very little sleep, and he knew that he must give a detailed briefing as soon as he reached the American capital. The Mossad, analyzing the material he brought back from the raid on the Black September leadership, acted instantly when the tape recording was played. There was a hurried conference at the American embassy and Kabakov was dispatched.

It had been clearly understood at the Tel Aviv meeting between American and Israeli intelligence that Kabakov was being sent to the United States to help the Americans determine if a real threat existed and to help identify the terrorists if they could be located. His official orders were clear.

But the high command of the Mossad had given him an additional directive that was flat and unequivocal. He was to stop the Arabs by whatever means necessary.

Negotiations for the sale of additional Phantom and Skyhawk jets to Israel were at a critical stage, and Arab pressure against the sale was intensified by the Western shortage of oil. Israel must have the airplanes. On the first day that no Phantoms flashed over the desert, the Arab tanks would roll.

A major atrocity within the United States would tip the balance of power in favor of the American isolationists. For the Americans, helping Israel must not have too high a price.

Neither the Israeli nor the American state depart-

ments knew about the three men sitting behind Kabakov. They would settle into an apartment near
National Airport and wait for him to call. Kabakov
hoped the call would not be necessary. He would
prefer to handle it himself, quietly.

Kabakov hoped the diplomats would not meddle
with him. He distrusted both diplomats and politicians.
His attitude and approach were reflected in his Slavic
features—blunt but intelligent.

Kabakov believed that careless Jews die young
and weak ones wind up behind barbed wire. He had
been a child of war, fleeing Latvia with his family
just ahead of the German invasion and later fleeing
the Russians. His father died in Treblinka. His mother
took Kabakov and his sister to Italy in a journey that
killed her. As she struggled toward Trieste, there was
a fire inside her that gave her strength while it con-
sumed her flesh.

When Kabakov remembered, across thirty years,
the road to Trieste, he saw it with his mother's arm
swinging diagonally across his vision as she walked
ahead, holding his hand, her elbow, knobby in the thin
arm, showing through her rags. And he remembered
her face, almost incandescent as she woke the children
before the first light reached the ditch where they
were sleeping.

In Trieste she turned the children over to the
Zionist underground and died in a doorway across the
street.

David Kabakov and his sister reached Palestine in
1946 and they stopped running. By the age of ten he
was a courier for the Palmach and fought in the defense of the Tel Aviv–Jerusalem road.

After twenty-seven years of war, Kabakov knew
better than most men the value of peace. He did not
hate the Arab people, but he believed that trying to
negotiate with Al Fatah was a lot of shit. That was the
term he used when he was consulted about it by his
superiors, which was not often.

The Mossad regarded Kabakov as a good intelligence officer, but his combat record was remarkable

and he was too successful in the field to be put behind
a desk. In the field, he risked capture and so he was
necessarily excluded from the inner councils of the
Mossad. He remained in the intelligence service's
executive arm, striking again and again at the Al Fatah
strongholds in Lebanon and Jordan. The innermost
circle of the Mossad called him "The final solution."

No one had ever said that to his face.

The lights of Washington wheeled beneath the
wing as the plane turned into the National Airport
traffic pattern. Kabakov picked out the Capitol, stark
white in its floodlights. He wondered if the Capitol
was the target.

The two men waiting in the small conference
room at the Israeli embassy looked carefully at Kabakov as he entered with Ambassador Yoachim Tell.
Watching the Israeli major, Sam Corley of the
Federal Bureau of Investigation was reminded of a
Ranger captain of twenty years ago, his commander
at Fort Benning.

Fowler of the Central Intelligence Agency had
never been in the military service. Kabakov made him
think of a pit bulldog. Both men had studied hastily
assembled dossiers on the Israeli, but the dossiers were
mostly concerned with the Six-Day War and the
October War, old Xeroxes from the CIA's Middle
East section. Clippings. "Kabakov, the Tiger of Mitla
Pass"—journalism.

Ambassador Tell, still wearing his dinner clothes
from an embassy function, made brief introductions.

The room fell silent and Kabakov pressed the
switch on his small tape recorder. The voice of Dahlia
Iyad filled the silence. "Citizens of America . . ."

When the tape had ended, Kabakov spoke slowly
and carefully, weighing his words. "We believe that
the Ailul al Aswad—Black September—is preparing to
strike here. They are not interested in hostages or
negotiations or revolutionary theatrics this time. They
want maximum casualties—they want to make you sick.
We believe the plan is well advanced and that this

woman is a principal." He paused. "We believe it likely that she is in this country now."

"Then you must have information to supplement the tape," Fowler said.

"It is supplemented by the fact that we know they want to strike here, and the circumstances in which the tape was found. They have tried before," Kabakov said.

"You took the tape from Najeer's apartment after you killed him?"

"Yes."

"You didn't question him first?"

"Questioning Najeer would have been useless."

Sam Corley saw anger in Fowler's face. Corley glanced at the file before him. "Why do you think it was the woman you saw in the room who made the tape?"

"Because Najeer had not had time to put it in a safe place," Kabakov said. "He was not a careless man."

"He was not careful enough to keep you from killing him," Fowler said.

"Najeer lasted a long time," Kabakov said. "Long enough for Munich to happen, Lod Airport, too long. If you are not careful now, American arms and legs will fly."

"Why do you think the plan would go on now that Najeer is dead?"

Corley looked up from the paper clip he was examining and answered Fowler himself. "Because the tape was dangerous. Making it would have been very nearly the final step. The orders would have been given. Am I right, Major?"

Kabakov recognized an expert interrogator when he saw one. Corley was being the advocate. "Exactly," he said.

"An operation might be mounted in another country and moved here at the last minute," Corley said. "Why do you think the woman is based here?"

"Najeer's apartment had been under surveillance

for some time," Kabakov explained. "She was not seen in Beirut before or after the night of the raid. Two linguists in the Mossad analyzed the tape independently and came to the same conclusion: She learned English as a child from a Briton, but has been exposed to American English for the last year or two. American-made clothing was found in the room."

"Maybe she was just a courier, taking final instructions from Najeer," Fowler said. "Instructions could be passed on anywhere."

"If she were only a courier, she would never have seen Najeer's face." Kabakov said. "Black September is compartmented like a wasp's nest. Most of their agents know only one or two others in the apparatus."

"Why didn't you kill the woman, too, Major?" Fowler was not looking at Kabakov when he said this. If he had been looking, he would not have looked long.

The ambassador spoke for the first time. "Because there was no reason to kill her at the time, Mr. Fowler. I hope you do not come to wish he had."

Kabakov blinked once. These men did not understand the danger. They would not be warned. Behind his eyes, Kabakov saw the Arab armor thundering across the Sinai and into the cities, herding Jewish civilians. Because there were no planes. Because the Americans had been sickened. Because he had spared the woman. His hundred victories were ashes in his mouth. The fact that he could not possibly have known that the woman was important did not excuse him in the slightest in his own eyes. The mission to Beirut had not been perfect.

Kabakov stared into Fowler's jowly face. "Do you have a dossier on Hafez Najeer?"

"He appears in our files on a list of Al Fatah officers."

"A complete dossier on him is included with my report. Look at the pictures, Mr. Fowler. They were taken after some of Najeer's earlier projects."

"I've seen atrocities."

"Not like these you haven't." The Israeli's voice was rising.

"Hafez Najeer is dead, Major Kabakov."

"And the good was interred with his bones, Fowler. If this woman is not found, Black September will rub your nose in guts."

Fowler glanced at the ambassador as though he expected him to intervene, but Yoachim Tell's small, wise eyes were hard. He stood with Kabakov.

When the major spoke again, his voice was almost too quiet. "You must believe it, Mr. Fowler."

"Would you recognize her again, Major?" Corley asked.

"Yes."

"If she were based here, why would she go to Beirut?"

"She needed something she could not get here. She needed something that only Najeer could get for her, and she had to confirm something personally for him in order to get it." Kabakov knew this sounded vague and he was not happy about it. He was also displeased with himself for using the word "something" three times in a row.

Fowler opened his mouth, but Corley interrupted him. "That wouldn't be guns."

"Coals to Newcastle, bringing guns here," Fowler said gloomily.

"It would have to be either equipment or access to another cell or to a highly placed agent," Corley continued. "I doubt that she needed access to an agent. As far as I can tell, U.A.R. intelligence here is a sorry lot."

"Yes," the ambassador said. "The embassy handyman sells them the contents of my wastebasket. He also buys from their handyman the contents of theirs. We load ours with junk mail and fictitious correspondence. Theirs runs heavily to duns from creditors and advertisements for unusual rubber products."

The meeting continued for another thirty minutes before the Americans rose to go.

"I'll try to get this on the agenda at Langley in the morning," Corley said.

"If you wish, I could—"

Fowler interrupted Kabakov. "Your report and the tape will be sufficient, Major."

It was after 3 A.M. when the Americans left the Embassy.

"Oy, the Arabs are coming," Fowler said to Corley as they walked to the cars.

"What do you think?"

"I think I don't envy you having to take up Blue Eyes Bennett's time with that stuff tomorrow," Fowler said. "If there are some crackpots here, the Agency is out of it, old buddy. No fooling around in the U.S.A." The CIA was still smarting from Watergate. "If the Middle East section turns up anything, we'll let you know."

"Why were you so pissed off in there?"

"I'm tired of it," Fowler said. "We've worked with the Israelis in Rome, in London, Paris, once even in Tokyo. You finger an Arab, cut them in on it, and what happens? Do they try to turn him? No. Do they watch him? Yes. Just long enough to find out who his friends are. Then there is a big bang. The Arabs are wiped out, and you are left holding your schwantz."

"They didn't have to send Kabakov," Corley said.

"Oh yes they did. You'll notice the military attaché Weisman wasn't there. We both know he has an intelligence function. But he's coordinating the Phantom sale. They don't want to connect the two things officially at all."

"You'll be at Langley tomorrow?"

"I'll be there all right. Don't let Kabakov get your ass in a crack."

Each Thursday morning the American intelligence community meets in a windowless, lead-shielded room in Central Intelligence Agency headquarters at Langley, Va. Represented are the CIA, FBI, National Security Agency, the Secret Service, the National Reconnaissance Office, and the military intelligence advisors to the Joint Chiefs of Staff. Specialists are called in when necessary. The agenda has a subscription list of fourteen. There are many subjects to be discussed and time is strictly limited.

Corley spoke for ten minutes, Fowler for five, and the representative from the Immigration and Naturalization subversive section had less time than that.

Kabakov was waiting in Corley's small office at FBI headquarters when he returned from the meeting.

"I'm supposed to thank you for coming," Corley said. "State is going to thank the ambassador. Our ambassador in Tel Aviv is going to thank Yigal Allon."

"You're welcome, now what are you going to do?"

"Damn little," Corley said, lighting his pipe. "Fowler brought a stack of tapes recorded off Radio Cairo and Radio Beirut. He said they were all threats of various kinds that came to nothing. The Agency is voiceprinting your tape against them."

"This tape is not a threat. It was made to be used afterward."

"The Agency is checking its sources in Lebanon."

"In Lebanon the CIA buys the same shit we do, from a lot of the same people," Kabakov said. "The kind of stuff that's two hours ahead of the newspapers."

"Sometimes not even two hours," Corley said. "In the meantime, you can look at pictures. We've got about a hundred known Al Fatah sympathizers on file, people we think are in the July 5th movement here. Immigration and Naturalization doesn't advertise it, but they have a file on suspicious Arab aliens. You'll have to go to New York for that."

"Can you put out a general customs alert on your own authority?"

"I've done that. It's our best bet. For a major job they probably would have to bring in the bomb from outside, that is *if* it's a bomb," Corley said. "We've had three small explosions linked to the July 5th movement in the past two years, all at Israeli offices in New York. From that—"

"One time they used plastic, the other two were dynamite," Kabakov said.

"Exactly. You do keep up, don't you? Apparently there's not much plastic available here or they wouldn't be lugging dynamite around and wouldn't blow themselves up trying to extract nitroglycerine."

"The July 5th movement is full of amateurs," Kabakov said. "Najeer would not have trusted them with this. The ordnance would be separate. If it's not already here, they'll bring it in." The Israeli rose and walked to the window. "So your government is making its files available to me and telling customs to watch out for fellows with bombs and that's all?"

"I'm sorry, Major, but I don't know what else we can do with the information we have."

"The U.S. could ask its new allies in Egypt to pressure Khadafy in Libya. He bankrolls Black September. The bastard gave them $5 million from the Libyan treasury as a reward for the Munich killings. He might be able to call it off if Egypt pushed him hard enough."

Colonel Muammar Khadafy, head of Libya's Revolutionary Command Council, was wooing Egypt again in his drive to build a solid power base. He might respond to pressure from the Egyptians now.

"The State Department is staying out of it," Corley said.

"U.S. intelligence doesn't think they're going to strike here at all, do they, Corley?"

"No," Sam Corley said wearily. "They think the Arabs wouldn't dare."

CHAPTER 4

AT THAT MOMENT the freighter *Leticia* was crossing the 21st meridian en route to the Azores and New York City. In her deepest forward hold in a locked compartment were 1,200 pounds of *plastique* packed in gray crates.

Beside the crates in the total darkness of the hold, Ali Hassan lay semiconscious. A large rat was on his stomach and it was walking toward his face. Hassan had lain there for three days, shot in the stomach by Captain Kemal Larmoso.

The rat was hungry, but not ravenous. At first Hassan's groans had frightened him, but now he heard only shallow, glottal breathing. He stood in the crust on the distended stomach and sniffed the wound, then moved forward onto the chest.

Hassan could feel the claws through his shirt. He must wait. In Hassan's left hand was the short crowbar Captain Larmoso had dropped when Hassan surprised him at the crates. In his right hand was the Walther PPK automatic he had drawn too late. He would not fire the gun now. Someone might hear. The traitor Larmoso must think him dead when he came into the hold again.

The rat's nose was almost touching Hassan's chin.

The man's labored breathing stirred the rat's whiskers.

With all his strength, Hassan jabbed the crowbar sideways across his chest and felt it gouge into the rat's side. The claws dug in as the rat leaped off him, and he heard the claws rasp on the metal deck as it ran.

Minutes passed. Then Hassan was aware of a faint rustling. He believed it came from inside his trouser leg. He could feel nothing below his waist and he was grateful for that.

The temptation to kill himself was with him all the time now. He had the strength to bring the Walther to his head. He would do it too, he told himself, as soon as Muhammad Fasil came. Until then he would guard the boxes.

Hassan did not know how long he had lain in the darkness. He knew his mind would be clear for only a few minutes this time, and he tried to think. The *Leticia* was a little more than three days from the Azores when he caught Larmoso snooping at the boxes. When Muhammad Fasil did not receive Hassan's scheduled cable from the Azores on November 2, he would have two days to act before the *Leticia* sailed again—and the Azores were the last stop before New York.

Fasil will act, Hassan thought. *I will not fail him.*

Every stroke of the *Leticia's* aged diesel vibrated the deck plates beneath his head. The red waves were spreading behind his eyes. He strained to hear the diesel and thought it was the pulse of God.

Sixty feet above the hold where Hassan lay, Captain Kemal Larmoso was relaxing in his cabin, drinking a bottle of Sapporo beer while he listened to the news. The Lebanese army and the guerrillas were fighting again. *Good,* he thought. *Turds to them both.*

The Lebanese threatened his papers and the guerrillas threatened his life. When he put into Beirut or Tyre or Tobruk, both had to be paid. The guerrillas not so much as the camel-fucking Lebanese customs.

He was in for it with the guerrillas now. He knew he was committed from the moment Hassan caught him at the boxes. Fasil and the others would be after him when he returned to Beirut. Maybe the Lebanese had learned from King Hussein and would drive the guerrillas out. Then there would be only one faction to pay. He was sick of it. "Take him there." "Bring the guns." "Speak nothing." *I know about speak nothing,* Larmoso thought. *My ear did not get this way from a hasty shave.* Once he had found a limpet mine attached to the *Leticia's* scaly hull, fuse ready to be set if he should refuse the guerrillas' demands.

Larmoso was a large, hairy man, whose body odor made even his crew's eyes water, and his weight sagged his bunk halfway to the floor. He opened another bottle of Sapporo with his teeth and brooded while he drank it, his small eyes fixed on an Italian magazine foldout depicting heterosexual buggery, which was taped to the bulkhead.

Then he lifted the small Madonna from the floor beside his bunk and stood it on his chest. It was scarred where he had probed it with his knife before realizing what it was.

Larmoso knew of three places where he might turn explosives into money. There was a Cuban exile in Miami with more money than sense. In the Dominican Republic there was a man who paid Brazilian cruzeiros for anything that would shoot or explode. The third possible customer was the U.S. government.

There would be a reward, of course, but Larmoso knew that there would also be other advantages in a deal with the Americans. Certain prejudices held against him by U.S. Customs might be forgotten.

Larmoso had opened the crates because he wanted to put the bite on the importer, Benjamin Muzi, for an unusually large payoff, and he needed to know the value of the contraband in order to figure out how much he could demand. Larmoso had never trifled with Muzi's shipments before, but persistent rumors had reached him that Muzi was going out of business in the Middle East, and if that happened Larmoso's illicit income would drop sharply. This could very well be Muzi's final shipment, and Larmoso wanted to make all he could.

He had expected to find a whopping shipment of hashish, a commodity Muzi often bought from Al Fatah sources. Instead he found *plastique*, and then Hassan was there, going for his pistol like a fool. *Plastique* was heavy business, not like a normal drug deal where friends could put the squeeze on one another.

Larmoso hoped that Muzi could solve the problem with the guerrillas and still turn a profit on the *plastique*. But Muzi would be furious at him for fooling with the crates.

If Muzi did not want to cooperate, if he refused to pay off Larmoso and make amends to the guerrillas for him, then Larmoso intended to keep the *plastique* and sell it elsewhere. Better to be a wealthy fugitive than a poor one.

But first he must take an inventory of what he had to sell, and he must get rid of certain garbage in the hold.

Larmoso knew that he had hit Hassan squarely. And he had given him plenty of time to die. He decided he would sack up Hassan, weight him in the harbor at Ponta Delgada while there was only an anchor watch aboard, and dump him in deep water when he cleared the Azores.

Muhammad Fasil checked the cable office in Beirut hourly all day. At first he hoped Hassan's cable from the Azores had only been delayed. Always before, the cables had come by noon. There had been three of them—from Benghazi, Tunis, and Lisbon—as the old freighter plowed westward. The wording varied in each, but they all meant the same thing—the explosives had not been disturbed. The next one should be "Mother much improved today" and it should be signed Jose. At 6 P.M., when the cable had still not arrived, Fasil drove to the airport. He was carrying the credentials of an Algerian photographer and a gutted speed graphic camera containing a .357 Magnum revolver. Fasil had made the reservations as a precaution two weeks before. He knew he could be in Ponta Delgada by 4 P.M. the next day.

Captain Larmoso relieved his first mate at the helm when the *Leticia* raised the peaks of Santa Maria early on the morning of November 2. He skirted the small island on the southwest side, then turned north for San Miguel and the port of Ponta Delgada.

The Portuguese city was lovely in the winter sun, white buildings with red-tiled roofs, and evergreens between them rising nearly as high as the bell tower. Behind the city were gentle mountain slopes, patched with fields.

The *Leticia* looked scalier than ever tied at the quay, her faded Plimsoll line creeping up out of the water as the crew off-loaded a consignment of re-conditioned light agricultural equipment and creeping down again as crates of bottled mineral water were loaded aboard.

Larmoso was not worried. The cargo handling involved only the aft hold. The small, locked compartment in the forward hold would not be disturbed.

Most of the work was completed by the afternoon of the second day, and he gave the crew shore leave, the purser doling out only enough cash to each man for one evening in the brothels and bars.

The crew trooped off down the quay, walking quickly in anticipation of the evening, the foremost sailor with a blob of shaving cream beneath his ear. They did not notice the thin man beneath the colonnade of the Banco Nacional Ultramarino, who counted them as they passed.

The ship was silent now except for Captain Larmoso's footsteps as he descended to the engine room workshop, a small compartment dimly lit by a bulb in a wire cage. Rummaging through a pile of cast-off parts he selected a piston rod, complete with wristpin assembly, which had been ruined when the *Leticia's* engine seized off Tobruk in the spring. The rod looked like a great metal bone as he hefted it in his hands. Confident that it was heavy enough to take Hassan's body down the long slide to the bottom of the Atlantic, Larmoso carried the rod aft and stowed it in a locker near the stern along with a length of line.

Next he took from the galley one of the cook's big burlap garbage bags and carried it forward through the empty wardroom toward the forward companionway. He draped the bag over his shoulder like a serape and whistled between his teeth, his footfalls loud in the passageway. Then he heard a slight sound behind him. Larmoso paused, listening. Probably the noise was only the old man on anchor watch walking on the deck above his head. Larmoso stepped through the wardroom hatch into the companionway and went down the metal steps to the level of the forward hold. But instead of entering the hold, he slammed its hatch loudly and stood against the bulkhead at the foot of the companionway, looking up the metal shaft to the hatch at the top of the dark steps. The five-shot Smith & Wesson Airweight looked like a child's licorice pistol in his big fist.

As he watched, the wardroom hatch swung open and, as slowly as a questing snake, the small, neat head of Muhammad Fasil appeared.

Larmoso fired, the blast incredible inside the metal walls, the bullet screaming off the handrail. He ducked into the hold and slammed the hatch behind him. He was sweating now, and the rank smell of him mixed with the smells of rust and cold grease as he waited in the darkness.

The footsteps descending the companionway were slow and evenly spaced. Larmoso knew Fasil was holding the railing with one hand and keeping his gun trained on the closed hatch with the other. Larmoso scrambled behind a crate twelve feet from the hatch Fasil had to enter. Time was on his side. Eventually the crew would straggle back. He thought of the deals and excuses he might offer Fasil. Nothing would work. He had four shots left. He would kill Fasil when he came through the hatch. It was settled.

The companionway was quiet for a second. Then Fasil's Magnum roared, the bullet blasting through the hatch and sending metal fragments flying through the hold. Larmoso fired back at the closed hatch, the .38 special bullet only dimpling the metal, and fired again and again as the hatch flew open and the dark shape tumbled through.

Even as he fired the last round, Larmoso saw by the muzzle flash that he had shot a sofa pillow from the wardroom. Now he was running, tripping and cursing, through the dark hold toward the forward compartment.

He would get Hassan's pistol. He would kill Fasil with it.

Larmoso moved well for a big man, and he knew the layout of the hold. In less than 30 seconds he was at the compartment hatch, fumbling with the key. The stench that puffed over him when he opened the hatch gagged him as he plunged inside. He did not want to show a light, and he crawled across the deck in the black compartment, feeling for Hassan and muttering softly to himself. He butted into the crates and crawled around them. His hand touched a shoe. Larmoso felt his way up the trouser leg and over the belly. The gun was not in the waistband. He felt on either side of the body. He found the arm, he felt it move, but he did not find the gun until it exploded in his face.

Fasil's ears were ringing and several minutes passed before he could hear the hoarse whisper from the forward compartment.

"Fasil. Fasil."

The guerrilla shone his small flashlight into the compartment, tiny feet scurrying from the beam. Fasil played the light over the red mask of Larmoso, lying dead on his back, then stepped inside.

Kneeling, he took the rat-ravaged face of Ali Hassan in his hands. The lips moved.

"Fasil."

"You have done well, Hassan. I'll get a doctor." Fasil could see that it was hopeless. Hassan, swollen with peritonitis, was beyond help. But Fasil could kidnap a doctor a half-hour before the *Leticia* sailed and make him come along. He could kill the physician at sea before the ship reached New York. Hassan deserved no less. It was the humane thing to do.

"Hassan, I will be back in five minutes with the medical kit. I will leave the light with you."

A faint whisper. "Is my duty done?"

"It is done. Hold on, old friend, I will bring morphine now and then a doctor."

Fasil was feeling his way aft through the dark hold when Hassan's pistol went off behind him. He paused and leaned his head against the ship's cold iron. "You will pay for this," he whispered. He was talking to a people that he had never seen.

The old man on anchor watch was still unconscious, with a swollen lump on the back of his head where Fasil had slugged him. Fasil dragged him to the first mate's cabin and laid him on the bunk, then sat down to think.

Originally the plan was to have the crates picked up at the Brooklyn dock by the importer, Benjamin Muzi. There was no way of knowing if Larmoso had contacted Muzi and enlisted his aid in this treachery. Muzi would have to be dealt with anyway because he knew far too much. Customs would be curious at the absence of Larmoso. Questions would be asked. It seemed unlikely that the others on the ship knew what was in the crates. Larmoso's keys were still dangling from the lock on the forward compartment when the captain was killed. Now they were in Fasil's pocket. The *plastique* must not go into New York Harbor, that was clear.

First Mate Mustapha Fawzi was a reasonable man and not a brave one. At midnight when he returned to the ship, Fasil had a brief conversation with him. In one hand Fasil held a large black revolver. In the other he held $2,000. He inquired about the health of Fawzi's mother and sister in Beirut, then suggested that their continued health depended largely on Fawzi's cooperation. The thing was quickly done.

It was 7 P.M. Eastern Standard Time when the telephone rang in Michael Lander's house. He was working in his garage and picked up the extension. Dahlia was mixing a can of paint.

From the amount of line noise, Lander guessed the caller was very far away. He had a pleasant voice with a British clip, similar to Dahlia's. He asked for the "lady of the house."

Dahlia was at the phone in an instant and began a rather tedious conversation in English about relatives and real estate. Then the conversation was punctuated with 20 seconds of rapid-fire slangy Arabic.

Dahlia turned from the phone, covering the mouthpiece with her hand.

"Michael, we have to pick up the *plastique* at sea. Can you get a boat?"

Lander's mind worked furiously. "Yes. Make sure of the rendezvous point. Forty miles due east of the Barnegat Light a half-hour before sunset. We'll make visual contact with the last light and close after dark. If the winds are over force five, postpone it for exactly 24 hours. Tell him to pack it in units one man can lift."

Dahlia spoke quickly into the telephone, then hung up.

"Tuesday the twelfth," she said. She was looking at him curiously. "Michael, you worked that out rather quickly."

"No, I didn't," Lander said.

Dahlia had learned very early never to lie to Lander. That would be as stupid as programming a computer with half-truths and expecting accurate answers. Besides, he could always tell when she had even the temptation to lie. Now she was glad that she had confided in him from the beginning on the arrangements for bringing in the *plastique*.

He listened calmly as she told him what had happened on the ship.

"Do you think Muzi put Larmoso up to it?" he asked.

"Fasil doesn't know. He never had a chance to question Larmoso. We have to assume Muzi put him up to it. We can't afford to do otherwise, can we, Michael? If Muzi dared to interfere with the shipment, if he planned to keep our advance payment and sell the *plastique* elsewhere, then he has sold us out to the authorities here. He would have to do that for his own protection. Even if he has not betrayed us, he would have to be dealt with. He knows far too much, and he has seen you. He could identify you."

"You intended to kill him all along?"

"Yes. He is not one of us, and he is in a dangerous business. If the authorities threatened him on some other matter, who knows what he might tell them?" Dahlia realized she was being too assertive. "I couldn't stand the thought of him always being a threat to you, Michael," she added in a softer voice. "You didn't trust him either, did you, Michael? You had a pickup at sea all worked out in advance, just in case, didn't you? That's amazing."

"Yeah, amazing," Lander said. "One thing. Nothing happens to Muzi until after we have the plastic. If he has gone to the authorities, to get immunity for himself in some other matter or whatever, the trap will be set at the dock. As long as they think we are coming to the dock, they are less likely to fly a stakeout team out to the ship. If Muzi is hit before the ship comes in, they'll know we're not coming to the dock. They'll be waiting for us when we go out to the ship." Suddenly Lander was furious and white around the mouth. "So Muzi was the best your camel-shit mastermind could come up with."

Dahlia did not flinch. She did not point out that it was Lander who went to Muzi first. She knew that this anger would be suppressed and added to Lander's general fund of rage as, irresistibly, his mind was drawn back to the problem.

He closed his eyes for a moment. "You'll have to go shopping," he said. "Give me a pencil."

CHAPTER 5

Now THAT Hafez Najeer and Abu Ali were dead, only Dahlia and Muhammad Fasil knew Lander's identity, but Benjamin Muzi had seen him several times, for Muzi had been Lander's first link to Black September and the plastic.

From the beginning, the great problem had been obtaining the explosives. In the first white heat of his epiphany, when he knew what he would do, it had not occurred to Lander that he would need help. It was part of the aesthetic of the act that he do it alone. But as the plan flowered in his mind, and as he looked down on the crowds again and again, he decided they deserved more than the few cases of dynamite that he could buy or steal. They should have more attention than the random shrapnel from a shattered gondola and a few pounds of nails and chain.

Sometimes, as he lay awake, the upturned faces of the crowd filled his midnight ceiling, mouths open, shifting like a field of flowers in the wind. Many of the faces became Margaret's. Then the great fireball lifted off the heat of his face and rose to them, swirling like the Crab nebula, searing them to charcoal, soothing him to sleep.

He must have plastic.

Lander traveled across the country twice looking for plastic. He went to three military arsenals to case the possibilities for theft and saw that it was hopeless. He went to the plant of a great corporation that manufactures baby oil and napalm, industrial adhesives and plastic explosives, and he found that plant security was as tight as that of the military and considerably more imaginative. The instability of nitroglycerine ruled out extracting it from dynamite.

Lander checked newspapers avidly for stories about terrorism, explosions, bombs. The pile of clippings in his bedroom grew. It would have offended him to know that this was patterned behavior, to know in how many bedrooms sick men keep clippings, waiting for their day. Many of Lander's clippings carried foreign datelines—Rome, Helsinki, Damascus, The Hague, Beirut.

In a Cincinnati motel in mid-July the idea came to him. He had flown over a fair that day and was getting mildly drunk in the motel lounge. It was late. A television set was suspended from the ceiling over the end of the bar. Lander sat almost directly beneath it, staring into his drink. Most of the customers were facing him, turned on their stools, the bloodless light of the TV playing over their uplifted faces.

Lander stirred and came alert. Something in the expression on the faces of the customers watching television. Apprehension. Anger. Not fear exactly, for they were safe enough, but they wore the look of a man watching wolves from his cabin window. Lander picked up his drink and walked down the bar until he could see the screen. Film of a Boeing 747 sitting in the desert with heat shimmer around it. The forward end of the fuselage exploded, then the center section, and the plane was gone in a belch of flame and smoke. The program was a rerun of a news special on Arab terrorism.

Cut to Munich. The horror at the Olympic village. The helicopter at the airport. Muffled gunfire inside it as the Israeli athletes were shot. The embassy at

Khartoum where the American and Belgian diplomats were slain. Al Fatah leader Yasir Arafat denying responsibility.

Yasir Arafat again at a news conference in Beirut, bitterly accusing England and the United States of aiding the Israelis in terrorist raids against the guerrillas. "When our revenge comes, it will be big," Arafat said, his eyes reflecting double moons from the television lights.

A statement of support from Col. Khadafy, student of Napoleon and Al Fatah's constant ally and banker: "The United States deserves a strong slap in the face." A further comment from Khadafy—"God damn America."

"Scumbag," said a man in a bowling jacket who stood next to Lander. "Bunch of scumbags."

Lander laughed loudly. Several of the drinkers turned to him.

"That funny to you, Jack?"

"No. I assure you, sir, that is not funny at all. You scumbag." Lander put money on the bar and walked out with the man shouting after him.

Lander knew no Arabs. He began to read accounts of the Arab-American groups sympathetic to the cause of the Palestinian Arabs, but the one meeting he attended in Brooklyn convinced him that Arab-American citizens' committees were far too straight for him. They discussed subjects such as "justice" and "individual rights" and encouraged writing to Congressmen. If he put out feelers there for militants, he rightly suspected, he would soon be approached by an undercover cop with a Kel transmitter strapped to his leg.

Demonstrations in Manhattan on the Palestinian question were no better. At United Nations Plaza and Union Square he found less than 20 Arab youngsters surrounded by a sea of Jews.

No, he needed a competent and greedy crook with good contacts in the Middle East. And he found one. Lander obtained the name of Benjamin Muzi from an airline pilot he knew who brought back interesting packages from the Middle East in his shaving kit and delivered them to the importer.

Muzi's office was gloomy enough, set in the back of a shabby warehouse on Sedgwick Street in Brooklyn. Lander was shown to the office by a very large and odorous Greek, whose bald head reflected the dim overhead light as they wound through a maze of crates.

Only the office door was expensive. It was of steel with two deadbolts and a Fox lock. The mail slot was belly-high, with a hinged metal plate in the inside that could be bolted shut.

Muzi was very fat, and he grunted as he lifted a pile of invoices off a chair and motioned for Lander to sit down.

"May I offer you something? A refreshment?"

"No."

Muzi drained his bottle of Perrier water and fished a fresh bottle out of his ice chest. He dropped in two aspirin tablets and took a long swallow. "You said on the telephone that you wished to speak to me on a matter of the utmost confidence. Since you haven't offered your name, do you have any objection to being called Hopkins?"

"None whatever."

"Excellent. Mr. Hopkins, when people say 'in confidence' they generally mean contravention of the law. If that is the case here, then I will have nothing whatever to do with you, do you understand me?"

Lander removed a packet of bills from his pocket and placed it on Muzi's desk. Muzi did not touch the money or look at it. Lander picked up the packet and started for the door.

"A moment, Mr. Hopkins." Muzi gestured to the Greek who stepped forward and searched Lander thoroughly. The Greek looked at Muzi and shook his head.

"Sit down, please. Thank you, Salop. Wait outside." The big man closed the door behind him.

"That's a filthy name," Lander said.

"Yes, but he doesn't know it," Muzi said, mopping his face with a handkerchief. He steepled his fingers under his chin and waited.

"I understand you are a man of wide influence," Lander began.

"I am certainly a wide man of influence."

"Certain advice—"

"Contrary to what you may believe, Mr. Hopkins, it is not necessary to indulge in endless Arabic circumlocutions in dealing with an Arab, especially since, for the most part, Americans lack the subtlety to make it interesting. This office is not bugged. You are not bugged. Tell me what you want."

"I want a letter delivered to the head of the intelligence section of Al Fatah."

"And who might that be?"

"I don't know. You can find out. I am told you can do nearly anything in Beirut. The letter will be sealed in several tricky ways and it must get there unopened."

"Yes, I expect it must." Muzi's eyes were hooded like a turtle's.

"You're thinking letter bomb," Lander said. "It's not. You can watch me put the contents in the envelope from ten feet away. You can lick the flap, then I'll put on the other seals."

"I deal with men who are interested in money. People with politics often don't pay their bills, or they kill you out of ineptitude. I don't think—"

"$2,000 now, $2,000 if the message gets there satisfactorily." Lander put the money back on the desk. "Another thing, I would advise you to open a numbered bank account in The Hague."

"To what purpose?"

"To put a lot of Libyan currency in if you should decide to retire."

There was a prolonged silence. Finally Lander broke it.

"You have to understand that this must go to the right man the first time. It must not be handed around."

"Since I don't know what you want, I am working blind. Certain inquiries could be made, but even inquiry is dangerous. You are aware that Al Fatah is fragmented, contentious within itself."

"Get it to Black September," Lander said.

"Not for $4,000."

"How much?"

"Inquiries will be difficult and expensive and even then you can never be sure—"

"How much?"

"For $8,000, payable immediately, I would do my best."

"$4,000 now and $4,000 afterward."

"$8,000 now, Mr. Hopkins. Afterward I will not know you and you will never come here again."

"Agreed."

"I am going to Beirut in a week's time. I do not want your letter until immediately before my departure. You can bring it here on the night of the seventh. It will be sealed in my presence. Believe me, I do not want to read what is in it."

The letter contained Lander's real name and address and said that he could do a great service for the Palestinian cause. He asked to meet with a representative of Black September anywhere in the Western Hemisphere. He enclosed a money order for $1,500 to cover any expenses.

Muzi accepted the letter and the $8,000 with a gravity just short of ceremony. It was one of his peculiarities that, when his price was met, he kept his word.

A week later, Lander received a picture postcard from Beirut. There was no message on it. He wondered if Muzi had opened the letter himself and gotten the name and address from it.

A third week passed. He had to fly four times out of Lakehurst. Twice in that week he thought he was being followed as he drove to the airfield, but he could not be sure. On Thursday, August 15, he flew a night-sign run over Atlantic City, flashing billboard messages from the computer-controlled panels of lights on the blimp's great sides.

When he returned to Lakehurst and got into his car, he noticed a card stuck under the windshield wiper. Annoyed, he got out and pulled it loose, expecting an advertisement. He examined the card under the dome light. It was a chit good for a swim at Maxie's Swim Club, near Lakehurst. On the back was written "tomorrow 3 P.M. flash once now for yes."

Lander looked around him at the darkened airfield parking lot. He saw no one. He flashed his headlights once and drove home.

There are many private swimming clubs in New Jersey, well maintained and fairly expensive, and they offer a variety of exclusionary policies. Maxie's had a predominantly Jewish clientele, but unlike some of the club owners Maxie admitted a few blacks and Puerto Ricans if he knew them. Lander arrived at the pool at 2:45 P.M. and changed into his swimsuit in a cinder-block dressing room with puddles on the floor. The sun and the sharp smell of chlorine and the noisy children reminded him of other times, swimming at the officers' club with Margaret and his daughters. Afterwards a drink at poolside, Margaret holding the stem of her glass with fingers puckered from the water, laughing and tossing her wet hair back, knowing the young lieutenants were watching.

Lander felt very much alone now, and he was conscious of his white body and his ugly hand as he walked out on the hot concrete. He put his valuables in a wire basket and checked them with the attendant, tucking the plastic check tag in his swimsuit pocket. The pool was an unnatural blue and the light danced on it, hurting his eyes.

There are a lot of advantages in a swimming pool, he reflected. Nobody can carry a gun or a tape recorder, nobody can be fingerprinted on the sly.

He swam back and forth lazily for half an hour. There were at least fifteen children in the pool with a variety of inflated seahorses and inner tubes. Several young couples were playing keepaway with a striped beach ball, and one muscle-bound young man was anointing himself with suntan oil on the side of the pool.

Lander rolled over and began a slow backstroke across the deep end, just out of range of the divers. He was watching a small, drifting cloud when he collided with a swimmer in a tangle of arms and legs, a girl in a snorkel mask who had been kicking along, apparently watching the bottom instead of looking where she was going.

"Sorry," she said, treading water. Lander blew water out of his nose and swam on, saying nothing. He stayed in the pool another half-hour, then decided to leave. He was about to climb out when the girl in the snorkel mask surfaced in front of him. She took off the mask and smiled.

"Did you drop this? I found it on the bottom of the pool." She was holding his plastic check tag.

Lander looked down to see that the pocket of his swimsuit was wrong side out.

"You'd better check your wallet and make sure everything is there," she said and submerged again.

Tucked inside the wallet was the money order he had sent to Beirut. He gave his basket back to the attendant and rejoined the girl in the pool. She was in a water fight with two small boys. They complained loudly when she left them. She was splendid to see in the water, and Lander, feeling cold and shriveled inside his swimming trunks, was angered at the sight.

"Let's talk in the pool, Mr. Lander," she said, wading to a depth where the water lapped just below her breasts.

"What am I supposed to do, shoot off in my pants and spill the whole business right here?"

She watched him steadily, multicolored pinpoints of light dancing in her eyes. Suddenly he placed his mangled hand on her arm, staring into her face, watching for the flinch. A gentle smile was the only reaction he saw. The reaction he did not see was beneath the surface of the water. Her left hand slowly turned over, fingers hooked, ready to strike if necessary.

"May I call you Michael? I am Dahlia Iyad. This is a good place to talk."

"Was everything in my wallet satisfactory to you?"

"You should be pleased that I searched it. I don't think you would deal with a fool."

"How much do you know about me?"

"I know what you do for a living. I know you were a prisoner of war. You live alone, you read very late at night, and you smoke a rather inferior grade of marijuana. I know that your telephone is not tapped, at least not from the telephone terminal in your basement or the one on the pole outside your home. I don't know for certain what you want."

Sooner or later he would have to say it. Aside from his distrust of this woman, it was difficult to say the thing, as hard as opening up for a shrink. All right.

"I want to detonate 1,200 pounds of plastic explosive in the Super Bowl."

She looked at him as though he had painfully admitted a sexual aberration that she particularly enjoyed. Calm and kindly compassion, suppressed excitement. Welcome home.

"You have no plastic, do you, Michael?"

"No." He looked away as he asked the question. "Can you get it?"

"That's a lot. It depends."

Water flew off his head as he snapped back to face her. "I don't want to hear that. That is not what I want to hear. Talk straight."

"If I am convinced you can do it, if I can satisfy my commander that you can do it and will do it, then yes, I can get the plastic. I'll get it."

"That's all right. That's fair."

"I want to see everything. I want to go home with you."

"Why not?"

They did not go directly to Lander's house. He was scheduled for a night-sign flight and he took Dahlia with him. It was not common practice to take passengers on night-sign flights, since most of the seats were removed from the gondola to make room for the on-board computer that controlled the 8,000 lights along the sides of the blimp. But with crowding there was room. Farley, the copilot, had inconvenienced everyone on two previous occasions by bringing his Florida girlfriend and was in no position to grumble at giving up his seat to this young woman. He and the computer operator licked their lips over Dahlia and entertained themselves with lewd pantomimes at the rear of the gondola when she and Lander were not looking.

Manhattan blazed in the night like a great diamond ship as they passed over at 2,500 feet. They dropped toward the brilliant wreath of Shea Stadium where the Mets were playing a night game, and the sides of the dirigible became huge flashing billboards, letters moving down its sides. "Don't forget, hire the Vet," was the first message. "Winston tastes God—" this message was interrupted while the technician cursed and fumbled with the perforated tape.

Afterward, Dahlia and Lander watched while the ground crew at Lakehurst secured the floodlit blimp for the night. They paid special attention to the gondola, as the men in coveralls removed the computer and reinstalled the seats.

Lander pointed out the sturdy handrail that runs around the base of the cabin. He led her to the rear of the gondola to watch while the turbojet generator that powers the lights was detached. The generator is a sleek, heavy unit shaped like a largemouth bass, and it has a strong, three-point attachment that would be very useful.

Farley approached them with his clipboard. "Hey, you people aren't going to stay *here* all night."

Dahlia smiled at him vacuously. "It's all so exciting."

"Yeah." Farley chuckled and left them with a wink.

Dahlia's face was flushed and her eyes were bright as they drove home from the airfield.

She made it clear from the first that, inside his house, she expected no performance of any kind from Lander. And she was careful not to show any distaste for him either. Her body was there, she had brought it because it was convenient to do so, her attitude seemed to say. She was physically deferential to Lander in a way so subtle that it does not have a name in English. And she was very, very gentle.

In matters of business it was quite different. Lander quickly found that he could not browbeat her with his superior technical knowledge. He had to explain his plan in minute detail, defining terms as he went along. When she disagreed with him it was usually on methods for handling people, and he found her to be a shrewd judge of people and greatly experienced in the behavior of frightened men under pressure. Even when she was adamant in disagreement she never emphasized a point with a body movement or a facial expression that reflected anything other than concentration.

As the technical problems were resolved, at least in theory, Dahlia could see that the greatest danger to the project was Lander's instability. He was a splendid machine with a homicidal child at the controls. Her role became increasingly supportive. In this area, she could not always calculate and she was forced to feel.

As the days passed, he began to tell her things about himself—safe things that did not pain him. Sometimes in the evenings, a little drunk, he carped endlessly about the injustices of the Navy until she finally went to her room after midnight, leaving him cursing at the television. And then one night, as she sat on the side of his bed, he brought her a story like a gift. He told her about the first time he ever saw a dirigible.

He was a child of eight with impetigo on his knees, and he was standing on the bare clay playground of a country school when he looked up and saw the airship. Silver, wearing for a reach across the wind, it floated over the schoolyard, scattering in the air behind it tiny objects that floated down—Baby Ruth candy bars on small parachutes. Running after the airship, Michael could stay in its shadow the length of the schoolyard, the other children running with him, scrambling for the candy bars. Then they reached the plowed field at the edge of the schoolyard and the shadow moved away, rippling over the rows. Lander in his short pants fell in the field and tore the scabs off his knees. He got to his feet again and watched the dirigible out of sight, rivulets of blood on his shins, a candy bar and parachute clutched in his hand.

While he was lost in the story, Dahlia stretched out beside him on the bed, listening. And he came to her from the playground, with wonder and the light of that old day still in his face.

After that he became shameless. She had heard his terrible wish and had accepted it as her own. She had received him with her body. Not with withering expectations, but with abundant grace. She saw no ugliness in him. Now he felt that he could tell her *anything*, and he poured it out—the things that he could never tell before, even to Margaret. Especially to Margaret.

Dahlia listened with compassion and concerned interest. She never showed a trace of distaste or apprehension, though she learned to be wary of him when he was talking about certain things, for he could become angry at her suddenly for injuries that others had done to him. Dahlia needed to know Lander, and she learned him very well, better than anyone else would ever know him—including the blue-ribbon commission that investigated his final act. The investigators had to rely on their piles of documents and photographs, their witnesses stiff upon the chair. Dahlia had it from the monster's mouth.

It is true that she learned Lander in order to use him, but who will ever listen for free? She might have done a great deal for him if her object had not been murder.

His utter frankness and her own inferences provided her with many windows on his past. Through them, she watched her weapon forged. . . .

Willett-Lorance Consolidated School, a rural school between Willett and Lorance, South Carolina, February 2, 1941:

"Michael, Michael Lander, come up here and read your paper. I want you to pay strict attention, Buddy Ives. And you too, Junior Atkins. You two have been fiddling while Rome burns. At six-weeks tests, this class will be divided into the sheep and the goats."

Michael has to be called twice more. He is surprisingly small walking up the aisle. Willett-Lorance has no accelerated program for exceptional children. Instead, Michael has been "skipped" ahead. He is eight years old and in the fourth grade.

Buddy Ives and Junior Atkins, both 12, have spent the previous recess dipping a second-grader's head in the toilet. Now they pay strict attention. To Michael. Not to his paper.

Michael knows he must pay. Standing before the class in his baggy short pants, the only pair in the room, reading in a voice barely audible, he knows he will have to pay. He hopes it will happen on the playground. He would rather be beaten than dipped.

Michael's father is a minister and his mother is a power in the PTA. He is not a cute, appealing child. He thinks there is something terribly wrong with him. For as long as he can remember he has been filled with horrible feelings that he does not understand. He cannot yet identify rage and self-loathing. He has a constant picture of himself as a prissy little boy in short pants, and he hates it. Sometimes he watches the other eight-year-olds playing cowboys in the shrubbery. On a few occasions he has tried to play, yelling "bang bang" and pointing his finger. He feels silly doing it. The others can tell he is not really a cowboy, does not believe in the game.

He wanders over to his classmates, the 11- and 12-year-olds. They are choosing sides to play football. He stands in the group and waits. It is not too bad to be chosen last, as long as you are chosen. He is alone between the two sides. He is not chosen. He notes which team chose last and walks over to the other team. He can see himself coming toward them. He can see his knobby knees beneath the short pants, knows they are talking about him in the huddle. They turn their backs to him. He cannot beg to play. He walks away, his face burning. There is no place on the red clay playground where he can get out of sight.

As a Southerner, Michael is deeply imprinted with the Code. A man fights when called on. A man is tough, straightforward, honorable, and strong. He can play football, he loves to hunt, and he allows no nasty talk around the ladies, although he discusses them in lewd terms among his fellows.

When you are a child, the Code without the equipment will kill you.

Michael has learned not to fight 12-year-olds if he can help it. He is told that he is a coward. He believes it. He is articulate and has not yet learned to conceal it. He is told that he is a sissy. He believes that this must be true.

He has finished reading his paper before the class now. He knows how Junior Atkins' breath will smell in his face. The teacher tells Michael he is a "good classroom citizen." She does not understand why he turns his face away from her.

September 10, 1947, the football field behind Willett-Lorance Consolidated:

Michael Lander is going out for football. He is in the tenth grade and he is going out without his parents' knowledge. He feels that he has to do it. He wants the good feeling his classmates have about the sport. He is curious about himself. The uniform makes him wonderfully anonymous. He cannot see himself when he

has it on. The tenth grade is late for a boy to begin
playing football, and he has much to learn. To his
surprise the others are tolerant of him. After a few
days of forearms and cleats, they have discovered that,
though he is naive about the game, he will hit and he
wants to learn from them. It is a good time for him.
It lasts a week. His parents learn that he is going out
for football. They hate the coach, a godless man who,
it is rumored, keeps alcohol in his home. The Reverend
Lander is on the school board now. The Landers drive
up to the practice field in their Kaiser. Michael does
not see them until he hears his name being called. His
mother is approaching the sideline, walking stiff-ankled
through the grass. The Reverend Lander waits in the
car.

"Take off that monkey suit."

Michael pretends not to hear. He is playing line-
backer with the scrubs in scrimmage. He assumes his
stance. Each blade of grass is distinct in his eyes. The
tackle in front of him has a red scratch on his calf.

His mother is walking the sideline now. Now she
is crossing it. She is coming. Two hundred pounds of
pondered rage. "I said take off that monkey suit and
get in that car."

Michael might have saved himself in that moment.
He might have yelled into his mother's face. The coach
might have saved him, had he been quicker, less afraid
for his job. Michael cannot let the others see any more.
He cannot be with them after this. They are looking
at each other now with expressions he cannot stand.
He trots toward the prefabricated building they use
for a dressing room. There are snickers behind him.

The coach has to speak to the boys twice to
resume the practice. "We don't need no mama's boys
no way," he says.

Michael moves very deliberately in the dressing
room, leaving his equipment in a neat pile on the
bench with his locker key on top. He feels only a
dull heaviness inside, no surface anger.

Riding home in the Kaiser, he listens to a torrent of
abuse. He replies that, yes, he understands how he has

embarrassed his parents, that he should have thought
of others. He nods solemnly when reminded that he
must save his hands for the piano.

July 18, 1948: Michael Lander is sitting on the
back porch of his home, a mean parsonage beside
the Baptist church in Willett. He is fixing a lawn
mower. He makes a little money fixing lawn mowers
and small appliances. Looking through the screen, he
can see his father lying on a bed, his hands behind his
head, listening to the radio. When he thinks of his
father, Michael sees his father's white, inept hands, the
ring from Cumberland-Macon Divinity School loose
behind the knuckle of his ring finger. In the South,
as in many other places, the church is an institution
of, by, and for women. The men tolerate it for the sake
of family peace. The men of the community have no
respect for the Reverend Lander because he could
never make a crop, could never do anything practical.
His sermons are dull and rambling, composed while
the choir is singing the offertory hymn. The Reverend
Lander spends much of his time writing letters to a
girl he knew in high school. He never mails the letters,
but locks them in a tin box in his office. The combination padlock is childishly simple. Michael has read the
letters for years. For laughs.

Puberty has done a great deal for Michael Lander.
At fifteen he is tall and lean. He has, by considerable
effort, learned to do convincingly mediocre school-
work. Against all odds, he has developed what appears
to be an affable personality. He knows the joke about
the bald-headed parrot, and he tells it well.

A freckle-faced girl two years older has helped
Michael discover that he is a man. This is a tremendous
relief to him after years of being told that he is a queer,
with no evidence to judge himself either way.

But in the blossoming of Michael Lander, part of
him has stood off to the side, cold and watchful. It is
the part of him that recognized the ignorance of the
classroom, that constantly replays little vignettes of
grade school making the new face wince, that flashes
the picture of the unlovely little scholar in front of

him in moments of stress, and can open under him a dread void when his new image is threatened.

The little scholar stands at the head of a legion of hate and he knows the answer every time, and his creed is *God Damn You All*. At fifteen Lander functions very well. A trained observer might notice a few things about him that hint at his feelings, but these in themselves are not suspicious. He cannot bear personal competition. He has never experienced the gradients of controlled aggression that allow most of us to survive. He cannot even endure board games, he can never gamble. Lander understands limited aggression objectively, but he cannot take part in it. Emotionally, for him there is no middle ground between a pleasant, uncompetitive atmosphere and total war to the death with the corpse defiled and burned. So he has no outlet. And he has swallowed his poison longer than most could have done.

Though he tells himself that he hates the church, Michael prays often during the day. He is convinced that assuming certain positions expedites his prayers. Touching his forehead to his knee is one of the most effective ones. When it is necessary for him to do this in public places, he must think of a ruse to keep it from being noticeable. Dropping something beneath his chair and bending to get it is a useful device. Prayers delivered in thresholds or while touching a door lock are also more effective. He prays often for persons who appear in the quick flashes of memory that sear him many times a day. Without willing it, despite his efforts to stop, he conducts internal dialogues often during his waking hours. He is having one now:

"There's old Miss Phelps working in the teacherage yard. I wonder when she'll retire. She's been at that schoolhouse for a long time."

"Do you wish she was rotten with cancer?"

"No! Dear Jesus forgive me, I don't wish she was rotten with cancer. I wish I was rotten with cancer first. [He touches wood.] Dear God, let me be rotten with cancer first, oh Father."

"*Would you like to take your shotgun and blow her rotten ignorant old guts out?*"

"*No! No! Jesus Father no I don't. I want her to be safe and happy. She can't help what she is. She's a kind and good lady. She's all right. Forgive me for saying God Damn.*"

"*Would you like to stick her face in the lawn mower?*"

"*I wouldn't, I wouldn't, Christ help me stop thinking that.*"

"*Fuck the Holy Ghost.*"

"*No! I mustn't think it, I won't think it, that's the mortal sin. I can't get forgiven. I won't think fuck the Holy Ghost. Oh, I thought it again.*"

Michael reaches behind him to touch the latch of the screen door. He touches his forehead to his knee. Then he concentrates hard on the lawn mower. He is anxious to finish it. He is saving his money for a flying lesson.

From the first, Lander was attracted to machinery and he had a gift for working with machines. This did not become a passion until he discovered machines that enveloped him, that became his body. When he was inside them, he saw his actions as those of the machine, he never saw the little scholar.

The first was a Piper Cub on a grass airfield. At the controls he saw nothing of Lander, but he saw the little plane banking, stalling, diving, and its shape was his and its grace and strength were his and he could feel the wind on it and he was free.

Lander joined the Navy when he was sixteen, and he never went home again. He was not accepted for flight school the first time he applied, and he served throughout the Korean War handling ordnance on the carrier *Coral Sea*. A picture in his album shows him standing before the wing of a Corsair with a ground crew and a rack of fragmentation bombs. The others in the crew are smiling, and they have their arms around one another's shoulders. Lander is not smiling. He is holding a fuse.

On June 1, 1953, Lander awoke in the enlisted men's barracks at Lakehurst, N.J., shortly after dawn. He had arrived at his new assignment in the middle of the night and he needed a cold shower to wake up. Then he dressed carefully. The Navy had been good for Lander. He liked the uniform, liked the way he looked in it and the anonymity it gave him. He was competent and he was accepted. Today he would report for his new job, handling pressure-actuated depth-charge detonators being prepared for experiments in anti-submarine warfare. He was good with ordnance. Like many men with deep-seated insecurities, he loved the nomenclature of weapons.

He walked through the cool morning toward the ordnance complex, looking around curiously at all he had not seen when he arrived in darkness. There were the giant hangars that held the airships. The doors on the nearest one were opening with a rumble. Lander checked the time, then stopped on the sidewalk, watching. The nose came out slowly and then the great length of it. The airship was a ZPG-1 with a capacity of a million cubic feet of helium. Lander had never been so close to one before. Three hundred twenty-four feet of silver airship, the rising sun touching it with fire. Lander trotted across the asphalt apron. The ground crew was swarming under the airship. One of the portside engines roared and a puff of blue smoke hung in the air behind it.

Lander did not want to arm airships with depth charges. He did not want to work on them or roll them in and out of hangars. He saw only the controls.

He qualified easily for the next competitive examination for officer candidate school. Two hundred eighty enlisted men took the test on a hot July afternoon in 1953. Lander placed first. His standing in OCS won him a choice of assignments. He went to the airships.

The extension of the kinesthetic sense in controlling moving machines has never been satisfactorily explained. Some people are described as "naturals," but the term is inadequate. Mike Hailwood, the great motorcycle racer, is a natural. So was Betty Skelton, as anyone will testify who has seen her do an outside Cuban Eight in her little biplane. Lander was a natural. At the controls of an airship, freed of himself, he was sure and decisive, pressure-proof. And while he flew, part of his mind was free to race ahead, weighing probabilities, projecting the next problem and the next.

By 1955, Lander was one of the most proficient airship pilots in the world. In December of that year, he was second officer on a series of hazardous flights from South Weymouth Naval Air Station in Massachusetts, testing the effects of ice accumulation in bad weather. The flights won for the crew the Harmon Trophy for that year.

And then there was Margaret. He met her in January at the officers' club at Lakehurst, where he was being lionized after the flights from South Weymouth. It was the beginning of the best year of his life.

She was twenty years old and good-looking and fresh from West Virginia. Lander the lion, in his perfect uniform, knocked her out. Oddly, he was the first man for her and, while teaching her was a great satisfaction to him, the memory of it made things much more difficult for him later when he believed that she had others.

They were married in the chapel at Lakehurst with its plaque made of wreckage from the airship *Akron*.

Lander came to define himself in terms of Margaret and his profession. He flew the biggest, longest, sleekest airship in the world. He thought Margaret was the best-looking woman in the world.

How different Margaret was from his mother! Sometimes when he awakened from dreaming of his mother, he looked at Margaret for a long time, admiring her as he checked off the physical differences.

They had two children, they went to the Jersey shore in the summer with their boat. They had some good times. Margaret was not a very perceptive person, but gradually she came to realize that Lander was not exactly what she had thought. She needed a fairly constant level of reinforcement, but he swung between extremes in his treatment of her. Sometimes he was cloyingly solicitous. When he was thwarted in his work or at home, he became cold and withdrawn. Occasionally he showed flashes of cruelty that terrified her.

They could not discuss their problems. Either he adopted an annoying pedantic attitude or he refused to talk at all. They were denied the catharsis of an occasional fight.

In the early sixties he was away much of the time, flying the giant ZPG-3W. At 403 feet, it was the biggest non-rigid airship ever built. The 40-foot radar antenna revolving inside its vast envelope provided a key link in the country's early warning system. Lander was happy, and his behavior while he was at home was correspondingly good. But the extension of the Distant Early Warning Line, the "DEW Line" of permanent radar installations, was eating into the airships' defense role, and in 1964 the end came for Lander as a Navy airship pilot. His group was disbanded, the airships were dismantled, and he was on the ground. He was transferred to Administration.

His behavior toward Margaret deteriorated. Scalding silences marked their hours together. In the evenings he cross-examined her about her activities during the day. She was innocent enough. He would not believe it. He grew physically indifferent to her. By the end of 1964, her activities in the daytime were no longer innocent. But, more than sex, she sought warmth and friendship.

Lander volunteered for helicopters during the Vietnam expansion, and he was readily accepted. He was distracted now by his training. He was flying again. He gave Margaret expensive presents. She felt uncomfortable and uneasy about them, but this was better than the way he had acted before.

On his final leave before shipping out to Vietnam

they went to Bermuda for a good vacation. If Lander's conversation was tiresomely larded with the technicalities of rotary-wing aircraft, he was at least attentive, sometimes loving. Margaret responded. Lander thought he had never loved her so much.

On February 10, 1967, Lander flew his 114th air-sea rescue mission off the carrier *Ticonderoga* in the South China Sea. A half-hour after moonset, he hung over the dark ocean off Dong Hoi. He was in a holding pattern 15 miles at sea, waiting for some F-4s and Skyraiders coming home from a raid. One of the Phantoms was hit. The pilot reported that his starboard engine had conked and he was showing a fire light. He would try to make it to the sea before he and the second officer ejected.

Lander, in the rattling cockpit of his helicopter, was talking to the pilot all the time, Vietnam a dark mass to his left.

"Ding Zero One, when you're well over the water gimme some lights if you gottem." Lander could find the Phantom crew on the water by their homing device, but he wanted to cut down on the time as much as possible. "Mr. Dillon," he said to the door gunner, "we'll go down with you facing landward. Ops confirms no friendly vessels are close by. Any boat that ain't rubber ain't ours."

The voice of the Phantom pilot was loud in his earphones. "Mixmaster, I've got a second fire light and she's filling up with smoke. We're punching out." He yelled the coordinates, and before Lander could repeat them for confirmation he was gone.

Lander knew what was happening—the two-man crew pulling down their face curtains, the canopy blowing off, the fliers rocketing up into the cold air, turning in their ejection seats, the seats falling away, and then the jar and the cool rush down through the darkness to the jungle.

He wheeled the big helicopter landward, blades slapping the heavy sea air. He had a choice now. He could wait for air cover, hang around trying to contact the men by radio, waiting for protection, or he could go in.

"There it is, sir." The copilot was pointing.

Lander could see a shower of fire a mile inland as the Phantom blew up in the air. He was over the beach when the homing signal came through. He called for air cover, but he did not wait for it. The helicopter, showing no lights, skimmed over the double canopy forest.

The light signal blinked from the narrow, rutted road. The two on the ground had the good sense to mark a landing zone for him. There was room for the rotor between the banks of trees flanking the road. Setting it down would be quicker than pulling them up with the hook one by one. Down, sinking between the banks of trees, blowing the weeds flat at the sides of the road, and suddenly the night was full of orange flashes and the cockpit ripped around him. Splattered with the copilot's blood, falling, rocking crazily, the smell of burning rubber.

The bamboo cage was not long enough for Lander to stretch out in it. His hand had been smashed by a bullet, and the pain was constant and terrible. He was delirious part of the time. His captors had nothing to treat him with except a little sulfa powder from an old French medical kit. They took a thin plank from a crate and bound the hand flat against it. The wound throbbed constantly. After three days in the cage, Lander was marched northward to Hanoi, prodded along by the small, wiry men. They were dressed in muddy black pajamas and carried very clean AK-47 automatic rifles.

During the first month of his confinement in Hanoi, Lander was half crazy with the pain in his hand. He was in a cell with an Air Force navigator, a thoughtful former zoology teacher named Jergens. Jergens put wet compresses on the mangled hand and tried to comfort Lander as best he could, but Jergens had been confined for a long time and he was very shaky himself. Thirty-seven days after Lander arrived,

Jergens reached the point where he could not stop yelling in the cell and they took him away. Lander cried when he was gone.

One afternoon in the fifth week, a young Vietnamese doctor came into the cell carrying a small black bag. Lander shrank away from him. He was seized by two guards and held while the doctor injected a powerful local anesthetic into his hand. The relief was like cool water flowing over him. In the next hour, while he could think, Lander was offered a deal.

It was explained to him that the Democratic Republic of Vietnam's medical facilities were terribly inadequate to treat even their own wounded. But a surgeon would be provided to repair his hand and drugs would be administered to ease the pain—if he signed a confession of his war crimes. It was clear to Lander that if the mangled meat at the end of his arm were not repaired, he would lose the hand and possibly the entire arm. He would never fly again. He did not believe that a confession signed under these circumstances would be regarded seriously at home. Even if it was, he preferred the hand to anyone's good opinion. The anesthetic was wearing off. Pain was beginning to shoot up his arm again. He agreed.

He was not prepared for what came next. When he saw the lectern, the room full of prisoners sitting like a class, when he was told that he must read his confession to them, he froze.

He was hustled into an anteroom. A powerful hand smelling of fish was clamped over his mouth while a guard twanged his metacarpals. He was about to faint. He nodded frantically, straining against the hand over his face. He was given another shot while the hand was tied out of sight beneath his jacket.

He read, blinking in the lights, while the movie camera whirred.

Sitting in the front row was a man with the leathery, scarred head of a plucked hawk. He was Colonel Ralph DeJong, senior American officer at the Plantation prison camp. In his four years of imprisonment, Colonel DeJong had done 258 days of solitary confinement. As Lander completed his confession, Colonel DeJong spoke suddenly, his voice carrying through the room. "It's a lie."

Two guards were on DeJong instantly. They dragged him from the room. Lander had to read the conclusion a second time. DeJong served 100 days in solitary confinement on reduced rations.

The North Vietnamese fixed Lander's hand at a hospital on the outskirts of Hanoi, a stark building whitewashed inside, with cane screens over the openings where the windows had been blown out. They did not do a pretty job. The red-eyed surgeon who worked on Lander did not have the training for cosmetic surgery on the red spider clamped to his table, and he had few drugs. But he had stainless-steel wire and ligatures and patience and, eventually, the hand functioned again. The doctor spoke English and exercised his English on Lander in maddeningly tedious conversations while he worked.

Lander, desperate for some distraction, looking anywhere but at his hand while the work went on, saw an old French-made resuscitator, obviously unused, in the corner of the operating room. It was driven by a DC motor with an eccentric flywheel pumping the bellows. Gasping, he asked about it.

The motor was burned out, the doctor said. No one knew how to fix it.

Driving his attention into any corner where it might escape the pain, Lander talked about armatures and how they are rewound. Beads of sweat stood out on his face.

"Could you repair it?" The doctor's brow was furrowed. He was tying a tiny knot. The knot was no bigger than the head of a fire ant, no bigger than a tooth pulp, bigger than the blazing sun.

"Yes." Lander talked about copper wire and reels, and some of the words were cut off in the middle.

"There," the doctor said. "That finishes you for now."

The majority of American POW's behaved in a manner admirable in the eyes of the American military. They endured for years to return to their country with a crisp salute slanting above their sunken eyes. They were determined men with strong, resilient egos. They were men for whom beliefs were possible.

Colonel DeJong was one of these. When he emerged from solitary confinement to resume command of the POW's he weighed 140 pounds. Deep in his skull his eyes glowed redly, as a martyr's eyes reflect the fire. He had not passed judgment on Lander until he saw him in a cell with a spool of copper wire, rewinding the armature on a North Vietnamese motor, a few fishbones beside him on a plate.

Colonel DeJong passed the word and Lander received the Silence in the compound. He became an outcast.

Lander had never been able to bring his usual level of craftsmanship to bear on the jerry-built system of defenses that allowed him to survive. His disgrace before the other prisoners, the isolation that came later, were all the old, bad times come back again. Only Jergens would talk to him and Jergens was often in solitary. He was taken away whenever he could not stop yelling.

Weakened by his wound, raddled with malaria, Lander was stripped down to his two ill-matched parts—the child, hated and hating, and the man he had created in the image of what he wanted to be. The old dialogues in his head resumed, but the voice of the man, the voice of sanity remained the stronger. He endured in this state for six years. It took more than prison for Lander to let go and allow the child to teach the man to kill.

On the last Christmas of his captivity, he was given one letter from Margaret. She had a job, it said. The children were all right. A picture was enclosed, Margaret and the children in front of the house. The children were longer. Margaret had gained a little weight. The shadow of the person who took the picture lay in the foreground. The shadow was wide.

It fell on their legs. Lander wondered who had taken the picture. He looked at the shadow more than he looked at his wife and children.

On February 15, 1973, Lander was led aboard an Air Force C-141 at Hanoi. An orderly fastened his seat belt. He did not look out the window.

Colonel DeJong was also on the plane, though he was hard to recognize. His nose had been broken and his teeth kicked out in the past two years as he set an example of noncooperation for his men. Now he set an example by ignoring Lander. If Lander noticed, he did not show it. He was gaunt and sallow and subject any second to a malarial chill. The Air Force doctor aboard the plane kept a close eye on him. A refreshment cart went up and down the aisle constantly.

A number of officers had been sent along on the plane to talk with the POW's, if they wanted to talk. One of these men sat by Lander. Lander did not want to talk. The officer called his attention to the goodie wagon. Lander took a sandwich and bit into it. He chewed several times, then spit the bite into his barf bag. He put the sandwich in his pocket. Then he put another sandwich in his pocket.

The officer beside him started to reassure him that there would be plenty of sandwiches, then decided against it. He patted Lander's arm. No response.

Clark Air Force Base, the Philippines. A band was there, and the base commander, ready to greet the men. Television cameras were waiting. Colonel DeJong was to be first off the plane. He walked down the aisle toward the door, saw Lander, and stopped. For a second there was hate in DeJong's face. Lander looked up at him and quickly turned away. He was trembling. DeJong opened his mouth, then his expression softened by a millimeter and he walked on, into the cheers, into the sun.

Lander was taken to St. Alban's Naval Hospital in Queens. There he began a journal, a project he would not continue long. He wrote very slowly and carefully. He was afraid that if he went any faster, the pen might get away from him and write something he did not wish to see.

Here are the first four entries:

St. Alban's, March 2.

I am free. Margaret came to see me every day for the first eight days. She has come three times this week. The other days she had car pool. Margaret looks well, but not like I thought about her back there. She looks like she is satisfied all the time. She brought the girls twice. They were here today. They just sat and looked at me and looked around the room. I kept my hand under the sheet. There is not much for them to do in the hospital. They can go down to the rec room and get a coke. I must remember to get some change. Margaret had to give them the change. I suppose I look strange to them. Margaret is very good and patient and they obey her. I dreamed about the Weasel again last night and I was absent-minded talking to them today. Margaret keeps up the conversation.

St. Alban's, March 12.

The doctors say I have falciparum malaria and that is why the chill cycle is irregular. They are giving me chloroquine, but it doesn't work immediately. A chill caught me today while Margaret was here. She has her hair cut short now. It does not look like her too much, but it smells good. She held me during the chill. She was warm, but she turned her face away. I hope I don't smell bad. Maybe it's my gums. I'm afraid Margaret will hear something. I hope she never saw the film.

Good news. The medics rate my hand only ten per cent impaired. It should not affect my flying status. Margaret and the kids will have to see it sooner or later.

St. Alban's, March 20.

Jergens is down the hall. He hopes to go back to teaching, but he is in bad shape. We were cellmates exactly two years, I think. He says it was 745 days. He is dreaming too. Sometimes the Weasel. He has to have the door of his room open. It was all the solitary toward the last that brought him down. They would not believe that he wasn't yelling deliberately in the cell at night. The Weasel yelled at him and called General Smegma. Smegma's real name was Capt. Lebron Nhu, I must remember that. Half French, half Vietnamese. They shoved Jergens back against the wall and slapped him and this is what Jergens said:

"Various species of plants and animals carry lethal factors which, when homozygous, stop development at some stage and the individual dies. A conspicuous case is that of the yellow race of the house mouse, *mus musculus*, which never breeds true. This should be of interest to you, Smegma. (That was where they started trying to drag him out of the cell.) If a yellow mouse is mated to some non-yellow, half the young are yellow and half are non-yellow (Jergens was holding onto the bars then and Weasel went outside to kick his fingers), a ratio to be expected from mating a heterozygous animal, yellow, with a homozygous recessive, any non-yellow such as agouti, a small voracious rodent, slender legged, resembling a rabbit but with smaller ears. If two yellows are mated together, the young average two yellow and one non-yellow, whereas the expected ratio among the young would be one pure yellow to two heterozygous yellow to one non-yellow. (His hands were bleeding and they were dragging him down the hall and him still yelling.) *But*, the 'homozygous yellow' dies as an embryo. That's you, Smegma. The 'creeper fowl' with short, crooked legs behaves genetically like the yellow mouse."

Jergens had six months solitary for that and lost his teeth on the diet. He had that about the yellow mouse scratched on the slats in his bunk and I used to read it after he was gone.

I am not going to think about that any more.

Yes I am. I can say it to myself during the other things. I must raise this mattress and see if anyone in the hospital has scratched on the slats.

St. Alban's, April 1, 1973.

In four days I can go home. I told Margaret. She will trade days in the car pool to come get me. I have to be careful with my temper, now that I am stronger. I blew up today when Margaret told me she had arranged to trade cars. She told me she ordered the station wagon in December, so it's already done. She should have waited. I could have gotten a better deal. She said the dealer was giving her a very special deal. She looked smug.

If I had a protractor, a level, navigation tables and a string I could figure out the date without a calendar. I get one hour of direct sunlight through my window. The strips of wood between the windowpanes make a cross on the wall. I know the time and I know the latitude and longitude of the hospital. That and the angle of the sun would give me the date. I could measure it on the wall.

Lander's return was difficult for Margaret. She had begun to build a different life with different people in his absence, and she interrupted that life to take him home. It is probable that she would have left him had he come home from his last tour in 1968, but she would not file for a divorce while he was imprisoned. She tried to be fair, and she could not bear the thought of leaving him while he was sick.

The first month was awful. Lander was very nervous, and his pills did not always help him. He could not stand to have the doors locked, even at night, and he prowled the house after midnight, making sure they were open. He went to the refrigerator twenty times a day to reassure himself that it was full of food. The children were polite to him, but their conversation was about people he did not know.

He gained strength steadily and talked of returning to active duty. The records at St. Alban's Hospital showed a weight gain of 18 pounds in the first two months.

The records of the Judge Advocate General of the Department of the Navy show that Lander was summoned to a closed hearing on May 24 to answer charges of collaboration with the enemy lodged by Colonel Ralph DeJong.

The transcript of the hearing records that Exhibit Seven, a piece of North Vietnamese propaganda film, was shown at the hearing, and that, immediately afterward, the hearing was recessed for fifteen minutes while the defendant excused himself. Subsequently, testimony by the defendant and by Colonel DeJong was heard.

The transcript on two occasions records that the accused addressed the hearing board as "Mam." Much later, these quotations were considered by the blue-ribbon commission to be typographical errors in the transcript.

In view of the accused's exemplary record prior to capture and his decoration for going after the downed air crew, the action that led to his capture, the officers at the hearing were inclined to be lenient.

A memorandum signed by Colonel DeJong is affixed to the transcript. It states that, in view of the Defense Department's expressed wish to avoid adverse publicity regarding POW misconduct, he is willing to drop the charges "for the larger good of the service" if Lander offers his resignation.

The alternative to resignation was court martial. Lander did not think he could sit through the film again.

A copy of his resignation from the United States Navy is attached to the transcript.

Lander was numb when he left the hearing room. He felt as if one of his limbs had been struck off. He would have to tell Margaret soon. Although she had never mentioned the film, she would know the reason for his resignation. He walked aimlessly through Washington, a solitary figure on a bright spring day, neat in the uniform he could never wear again. The film kept running in his head. Every detail was there, except that, somehow, his POW uniform was replaced with short pants. He sat down on a bench near the Ellipse. It was not so far to the bridge into Arlington, not so far to the river. He wondered if the undertaker would cross his hands on his chest. He wondered if he could write a note requesting that the good hand be placed on top. He wondered if the note would dissolve in his pocket. He was staring at the Washington Monument without really seeing it. He saw it with the tunnel vision of a suicide, the monument standing up in the bright circle like a post reticule in a telescopic sight. Something moved into his field of vision, crossing the bright circle, above and behind the pointed reticule.

It was the silver airship of his childhood, the Aldrich blimp. Behind the still point of the monument he could see it porpoising gently in a headwind and he gripped the end of his bench as though it were the elevator wheel. The ship was turning, turning faster now as it caught the wind on the starboard side, making a little leeway as it droned over him. Hope drifted down upon Lander through the clear spring air.

The Aldrich Company was glad to have Michael Lander. If the company officials were aware that for 98 seconds his face had appeared on network television denouncing his country, they never mentioned it. They found that he could fly superbly and that was enough.

He trembled half the night before his flight test. Margaret had great misgivings as she drove him to the airfield, only five miles away from their house. She needn't have worried. He changed even as he walked toward the airship. All the old feeling flooded him and invigorated him and left his mind calm and his hands steady.

Flying appeared to be marvelous therapy for him, and for part of him it was. But Lander's mind was jointed like a flail, and as he regained his confidence the half of his mind held steady by that confidence gave strength to the blows from the other half. His humiliation in Hanoi and Washington loomed ever greater in his mind during the fall and winter of 1973. The contrast between his self-image and the way he had been treated grew larger and more obscene.

His confidence did not sustain him through the hours of darkness. He sweated, he dreamed, he remained impotent. It was at night that the child in him, the hater, fed by his suffering, whispered to the man.

"What else has it cost you? What else? Margaret tosses in her sleep, doesn't she? Do you think she gave away a little while you were gone?"

"No."

"Fool. Ask her."

"I don't have to ask her."

"You stupid limpdick."

"Shut up."

"While you were squalling in a cell, she was straddling one."

"No. No. No. No. No. No."

"Ask her."

He asked her one cold evening near the end of October. Her eyes filled with tears and she left the room. Guilty or not?

He became obsessed with the thought that she had been unfaithful to him. He asked her druggist if her prescription for birth control pills had been renewed regularly over the past two years and was told that it was none of his business. Lying beside her after yet another of his failures, he was tormented by graphic scenes of her performing acts with other men. Sometimes the men were Buddy Ives and Junior Atkins, one on Margaret, the other awaiting his turn.

He learned to avoid her when he was angry and suspicious, and he spent some of his evenings brooding in his garage workshop. Others he passed trying to make light conversation with her, feigning an interest in the details of her daily routine, in the doings of the children at school.

Margaret was deceived by his physical recovery, and his success at his job. She thought he was practically well. She assured him that his impotence would pass. She said the Navy counselor had talked to her about it before he came home. She used the word impotence.

The blimp's first spring tour in 1974 was confined to the Northeast, so Lander could stay at home. The second was to be a run down the East Coast to Florida. He would be away three weeks. Some of Margaret's friends had a party the night before his departure and the Landers were invited. Lander was in a good humor. He insisted that they attend.

It was a pleasant gathering of eight couples. There was food and dancing. Lander did not dance. Talking rapidly, a film of sweat on his forehead, he told a captive group of husbands about the balonet and damper systems in airships. Margaret interrupted his discourse to show him the patio. When he returned, the talk had turned to professional football. He took the floor to resume his lecture where he had left off.

Margaret danced with the host. Twice. The second time, the host held her hand for a moment after the music had stopped. Lander watched them. They were talking quietly. He knew they were talking about him. He explained all about catenary curtains while his audience stared into their drinks. Margaret was being very careful, he thought. But he could see her soaking up the attention of the men. She drew it in through her skin.

Driving home he was silent, white with rage.

Finally, in the kitchen of their house, she could stand his silence no longer.

"Why don't you just start yelling and get it over with?" she said. "Go ahead and say what you're thinking."

Her kitten came into the kitchen and rubbed itself on Lander's leg. She scooped it up, fearful that he might kick it.

"Tell me what I did, Michael. We were having a good time, weren't we?"

She was so very pretty. She stood convicted by her loveliness. Lander said nothing. He approached her quickly, looking into her face. She did not back away. He had never struck her, could never strike her. He grabbed the kitten and went to the sink. When she realized what he was doing, the kitten was already in the garbage disposal. She ran to the sink and tore at his arms as he switched it on. She could hear the kitten until the disposal's ablative action disposed of its extremities and reached its vitals. All the time, Lander was staring into her face.

Her screams woke the children. She slept in their room. She heard him when he left shortly after daylight.

He sent her flowers from Norfolk. He tried to call her from Atlanta. She did not answer the telephone. He wanted to tell her that he realized his suspicions were groundless, the product of a sick imagination. He wrote her a long letter from Jacksonville, telling her he was sorry, that he knew he had been cruel and unfair and crazy and that he would never behave that way again.

On the tenth day of the scheduled three-week tour, the copilot was bringing the blimp to the landing mast when a freak gust of wind caught it and swung it into the maintenance truck, tearing the fabric of the envelope. The airship would stand down for a day and a night while repairs were made. Lander could not face a motel room for a day and a night with no word from Margaret.

He caught a flight to Newark. At a Newark pet store he bought a fine Persian kitten. He arrived at his house at midday. The house was quiet, the children were at camp. Margaret's car was in the driveway. Her teapot was heating on a low fire. He would give her the kitten and tell her he was sorry and they could hold each other and she would forgive him. He took the kitten out of the carrier and straightened the ribbon around its neck. He climbed the stairs.

The stranger was reclining on the daybed, Margaret astride him pumping, her breasts bouncing. They did not see Lander until he screamed. It was a short fight. Lander did not have all his strength back and the stranger was big, fast and frightened. He slugged Lander hard on the temple twice and he and Margaret fled together.

Lander sat on the playroom floor, his back against the wall. His mouth was open and bleeding and his eyes were vacant. The teapot whistle shrilled for half an hour. He did not move, and when the water boiled away, the house was filled with the smell of scorched metal.

When pain and rage reach levels far above the mind's capacity to cope, a curious relief is possible but it requires a partial death.

Lander smiled an awful smile, a bloody rictus smile, when he felt his will die. He believed that it passed out through his mouth and nose in a thin smoke riding on a sigh. The relief came to him then. It was over. Oh, it was over. For half of him.

The remains of the man Lander would feel some pain, would jerk galvanically like frogs' legs in a skillet, would cry out for relief. But he would never again sink his teeth into the pumping heart of rage. Rage would never again cut out his heart and rub it pumping in his face.

What was left could live with rage because it was made in rage and rage was its element and it thrived there as a mammal thrives in air.

He rose and washed his face, and when he left the house, when he returned to Florida, he was steady. His mind was as cool as snake's blood. There were no more dialogues in his head. There was only one voice now. The man functioned perfectly because the child needed him, needed his quick brain and clever fingers. To find its own relief. By killing and killing and killing and killing. And dying.

He did not yet know what he would do, but as he hung over the crowded stadiums week after week, it would come to him. And when he knew what he must do, he sought the means, and before the means came Dahlia. And Dahlia heard some of these things and inferred much of the rest.

He was drunk when he told her about finding Margaret and her lover in the house and afterward he became violent. She caught him behind the ear with the heel of her hand, knocking him unconscious. In the morning, he did not remember that she had hit him.

Two months passed before Dahlia was sure of him, two months of listening, of watching him build and scheme and fly, of lying next to him at night.

When she was sure, she told Hafez Najeer these things and Najeer found it good.

Now, with the explosives at sea, moving toward the United States at a steady 12 knots in the freighter *Leticia*, the entire project was threatened by Captain Larmoso's treachery and perhaps by the treachery of Benjamin Muzi himself. Had Larmoso interfered with the crates at Muzi's orders? Perhaps Muzi had decided to keep the advance payment, sell Lander and Dahlia to the authorities, and peddle the plastic elsewhere. If so, they could not risk picking up the explosives on the New York dock. They must pick up the plastic at sea.

CHAPTER 6

THE BOAT WAS fairly standard in appearance—a sleek
sportfisherman 38 feet long—a "canyon runner" of the
kind used by men with a lot of money and not much
time. Each weekend in the season many of them blast
eastward through the swells, carrying paunchy men in
Bermuda shorts to the sudden deeps off the New
Jersey coast where the big fish feed.

But in an age of fiberglass and aluminum boats,
this one was made of wood—double planked with
Philippine mahogany. It was beautifully and strongly
made and it had cost a great deal. Even the superstructure was wood, but this was not noticeable because much of the brightwork had been painted over.
Wood is a very poor radar reflector.

Two big turbocharged diesels were crammed into
the engine room and much of the space used for dining and relaxing in ordinary craft had been sacrificed
to make room for extra fuel and water. For much of
the summer, the owner used it in the Caribbean, running hashish and marijuana out of Jamaica into Miami
in the dark of the moon. In the winter he came north
and the boat was for hire, but not to fishermen. The
fee was $2,000 a day, no questions asked, plus a

staggering deposit. Lander had mortgaged his house to get the deposit.

It was in a boathouse at the end of a row of deserted piers in Toms River off Barnegat Bay, fully fueled, waiting.

At 10 A.M. on November 12 Lander and Dahlia arrived at the boathouse in a rented van. A cold, drizzling rain was falling and the winter piers were deserted. Lander opened the double doors on the landward side of the boathouse and backed the van in until it was 6 feet from the stern of the big sportfisherman. Dahlia exclaimed at the sight of the boat, but Lander was busy with his checklist and paid no attention. For the next 20 minutes they loaded equipment aboard: extra coils of line, a slender mast, two long-barreled shotguns, a shotgun with the barrel sawed off to 18 inches, a high-powered rifle, a small platform lashed onto four hollow floats, charts to supplement the already well-stocked chart bin, and several neat bundles that included a lunch.

Lander lashed every object down so tightly that even if the boat had been turned upside down and shaken, nothing would have fallen out.

He flicked a switch on the boathouse wall and the big door on the water side creaked upward, admitting the gray winter light. He climbed to the flying bridge. First the port diesel roared and then the starboard, blue smoke rising in the dim boathouse. His eyes darted from gauge to gauge as the engines warmed up.

At Lander's signal, Dahlia cast off the stern lines and joined him on the flying bridge. He eased the throttles forward, the water swelling like a muscle at the stern, the exhaust ports awash and burbling, and the boat nosed slowly out into the rain.

When they had cleared Toms River, Lander and Dahlia moved to the lower control station inside the heated cabin for the run down the bay to Barnegat Inlet and the open sea. The wind was from the north, raising a light chop. They sliced through it easily, the windshield wipers slowly swiping away fine raindrops. No other boats were out that they could see. The long sandspit that protected the bay lay low in the mist off to port and on the other side they could make out a smokestack at the head of Oyster Creek.

In less than an hour they reached Barnegat Inlet. The wind had shifted to the northeast and the ground swells were building in the inlet. Lander laughed as they met the first of the big Atlantic rollers, spray bursting from the bows. They had mounted to the exposed upper control station again to run the inlet, and cold spray stung their faces.

"The waves won't be so big out there, sport," Lander said as Dahlia wiped her face with the back of her hand.

She could see that he was enjoying himself. He loved to feel the boat under him. Buoyancy had a fascination for Lander. Fluid strength, giving, pushing with support reliable as rock. He turned the wheel slowly from side to side, slightly altering the angle at which the boat met the seas, extending his kinesthetic sense to feel the changing forces on the hull. The land was falling astern now on both sides, the Barnegat Light flashing off to starboard.

They ran out of the drizzle into watery winter sunlight as they cleared the shore and, looking back, Dahlia watched the gulls wheeling, very white against the gray clouds banked behind them. Wheeling as they had above the beach at Tyre when she was a child standing in the warm sand, her feet small and brown beneath her ragged hem. She had followed too many strange corridors in Michael Lander's mind for too long. She wondered how the presence of Muhammad Fasil would change the chemistry between them, if Fasil was still alive and waiting with the explosives out there beyond the 90-fathom curve. She would have to speak with Fasil quickly. There were things that Fasil must understand before he made a fatal mistake.

When she turned back to face the sea, Lander was watching her from the helmsman's seat, one hand on the wheel. The sea air had brought color to her cheeks and her eyes were bright. The collar of her sheepskin coat was turned up around her face and her Levis were taut around her thighs as she balanced against the motion of the boat. Lander, with two big diesels beneath his hand, doing something that he did well, threw back his head and laughed and laughed again. It was a real laugh and it surprised her. She had not heard it often.

"You are a dynamite lady, you know that?" he said, wiping his eye with his knuckle.

She looked down at the deck and then raised her head again, smiling, looking into him. "Let's go get some plastic."

"Yeah," Lander said, bobbing his head. "All the plastic in the world."

He held a course of 110 degrees magnetic, a hair north of east with the compass variation, then altered it north 5 more degrees as the bell and whistle buoys off Barnegat showed him more precisely the effect of the wind. The seas were on the port bow, moderating now, and only a little spray blew back as the boat sliced through them. Somewhere out there beyond the horizon, the freighter was waiting, riding the winter sea.

They paused at mid-afternoon while Lander made a fix of their position with the radio direction finder. He did it early to avoid the distortion that would be present at sundown and he did it very carefully, taking three bearings and plotting them on his chart, noting times and distances in meticulous little figures.

As they roared on eastward toward the "X" on the chart, Dahlia made coffee in the galley to go with the sandwiches she had brought, then cleared away the counter. With small strips of adhesive tape, she fastened to the countertop a pair of surgical scissors, compress bandages, three small disposable syringes of morphine, and a single syringe of Ritalin. She laid a set of splints along the fiddle rail at the counter edge and fastened them in place with a strip of tape.

They reached the approximate rendezvous point, well beyond the northbound Barnegat-to-Ambrose sealane, an hour before sunset. Lander checked his position with the RDF and corrected it slightly north-ward.

They saw the smoke first, a smudge on the horizon to the east. Then two dots under the smoke as the freighter's superstructure showed. Soon she was hull up, steaming slowly. The sun was low in the southwest, behind Lander as he ran toward the ship. It was as he had planned. He would come out of the sun to look her over, and any gunman on the ship with a telescopic sight would be dazzled by the light.

Throttled back, the sportsfisherman eased toward the scabby freighter, Lander studying her through his binoculars. As he watched, two signal flags shot up the outboard halyards on the port side. He could make out a white "X" on a blue field and, below it, a red diamond on a white field.

"M.F.," Lander read.

"That's it. Muhammad Fasil."

Forty minutes of sunlight remained. Lander decided to take advantage of it. With no other vessels in sight, it was better to risk the transfer in daylight than to take a chance on mischief from the freighter in the dark. While there was light, he and Dahlia could keep the rail of the freighter covered.

Dahlia broke out the Delta pennant. Closer and closer the boat crept, its exhaust burbling. Dahlia and Lander pulled on stocking masks.

"Big shotgun," Lander said.

She put it in his hand. He opened the windshield in front of him and laid the shotgun on the instrument panel, muzzle out on the foredeck. It was a Remington 12-gauge automatic with a long barrel and full choke, and it was loaded with 00 buckshot. Lander knew it would be impossible to fire a rifle accurately from the moving boat. He and Dahlia had gone over it many times. If Fasil had lost control of the ship and they were fired on, Lander would shoot back, blast the stern around, and run into the sun while Dahlia emptied the other long shotgun at the freighter. She would switch to the rifle when the range increased.

"Don't worry about trying to hit somebody with

the boat pitching," he had told her. "Rattle enough lead around their ears and you'll suppress their fire." Then he remembered that she had more experience with small arms than he.

The freighter turned slowly and hove to with the seas nearly abeam. From 300 yards, Lander could see only three men on her deck and a single lookout high on the bridge. One of the men ran to the signal halyard and dipped the flags once, acknowledging the Delta Lander was flying. It would have been easier to use radio, but Fasil could not be on deck and in the radio shack at the same time.

"That's him, that's Fasil in the blue cap," Dahlia said, lowering her binoculars.

When Lander was within 100 yards, Fasil spoke to the two men beside him. They swung a lifeboat davit out over the side, then stood with their hands in sight on the rail.

Lander idled his engines and scrambled aft to rig a fender board on the starboard side, then mounted to the flying bridge carrying the short shotgun.

Fasil appeared to be in control of the ship. Lander could see a revolver in his belt. He must have ordered the deck cleared except for the mate and one crewman. The rust streaks on the freighter's side glowed orange in the lowering sun as Lander brought the boat under her lee and Dahlia threw a line to the crewman. The sailor started to make it fast to a deck cleat, but Dahlia shook her head and beckoned. Then he understood and passed the line around the cleat and threw the end back.

She and Lander had rehearsed this carefully, and she quickly rigged a doubled after bowspring—a connection that could be cast off instantly from the smaller craft. With the rudder hard over, the engines held the boat's stern against the ship.

Fasil had repacked the plastic explosive in 25-pound bags. Forty-eight of them were piled on the deck beside him. The fender board scraped against the side of the freighter as the boat rose and fell on the muted seas in the lee of the ship. A ladder was flung over the *Leticia's* side.

Fasil called down to Lander, "The mate is coming down. He is not armed. He can help stow the bags."

Lander nodded and the man scrambled down the side. He obviously was trying not to look at Dahlia or Lander, sinister in their masks. Using the lifeboat davit as a miniature cargo crane, Fasil and the sailor lowered a cargo net containing the first six bags and the automatic weapons in a canvas-wrapped bundle. It was a tricky business in the lively boat to time exactly the moment to release the load from the hook, and once Lander and the mate went sprawling.

With twelve bags in the cockpit, the loading operation paused while the three in the boat passed the bags forward, stowing them in the cabin in the bow. It was all Lander could do to keep himself from ripping open a bag and looking at the stuff. It felt electric in his hands. Then came the next twelve bags and the next. The three working in the boat were wet with sweat despite the cold.

The hail from the lookout on the bridge was nearly carried away by the wind. Fasil spun around and cupped his hands behind his ears. The man was waving his arms and pointing. Fasil leaned over the rail and yelled down, "Something's coming, from that way —east. I'm going to look."

In less than 15 seconds he was on the bridge, snatching the binoculars from the frightened lookout. He was back on the deck in an instant, wrestling with the cargo net, yelling over the side.

"It's white with a stripe near the bow."

"Coast Guard," Lander said. "What's the range—how far away?"

"About 8 kilometers, he's coming fast."

"Swing it down, God dammit."

Fasil slapped the face of the crewman beside him and put the man's hands on the lifting tackle. The cargo net bulging with the last twelve bags of plastic swayed over the sea and dropped quickly, ropes squealing in the blocks. It dropped into the cockpit with a heavy thump and was quickly lashed down.

On the freighter deck, Muhammad Fasil turned to the sweating crewman. "Stand at the rail with your hands in sight." The man fixed his eyes on the horizon and appeared to be holding his breath as Fasil went over the side.

The mate standing in the cockpit could not take his eyes off Fasil. The Arab handed the man a roll of bills and pulled out his revolver, touching the muzzle to the man's upper lip. "You have done well. Silence and health are one. Do you understand me?"

The man wanted to nod, but was prevented by the pistol under his nose.

"Go in peace."

The man went up the ladder as rapidly as an ape. Dahlia was casting off the bowspring.

While this was going on, Lander looked almost pensive. He had demanded from his mind a projection of possibilities based on all he knew.

The patrol boat, approaching from the other side of the ship, could not see him yet. Probably the sight of the freighter hove to had aroused the Coast Guard's curiosity, unless they had been tipped off. Patrol boat. Six in these waters, all 82 feet, twin diesels, 1,600 shaft horsepower, good for 20 knots. Sperry-Rand SPB-5 radar, crew of eight. One .50 caliber machine gun and an 81 mm mortar. In a flash Lander considered setting fire to the freighter, forcing the cutter to stop and render aid. No, the first mate would scream piracy and the hue and cry would go up. Search planes would come, some of them with infrared equipment that would pick up the heat of his engines. Darkness coming. No moon for five hours. Better a chase.

Lander snapped back to the present. His deliberations had taken five seconds.

"Dahlia, rig the reflector." He slammed the throttles open and heeled the big boat over in a foaming curve away from the freighter. He headed toward the land, forty miles away, the engines roaring at full throttle and spray flying back as they smashed through moderate seas. Even heavily laden, the powerful boat was doing close to 19 knots. The cutter had a slight edge in speed. He would keep the freighter between them as long as he could. He yelled down to Fasil in the cockpit. "Monitor 2182 kilocycles." This was the International Radio-Telephone Distress frequency and a "calling frequency" used in initial contacts between vessels.

The freighter was well astern now, but as they watched, the cutter appeared, still beyond the freighter but coming hard, throwing a big bow wave. As Lander looked back over his shoulder he saw the cutter's bow swing slightly until it pointed dead at him.

Fasil scrambled up the ladder until his head was above the level of the flying bridge. "He's ordering us to halt."

"Fuck him. Switch to the Coast Guard frequency. It's marked on the dial. We'll see if he calls for help."

With the running lights off, the boat raced toward the last glow in the west. Behind them, graceful white bow and bow wave gleaming in the last light, the Coast Guard cutter charged like a terrier.

Dahlia had finished clamping the passive radar reflector to the handrail on the bridge. It was a kite-shaped assembly of metal rods which she had bought in a marine supply store for $12, and it trembled as the boat plunged through the seas.

Lander sent her below to check the lashings. He wanted nothing to come adrift in the pounding the boat would have to take.

She checked the cockpit first and then worked forward to the cabin where Fasil frowned at the radio.

"Nothing yet," he said in Arabic. "Why the radar reflector?"

"The Coast Guard would have seen us anyway," Dahlia said. She had to yell in his ear to be heard in the plunging boat. "When the Coast Guard captain sees that the chase will continue into darkness, he will have his radar operator get a fix on us and track us while he can still follow visually—then there will be no problem identifying the blip we make on his screen after the light is gone." Lander had explained all this at tiresome length. "With that reflector, it is a big, fat blip, distinct from interference from the waves. Like the image of a metal boat."

"Is—"

"Listen to me," she said urgently, glancing upward toward the bridge above their heads. "You must not act familiar with me in any way, or touch me, do you understand? You must speak only English in his presence. Never come upstairs in his house. Never surprise him. For the sake of the mission."

Fasil's face was lit from beneath by the radio dials, his eyes glowing in their shadowed sockets. "For the mission, then, Comrade Dahlia. As long as he functions, I will humor him."

Dahlia nodded. "If you don't humor him, you may find out how well he functions," she said, but the words were lost in the wind as she climbed aft.

It was dark now. There was only the faint light of the binnacle on the bridge, visible to Lander alone. He could see the red and green running lights of the cutter clearly and its big searchlight boring into the dark. He estimated that the government vessel had about a half-knot advantage and his lead was about four-and-a-half miles. Fasil climbed up beside him. "He's radioed customs about the *Leticia*. He says he's going to take us himself."

"Tell Dahlia it's almost time."

They were pounding toward the sealanes now. Lander knew that the men in the cutter could not see him, yet the vessel matched every slight course alteration he made. He could almost feel the fingers of the radar on his back. It would be better if there were some ships . . . yes! Off the port bow were the white range lights of a ship, and as the minutes passed he raised her running lights. A freighter northbound and plowing along at a good rate. He altered course slightly to pass under her bows as closely as possible. Lander saw in his mind the patrol boat's radar screen, its green light glowing on the face of the operator watching the big image of the freighter and the smaller one of the speedboat converge, the blips glowing bright each time the sweep went around.

"Get ready," he yelled to Dahlia.

"Let's go," she said to Fasil. He did not ask questions. Together they pulled the little platform with the floats clear of the lashed-down explosives. Each float was made of a five-gallon drum and each had a pinhole in the top and an ordinary faucet in its underside. Dahlia brought the mast from the cabin and the radar reflector from the bridge. They clamped the reflector to the top of the mast and set the mast in a socket on the platform. With Fasil's help she attached a 6-foot line to the underside of the platform and secured the other end to a heavy lead weight. They looked up from their work to see the lights of the freighter hanging almost over them, its bow like a cliff. In a flash they were past it.

Lander, angling north, looked back over the stern to keep the freighter between him and the patrol boat. Now the radar blips had merged, the greater height of the freighter shielding Lander's boat from the radar impulses.

He estimated the distance back to the cutter. "Half turn on the faucets." A moment later, he cut the engines. "Overboard."

Dahlia and Fasil dropped the floating platform over the side, the mast wagging wildly until the weight hanging down beneath the platform steadied it like a keel, holding the radar reflector high above the water. The device rocked again as Lander rammed the throttles home and headed straight south in the blacked-out boat.

"The radar operator can't be sure if the image of the reflector is us or something new, or if we're running along on the other side of the freighter," Fasil said. "How long will it float?"

"Fifteen minutes with the faucets half open," Dahlia said. "It will be gone when the cutter gets there."

"Then he will follow the ship north to see if we're alongside?"

"Perhaps."

"How much can he see of us now?"

"A wooden boat at this range, not much if anything. Even the paint is not lead-based. There will be some wake interference from the ship. The engine noise from the ship will help too, if he stops to listen. We don't know yet if he's taken the bait."

From the bridge, Lander watched the lights of the patrol boat. He could see the two high white range lights and the red portside running light. If she turned toward him, he would see the green starboard light come around.

Dahlia was beside him now and together they watched the cutter's lights. They saw only red, and then as the distance increased they could make out only the white range lights, then nothing but an occasional beam of the searchlight, raised by a wave, probing the empty dark.

Lander was aware of a third presence on the bridge.

"A nice piece of work," Muhammad Fasil said.

Lander did not answer him.

CHAPTER 7

MAJOR KABAKOV'S eyes were red and he was irritable. The clerks in the New York office of the Immigration and Naturalization Service had learned to walk softly around him as he sat, day after day, studying mug shots of Arab aliens living in the United States.

The ledger-sized books piled on either side of him at the long table contained, in all, 137,000 photos and descriptions. He was determined to look at every one. If the woman was on a mission in this country, she would have established a cover first, he was convinced of it. The "suspicious Arab" file maintained sub rosa by Immigration had contained few women, and none of them resembled the woman in Hafez Najeer's bedroom. Immigration and Naturalization estimated there were some 85,000 Arabs on the Eastern Seaboard who had entered the country illegally over the years and appeared in nobody's file. Most of them worked quietly at inconspicuous jobs, bothered no one and rarely came to the attention of the authorities. The possibility plagued him that the woman might be one of these.

Wearily, he turned another page. Here's a woman. Katherine Ghalib. Working with retarded children in Phoenix. Fifty years old and looks it.

A clerk was at his elbow. "Major, there's a call for you in the office."

"Very well. Don't move these damned books. I'll lose my place."

The caller was Sam Corley in Washington.

"How's it going?"

"Nothing yet. I've got about 80,000 Arabs to go."

"I got a report from the Coast Guard. It may not be anything, but one of their cutters spotted a power boat next to a Libyan freighter off the Jersey coast yesterday afternoon. The boat ran from them when they went to take a look."

"*Yesterday?*"

"Yeah, they had been busy with a ship fire way out and they were coming back. The freighter was out of Beirut."

"Where's the ship now?"

"Impounded in Brooklyn. Captain's missing. I don't know the details yet."

"What about the boat?"

"Gave them the slip in the dark."

Kabakov swore viciously. "Why did it take them so long to tell us?"

"Damned if I know, but there it is. I'll call Customs up there. They'll give you a rundown."

The *Leticia's* first mate and acting captain, Mustapha Fawzi, talked with customs officers for an hour in his little cabin, waving his arms in air thick with the acrid smoke of his Turkish cigarettes.

Yes, the boat approached his ship, Fawzi told them. The boat was low on petrol and requested assistance. Following the law of the sea, he helped them. His description of the boat and its occupants was vague. This event took place in international waters, he stressed. No, he would not voluntarily permit a search of his vessel. The ship, under international law, was Libyan territory and was his responsibility after the most unfortunate falling overboard of Captain Larmoso.

Customs did not want an incident with the Libyan

government, particularly now with the Middle East inflamed. What the Coast Guard saw would not constitute sufficient probable cause for a search warrant to be issued. Fawzi promised a deposition on Larmoso's accident, and the customs officers left the ship to confer with the departments of Justice and State.

Fawzi drank a bottle of the late Captain's beer and fell soundly asleep for the first time in days.

A voice seemed to be calling Fawzi from far away. His name was repeated in a deep voice and something was hurting his eyes. Fawzi awoke and raised his hand to shield his eyes from the blinding flashlight beam.

"Good evening, Mustapha Fawzi," Kabakov said. "Please keep your hands above the sheet."

Sergeant Moshevsky, looming huge behind Kabakov, flicked on the lights. Fawzi sat up in bed and called upon God.

"Freeze," Moshevsky said, holding a knife beneath Fawzi's ear.

Kabakov pulled up a chair and sat down at the bedside. He lit a cigarette. "I would appreciate a quiet conversation now. Will it be quiet?"

Fawzi nodded and Kabakov motioned Moshevsky away. "Now Mustapha Fawzi, I am going to explain to you how you will help me at no risk to yourself. You see, I will not hesitate to kill you if you do not cooperate, but I have no reason to kill you if you are helpful. It's very important that you understand that."

Moshevsky stirred impatiently and delivered his line. "First let me cut—"

"No, no," Kabakov said, raising his hand. "You see, Fawzi, with men less intelligent than yourself it is often necessary to establish, first, that you will suffer terrible pain and mutilation if you displease me and, second, that you will get some marvelous reward if you are useful. We both know what the reward usually is." Kabakov flicked the ash from his cigarette with the tip of his little finger. "Ordinarily, I would let my friend break your arms before we talked. But you see, Fawzi, you have nothing to lose by telling me what has happened here. Your noncooperation with customs is a matter of record. Your cooperation with me will remain our secret." He flipped his Israeli identification onto the bed. "Will you help me?"

Fawzi looked at the card and swallowed hard. He said nothing.

Kabakov rose and sighed. "Sergeant, I am going out for a breath of air. Perhaps Mustapha Fawzi would like some refreshments. Call me when he has finished eating his testicles." He turned toward the cabin door.

"I have relatives in Beirut." Fawzi was having trouble controlling his voice. Kabakov could see the heart pounding in his thin body as he sat half-naked in the bunk.

"Of course you do," Kabakov said. "And they have been threatened, I am sure. Lie to Customs all you like. But don't lie to me, Fawzi. There is no place where you will be safe from me. Not here, not at home, not in any port on earth. I have respect for your relatives. I understand these things and I'll cover for you."

"The Lebanese killed Larmoso in the Azores," Fawzi began.

Moshevsky had no taste for torture. He knew Kabakov hated it as well. It took a conscious effort for Moshevsky to keep from smiling as he searched the cabin. Each time Fawzi's recitation faltered, Moshevsky paused in his work to scowl at him, trying to look disappointed at not getting to carve him up.

"Describe the Lebanese."

"Slender, medium height. He had a cut on his face, scabbed over."

"What was in the bags?"

"I don't know. As Allah is my witness. The Lebanese packed them from the crates in the forward hold. He allowed no one near them."

"How many were in the boat?"

"Two."

"Describe them."

"One tall and thin, the other smaller. They wore masks. I was frightened, I did not look."

"What did they speak?"

"The bigger spoke English with the Lebanese."

"The smaller?"

"The smaller said nothing."

"Could the smaller have been a woman?"

The Arab flushed. He did not want to admit being frightened by a woman. It was unthinkable.

"With the Lebanese holding a gun, with your relatives threatened—it was these thoughts that made you cooperate, Fawzi," Kabakov said gently.

"The smaller could have been a woman," Fawzi said finally.

"You saw her hands on the bags?"

"She wore gloves. But there was a lump at the back of her mask that might have been her hair. And there is the thing of her bottom."

"The thing of her bottom?"

"Rounded, you know. Wider than a man's. Perhaps a shapely boy?"

Moshevsky, rummaging through the refrigerator, helped himself to a bottle of beer. Something was behind the bottle. He pulled it out and handed it to Kabakov.

"Did Captain Larmoso's religion require him to keep religious articles in his refrigerator?" Kabakov asked, holding the knife-scarred figure of the Madonna close to Fawzi's face.

Fawzi looked at it with genuine incomprehension and the distaste a Moslem feels toward religious statuary. Kabakov, deep in thought, smelled the statue and dug into it with his fingernail. Plastic. Larmoso had known what it was, but had not known much about its properties, he reasoned. The captain had thought it safest to keep the thing cold, as cold as the rest of the explosive down in the hold. He needn't have bothered, Kabakov thought. He turned the statue in his hands. If they went to this trouble to disguise the plastic, then they originally had planned to bring it through Customs.

"Get me the ship's books," Kabakov snapped.

Fawzi found the manifest with the bill of lading

after a short delay. Mineral water, unrestricted hides, flatware—there it was. Three crates of religious statues. Made in Taiwan. Shipped to Benjamin Muzi.

Muzi watched from Brooklyn Heights as the *Leticia* labored into New York harbor escorted by the Coast Guard cutter. He swore in several languages. What had Larmoso done? Muzi walked to a telephone booth at top speed, approximately two-and-a-half miles per hour. He moved with the dignity of an elephant, and like an elephant he had surprising grace in his extremities and loved orderly progressions. This business was most disorderly.

His size prevented him from entering the booth, but he could reach inside and dial. He called Coast Guard Search and Rescue, identifying himself as a reporter for El Diario-La Prensa. The helpful young man at the Coast Guard communications center told him the details that could be gleaned from radio traffic concerning the *Leticia* and her missing captain and the pursuit of the speedboat.

Muzi drove along the Brooklyn-Queens Expressway overlooking the Brooklyn docks. On the pier beside the *Leticia* he could see both Customs and Port Authority police. He was relieved that neither the freighter nor the cutter flew the red swallow-tailed Bravo that means dangerous cargo aboard. Either the authorities had not yet found the explosives or the speedboat had taken the plastic off the ship. If the speedboat had taken the plastic, which was very likely, then he had a little time as far as the law was concerned. It would take days for the authorities to inventory the *Leticia's* cargo and pinpoint the missing shipment. Probably he was not yet hot with the law. But he was hot all right, and he could feel it.

Something was terribly wrong. It did not matter whose fault it was, he would be blamed. He had a quarter of a million dollars of Arab money in a bank in the Netherlands and his employers would accept no excuse. If they took the plastic at sea, then they believed he was ready to betray them, had betrayed them. What had that fool Larmoso done? Whatever it was, Muzi knew he would never get a chance to explain that he was innocent. Black September would kill him at the first opportunity. Clearly he would have to take early retirement.

From his safe deposit box in a lower Manhattan bank, Muzi took a thick wad of banknotes and a number of bankbooks. One of the bankbooks bore the name of the Netherland's oldest and most prestigious financial house. It showed a balance of $250,000, all deposited at once and available only to him.

Muzi sighed. It would have been so nice to collect the second $250,000 when the plastic was delivered. Now the guerrillas would stake out the bank in Holland for a while, he was sure. Let them. He would transfer the account and pick up the money elsewhere.

The items that worried him most were not in the lockbox. His passports. For years he had kept them in the lockbox, but after his last trip to the Middle East, inexcusably he had left them in his home. He would have to get them. Then he would fly from Newark to Chicago to Seattle and over the Pole to London. Where was it that Farouk had dined in London? Muzi, who greatly admired Farouk's taste and style, determined to find out.

Muzi had no intention of returning to his office. Let them interrogate the Greek. His ignorance would astound them. The odds were very good that the guerrillas were watching his home as well. But they would not watch long. With the explosives in hand, they would have other things to do. It would be stupid to rush home immediately. Let them think that he had already fled.

He checked into a motel on the West Side, signing the register "Chesterfield Pardue." He iced down 12 bottles of Perrier in the bathroom sink. For a moment he felt a nervous chill. He had a sudden urge to sit in the dry bathtub with the shower curtain closed, but he feared that his wide behind would get stuck in the tub as it had in Atlantic City once.

The chill passed and he lay on the bed, hands

folded on his great mound of a stomach, frowning at the ceiling. Fool that he was to get mixed up with those scabby guerrillas. Skinny, oafish fellows, all of them, enjoying nothing but politics. Beirut had been bad news for him before, in the failure of the Intra Bank in 1967. The bank failure had put a dent in his retirement fund. If it had not occurred he would have retired already.

He had been close to recouping when the Arab offer came along. The whopping fee for bringing in the plastic would put him over the top. For that reason, he had decided to take the risk. Well, half the guerrilla money would still do it.

Retirement. To his exquisite little villa near Naples with no difficult steps to climb. It had been a long time coming.

He had started as a cabin boy on the freighter *Ali Bey*. At 16, his bulk already made climbing the companionways a chore. When the *Ali Bey* came to New York in 1938, Muzi took one look at the city and immediately jumped ship. Fluent in four languages and quick with figures, he soon found employment on the Brooklyn waterfront as a warehouse checker for a Turk named Jahal Bezir, a man of almost Satanic cunning who cleaned up in the black market during World War II.

Bezir was greatly impressed with Muzi, for he could never catch him stealing. By 1947 Muzi was keeping books for Bezir, and as time passed the old man relied on him more and more.

The old Turk's mind remained clear and active, but increasingly he lapsed into the Turkish of his childhood, dictating his correspondence in that language and leaving the translation to Muzi. Bezir made a great show of reading the translations, but if there were several letters, he sometimes was unaware of which one was in his hand. This puzzled Muzi. The old man's eyesight was good. He was far from senile. He was fluent in English. With a few judicious tests, Muzi confirmed that Bezir could no longer read. A visit to the public library told Muzi a great deal about aphasia. The old man had it all right. Muzi thought about this development for a long time. Then he began to make modest currency speculations on the foreign exchanges, taking advantage of the Turk's credit without his knowledge or consent.

The postwar currency fluctuations were good for Muzi. Almost the only exception was one awful three-day period, when a cartel of speculators red-dogged Muscat military scrip with Muzi holding 10,000 certificates at 27 to the pound sterling and the Turk snoring peacefully upstairs. That cost him $3,000 U.S. out of his own pocket, but by then he could afford it.

Meanwhile he had delighted Bezir by devising a hollow docking hawser for the importation of hashish. When the Turk died, distant relatives appeared to seize his business and ruin it. Muzi was left with $65,000 he had made in currency speculation and some excellent smuggling connections. That was all he needed to become a dealer in anything and everything that would turn a dollar, with the exception of hard narcotics. The astronomical profit potential of heroin tempted him, but Muzi saw past the fast buck. He did not want to be branded for the rest of his life. He did not want to have to sleep in a safe at night. He did not want the risks, and he did not like the people who dealt in heroin. Hashish was another matter entirely.

By 1972, the Jihaz al-Rasd section of Al Fatah was heavily engaged in the hashish trade. Many of the half-kilo sacks Muzi bought in Lebanon were decorated with their trademark—a feda'i holding a submachine gun. It was through his hashish connections that Muzi had delivered the letter for the American, and it was through them that he had been approached about smuggling in the plastic.

In recent months, Muzi had been extricating himself from the hash trade and systematically closing out his other interests in the Middle East. He wanted to do it gradually and leave no one on the hook. He wanted to make no enemies who might interfere with

a peaceful retirement and an endless succession of
dinners *al fresco* on his terrace overlooking the Bay
of Naples. Now this business of the *Leticia* threatened
everything. Perhaps the guerrillas were unsure of
him because he was pulling out of the Middle East.
Larmoso, too, must have gotten wind of his liquida-
tions and been uneasy, ready for a chance to go into
business for himself. Whatever Larmoso had done,
he had spooked the Arabs badly.

Muzi knew he could manage all right in Italy. He
had to take one sizable chance here in New York,
and then he was home free. Lying on his motel bed,
waiting to make his move, his stomach rumbling, Muzi
pretended he was dining at Lutèce.

Kabakov sat on a coil of garden hose, shivering.
A cold draft whistled through the tool shed atop the
warehouse and there was frost on the walls, but the
shed offered concealment and a good view of Muzi's
house across the street. The sleepy man watching out
the side window of the shack unwrapped a chocolate
bar and began to gnaw it, the cold chocolate breaking
off with little popping sounds. He and the other two
members of the tactical incursion team had driven up
from Washington in a rented van after they received
Kabakov's call.

The hard five-hour drive on the turnpike had
been necessary because the team's luggage would have
aroused a great deal of interest under an airport fluoroscope—submachine guns, snipers' rifles, grenades. Another member of the team was on a roof down the
block on the opposite side of the street. The third
was with Moshevsky at Muzi's office.

The sleepy Israeli offered Kabakov some of the
chocolate. Kabakov shook his head and continued to
watch the house through his binoculars, peering
through the crack in the partially opened shed door.
Kabakov wondered if he had been right in not telling
Corley and the other American authorities about Muzi
and the Madonna. He snorted through his nose. Of
course he was right. At best, the Americans might

have let him talk to Muzi in some precinct anteroom with a lawyer present. This way he would speak to Muzi under more favorable circumstances—if the Arabs hadn't killed him already.

Muzi lived on a pleasant, tree-lined street in the Cobble Hill section of Brooklyn. His building, a brownstone, contained four apartments. His was the largest apartment on the ground floor. The only entrance was in the front and Kabakov felt sure that he would use it, if he came. Muzi was far too fat to go in a window, judging from the enormous clothes in his closet.

Kabakov hoped to complete his business very quickly, if Muzi gave him a good lead on the explosives. He would tell Corley when it was over. He looked at his watch through red-rimmed eyes: 7:30 A.M. If Muzi did not come during the day, he would have to set up alternating watches so that his men could sleep. Kabakov told himself again and again that Muzi would come. The importer's passports—three of them in various names—were in Kabakov's breast pocket. He had found them in a quick search of Muzi's bedroom. He would have preferred to wait in the apartment, but he knew that Muzi's time of greatest danger would be on the street and he wanted to be in a position to cover him.

Once again he scanned the windows across the street. In one apartment building to the left a window shade went up. Kabakov tensed. A woman stood at the window in her slip. As she turned away, he could see a child behind her, sitting at a kitchen table.

A few early commuters were on the sidewalk now, still pale with sleep and hurrying to the bus stop on Pacific Street, a block away. Kabakov flicked open the passports and studied Muzi's fat face for the fiftieth time. His legs were cramping and he rose to stretch them. The walkie-talkie beside him crackled.

"Jerry Dimples, front door your position a man with keys."

"Roger Dimples," Kabakov said into the microphone. With any luck it was the relief for the watchman who had snored the night away on the ground floor of the warehouse. A moment later the radio spat again, and the Israeli on the rooftop down the street confirmed that the night watchman was leaving the building. The watchman crossed the street into Kabakov's field of vision and walked to the bus stop.

Kabakov turned back to watch the windows, and when he looked at the bus stop again, the big green city bus was there, discharging a clutch of cleaning ladies. They began to waddle along the block, sturdy, middle-aged women with shopping bags. Many of them had Slavic features similar to Kabakov's own. They looked much like the neighbors he had had as a small child. He followed them with his field glasses. The group grew smaller as the women, one by one, dropped out at the buildings where they worked. They were passing Muzi's house now, and a fat one from the center of the group turned up the walk toward the entrance, umbrella under one arm and a shopping bag in each hand. Kabakov focused his glasses on her. Something peculiar—the shoes. They were large Cordovans and one of the bulging calves above them bore a fresh razor cut.

"Dimples Jerry," Kabakov said into his walkie-talkie. "I think the fat woman is Muzi. I'm going in. Cover the street."

Kabakov put his rifle aside and picked up a sledge-hammer from the corner of the shed. "Cover the street," he repeated to the man beside him. Then he was pounding down the stairwell, not caring if the day watchman heard him. A quick look outside, a dash across the street, carrying the hammer at port arms.

The building entrance was unlocked. He stood outside Muzi's door, straining to hear. Then he swung the hammer sideways with all his strength, dead center on the lock.

The door smashed open, carrying part of the door facing with it, and Kabakov was inside before the splinters hit the floor, leveling a large pistol at the fat man in the dress.

Muzi stood in the doorway to his bedroom, his

hands full of papers. His jowls quivered, and he had a sick, dull look in his eyes as he watched Kabakov. "I swear I didn't—"

"Turn around, hands on the wall." Kabakov searched Muzi carefully, removing a small automatic pistol from his purse. Then he closed the scarred door and leaned a chair against it.

Muzi had composed himself with the speed of thought. "Do you mind if I remove this wig? It itches, you know."

"No. Sit down." Kabakov spoke into the radio. "Dimples Jerry. Get Moshevsky. Tell him to bring the truck." He took the passports from his pocket. "Muzi, do you want to live?"

"A rhetorical question, no doubt. May I ask who you are? You have neither displayed a warrant nor killed me. Those are the only two credentials I would recognize immediately."

Kabakov passed Muzi his identification. The fat man's expression did not change, but inside his head the wet implements of scheming were pumping hard, for he saw a chance that he might live. Muzi folded his hands across his apron and waited.

"They've already paid you, haven't they?"

Muzi hesitated. Kabakov's pistol bucked, silencer hissing, and a bullet slammed through the chair back beside Muzi's neck.

"Muzi, if you do not help me, you are a dead man. They will not let you live. If you stay here, you will go to prison. It should be obvious to you that I am your only hope. I will make this proposal once. Tell me everything and I will put you on an airplane at Kennedy Airport. I and my men are the only ones who can get you on a plane alive."

"I recognize your name, Major Kabakov. I know what you do and I think it rather unlikely that you would leave me alive."

"Do you keep your word in business?"

"Frequently."

"So do I. You have their money already, or a lot of it, I expect. Tell me and go spend it."

"In Iceland?"

"That's your problem."

"All right," Muzi said heavily. "I'll tell you. But I want to fly out tonight."

"If the information checks out, agreed."

"I don't know where the plastic is, that's the truth. I was approached twice, once here and once from Beirut." Muzi mopped his face with his apron, relief spreading through his body like brandy. "Do you mind if I get a Perrier? This talking is thirsty work."

"You know the house is surrounded."

"Believe me, Major, I do not want to run."

Only a serving counter separated the kitchen area from the living room. Kabakov could watch him all the time. He nodded.

"First there was the American," Muzi said at the refrigerator.

"The *American?*"

Muzi opened the refrigerator door and he saw the device for an instant before the explosion blew him piecemeal through the kitchen wall. The room heaved, Kabakov turning in the air, blood flying from his nose, falling, shattered furniture rattling around him. Blackness. A ringing silence and then the crackle of flames.

The first alarm went in at 8:05. The fire dispatcher called it "a four-brick, 75 by 125, fully involved, Engine 224, Ladder 118 and Emergency Service responding."

Police teleprinters rattled in the stationhouses, printing this message:

SLIP 12 0820 HRS 76 PRECINCT REPORTS SUSPICIOUS EXPLOSION AND FIRE 382 VINCENT ST. TWO DOAS TO KINGS COUNTY HOSP OPR 24 ZZZZZZZZZZZZZZZZZZZZZZZZZZ

The paper feed clanked twice, the carriage returned, then this message:

SLIP 13 0820 HRS CQN SLIP 12 ONE DOA ONE INJURED AUTH LONG ISLAND COLLEGE HOSP OPR 24 ZZZZZZZZZZZZZZZZZZZZZZZZZZ

Reporters from the *Daily News, The New York*

Times, and AP were waiting in the corridor of Long Island College Hospital when the fire marshal came out of the room red-faced and angry. Beside him were Sam Corley and a deputy chief. The fire marshal cleared his throat.

"I think it was a gas explosion in the kitchen," the fire marshal said, looking away from the cameras. "We're checking it out."

"ID's?"

"Only on the dead guy." He consulted the slip of paper in his hand. "Benjamin Muzi, or maybe you say it 'Muzzy.' Community relations will give it to you." He brushed past the reporters and stalked out. The back of his neck was very red.

CHAPTER 8

THE BOMB that killed Benjamin Muzi on Thursday morning had been placed in the refrigerator 28 hours before by Muhammad Fasil, and it had almost cost Fasil his hand before a detonator was ever stuck into the plastic. For Fasil had made an error, not with the explosive, but with Lander.

It had been nearly midnight Tuesday when Lander, Fasil, and Dahlia secured the boat and it was almost 2 A.M. when they arrived at Lander's house with the plastic.

Dahlia could still feel the boat moving under her as she walked into the house. She fixed a quick hot meal and Fasil wolfed it down at the kitchen table, his face gray with fatigue. She had to take Lander's food into the garage. He would not leave the plastic. He had opened a bag and lined up six Madonnas on his workbench. Like a raccoon with a clam, he turned one in his hand and sniffed and tasted it. It must be Hexogen of Chinese or Russian manufacture mixed with TNT or kamnikite and some kind of synthetic rubber binder, he decided. The bluish-white substance had a faint smell that touched the back of the nasal passages, like the smell of a garden hose left in the sun, the smell of a body bag. Lander knew he must pace himself to get everything done in the remaining six weeks before the Super Bowl. He put down the statuette and forced himself to sip his soup until his hands were steady. He hardly glanced at Dahlia and Fasil as they came into the garage, Fasil popping an amphetamine tablet into his mouth. The guerrilla started for the workbench and the row of Madonnas, but Dahlia stopped him with a touch on the arm.

"Michael, I need a half-kilo of plastic, please," she said. "For what we were discussing." She spoke as a woman speaks to her lover, leaving things half-said in the presence of a third person.

"Why don't you shoot Muzi?"

Fasil had been under a strain for a week guarding that plastic on the ship, and his bloodshot eyes narrowed at Lander's indifferent tone. " 'Why don't you shoot Muzi?' " he mimicked. "You don't have to do anything, just give me the plastic." The Arab moved to the workbench. Lander's arm blurred with speed as he brought the electric saw off the bottom shelf and pulled the trigger, the shrieking blade a half-inch from Fasil's reaching hand.

Fasil stood very still. "I'm sorry, Mr. Lander. I meant no disrespect." Carefully, carefully. "We may not get a shot. I want to cover every eventuality. Your project must not be interrupted."

"All right," Lander said. He spoke so quietly Dahlia could not hear him over the sound of the saw. He released the trigger and the blade whirred to a stop, each black tooth distinct. Lander cut a Madonna in two with a knife. "You have a detonator and wire?"

"Yes, thank you."

"Will you need a battery? I have several."

"No, thank you."

Lander turned back to his work and did not look up as Dahlia and Fasil drove away in his car, heading north toward Brooklyn to arrange the death of Muzi.

WCBS "Newsradio 88" broadcast the first bulletin on the explosion at 8:30 A.M. Thursday and confirmed Muzi's identity by 9:45. Now the deed was done. The last possible connection between him and the plastic was cut. Thursday was beginning auspiciously. Lander heard Dahlia come into the workshop. She brought him a cup of coffee. "Good news," he said.

She listened carefully as the newcast recycled. She was eating a peach. "I wish they would identify the injured one. There's a fair chance it's the Greek."

"I'm not worried about the Greek," Lander said. "He only saw me once and he didn't hear what we said. Muzi showed no respect for him. I doubt if he trusted him at all."

Lander paused in his work to watch her as she leaned against the wall eating the peach. Dahlia relished fruit. He liked to see her absorbed in a simple pleasure. Displaying appetite. It made him feel that she was uncomplicated, unthreatening, that he moved around her unseen. He was the benign bear watching the camper unload the goodies in the firelight. When she first came to him, he had often turned suddenly to look at her, expecting to see malice or cunning or distaste. But she was always the same—insolence in her posture and welcome in her face.

Dahlia was aware of all this. She appeared to be watching with interest as he turned back to the wiring harness he was making. Actually she was worrying.

Fasil had slept most of yesterday and most of this morning. But soon he would awaken. He would be elated at the success of his device, and he must be restrained from showing it. Dahlia was sorry that Fasil had completed his training before 1969, when the Chinese instructors came to Lebanon. They could have taught him much about self-effacement, something he never learned in training in North Vietnam and certainly not in East Germany. She watched Lander's long fingers deftly moving the soldering iron. Fasil had made a near-fatal mistake with Lander, and she must make sure it did not happen again. She must make Fasil understand that if he were not very careful, the project might come to a bloody end here in Lander's house. The project needed Fasil's quick, savage mind, and his muscle and firepower would be essential at the penultimate moment, when the explosive was being attached to the blimp. But she had to keep him in line.

Fasil nominally was her superior in the terrorist organization, but this mission had been acknowledged as hers by no less than Hafez Najeer himself. Further, she was the key to Lander and Lander was irreplaceable. On the other hand, Hafez Najeer was dead and Fasil no longer feared his wrath. And Fasil was not very progressive in his view of women. It would be so much easier if they all spoke French. That simple difference would have been invaluable, she thought.

Like many educated Arabs, Fasil practiced two sets of social behavior. In Western-style social situations, speaking French, his treatment of women was as gracious and egalitarian as anyone could wish. Back among traditional Arabs, his ingrained sexual chauvinism reasserted itself strongly. A woman was a vessel, a servant, a draft animal with no control over her sexual urges, a sow perpetually in heat.

Fasil might be cosmopolitan in his manners and radical in his politics, but Dahlia could tell that in the send and ebb of his emotions he was not greatly removed from the time of his grandfather, the time of female circumcision, clitoridectomy and infibulation, the bloody rites which ensured that female children would not bring dishonor on their houses. She always detected a faint sneer in his voice when he called her comrade.

"Dahlia." Lander's voice shifted her attention back to him. The change did not register in her face at all. It was a trick she had. "Hand me the needle-nosed pliers." His voice was calm, his hands steady. Good omens for what might be a difficult day. She was determined there would be no wasteful squabbling. Dahlia had confidence in Fasil's basic intelligence and dedication, if not in his attitude. She had confidence in the strength of her own will. She believed in the genuine understanding and affection she shared with Lander, and she believed in the 50 milligrams of chlorpromazine she had dissolved in his coffee.

CHAPTER 9

KABAKOV STRUGGLED back to consciousness like a desperate diver thrashing upward to the air. He felt the fire in his chest and tried to raise his hands to his burning throat, but his wrists were held with a grip like padded iron. He realized that he was in a hospital. He felt the rough-dried hospital sheet under him and felt the loom of someone standing beside the bed. He did not want to open his smarting eyes. His body was seized by his will. *He would relax. He would not struggle and bleed.* It was not the first time he had regained consciousness in a hospital.

Moshevsky, towering over the bed, relaxed his grip on Kabakov's wrists and turned to an orderly at the door of the room. He used his softest growl. "He's coming around. Tell the doctor to get in here. Move!"

Kabakov opened and shut one hand, then the other. He moved his right leg, then his left. Moshevsky nearly smiled with relief. He knew what Kabakov was doing. He was taking inventory. Moshevsky had done it himself on several occasions.

Minutes passed as Kabakov drifted back and forth between the darkness and the hospital room. Moshevsky, swearing softly, had started for the door when the doctor came in with a nurse following him. The doctor was a slight young man with sideburns.

He glanced at the chart while the nurse opened the oxygen tent and peeled back the top sheet, suspended tentlike on a metal frame to keep it from touching the patient. The doctor shined a penlight into each of Kabakov's eyes. The eyes were red and tears welled out when he opened them. The nurse administered eyedrops and shook down a thermometer while the doctor listened to Kabakov's breathing.

The skin quivered under the cold stethoscope and the doctor was inconvenienced by the tape covering the left side of the rib cage. The emergency room had done a neat job. The doctor looked with some professional curiosity at the old scars that dotted and seamed Kabakov's body. "Do you mind standing out of the light?" he said to Moshevsky.

Moshevsky shifted from one foot to the other. Finally, in a position that resembled parade rest, he stared fixedly out the window until the examination was completed. He followed the doctor outside.

Sam Corley was waiting in the hall. "Well?"

The young doctor raised his eyebrows and looked annoyed. "Oh, yes. You're the FBI." He might have been identifying a plant. "He has a mild concussion. The X-rays look good. Three fractured ribs. Second-degree burns on the left thigh. Smoke inhalation has him very raw in the throat and lungs. He's got a ruptured sinus that may require a drain. An ENT man will be in this afternoon. His eyes and ears appear to be okay, but I expect his ears are ringing. It's not unusual."

"The hospital administrator spoke to you about listing him as very critical?"

"The administrator can list him any way he pleases. I would call his condition fair or even good. He has a remarkably tough body, but he's battered it around a lot."

"But you'll—"

"Mr. Corley, the administrator can tell the public

he's pregnant for all I care. I won't contradict him. How did this happen, or may I ask?"

"I think a stove exploded."

"Yes, I'm sure it did." The doctor snorted through his nose and walked off down the hall.

"What's an ENT man?" Moshevsky asked Corley.

"An ear, nose, and throat specialist. By the way, I thought you didn't speak English."

"Poorly, if at all," Moshevsky said, hurriedly re-entering the room with Corley staring balefully at his back.

Kabakov slept through most of the afternoon. As his sedative wore off, his eyes began to twitch beneath the lids and he dreamed, the colors in his dreams drug-bright. He was in his apartment in Tel Aviv and the red telephone was ringing. He could not reach it. He was entangled in a pile of clothing on the floor, and the clothing stank of cordite.

Kabakov's hands clutched the hospital sheet. Moshevsky heard the cloth rip and came out of his chair with the speed of a Cape buffalo. He unclenched Kabakov's fists and put them back at his sides, relieved to see that only the sheet was torn and not the bandage.

Kabakov woke remembering. The events at Muzi's house did not come back to him in order, and it was maddening to have to rearrange the pieces as he recalled them. By nightfall the oxygen tent had been removed and the ringing in his ears had subsided enough for him to listen while Moshevsky filled him in on the aftermath of the explosion—the ambulance, the cameramen, the press temporarily deceived but suspicious.

And Kabakov had no trouble hearing Corley when he was admitted to the room.

"What about Muzi?" Corley was pale with anger.

Kabakov did not want to talk. Talking made him cough and coughing aggravated the fire in his chest. He nodded to Moshevsky. "Tell him," he croaked.

Moshevsky's accent showed marked improvement. "Muzi was an importer—"

"Jesus Christ, I know all that. I've got the paper on him. Tell me what you saw and heard."

Moshevsky cut his eyes toward Kabakov and received a slight nod. He began with the questioning of Fawzi, the discovery of the Madonna, and the examination of the ship's papers. Kabakov filled in the scene in Muzi's apartment. When they had finished, Corley picked up Kabakov's bedside telephone and issued a rapid series of orders—warrants for the *Leticia* and crew, a lab team for the ship. Kabakov interrupted him once.

"Tell them to abuse Fawzi in front of the crew."

"What?" Corley's hand was over the mouthpiece.

"Say he's being arrested for not cooperating. Shove him around a little. I owe him a favor. He has relatives in Beirut."

"It's our ass if he complains."

"He won't."

Corley turned back to the telephone and continued his instructions for several minutes. ". . . yeah, Pearson, and call Fawzi a—"

"Pig-eating crotch cannibal," prompted Moshevsky.

". . . yeah, that's what I said call him," Corley said finally. "When you advise him of his rights, yeah. Don't ask questions, Pearson, just do it." He hung up the receiver.

"Okay, Kabakov. You were dragged out of that house by two guys with golf bags who just *happened* to be passing by, the fire department's report says. Some *golfers*." Corley stood in the middle of the room in his rumpled suit, flipping his keys. "These fellows just *happened* to leave the scene in a panel truck as soon as the ambulance arrived. What was the truck—a shuttle to some golf club where everybody talks funny? I quote to you from the police 'aided card': 'They both talked funny.' Like you talk funny. What are you running here, Kabakov? Are you gonna shit me or what?"

"I would have called you when I knew something." Kabakov's faint croak carried no apology.

"You would have sent me a postcard from fucking Tel Aviv. 'Sorry about the crater and the tidal wave.' " Corley looked out the window for a full minute. When he turned back to the bed, the anger had gone out of him. He had beaten the anger and he was ready to go again. It was a capacity Kabakov appreciated. "An American," Corley muttered. "Muzi said an American. Muzi was very clean, by the way. The police yellow sheet listed only one arrest. Assault and battery and disorderly conduct in a French restaurant. Charges dropped.

"We didn't get much from the house. The bomb was plastic, a little over a pound. We think it was wired into the light bulb socket inside the refrigerator. Someone unplugged the box, wired it up, closed the refrigerator door and plugged it back again. Unusual."

"I have heard of it once before," Kabakov said quietly, too quietly.

"I'm having you transferred to Bethesda Naval Hospital first thing tomorrow. We can set up adequate security there."

"I'm not staying—"

"Oh, yes you are." Corley took the late edition of the New York *Post* from his jacket pocket and held it up. Kabakov's picture was on page 3. It had been shot over the shoulder of an ambulance attendant as Kabakov was carried into the emergency room. The face was smoke-stained but the features were distinct. "They have your name as 'Kabov,' no address or occupation. We put the lid on the police community news unit before your identity was cleared up. Washington is climbing my ass. The director thinks the Arabs might recognize this picture and hit you."

"Splendid. We can take one alive and discuss it with him."

"Oh, no. Not in this hospital we can't. The whole wing would have to be evacuated first. Besides, they might succeed. You're no good to me dead. We don't want you to be another Yosef Alon."

Colonel Alon, the Israeli air attaché in Washington, was shot down in his driveway in Chevy Chase,

Md., by guerrilla assassins in 1973. Kabakov had known and liked Alon, had stood beside Moshe Dayan at Lod Airport when his body was carried off the plane, wind rippling the flag that draped his casket.

"Possibly they would send the same people who killed Colonel Alon," Moshevsky said with the smile of a crocodile.

Corley shook his head wearily. "They'd send goons and you know it. No. We're not going to have a hospital shot up. Later, if you want to, you can make a speech on the steps of the UAR mission in a red jumpsuit for all I care. My orders are to keep you alive. The doctor says you must be flat on your back for a week, minimum. In the morning, pack your bedpan. You're moving to Bethesda. The press will be told you're transferred to the Brooke Army burn unit in San Antonio."

Kabakov closed his eyes for several seconds. If he were in Bethesda, he would be in the hands of the bureaucrats. They would have him looking at pictures of suspicious Arab pita bakers for the next six months.

But he had no intention of going to Bethesda. He needed a little medical attention, absolute privacy, and a place to rest for a day or two, with nobody giving orders about his convalescence. And he knew where he might get these things. "Corley, I can make better arrangements for myself. Did they tell you specifically Bethesda?"

"They said it was my responsibility to see that you were safe. You *will* be safe." The unspoken threat was there. If Kabakov did not cooperate, the State Department would see to it that he was ordered back to Israel.

"All right, look. By morning I'll have things set up. You can check it out until you're satisfied."

"I'll promise nothing."

"But you'll keep an open mind?" Kabakov hated to wheedle.

"We'll see. Meanwhile, I'm keeping five men on this floor. It really burns you to lose a round, doesn't it?"

Kabakov looked at him, and suddenly Corley was reminded of a badger he had trapped in Michigan as a boy. The badger had come at him dragging the trap, the broken end of his femur furrowing the dirt. His eyes had looked like Kabakov's.

As soon as the FBI agent had left the room, Kabakov tried to sit up, then fell back dizzy with the effort.

"Moshevsky, call Rachel Bauman," he said.

Bauman, Rachel, M.D., was in the medical listings of the Manhattan Telephone Directory. Moshevsky dialed the number with his little finger, the only finger that would go in the holes, and got an answering service. Dr. Bauman was away for three days.

He found "Bauman, R." in the Manhattan residence listing. The same answering service operator replied. Yes, she said, Dr. Bauman might check in, but she wasn't sure. Did she have a number where Dr. Bauman might be reached? Sorry, but she couldn't give out that information.

Moshevsky got one of the federal marshals on guard in the corridor to speak to the answering service. They waited while the operator checked his identification and called back.

"Dr. Bauman's at Mt. Murray Lodge in the Pocono Mountains," the marshal said at last. "She told the answering service she'd call with the room number later. That was yesterday. She hasn't called yet. If she planned to call back with the room number, she knew she wouldn't be registering in her own name."

"Yes, yes," Kabakov croaked.

"Shacked up, probably." The man would not be quiet.

Well, Kabakov was thinking, what can you expect when you don't call somebody for seven years? "How far away is this place?"

"About three hours."

"Moshevsky, go get her."

Seventy miles from the hospital, in Lakehurst, N.J., Michael Lander fiddled with the controls on his television set. It had an excellent picture—all of his appliances worked flawlessly—but he was never satisfied. Dahlia and Fasil gave no sign of their impatience. The 6 P.M. newscast was well underway before Lander finally left the set alone.

"An explosion in Brooklyn early today took the life of importer Benjamin Muzi. A second man was critically injured," the newscaster was saying. "Here's Frank Frizzell with an on-the-scene report.

The newscaster stared into the camera for an awkward moment before the film rolled. There was Frank Frizzell standing in a tangle of fire hoses on the sidewalk in front of Muzi's house.

". . . blew out the kitchen wall and caused minor damage to the house next door. Thirty-five firemen with six pieces of equipment battled the fire for more than half an hour before bringing it under control. Six firemen were treated for smoke inhalation."

The scene switched to the side of the house, with its gaping hole. Lander leaned forward eagerly, trying to gauge the force of the blast. Fasil watched as though hypnotized.

The firemen were taking up their hoses. Clearly the TV crew had arrived when the operation was almost completed. Now film from the ramp outside the hospital. Some intelligent television deskman, knowing Long Island College Hospital was the designated receiver for disaster victims in the 76th Precinct, must have sent a camera crew directly to the hospital immediately after the alarm. The news team had arrived just before the ambulance. Here was the ambulance crew bringing out the stretcher, two men rolling it and a third holding up a bottle of intravenous fluid. The picture jerked as the cameraman was jostled by the crowd. Picture bouncing now as the cameraman trotted along with the stretcher. A pause as they reached the emergency room ramp. A closeup of the smoke-stained face. "David Kabov, no address, remained in Long Island College Hospital, his condition described as very critical."

"Kabakov!" Fasil shouted. His lip was drawn back

from his teeth and he lapsed into Arabic in a string of filthy oaths. Now Dahlia was speaking Arabic too. She was pale, remembering the room in Beirut, the black muzzle of the machine gun swinging toward her, Najeer slack against the splattered wall.

"Speak English." Lander repeated it twice before they heard him. "Who is that?"

"I can't be positive," Dahlia said, breathing deeply.

"I can." Fasil held the bridge of his nose between thumb and forefinger. "It's a filthy Israeli coward who comes in the night to kill and kill and kill, women, children . . . he doesn't care. The bastard Jew killed our leader, killed many others, nearly killed Dahlia." Unconsciously, Fasil's hand had moved to the bullet stripe on his cheek, suffered in the Beirut raid.

Lander's mainspring was hate, but his hate came from injury and madness. Here was conditioned hatred, and though Lander could not have defined the difference, was not consciously aware of the difference, it made him uneasy. "Maybe he'll die," he said.

"Oh, yes," Fasil said. "He will."

CHAPTER 10

KABAKOV LAY AWAKE for hours in the middle of the night, after the noise of the hospital had diminished to the rustle of nylon uniforms, the squeak of soft-soled shoes on waxed floors, the toothless cry of an elderly patient down the hall calling for Jesus. He was holding onto himself as he had before, lying awake listening to the traffic in a hospital hall. Hospitals threaten us all with the old disasters of childhood, the uncontrolled bowel, the need to weep.

Kabakov did not think in terms of bravery and cowardice. When he thought about it at all, he was a behaviorist. His citations credited him with various virtues, some of which he believed to be nonexistent. The fact that his men were somewhat in awe of him was useful in leading them, but it was not a source of pride to him. Too many had died beside him.

He had seen courage. He would define it as doing what was necessary, regardless. But the operative word was *necessary*. Not *regardless*. He had known two or three men who had been utterly without fear. They were all psychotic. Fear could be controlled and channeled. It was the secret of a successful soldier.

Kabakov would laugh at the suggestion that he

was an idealist, but there was inside him a dichotomy that is close to the center of what is called Jewishness. He could be utterly pragmatic in his view of human behavior and still feel on the very heart of his heart the white hot fingerprint of God.

Kabakov was not a religious man as the world sees religious men. He was not learned in the rites of Judaism. But he had known that he was a Jew every day that he lived. He believed in Israel. He would do his best and leave the rest to the rabbis.

He was itching under the tape on his ribs. He found that by twisting slightly, he could make the tape pull on the itching place. It was not as satisfactory as scratching, but it helped. The doctor, young what's-his-name, had kept asking questions about his old scars. Kabakov laughed to himself, remembering how the doctor's curiosity had offended Moshevsky. Moshevsky told the man Kabakov was a professional motorcycle racer. He did not tell the doctor about the fight for Mitla Pass in 1956, or the Syrian bunkers at Rafid in 1967, or the other, less conventional battlefields that had marked Kabakov—a hotel roof in Tripoli, the docks on Crete with the bullets splintering the planks—all the places where the Arab terrorists had nested.

It was the doctor's question about old wounds that had started Kabakov thinking about Rachel. Now, lying in the dark, he thought about how it began with her.

June 9, 1967: He and Moshevsky lying on stretchers outside a field hospital in Galilee, the wind blowing sand against the canvas sides with a hissing sound and the generator roaring over the moans of the wounded. A doctor, stepping high like an ibis over the litters, carrying on the awful business of triage. Kabakov and Moshevsky, both hit with small arms fire storming the Syrian Heights in darkness, were carried inside the field hospital, into the light, emergency lanterns swinging beside the operating room lamps. Numbness spreading from the needle, the masked doctor bending over him. Kabakov, watching like a stranger, not looking down at himself, mildly surprised to see that the doctor's hands, extended for fresh sterile gloves, were the hands of a woman. Dr. Rachel Bauman, psychiatric resident at Mt. Sinai Hospital in New York turned volunteer battlefield surgeon, removed the slug that had notched Kabakov's collarbone.

He was recuperating in a Tel Aviv hospital when she came into his ward on a round of postoperative examinations. She was an attractive woman of about 26 with dark red hair gathered into a bun. Kabakov's eyes never left her after she began her rounds with an older staff doctor and a nurse.

The nurse pulled down the sheet. Dr. Bauman did not speak to Kabakov. She was engrossed by the wound, pressing the skin around it with her fingers. The staff doctor examined it in turn.

"A very nice job, Dr. Bauman," he said.

"Thank you, Doctor. They gave me the easier ones."

"You did this?" Kabakov said.

She looked at him as though she had just realized he was there. "Yes."

"You have an American accent."

"Yes, I'm an American."

"Thank you for coming."

A pause, a blink, she reddened. "Thank you for breathing," she said and walked away down the ward. Kabakov's face showed his surprise.

"Dummy," the older doctor said. "How would you like it if a Jew said to you 'Thank you for acting like a Jew all day today'?" He patted Kabakov's arm as he left the bedside.

A week later, leaving the hospital in uniform, he saw her on the front steps.

"Dr. Bauman."

"Major Kabakov. I'm glad to see you out." She did not smile. The wind pressed a strand of hair across her cheek.

"Have dinner with me."

"There isn't time, thank you. I have to go." She disappeared into the hospital.

Kabakov was away from Tel Aviv for the next

two weeks, reestablishing contact with intelligence sources along the Syrian front. He conducted one probe across the ceasefire line, moving through a moonless night to a Syrian rocket launcher position that persisted in violation of the ceasefire despite United Nations surveillance. The Russian-made rockets all detonated simultaneously in their storage racks, leaving a crater in the hillside.

When his orders brought him back to the city, he sought out some of the women he knew and found them to be as satisfactory as ever. And he persisted in his invitations to Rachel Bauman. She was helping in the operating room and working with head injury cases as much as 16 hours a day now. Finally, wearily, smelling of disinfectant, she began to meet Kabakov near the hospital for hurried meals. She was a reserved woman and she protected herself, protected the direction of her life. Sometimes, after the last surgery of the evening, they sat on a park bench and sipped brandy from a flask. She was too tired for much conversation, but she drew comfort from sitting beside the large, dark form of Kabakov. She would not come to his apartment.

This arrangement ended suddenly. They were in the park and, though Kabakov could not tell it in the darkness, she was close to tears. A desperate four-hour operation had failed, a case of brain damage. Knowledgeable in head trauma, she had been called in to aid in the diagnosis, had confirmed the signs of subdural hemotoma in a seventeen-year-old Arab soldier. The increased cerebrospinal fluid pressure and the presence of blood in the fluid left no doubt. She helped the neurosurgeon. There was an unavoidable intracerebral hemorrhage and the young man was dead. Wasted even as she watched his face.

Kabakov, laughing and unaware, told her a story about a tank driver with a scorpion in his underwear, who flattened a Quonset hut. She did not respond.

"Thinking?" he said.

A column of armored personnel carriers rumbled along the street behind them, and she had to speak loudly to be heard. "I'm thinking that in some Cairo hospital they're working just as hard to clean up the messes *you* make. Even in peacetime you do it, don't you? You and the fedayeen."

"There is no peacetime."

"They gossip at the hospital. You're some sort of super commando, aren't you?" She could not stop now and her voice was shrill. "Do you know what? I was passing through the lounge at the hotel, going to my room, and I heard your name. A little fat man, a second secretary from one of the foreign missions, was drinking with some Israeli officers. He was saying that if real peace ever comes they'll have to gas you like a war dog."

Nothing. Kabakov still, his profile indistinct against against the dark trees.

The anger went out of her suddenly, leaving her slack, sick that she had struck at him. It was an effort for her to speak, but she owed him the rest of the story. "The officers stood up. One of them slapped the fat man's face and they walked away with their drinks still on the table," she finished miserably.

Kabakov stood in front of her. "Get some sleep, Dr. Bauman," he said, and then he was gone.

Kabakov's duties chafed him in the next month— office work. He had been transferred back to the Mossad, which was working furiously to determine the full damage wrought on Israel's ring of enemies in the Six-Day War and to estimate their potential for a second strike. There were exhaustive debriefings of pilots, unit commanders, and individual soldiers. Kabakov conducted many of the debriefings, collating the material with information provided by sources within the Arab countries and reducing the results to terse memoranda carefully studied by his chiefs. It was tiresome, tedious work and Rachel Bauman intruded only occasionally into his thoughts. He neither saw nor called her. Instead, he confined his attentions to a ripe Sabra sergeant with a bulging blouse, who could have ridden a Brahma bull without holding onto the rope. His Sabra was soon transferred and he was alone again, remaining alone by choice, numbed by the routine of his work, until a party brought him out.

The party was his first real celebration since the war ended. It was organized by two dozen of the men who served in Kabakov's paratroop section and was attended by a wild and friendly group of fifty—men and women, soldiers all. They were bright-eyed and sunburned and most of them were younger than Kabakov. The Six-Day War had scorched the youth off their faces, and now, indomitable as a hardy crop, it was coming back again. The women were glad to be in skirts and sandals and bright blouses instead of uniform, and it was good to look at them. There was little discussion of the war, no mention of the men they had lost. *Kaddish* had been said and would be said again.

The group took over a café on the outskirts of Tel Aviv beside the road to Haifa, an isolated building blue-white under the moon. Kabakov heard the party from 300 yards away as he approached in his jeep. It sounded like a riot with musical accompaniment. Couples were dancing inside the café and under an arbor on the terrace. A ripple of attention swept over the room as Kabakov entered, weaving his way through the dancers, acknowledging a dozen greetings yelled above the crashing music. Some of the younger soldiers pointed him out to their companions with a glance and a nod of the head. Kabakov was pleasantly aware of all this, though he made an elaborate effort not to show it. He knew that it was wrong to make anything special of him. Every man took his own chances. These people were just young enough to want to indulge themselves in this bullshit, he thought. He wished Rachel were here, wished she had come in with him, and he believed innocently that the wish had nothing to do with his welcome. Damn Rachel!

He made his way to a long table at the end of the terrace, where Moshevsky was seated with some lively girls. Moshevsky had an assortment of bottles before him, and he was telling lewd knock-knock jokes as fast as he could think of them. Kabakov felt good and the wine made him feel better. The men at the party held a variety of ranks, commissioned and noncommissioned, and no one thought it strange that a major and a sergeant should carouse side-by-side. The discipline that had carried the Israelis across the Sinai was born of mutual respect and sustained by *esprit*, and it was like a coat-of-mail that could be hung by the door on these occasions. This was a good party: the people understood each other, the wine was Israeli, and the dances were the dances of the kibbutz.

Just before midnight, through the whirling dancers, Kabakov spotted Rachel hesitating at the edge of the light. She walked toward the arbor where the couples danced, clapping their hands and singing.

The air was soft on her arms and brushed her legs beneath the short denim dress, air scented with wine and strong tobacco and warm flowers. She saw Kabakov, lounging back like Nero at his long table. Someone had put a flower behind his ear and a cigar was in his teeth. A girl leaned toward him talking.

Shyly, Rachel approached his table, through the dancers and the music. A very young lieutenant grabbed her and spun her in the dance and, when the room stopped whirling, Kabakov was standing before her, his eyes wine-bright. She had forgotten how big he was. "David," she said, looking up into his face, "I want to tell you—"

"That you need a drink," Kabakov said, holding out a glass.

"I go home tomorrow—they said you were here and I couldn't leave without—"

"Without dancing with me? Of course not."

Rachel had danced during her kibbutz summer years before, and the steps came back to her now. Kabakov had a remarkable facility for dancing with a glass in his hand, obtaining refills in full flight, and they drank from it by turns. With his other hand he reached behind her and plucked the pins from her hair. It tumbled in a dark red mass down her back and around her cheeks, more hair than Kabakov would have believed possible. The wine warmed Rachel, and she found herself laughing as she danced. The other, the pain and mutilation she had been steeped in, seemed distant.

Quite suddenly it was late. The noise had dropped and many of the revelers had left without Kabakov or Rachel noticing. Only a few couples still danced beneath the arbor. The musicians were asleep, their heads down on a table by the bandstand. The dancers were very close together, moving to an old Edith Piaf song played on the jukebox near the bar. The terrace was strewn with crushed flowers and cigar ends and puddled with wine. A very young soldier, his foot in a cast propped up on a chair, was singing along with the record, holding a bottle at his side. It was late, late, the hour when the moon fades and objects harden in the half-light to take the weight of day. Kabakov and Rachel barely moved to the music. They stopped entirely, warm against each other. Kabakov kissed away a trickle of sweat on the side of her neck, tasted the sweat, a drop of the moving sea. The air that she had warmed and scented rose to touch his eyes and throat. She swayed, a short sidestep to keep her balance, thigh sliding over his, around his, holding, remembering absurdly the first time she had laid her cheek on the warm hard side of a horse's neck.

They parted slowly in a deepening V that let the light between them, and walked outside in the still dawn, Kabakov hooking a bottle of brandy off a table as he passed. The beaded grass wet Rachel's ankles as they climbed the hillside path, and they saw details of the rocks and brush with the unnatural clarity of vision that follows a sleepless night.

Sitting with their backs against a rock, they watched the sun come up. In the light of that clear day, Kabakov could see the tiny flaws in her complexion, the freckles, the lines of fatigue beneath her eyes, the good cheekbones. He wanted her very much and time had run out.

He kissed her for minutes, his hand warm beneath her hair.

A couple came down the path from the thickets

above, bashful in the light, brushing leaves from their clothing. They stumbled over the feet of Kabakov and Rachel sitting beside the path, and passed on, unnoticed.

"David, I am shook," Rachel said at last, shredding a blade of grass. "I didn't mean for this to get started, you know?"

"Shook?"

"Disturbed, upset. Slang."

"Well, I—" Kabakov tried to think of a nice phrase, then snorted at himself. He liked her. Talk was nothing. Damn talking. He talked. "Wet drawers and vague regrets are fifth-form nonsense. Come with me to Haifa. I can get a week's leave. I want you to come with me. We'll talk about your responsibilities next week."

"Next week. Next week I might not have any sense at all. I have obligations in New York. What would be different about it next week?"

"Knocking the slats out of a bed and lying in the sun and looking at each other would make it different."

She turned away quickly.

"Don't get pissed off, either."

"I'm not pissed off," she said.

"Stop saying words like pissed off, then. It sounds like you are." He was smiling. She smiled too. An awkward silence.

"Will you come back?" Kabakov said.

"Not soon. I have my residency to finish. Not unless the war breaks out again. But it hasn't stopped for you, not even for a little while, has it, David? It's never over for you."

He said nothing.

"It's funny, David. Women are supposed to have busy little flexible lives, men have Their Duty. What I do is real and valuable and important. And if I say it's *my* duty, because I want it to be my duty, then that is just as real as your uniform. We won't 'talk about it next week.'"

"Fine," Kabakov said. "Go do your duty."

"Don't get pissed off, either."

"I'm not pissed off."

"Hey, David, thank you for asking me. If I could, I would ask you. To go to Haifa. Or somewhere. And knock the slats out of a bed." A pause, then quickly, "Goodbye, Major David Kabakov. I'll remember you."

And then she was running down the trail. She did not realize she was crying until her jeep picked up speed and the wind spread the tears in cold patches on her cheeks. Tears the wind dried, seven years ago, in Israel.

A nurse came into Kabakov's room, interrupting his thoughts, and the hospital walls closed in on him again. She carried a pill in a paper cup. "I'm going off now, Mr. Kabov," the nurse said. "I'll see you tomorrow afternoon." Kabakov looked at his watch. Moshevsky should have called from the lodge by now, it was nearly midnight.

From a car parked across the street, Dahlia Iyad watched a group of late-shift nurses filing through the front entrance of the hospital. She, too, made a note of the time. Then she drove away.

CHAPTER 11

As KABAKOV took his pill, Moshevsky was standing just inside the doorway of the Boom-Boom Room, the nightclub at Mt. Murray Lodge. He was glowering at the crowd. It had been a tiresome three-hour drive through the runty Pocono Mountains in a light snow, and he was disgruntled. As he had expected, the registration desk did not list a Rachel Bauman. He had not spotted her in the dinner crowd downstairs, though his surveillance had on three occasions attracted the headwaiter, who uneasily offered him a table. The band in the Boom-Boom Room was loud, but not bad, and the "activities director" was master of ceremonies. A moving spotlight slid over the tables, pausing on each. Often the patrons waved when the light touched them.

Rachel Bauman, sitting with her current fiancé and a couple they had met at the lodge, did not wave in the spotlight. She thought this was an ugly lodge with no view. She thought the Poconos were stupid little mountains. She thought the crowd was frumpy. Numerous new art-carved engagement and wedding rings made the room flash like a muddy constellation. This depressed her because she was reminded that she had agreed, sort of, to marry the personable, dull young lawyer at her side. He was not the type to interfere with her life.

Furthermore, their room was vulgar, cost $60 a day, and had hairs in the bathtub. The furniture was Brooklyn oriental, the bathtub hairs unmistakably pubic. Her fiancé, sort of, sported an ascot with his dressing gown and wore his watch to bed. Holy God, look at me, Rachel was thinking. I have little enameled rings on my fingers.

Moshevsky appeared beside the table like a whale peering down into a rowboat. He had gone over what he would say. He would open with humor.

"Dr. Bauman, I always see you making a party. You remember me, Moshevsky, Israel 1967, now could we have some words?"

"I beg your pardon?"

That was all Moshevsky had been prepared to say for openers. He hesitated, then rallied, bending over as though showing his face to a short dermatologist. "Robert Moshevsky, Israel 1967. With Major Kabakov? At the hospital and the party?"

"Of course! Sergeant Moshevsky. I didn't recognize you in your civvies."

Moshevsky was nonplussed. He thought she had said "skivvies," a term he understood. He looked down at himself quickly. No problem there. Rachel's boyfriend and the other couple were staring at him now.

"Marc Taubman, this is Robert Moshevsky, a good friend of mine," Rachel was saying to her escort. "Please sit down, Sergeant."

"Yes, do," Taubman said dubiously.

"What in the world—" Rachel's face changed suddenly. "Is David all right?"

"Almost." Enough of this social stuff. His instructions did not include sitting around and talking. What would Kabakov say? He bent close to her ear. "I have to speak with you privately, please," he rumbled. "Most urgent."

"Would you excuse us?" She put her hand on Taubman's shoulder as he started to rise. "I'll only be a moment, Marc. It's all right."

In five minutes Rachel returned to the table to summon Marc Taubman outside. Ten minutes later he was sitting alone in the bar with his chin in his hand. Rachel and Moshevsky were speeding back to New York, snow streaking level into the windshield like tracer fire.

To the south, the snow had changed to sleet that rattled off the roof and windshield of Lander's station-wagon as Dahlia Iyad drove down the Garden State Parkway. The parkway had been sanded, but Route 70 was slick as she turned west toward Lakehurst. It was 3 A.M. when she reached Lander's house and ran inside. Lander was pouring a cup of coffee. She put the two-star edition of the *Daily News* on the kitchen counter and opened it to the centerfold picture section. The face of the man on the stretcher was clear. It was Kabakov all right. Cold drops of water trickled onto her scalp as the sleet melted in her hair.

"So it's Kabakov, so what?" Lander said.

"So what indeed," Fasil said, coming out of his room. "He had a chance to talk to Muzi, he may have your description. He must have found Muzi through the ship, and at the ship he would have gotten my description also. He may not have fixed on my identity yet, but he knows of me. It will occur to him. He has seen Dahlia. He has to go."

Lander set his cup down with a clatter. "Don't shit me, Fasil. If the authorities knew anything they'd have been here by now. You just want to kill him for revenge. He shot your leader, didn't he? Strolled right in and blew off his ass."

"In his sleep, he sneaked—"

"You people really get me. This is why the Israelis beat you with such regularity, you're always thinking about revenge, trying to get them back for what happened last week. And you're willing to risk this whole thing, just for revenge."

"Kabakov must die," Fasil said, his voice rising.

"It's not just revenge, either. You're afraid that

if you don't get him while he's injured, sooner or later he'll come to see *you* in the middle of the night."

The word "afraid" hung in the air between them. Fasil was exerting a tremendous effort to hold his temper. An Arab could swallow a toad more easily than an insult. Dahlia moved quietly to the coffeepot, breaking their eye contact. She poured a cup and stood leaning against the counter, her behind firmly against the drawer containing the butcher knives.

When Fasil spoke, his throat seemed very dry. "Kabakov is the best they have. If he dies, he will be replaced, true, but it will not be the same. Let me point out, Mr. Lander, that Muzi was destroyed because he had seen you. He had seen your face and your—" Fasil's Arab tongue could be artful when he wished. He hesitated just long enough for Lander to anticipate the word "hand," then diverted the sentence with what appeared to be tact—"your accent was known to him. Besides, are we not all marked with our wounds?" He tapped the scar on his cheek. Lander said nothing, so Fasil continued. "Now we have a man who knows Dahlia on sight. There are places where he might find her picture."

"Where?"

"My picture is in the alien registry. I was well disguised in that one," she said. "But in the annuals of the American University at Beirut—"

"School annuals? Come on, he'd never—"

"They have done it before, Michael. They know we are often recruited there and at the university in Cairo. Many times the pictures are taken and the annual published before a person becomes involved in the movement. He will be looking."

"If Dahlia is identified, her picture will be circulated," Fasil added. "When the time comes for you to strike, there will be Secret Service all around—if the President attends."

"He'll attend, he'll attend. He's said he would attend."

"Then Secret Service likely will come to the airfield. They might have seen Dahlia's picture, perhaps a picture of me, probably a description of you," Fasil said. "All because of Kabakov—if he is allowed to live."

"I will not risk you or Dahlia being captured," Lander snapped. "It would be stupid to go myself."

"That is not necessary," Dahlia said. "We can do it by remote control." She was lying.

At Long Island College Hospital, Rachel had to show her identification at two federal checkpoints before she could accompany Moshevsky to Kabakov's floor.

Kabakov awakened at the slight sound of the opening door. She crossed the dark room and put her hand on his cheek, felt his eyelashes brush her hand, knew he was awake.

"David, I'm here," she said.

Six hours later Corley returned to the hospital. Visiting hours had begun and patients' relatives were carrying flowers down the halls and conferring in worried groups outside the doors where the signs said "No visitors. No smoking, oxygen in use."

Corley found Moshevsky seated on a bench outside Kabakov's room eating a Big Mac hamburger. Beside him in a wheelchair was a girl of about eight. She also was eating a Big Mac.

"Kabakov asleep?"

"Bathing," Moshevsky said, his mouth full.

"Good morning," the child said.

"Good morning. When will he be finished, Moshevsky?"

"When the nurse finishes scrubbing him," the child said. "It tickles. Did a nurse ever bathe you?"

"No. Moshevsky, tell her to hurry up. I've got to—"

"Would you like a bite of this hamburger?" the child said. "Mr. Moshevsky and I send out for them. The food here is terrible. Mr. Moshevsky won't let Mr. Kabakov have a hamburger. Mr. Kabakov said some very bad words about it."

"I see," Corley said, biting his thumbnail.

"I have a burn just like Mr. Kabakov."

"I'm sorry to hear it."

She gingerly leaned sideways in her wheelchair to take some french-fried potatoes from a sack in Moshevsky's lap. Corley opened the door, stuck his head in, spoke briefly to the nurse and withdrew again. "One leg to go," he muttered. "One leg to go."

"I was cooking and I spilled a pan of hot water on myself," the child said.

"I beg your pardon?"

"I said I was cooking and I burned myself with some hot water."

"Oh, I'm sorry."

"I was telling Mr. Kabakov, the same thing happened to him you know, I was telling him that most home accidents happen in the kitchen."

"*You've* been talking to Mr. Kabakov?"

"Sure. We watched the softball game on the playground across the street from his window. They play before school every morning. I can just see a brick wall from the window in my room. He knows some pretty good jokes. Want to hear one?"

"Thank you, no. He's told me a few already."

"I have one of those tent beds too, and—"

The nurse came out into the hall carrying a basin of water. "You can go in now."

"Good," the child said.

"Wait, Dotty," Moshevsky rumbled. "Stay with me. We haven't finished these chips."

"French fries," she said.

Corley found Kabakov propped up in bed. "Now that you're clean, here's what we have. We got warrants for the *Leticia*. Three crew members saw the boat. Nobody remembers the numbers, but they would be fake anyway. We got a little paint where they scraped the side of the ship. It's being analyzed."

Kabakov made a small gesture of impatience. Corley ignored it and went on. "The electronics people talked to the radar operator on the Coast Guard cutter. They think the boat was wood. We know it's fast. We're guessing it has turbo-charged diesels from the description of the sound. It adds up to a smuggler's boat. Sooner or later we'll find it. It had to be built somewhere, at a very good yard."

"What about the American?"

"Nothing. This country is lousy with them. We've got the *Leticia* crewmen working with an Identikit trying to make up a composite of the man who came over on the ship. We're having to work through an interpreter, though. It's slow going. 'Eyes like a pig's ass,' they tell us. Descriptions like that. I'll get you an Identikit and you can do one on the woman. Lab's working on the Madonna."

Kabakov nodded.

"Now, I've got a medevac laid on for 11:30. We'll leave here at 11, drive to the Marine Air Terminal at La Guardia—"

"May I talk to you, Mr. Corley?" Rachel spoke from the doorway. She carried Kabakov's X-rays and charts and wore her stiffest white coat.

"I could have gone to the Israeli mission already," Kabakov said. "You couldn't touch me there. Talk to her, Corley."

Half an hour later, Corley spoke to the hospital administrator, who spoke to the hospital's public information officer, who was trying to leave early on this Friday. The information officer stuck a memo for the press under the telephone and did not bother to post the patient condition book.

The television stations, putting together their six o'clock news, called at mid-afternoon to check on the victims of various disasters. Referring to the memo, the clerk told them "Mr. Kabov" had been medevaced to Brooke Army Hospital. It was a crowded news day. None of them used the story.

The New York Times, thorough as always, prepared a brief item on Mr. Kabov being moved. The *Times*' call was the last and the memo was thrown away. The first edition of the *Times* does not appear on the street until 10:30 P.M. By then it was too late. Dahlia was on the road.

CHAPTER 12

THE IRT EXPRESS train rumbled under the East River and stopped in the Boro Hall station near Long Island College Hospital. Eleven nurses, due to report at 11:30 P.M. for the overnight shift, got off the train. By the time they had climbed the stairs to the street, they numbered an even dozen. The women moved in a tight group along the dark Brooklyn sidewalk, turning their heads only slightly to scan the shadows with the keen survival instincts of city women. A wino was the only other person visible. He swayed toward them. The nurses had sized him up from 25 yards away and, pocketbooks shifted to their inboard arms, they skirted him and passed on, leaving in the air a pleasant scent of toothpaste and hairspray that he could not appreciate because his nose was stopped up. Most of the hospital windows were dark. An ambulance siren wailed and wailed again, louder this time.

"They're playing our song," a resigned voice said.

A yawning security guard opened the glass doors. "ID cards, ladies, let's see 'um."

Grumbling, the women rummaged their purses and held up their identification—building passes for the staff nurses, lime-green State University of New

York ID cards for the private nurses. This was the only special security measure they would encounter.

The guard swept the upheld cards with a glance as though he were polling a class. He waved the nurses on and they scattered toward their duty stations in the big building. One of them entered the women's restroom opposite the elevator bank on the ground floor. The room was dark, as she had expected.

She switched on the light and looked in the mirror. The blonde wig was a flawless fit and the effect of bleaching her eyebrows had been well worth the effort. With cotton pads filling out her cheeks and the glasses with fancy frames altering the proportions of her face, it was difficult to recognize Dahlia Iyad.

She hung her coat inside the toilet stall and took from its inside pocket a small tray. She placed two bottles, a thermometer, a plastic tongue depressor, and a paper pill cup on the tray and covered them with a cloth. The tray was a prop. The important piece of equipment was in her uniform pocket. It was a hypodermic syringe filled with potassium chloride, enough to cause cardiac arrest in a robust ox.

She put the crisp nurse's cap on her head and secured it carefully with hairpins. She gave her appearance a final check in the mirror. The loose-fitting nurse's uniform did her figure no justice, but it concealed the flat Beretta automatic stuffed into the top of her pantyhose. She was satisfied.

The ground-floor hall containing the administrative offices was dim and deserted, lighting cut to a minimum in the energy shortage. She ticked off the signs as she passed along the hall. Accounting, Records, there it was—Patient Information. The inquiry window with its round conversation hole was dark.

A simple snap lock secured the door. Thirty seconds' work with the tongue depressor forced back the beveled bolt and the door swung open. She had given considerable thought to her next move, and though it went against her instinctive wish to be hidden, she turned on the office lights instead of using the flashlight. One by one the banks of fluorescent lights buzzed and lit up.

She went to the large ledger on the inquiry desk and flipped it open. K. No Kabakov. Now she would have to go from door to door checking the nurses' stations, watching out for guards, risking exposure. Wait. The television news had pronounced it Kabov. The papers had spelled it Kabov. Bottom of the page, here it was. Kabov, D. No address. All inquiries to be directed to the hospital administrator. Inquiries in person reported to administrator, hospital security, and the Federal Bureau of Investigation, LE 5-7700. He was in Room 327.

Dahlia took a deep breath and closed the book.

"How did you get in there?"

Dahlia in a double reflex nearly jumped, did not jump, looked up calmly at the security guard peering at her through the inquiry window. "Hey, you want to make yourself useful," she said, "you could take this book up to the night administrator and I won't have to go all the way back upstairs. It weighs ten pounds."

"How did you get in there?"

"The night administrator's key." If he asked to see the key, she would kill him.

"Nobody is supposed to be in here at night."

"Look, you want to call upstairs and tell them they have to have your permission, that's fine with me. I was just told to come bring it, that's all." If he tried to call, she would kill him. "What, should I check in with you if they send me down here? I would have done that, but I didn't know."

"I'm responsible for this, see. I have to know who is here. I see this light, I don't know who's here. I have to leave the door to find out. What if somebody is waiting at the front to come in? Then they're mad at me, see, because I'm not at the door. You check with me when you come down here, all right?"

"All right, sure. I'm sorry."

"Be sure you lock this up and turn out the light, all right?"

"Sure."

He nodded and walked slowly down the hall.

Room 327 was quiet and dark. Only the street-lights below shone through the venetian blinds, casting faint bars of light on the ceiling. Eyes accustomed to the dark could make out the bed, fitted with its aluminum frame to hold the covers up off the patient. In the bed, Dotty Hirschburg slept the deep sleep of childhood, the tip of her thumb just touching the roof of her mouth, fingers spread on the pillow. She had watched the playground from the window of her new room all afternoon, and she had tired herself out. She was accustomed by now to the comings and goings of the night nurses and she did not stir when the door slowly opened. A column of light widened on the opposite wall, was blotted by a shadow, and then narrowed again as the door quietly closed.

Dahlia Iyad stood with her back against the door, waiting for her pupils to dilate. The light from the hall had shown her that the room was empty except for the patient, the cushions of the chair still deeply dented from Moshevsky's vigil. Dahlia opened her mouth and throat to silence her breathing. She could hear other breathing in the darkness. Nurse's footsteps in the hall behind her, pausing, entering the room across the hall.

Dahlia moved silently to the foot of the tentlike bed. She set her tray down on the rolling bed table and took the hypodermic from her pocket. She removed the cap from the long needle and depressed the plunger until she could feel a tiny bead of the fluid at the tip of the needle.

Anywhere would do. The carotid then. Very quick. She moved up beside the bed in the dark and felt gently for the neck, touched hair and then the skin. It felt soft. Where was the pulse? There. Too soft. She felt with thumb and fingers around the neck. Too small. The hair too soft, the skin too soft, the neck too small. She put the hypo in her pocket and switched on her penlight.

"Hello," said Dotty Hirschburg, blinking against the light. Dahlia's fingers rested cool on her throat.

"Hello," Dahlia said.

"The light hurts my eyes. Do I have to have a shot?" She looked up anxiously at Dahlia's face, lighted from beneath. The hand moved to her cheek.

"No. No, you don't have to have a shot. Are you all right? Do you want anything?"

"Do you go around and see if everybody is asleep?"

"Yes."

"Why do you wake them up then?"

"To make sure they're all right. You go back to sleep now."

"It seems pretty silly to me. Waking people up to see if they're asleep."

"When did you move in here?"

"Today. Mr. Kabakov had this room. My mother asked for it so I can see the playground."

"Where is Mr. Kabakov?"

"He went away."

"Was he very sick, did they take him away covered up?"

"You mean dead? Heck no, but they shaved a place on his head. We watched the ballgame together yesterday. The lady doctor took him away. Maybe he went home."

Dahlia hesitated in the hall. She knew she should not push it now. She should leave the hospital. She should fail. She pushed it. At the icemaker behind the nurses' station, she spent several minutes packing a pitcher with cubes. The head nurse, all starch and spectacles and iron gray hair, was talking with a nurse's aide in one of those listless conversations that drift on through the night with no beginning or end. At last the head nurse rose and marched down the hall in response to a call from a floor nurse.

Dahlia was at her desk in a second, flipping through the alphabetical index. No Kabakov. No Kabov. The nurse's aide watched her. Dahlia turned to the woman.

"What happened to the patient in 327?"

"Who?"

"The man in 327."

"I can't keep up with them. I haven't seen you before, have I?"

"No, I've been at St. Vincent's." This was true—she had stolen her credentials at St. Vincent's Hospital in Manhattan during the afternoon shift change. Dahlia had to hurry this up, even if she aroused the woman's suspicions. "If he was moved, there would be a record, right?"

"It would be downstairs locked up. If he's not in the file, he's not on this floor, and if he's not on this floor he's most likely not in this hospital."

"The girls were saying there was such a flap when he came in."

"There's a flap all the time, honey. Woman doctor come in here yesterday morning about 3 A.M. wanting to see his X-rays. Had to go upstairs and open up radiology. They must have moved him in the daytime after I left."

"Who was the doctor?"

"I don't know. Nothing would do but she was going to have those X-rays."

"Did she sign for them?"

"Up in radiology she had to sign them out, just like everybody signs them out."

The head nurse was coming. Quickly now. "Is radiology on four?"

"Five."

The head nurse and the aide were talking as Dahlia entered the elevator. The doors closed. She did not see the aide nod toward the elevator, did not see the head nurse's expression change as she remembered instructions from the night before, did not see her reach for the telephone fast.

In the emergency room Policeman John Sullivan's belt beeper sounded. "Now shut your mouth!" he said to the cursing, bloody drunk his partner was holding. Sullivan unclipped his walkie-talkie and responded to the call.

"Complainant third-floor head nurse Emma Ryan reports a suspicious person, white female, blonde, about five-seven, late twenties, nurse's uniform, possibly in radiology on the fifth floor," the precinct dispatcher told Sullivan. "Security guard will meet you at the elevators. Unit seven-one is on the way."

"Ten-four," Sullivan said, switching off. "Jack, cuff this bastard to the bench and cover the stairs until seven-one gets here. I'm going up."

The security guard was waiting with a bunch of keys.

"Freeze all the elevators except the first one," Sullivan said. "Let's go."

Dahlia had no trouble with the lock on the radiology lab. She closed the door behind her. In a moment she made out the bulk of the X-ray table, the vertical slab of the fluoroscope. She rolled one of the heavy leaded screens in front of the frosted glass door and turned on her penlight. The small beam played over the coiled barium hose, the goggles and gloves hanging beside the fluoroscope. Faintly a siren. An ambulance? Police? Looking around quickly. This door—a darkroom. An alcove lined with big filing cabinets. Drawer opening on loud rollers—X-rays in envelopes. Here a small office, a desk, and a book. Footsteps in the hall. A circle of light on the pages. Flip, flip. Yesterday's date. A page of signatures and case numbers. It had to be a woman's name. Go by the time in the left column —4 A.M., case number, no patient's name, X-ray signed out to Dr. Rachel Bauman. Not signed back in.

The footsteps stopping at the door. A tinkle of keys. The first one didn't work. Throw the wig behind the cabinet, glasses with it. Door bumping against the leaded screen. A bulky policeman and a security guard coming in.

Dahlia Iyad was standing before an illuminated X-ray viewer. A chest X-ray was clamped over the lighted screen of the viewer, ribs projecting bars of light and shadow on her uniform. The shadows of the bones moved over her face as she turned her head toward the men. The policeman's gun was out.

"Yes, officer?" Pretending to notice the gun for the first time. "My goodness, is something wrong?"

"Stand right there, ma'am." With his free hand, Sullivan fumbled for the light switch and found it. The room lit up, Dahlia seeing details of the office she had not noticed in the darkness. The policeman looked over the room with quick snaps of his head.

"What are you doing in here?"

"Examining an X-ray, obviously."

"Is anyone else in here?"

"Not now. There was a nurse a few minutes ago."

"Blonde, about your height?"

"Yes, I think so."

"Where did she go?"

"I have no idea. What's happening?"

"We're finding out."

The security guard looked in the other rooms adjoining the X-ray lab and returned, shaking his head. The policeman stared at Dahlia. Something about her did not seem quite right to him but he couldn't identify it. He should search her and take her downstairs to the complainant. He should secure the floor. He should radio his partner. Nurses make the air white around them. He did not want to put his hands on the white uniform. He did not want to offend a nurse. He did not want to appear a fool, handcuffing a nurse.

"You'll have to come with me for a few minutes, ma'am. We'll have to ask you some questions."

She nodded. Sullivan put away his gun, but did not fasten the retaining strap. He told the security guard to check the other doors along the hall and unclipped his radio from his belt.

"Six-five, six-five."

"Yeah, John," came the reply.

"One woman in the lab. She says the perpetrator was here and left."

"Back and front are covered. Want I should come up? I'm at the third-floor landing now."

"I'll bring her down to three. Ask the complainant to stand by."

"John, the complainant advises no one should be in the lab at this time."

"I'll bring her down. Stand by."

"Who said that?" Dahlia asked hotly. "She—honestly."

"Let's go." He walked behind her to the elevator, watching her, his thumb hooked in his holster. She stood by the panel of buttons in the elevator. The doors closed.

"Three?" she said.

"I'll do it." He reached for the button with his gun hand.

Dahlia's hand snaked to the light switch. Black in the elevator. The sound of scuffling feet, rasp of a holster, a grunt of pain, a curse, thrashing, a wheezing effort to breathe, the indicator lights blinking in succession in the dark elevator.

On the third floor, Officer Sullivan's partner watched the blinking lights over the door to the elevator shaft. Three. He waited. It did not stop. Two. It stopped.

Puzzled, he pushed the "up" button, and waited while the elevator rose again. He stood before the doors. They opened.

"John? My God, John!"

Officer John Sullivan sat against the back wall of the elevator, his mouth open, his eyes wide, the hypodermic needle hanging from his neck like a banderilla.

Dahlia was running now, the long second-floor hall rocking in her vision, lights whipping overhead, past a startled orderly and around the corner into a linen room. Slipping into a light green surgical smock. Tucking her hair into a cap. Hanging the cloth mask around her neck. Down the stairs to the emergency room at the rear of the ground floor. Walking slowly now, seeing the policemen, three of them, looking around like bird dogs. Worried relatives sitting in chairs. The howls of a stabbed drunk. Victims of minor fights waiting for treatment.

A small Puerto Rican woman was sitting on a

bench, sobbing into her hands. Dahlia went to her, sat down beside her, and put her arm around the plump little woman. "No tenga miedo," Dahlia said.

The woman looked up at her, tooth gold in her nut-brown face. "Julio?"

"He's going to be all right. Come, come with me. We'll walk around and get some air, you'll feel better."

"But—"

"Shush now, do as I say."

She had the woman up now, standing childlike under the comforting arm with her ruined, blown-out belly and her split shoes.

"I tole him. Ten times I tole him—"

"Don't worry now."

Walking toward the side exit of the emergency room. A cop in front of the door. A very big man, sweating in his blue coat.

"Why he don't come home to me? Why is this always to fight?"

"It's all right. Would you like to say a rosary?"

The woman's lips moved. The policeman did not move. Dahlia looked up at him.

"Officer, this lady needs some air. Could you walk her around outside for a few minutes?"

The woman's head was bowed and her lips were moving. Belt radios were crackling across the room. The alarm would be up any second now. Dead cop.

"I can't leave the door, lady. This way out is closed right now."

"Could I walk her around for a few minutes? I'm afraid she'll faint in here."

The woman was murmuring, beads between the thick brown fingers. The policeman rubbed the back of his neck. He had a big, scarred face. The woman swayed against Dahlia.

"Uh, what's your name?"

"Dr. Vizzini."

"All right, doctor." Leaning his weight on the door. Cold air in their faces. The sidewalk and the street lit in red flashes by the squadcar lights. No running, police around.

"Take deep breaths," Dahlia said. The woman bobbed her head. A yellow cab stopped. An intern got out. Dahlia caught the cabbie's attention, stopped the intern.

"You're going in, right?"

"Yeah."

"Would you walk this lady back inside? Thanks."

Blocks away now, on the Gowanus Parkway. Leaning back in the taxi, arching her neck back against the seat, eyes closed, she spoke to herself. "I really do care about her, you know."

Officer John Sullivan was not a dead cop, not yet, but he was close to death. Kneeling in the elevator, ear against Sullivan's chest, his partner could hear a confused murmuring beneath the rib cage. He pulled Sullivan around and laid him flat on the floor of the elevator. The door was trying to close and the policeman blocked it with his boot. Emma Ryan was not a head nurse for nothing. Her liver-spotted hand slammed down the stop switch on the elevator, and she bellowed once for the trauma team. Then she was kneeling over Sullivan, gray eyes flicking up and down him and her round back rising and falling as she gave him external heart massage. The officer at Sullivan's head gave mouth-to-mouth artificial respiration. The aide took over from the officer so that he could radio the alarm, but precious seconds had been lost.

A nurse arrived with a rolling stretcher. They lifted the heavy body onto it, Emma Ryan hoisting with surprising strength. She plucked the hypodermic from Sullivan's neck and handed it to a nurse. The needle had stitched through the skin, leaving two red holes, like a snake bite. Part of the dose had squirted against the elevator wall after the tip of the needle exited. It had trickled down to form a tiny pool on the floor. "Get Dr. Field, give him the hypo," Ryan snapped to the nurse. Then to another, "Get the blood sample while we're rolling, let's go."

In less than a minute, Sullivan was in a heart-lung machine in the intensive care unit, Dr. Field at his side. Armed with the results of blood test and urinalysis and with a tray of countermeasures at his elbow, Field sweated over Sullivan. He would live. They would make him live.

CHAPTER 13

ATTEMPTING TO KILL a New York City policeman is like touching a lit cigarette to an anaconda. New York's finest have a sudden and terrible wrath. They never stop hunting a cop killer, never forget, never forgive. A successful attempt on Kabakov—with the resultant diplomatic flap and heat from the Justice Department—might have resulted in news conferences by the mayor and the police commissioner, harangues and exhortations by Brooklyn borough command, and the full-time efforts of twenty to thirty detectives. Because a needle had been stuck in Officer John Sullivan's neck, more than 30,000 policemen in the five boroughs were ready to take care of business.

Kabakov, despite Rachel's objections, left the hospital bed she had set up in her spare bedroom and went to Sullivan's bedside at noon the following day. He was beyond rage and had throttled despair. Sullivan was strong enough to use an Identikit, and he had seen the woman, both full face and profile, in good light. Together, with the Identikit and a police artist, Kabakov, Sullivan, and the hospital security guard put together a composite picture that strongly resembled Dahlia Iyad. When the 3 P.M. police shift turned out, every patrolman and every detective had a copy of the composite. The early edition of the *Daily News* carried it on page two.

Six policemen from the Identification Division and four clerks from Immigration and Naturalization, each with a copy of the picture, pored over the Arab alien file.

The connection between the hospital incident and Kabakov was known only to head nurse Emma Ryan, the FBI agents working on the case, and the highest echelon of the New York Police Department. Emma Ryan could keep her mouth shut.

Washington did not want a terrorist scare and neither did the enforcement agencies. They did not want the media breathing down their necks in a case that could end as badly as this one. Police pointed out publicly that the hospital contained both narcotics and valuable radioactive elements, that the intruder might have been after these. This was not entirely satisfactory to the press, but in the crushing work-load of New York City news coverage, newsmen can easily forget yesterday's stories. Authorities hoped that in a few days the media's interest would flag.

And Dahlia hoped that in a few days Lander's anger would subside. He was enraged when he saw her likeness in the paper and knew what she had done. For a moment, she thought he would kill her. She nodded meekly when he forbade any further attempt on Kabakov. Fasil stayed in his room for two days.

David Kabakov's convalescence in Dr. Rachel Bauman's apartment was a strange, almost surreal time for her. Her home was bright and oppressively orderly and he came into it like a grizzled tomcat home from a fight in the rain. The sizes and proportions of her rooms and furnishings seemed all changed to Rachel with Kabakov and Moshevsky in the place. For large men, they did not make much noise. This was a relief to Rachel at first, and then it bothered her a little. Size and silence are a sinister combination in nature. They are the tools of doom.

Moshevsky was doing his best to be accommodating. After he had spooked her several times, appearing suddenly in the kitchen with a tray, he began clearing his throat to announce his movements. Rachel's friends across the hall were in the Bahamas and had left their keys with her. She installed Moshevsky in that apartment after his snoring on her couch became unbearable. Kabakov listened respectfully to her instructions regarding his treatment and followed them, with the one angry exception of the trip to Sullivan's bedside. She and Kabakov did not talk much at first. They did not chat at all. He seemed distracted, and Rachel did not disturb his thoughts.

Rachel had changed since the Six-Day War, but the change was one of degree. She had become more intensely what she was before. She had a busy practice, an ordered life. One man, two men over the years. Two engagements. Dinners in smart and hollow places, where the chefs put coy signatures of garnishment on uninspired dishes—places chosen by her escorts. None of her experiences roared in her ears. Men who could have struck fire from her, she rebuffed. Her only high was the best one—working well—and that sustained her. She did much volunteer work, therapy sessions with ex-addicts, parolees, disturbed children. During the October War of 1973, she worked a double shift at Mt. Sinai Hospital in New York so that a staff doctor with more recent surgical experience could go to Israel.

Externally she was molding fast. Bloomingdale's and Bonwit Teller, Lord & Taylor and Saks were the touchstones in her Saturday rounds. She would have looked like a trim Jewish matron, expensively turned out and just a little behind the trends, if she had not spoiled the effect with defiant touches, a hint of the street. For a time she had resembled a woman fighting her thirties with her daughter's accessories. Then she didn't give a damn what she wore anymore and lapsed into quiet business dress because she didn't have to think about it. Her working hours grew longer, her apartment grew tidier and more sterile. She paid an exorbitant price for a cleaning woman who could remember to put everything back precisely as it had been before.

Now, here was Kabakov, poking through her bookshelves and gnawing on a piece of salami. He seemed to delight in examining things and not putting them back where he found them. He had not put on his slippers and he had not buttoned up his pajama jacket. She would not look at him.

Rachel was no longer so concerned about the concussion. He did not seem to worry about it at all. As his periods of dizziness grew less frequent, then abated altogether, their relationship changed. The impersonal doctor-patient attitude she had tried to maintain began to soften.

Kabakov found Rachel's company stimulating. He felt a pleasant necessity to think when talking with her. He found himself saying things that he had not realized he felt or knew. He liked to look at her. She was long-legged and given to angular positions, and she had durable good looks. Kabakov had decided to tell her about his mission, and because he liked her he found it difficult to do. For years he had guarded his tongue. He knew that he was susceptible to women, that the loneliness of his profession tempted him to talk about his problems. Rachel had given him help when he needed it, immediately and with no unnecessary questions. She was involved now and could be in danger—the reason for the assassin's visit to the radiology lab was not lost on Kabakov.

Still, it was not his sense of justice that led him to tell her, no feeling that she had a right to know. His considerations were more practical. She had a first-rate mind and he needed it. Probably one of the plotters was Abu Ali—a psychologist. Rachel was a psychiatrist. One of the terrorists was a woman. Rachel was a woman. Her knowledge of the nuances of human behavior, and the fact that, with this knowledge, she was a product of the American culture, might give her some useful insights. Kabakov believed that he could think like an Arab, but could he think like an

American? *Was* there any way to think like an American? He had found them inconsistent. He thought that perhaps when the Americans had been here longer, they might have a way of thinking.

Sitting by a sunny window, he explained the situation to her as she dressed the burn on his leg. He started with the fact that a Black September cell was hidden in the Northeast, ready to strike somewhere with a large quantity of plastic explosive, probably half a ton or more. He explained from Israel's point of view the absolute necessity of his stopping them, and he hastily added the humanitarian considerations. She finished the bandaging and sat cross-legged on the rug listening. Occasionally she looked up at him to ask a question. The rest of the time he could only see the top of her bent head, the part in her hair. He wondered how she was taking it. He could not tell what she was thinking, now that the deadly struggle she had witnessed in the Middle East had come home to this safe place.

Actually, she was feeling relieved about Kabakov himself. Always she wanted to know specifics. Exactly what had been done and said—especially just before the blast at Muzi's house. She was glad to see that his answers were immediate and consistent. When questioned at the hospital about his most recent memories he had given the doctor vague replies, and Rachel could not be sure whether this was deliberate evasion or the result of head trauma. She had been handicapped in evaluating Kabakov's injury by her reluctance to ask him specifics. Now, her minute questioning served two purposes. She needed the information if she was to help him, and she wanted to test his emotional response. She was watching for the irritability under questioning that marks the Korsakoff, or amnesic-confabulatory syndrome, which frequently follows concussion.

Satisfied with his patience, pleased with his clarity, she concentrated on the information. He was more than a patient, she was more like a partner as the story was completed. Kabakov concluded with the questions that were eating at him: Who was the American? Where would the terrorists strike? When he had finished talking he felt vaguely ashamed, as though she had seen him crying.

"How old was Muzi?" she asked quietly.

"Fifty-six."

"And his last words were 'First there was the American'?"

"That's what he said." Kabakov did not see where this was leading. They had talked enough for now.

"Want an opinion?"

He nodded.

"I think there's a fair probability that your American is a non-Semitic Caucasian male, probably past his middle twenties."

"How do you know?"

"I don't know, I'm guessing. But Muzi was a middle-aged man. The person I described is what many men his age call an 'American.' Very likely, if the American he saw was black, he would have mentioned it. He would have used a racial designation. You spoke English the entire time?"

"Yes."

"If the American was a woman, very likely he would have said 'the woman' or 'the American woman.' A man of Muzi's age and ethnic background would not think of an Arab-American or an American Jew as 'the American.' In all cases, black, female, Semitic or Latin, the word 'American' is an adjective. It's a noun only for non-minority Caucasian males. I'm sounding pedantic probably, but it's true."

Kabakov, conferring with Corley by telephone, told the FBI agent what Rachel had said.

"That narrows it down to about forty million people," Corley said. "No, listen, anything helps, for Christ's sake."

Corley's report on the search for the boat was not encouraging. Customs agents and New York City police had checked every boatyard on City Island.

Nassau and Suffolk police had checked every marina on Long Island. The New Jersey state police had questioned boatyard owners along their coast. FBI agents had gone to the best boatyards—to legendary craftsmen like Rybovich, Trumpy, and Huckins—and to the lesser-known yards where craftsmen still built fine wooden boats. None of the yards could identify the fugitive craft.

"Boats, boats, boats," Rachel said to herself.

Kabakov stared out the window at the snow while Rachel fixed dinner. He was trying to remember something, going at it indirectly, the way he would use peripheral vision to see in the dark. The technique employed in blowing up Muzi teased Kabakov ceaselessly. Where had it happened before? One of the thousands of reports that had crossed his desk in the past five or six years had mentioned a bomb in a refrigerator. He remembered that the report had an old-style jacket, the manila kind, bound along the spine. That meant he had seen it before 1972, when the Mossad changed the bindings to facilitate microfilming. One other flash came to him. A memo on booby-trap techniques issued to commando units on his orders years ago. The memo had explained mercury switches, then in fashion among the fedayeen, with an addendum on electrical appliances.

He was composing a cable to Mossad headquarters with the scraps of information he recalled when quite suddenly he remembered. Syria 1971. A Mossad agent was lost in an explosion at a house in Damascus. The charge had not been heavy, but the refrigerator was shattered. A coincidence? Kabakov called the Israeli consulate and dictated the cable. The cable clerk pointed out that it was 4 A.M. in Tel Aviv.

"It's 0200 Zulu all over the world, my friend," Kabakov said. "We never close. Get that cable out."

A cold December drizzle stung Moshevsky's face and neck as he waited on the corner to flag a cab. He let three Dodges pass and finally spotted what he was looking for, a big Checker barging through the morning rush. He wanted the extra room so Kabakov would not have to bend his sore leg. Moshevsky told the driver to stop in front of Rachel's apartment building in the middle of the block. Kabakov hobbled out and climbed in beside him. He gave the address of the Israeli consulate.

Kabakov had rested as Rachel prescribed. Now he would roll. He could have called Ambassador Tell from the apartment, but his business required the safest of telephones—one equipped with a scrambler. He had decided to ask Tel Aviv to suggest that the U.S. State Department approach the Russians for help. Kabakov's request must be cleared through Tell. Going to the Russians was not a pleasant thought from the standpoint of his professional pride. At the moment, Kabakov could not afford professional pride. He knew that and accepted it, but he did not like it.

Since the spring of 1971, the Soviet Komitet Gosudarstvennoy Bezopastveny, the infamous KGB, has had a special section providing technical assistance to Black September through Al Fatah field intelligence. This was the source Kabakov wanted to tap.

He knew the Russians would never help Israel, but in light of the new East-West detente, he thought they might cooperate with the United States. The request to Moscow must come from the Americans, but Kabakov could not suggest the move without the approval of Tel Aviv. Precisely because he hated so much to ask, he would sign the message to Tel Aviv himself, instead of putting the primary responsibility on Tell.

Kabakov decided to swear that the plastic was Russian, whether it was or not. Maybe the Americans would swear to it too. That ought to put the onus on the Russians.

Why such a large quantity of explosives? Did the amount signify some special opportunity the Arabs had in this country? On that point the KGB might be of help.

The Black September cell in America would be sealed off now, even from the guerrilla leadership in Beirut. It would be hell to find. The heat from the woman's picture would drive the terrorists far down in their burrow. They had to be close by—they had reacted too fast after the explosion. Damn Corley for not staking out the hospital. Damn that pipe-smoking son of a bitch.

What had been planned in the Black September headquarters in Beirut, and who had taken part? Najeer. Najeer was dead. The woman. She was hiding. Abu Ali? Ali was dead. There was no way to be positive that Ali was in on the plot, but it was very likely, for he was one of the few men in the world Najeer trusted. Ali was a psychologist. But then Ali was many things. Why might they need a psychologist? Ali would never be able to tell anyone.

Who was the American? Who was the Lebanese who brought in the explosives? Who blew up Muzi? Was it the woman he saw in Beirut—the woman who came to the hospital to kill him?

The taxi driver pushed the big car to the limit the wet pavement would allow, slamming over the potholes and nosediving to a halt at the first red light. Moshevsky, with a resigned expression, climbed out and got into the front seat beside the driver. "Take it slowly. Neither bang nor jar," he said.

"Why?" the driver said. "Time is money, buddy."

Moshevsky leaned toward him confidentially. "Why is to keep me from breaking your fucking neck, that's why."

Kabakov looked absently at the crowds hurrying along the sidewalk. Midafternoon and already the light was failing. What a place. A place with more Jews than Tel Aviv. He wondered how the Jewish immigrants had felt, crowded on the ships, herded through Ellis Island, some of them even losing their names as semiliterate immigration officials scrawled "Smith" and "Jones" on the entry papers. Spilled from Ellis Island into a bleak afternoon on this cold rock where nothing was free except what they could give each other. Broken families, men alone.

What happened here then to a man alone who died before he could make a place and send for his family? A man alone? Who sat *shivah*—the neighbors?

The plastic madonna on the dashboard of the taxi caught Kabakov's attention, and his thoughts shifted guiltily back to the problem that plagued him. Closing his eyes against the cold afternoon, he started over from the beginning, with the mission to Beirut that had ultimately brought him here.

Kabakov had been briefed minutely before the raid. The Israelis knew Najeer and Abu Ali would be in the apartment house and that other Black September officers might be present. Kabakov had studied the dossiers on guerrilla leaders known to be in Lebanon until he knew what was in them by heart. He could see the folders now, stacked alphabetically on his desk.

First, Abu Ali. Abu Ali, killed in the Beirut raid, had no relatives, no family except his wife, and she, too, was dead. He—*a man alone!* Before the thought was completed, Kabakov was rapping on the plastic shield that separated him from the driver. Moshevsky slid open the partition.

"Tell him to step on it."

"So now you want me to step on it," the driver said over his shoulder.

Moshevsky showed the man his teeth.

"So I'm stepping," the driver said.

The Israeli consulate and mission to the United Nations share a white brick building at 800 Second Avenue in Manhattan. The security system is well thought-out and thorough. Kabakov fumed in the confines of the holding room, then went quickly to the communications center.

His coded cable to Tel Aviv regarding Abu Ali was acknowledged in less than a minute. It set delicate machinery in motion. Within fifteen minutes, a stocky young man left Mossad headquarters for Lod Airport. He would fly to Nicosia, Cyprus, switch passports and catch the next flight into Beirut. His first business in the Lebanese capital would be to enjoy a cup of coffee in a small café with an excellent view of the central Beirut police station, where, hopefully, waiting for the statutory period in the police property room was a numbered carton containing the effects of Abu Ali. Now there was someone to claim them.

Kabakov was on the scrambler with Tell for half an hour. The ambassador expressed no surprise at Kabakov's request for roundabout Russian aid. Kabakov had the feeling that Yoachim Tell had never been surprised in his life. He thought he had detected a bit of extra warmth in the ambassador's voice as he said goodbye. Was it sympathy? Kabakov reddened and stalked toward the door of the communications center. The telex in the corner rattled and the clerk's voice stopped him in the doorway. An answer was coming to his query about the Syrian bombing in 1971.

The bombing took place August 15, the telex said. It occurred during Al Fatah's major recruiting effort in Damascus that year. Three organizers were known to have been in Damascus at that time:

—Fakhri al-Amari, who led the team that assassinated Jordanian prime minister Wasfi el-Tel and drank his blood. Amari was believed to be in Algeria at the present time. Inquiries were underway.

—Abdel Kadir, who once bazookaed an Israeli school bus; killed when his bomb factory near Cheikh Saad blew up in 1973. The telex added that doubtless Kabakov would not need his memory refreshed on Kadir's demise, as he had been present at the time.

—Muhammad Fasil, alias Yusuf Halef, alias Sammar Tufiq. Believed to be the architect of the Munich atrocity and one of the men most wanted by the Mossad. Fasil was last reported operating in Syria. The Mossad believed him to be in Damascus at the time of Kabakov's Beirut raid, but recent reports, not yet confirmed, placed him in Beirut within the past three weeks. Israeli intelligence was pressing sources in Beirut and elsewhere on Fasil's whereabouts.

Photos of el-Amari and Fasil were being transmitted via satellite to the Israeli embassy in Washington to be forwarded to Kabakov. The negatives would follow. Kabakov winced at that. If they were sending negatives, the pictures must be poor—too poor to be very useful when transmitted electronically. Still, it was something. He wished that he had waited to ask about the Russians. "Muhammad Fasil," Kabakov muttered. "Yes. This is your kind of show. I hope you came personally this time."

He went back into the rain for the trip to Brooklyn. Moshevsky and the trio of Israelis under his direction combed the Cobble Hill bars and short-order restaurants and klabash games looking for traces of Muzi's Greek assistant. Perhaps the Greek had seen the American. Kabakov knew the FBI had covered this ground, but his own men did not look like police, they fit better into the ethnic mix of the neighborhood and they could eavesdrop in several languages. Kabakov stationed himself in Muzi's office, examining the incredible rat's nest of papers the importer had left, in the hope that he could find some scrap of information about the American or about Muzi's contacts in the Middle East. A name, a place, anything. If there was one person between Istanbul and the Gulf of Aden who knew the nature of the Black September mission in the United States, and Kabakov could find out his name, he would kidnap that person or die trying. By mid-evening he had discovered that Muzi kept at least three sets of books, but he had learned little else. Wearily, he returned to Rachel's apartment.

Rachel was waiting up for him. She seemed somehow different and, looking at her, he was no longer weary. Their separation during the day had made something clear to both of them.

Very gently they became lovers. And their encounters thereafter began and ended with great gentleness, as though they feared they might tear the fragile tent their feelings built in air around their bed.

"I'm silly," she said once, resting. "I don't care if I'm silly."

"I certainly don't care if you're silly," Kabakov said. "Want a cigar?"

Ambassador Tell's call came at seven A.M., while Kabakov was in the shower. Rachel opened the bathroom door and called his name into the steam. Kabakov came out quickly, while Rachel was still in the doorway. He wrapped a towel around himself and padded to the telephone. Rachel began to work very hard on her fingernails.

Kabakov was uneasy. If the ambassador had an answer on the Russians, he would not have used this telephone. Tell's voice was calm and very businesslike.

"Major, we've gotten an inquiry about you from *The New York Times.* Also some uncomfortable questions about the incident on the *Leticia.* I'd like for you to come down here. I'll be free a little after three, if that's convenient."

"I'll be there."

Kabakov found the *Times* on Rachel's doormat. *Page one:* ISRAELI FOREIGN MINISTER IN WASHINGTON FOR MIDEAST TALKS. *Read that later.* COST OF LIVING. GM RECALLS TRUCKS. *Page two. Oh, hell. Here it is:*
ARAB TORTURED HERE
BY ISRAELI AGENTS,
CONSUL ALLEGES
By Margaret Leeds Finch

A Lebanese seaman was questioned under torture by Israeli agents aboard a Libyan merchant vessel in New York harbor last week prior to his arrest by U.S. customs officials on smuggling charges, the Lebanese consul said Tuesday night.

In a strongly worded protest to the U.S. State Department, Consul Yusuf el-Amedi said first mate Mustapha Fawzi of the freighter *Leticia* was beaten and subjected to electric shock by two men who identified themselves as Israelis. He said he did not know what the agents were after and refused to comment on smuggling conspiracy charges pending against Fawzi.

An Israeli spokesman emphatically denied the allegations, saying the charge was "a clumsy attempt to arouse anti-Israeli feeling."

Department of Corrections physician Carl Gillette said he examined Fawzi at the Federal House of Detention on West Street and found no evidence of a beating.

Consul Amedi said Fawzi was attacked by Major David Kabakov of the Israeli Defense Force and another unidentified man. Kabakov is attached to the Israeli embassy in Washington.

The *Leticia* was impounded. . . .

Kabakov skimmed the rest of the article. The customs authorities had kept their mouths shut on the investigation of the *Leticia* and the newspaper did not have the Muzi connection yet, thank God.

"You are being ordered home, officially," Ambassador Tell said.

The corner of Kabakov's mouth twitched. He felt as though he had been kicked in the stomach.

Tell moved the papers on his desk with the tip of his pen. "The arrest of Mustapha Fawzi was reported routinely to the Lebanese consul, as Fawzi is a Lebanese citizen. A lawyer was provided by the consulate. The lawyer apparently is acting on orders from Beirut and he's playing Fawzi like a calliope. The Libyans were informed, since the vessel is of Libyan registry. Once your name came into it, I have no doubt Al Fatah was alerted and so was Colonel Khadafy, the enlightened Libyan statesman. I haven't seen the deposition supposedly authored by Fawzi, but I understand it's very colorful. Very graphic anatomically. Did you hurt him?"

"I didn't have to."

"The Lebanese and the Libyans will continue to protest until you are withdrawn. Probably the Syrians will join it too. Khadafy owns more than one Arab diplomat. And I doubt that any of them know why you are really here, with the possible exception of Khadafy."

"What does the U.S. State Department say?" Kabakov felt sick inside.

"They don't want a diplomatic uproar over this. They want to quash it. Officially, you are no longer welcome here as an arm of Israel."

"The fat-faced idiots! They deserve—" Kabakov shut his mouth with a snap.

"As you know, Major, the United Nations entertains the U.A.R. motion for a censure of Israel this week over the action against the fedayeen camps in Syria last month. This matter should not be exacerbated by another disturbance now."

"What if I resign my commission and get an ordinary passport? Then Tel Aviv could disown me if it became necessary."

Ambassador Tell was not listening. "It's tempting to think that if the Arabs succeed in this project, God forbid, the Americans would be enraged and would redouble their support for Israel," he said. "You and I both know that won't happen. The salient fact will be that the atrocity happened *because* the United States has helped Israel. Because they got involved in another dirty little war. Indochina has made them sick of involvement, just as it did the French, and understandably so. I wouldn't be surprised to see Al Fatah strike in Paris if the French sell us Mirages.

"Anyway, if it happens here, the Arab governments will denounce Al Fatah for the four hundredth time and Khadafy will give Al Fatah some millions of dollars. The United States can't afford to be angry at the Arabs too long. It sounds horrible, but the U.S. will find it convenient to blame only Al Fatah. This country consumes too much oil for it to be otherwise.

"If the Arabs succeed, and we have tried to stop them, then it won't be quite so bad for us. If we stop helping, even at State Department request, and the Arabs are successful, then we are still at fault.

"The Americans won't ask the Russians for any

intelligence from the Middle East, by the way. The State Department gave us the news that the Middle East is a 'sphere of continuing East-West tension' and no such request is possible. They don't want to admit to the Russians that the CIA can't get the information themselves. You were right to try it anyway, David.

"And now there is this." Tell passed Kabakov a cable from Mossad headquarters. "The information has also been relayed to you in New York."

The cable reported that Muhammad Fasil was seen in Beirut the day after Kabakov's raid. He had a wound on his cheek similar to the one described by Mustapha Fawzi, the first mate of the *Leticia*.

"Muhammad Fasil," Tell said quietly, "the worst one of all."

"I'm not going—"

"Wait, wait, David. This is a time for utter frankness. Is there anyone you know, in the Mossad or elsewhere, who might be better equipped to deal with this matter than you?"

"No sir." Kabakov wanted to say that if he had not taken the tape in Beirut, had not questioned Fawzi, if he had not searched the cabin on the ship, checked the ship's books, caught Muzi at a disadvantage, they would know nothing at all. All he said was "No sir."

"That's our consensus also." Tell's telephone rang. "Yes? Five minutes, very well." He turned back to Kabakov. "Major, would you please report to the conference room on the second floor? And you might straighten your tie."

Kabakov's collar was cutting into his neck. He felt as though he were strangling, and he paused outside the conference room to get hold of himself. Maybe the military attaché was about to read him his orders to go home. Nothing would be accomplished by screaming in the man's face. What was Tell talking about anyway, what consensus? If he had to go back to Israel he would by God go, and the guerrillas in Syria and Lebanon would wish to hell he was back in the United States.

Kabakov opened the door. The thin man at the window turned.

"Come in, Major Kabakov," said the foreign minister of Israel.

In 15 minutes Kabakov was back in the hall, trying to suppress a smile. An embassy car took him to National Airport. He arrived at the El Al terminal at Kennedy International 20 minutes before the scheduled departure of Flight 601 to Tel Aviv. Margaret Leeds Finch of the *Times* was lurking near the counter. She asked him questions while he checked his bag and while he went through the metal detector. He answered in polite monosyllables. She followed him into the gate, waving her press pass at the airline officials, and dogged him down the very boarding ramp to the door of the plane where she was politely but firmly stopped by El Al security men.

Kabakov passed through first class, through the tourist section, back to the galley where hot dinners were being loaded aboard. With a smile at the stewardess, he stepped out the open door into the elevated bed of the catering truck. The bed whirred downward, and the truck returned to its garage. Kabakov climbed out and entered the car where Corley and Moshevsky were waiting.

Kabakov had been officially withdrawn from the United States. Unofficially, he had returned.

He must be very careful now. If he fouled up, his country would lose a great deal of face. Kabakov wondered what had been said at the foreign minister's luncheon with the Secretary of State. He would never know the details, but clearly the situation had been discussed at some length. His instructions were the same as before: stop the Arabs. His team was being withdrawn, with the exception of Moshevsky. Kabakov was to be an ex officio advisor to the Americans. He felt sure the last part of his instructions had not been discussed over lunch; if it was necessary to do more than advise, he was to leave no unfriendly witnesses.

There was a strained silence in the car on the way back into Manhattan. Finally Corley broke it. "I'm sorry this happened, old buddy."

"I am not your old buddy, old buddy," Kabakov said calmly.

"Customs saw that piece of plastic and they were screaming to bust those guys. We had to bust them."

"Never mind, Corley. I'm here to help you, old buddy. Here, look at this." Kabakov handed him one of the pictures given him as he left the embassy. It was still wet from the darkroom.

"Who is it?"

"Muhammad Fasil. Here, read the file."

Corley whistled. "Munich! How can you be sure he's the one? The *Leticia* crew won't identify him. On advice of counsel, you can bet on that."

"They won't have to identify him. Read on. Fasil was in Beirut the day after our raid. We should have gotten him with the others, but we didn't expect him to be there. He got a bullet stripe on the cheek. The Lebanese on the freighter had a scab across his cheek. Fawzi said so."

The picture had been taken in a Damascus café in poor light and it was fuzzy.

"If you've got the negative, we can improve it with the NASA computer," Corley said. "The way they enhance the pictures from the Mariner project." Corley paused. "Has anybody from State talked to you?"

"No."

"But your own people have talked to you."

"Corley, 'my own people' always talk to me."

"About working through us. They made it clear you're going to help with the thinking and we're stuck with the work, right?"

"Right. You bet, old buddy."

The car dropped Kabakov and Moshevsky at the Israeli mission. They waited until it was out of sight and took a cab to Rachel's building.

"Corley knows where we are anyway, doesn't he?" Moshevsky said.

"Yes, but I don't want the son of a bitch to think he can drop by whenever he feels like it," Kabakov said. As he spoke, he was not thinking about Corley or Rachel's apartment at all. He was thinking about Fasil, Fasil, Fasil.

Muhammad Fasil was also deep in thought as he lay on his bed in Lander's ground-floor guestroom. Fasil had a passion for Swiss chocolates, and he was eating some now. In the field he ate the rough fare of the fedayeen, but in private he liked to rub Swiss chocolates between his fingers until the chocolate melted. Then he licked the chocolate off his fingers. Fasil had a number of little private pleasures of this kind.

He had a certain amount of surface passion and a range of visible emotion that was wide and not deep. But he was deep, all right, and cold, and those cold depths held sightless, savage things that brushed and bit one another in the dark. He had learned about himself very early. At the same time he had taught his schoolmates about himself and then he was left alone. Fasil had splendid reflexes and wiry strength. He had no fear and no mercy, but he did have malice. Fasil was living proof that physiognomy is a false science. He was slim and fairly good-looking. He was a monster.

It was curious how only the most primitive and the keenest found him out. The fedayeen admired him from a distance and praised his behavior under fire, not recognizing that his coolness was something other than courage. But he could not afford to mix with the most illiterate and ignorant among them, the ones gnawing mutton and gobbling chickpeas around a fire. These superstitious men had no calluses on their instincts. They soon became uneasy with him, and as quickly as manners permitted they moved away. If he was to lead them all someday, then he must solve that problem.

Abu Ali, too. That clever little man, a psychologist who made a long, circuitous trip through his own mind, had recognized Fasil. Once, over coffee, Ali had described one of his own earliest memories—a lamb walking around in the house. Then he asked Fasil his earliest memory. Fasil had replied that he remembered his mother killing a chicken by holding its head in the fire. After Fasil had spoken, he realized that this was not an idle conversation at all. Fortunately, Abu Ali had not been able to hurt Fasil in the eyes of Hafez Najeer, for Najeer was strange enough himself.

The deaths of Najeer and Ali had left a gap in the leadership of Black September that Fasil intended to fill. For this reason, he was anxious to get back to Lebanon. In the internecine slaughterhouse of fedayeen politics, a rival might grow too strong in Fasil's absence. He had enjoyed considerable prestige in the movement after the Munich massacre. Had not President Khadafy himself embraced Fasil when the surviving guerrillas arrived in Tripoli to a hero's welcome? Fasil thought the ruler of Libya had embraced the men who had actually been at Munich with somewhat greater fervor than he embraced Fasil, who planned the mission, but Khadafy had definitely been impressed. And had not Khadafy given $5 million to Al Fatah as a reward for Munich? That was another result of his efforts. If the Super Bowl strike was successful, if Fasil claimed credit for it, he would be the most prestigious guerrilla in the world, even better known than that idealist Guevara. Fasil believed that he could then count on support from Khadafy—and the Libyan treasury—in taking over Black September, and eventually he might replace Yasir Arafat as maximum leader of Al Fatah. Fasil was well aware that all those who had tried to replace Arafat were dead. He needed lead time to set up a secure base, for when he made his move to take over, Arafat's assassins would come.

None of his ends would be served by getting himself killed in New Orleans. Originally, he had not intended to take part in the action, anymore than he had at Munich. He was not afraid to do it, but he was fixed on the thought of what he might become if he lived. If the trouble on the *Leticia* had not occurred, he would still be in Lebanon.

Fasil could see that the odds of his getting away clean from New Orleans were not good under the current plan. His job was to provide muscle and covering fire at New Orleans Lakefront Airport while the bomb was being attached to the blimp. It was not possible to clamp the nacelle to the blimp at some other location—the ground crew and the mooring mast were necessary because the airship must be held rock-steady while the work was going on.

Lander might be able to fool the ground crew for a few vital seconds by claiming the nacelle contained some esoteric piece of television equipment, but the ruse would not last long. There would be violence, and after the takeoff Fasil would be left in the open on the airfield, possibly in a converging ring of police. Fasil did not think his role worthy of his abilities. Ali Hassan would have performed this function if he had not been killed on the freighter. It was certainly not a job that would justify the loss of Muhammad Fasil.

If he was not trapped at the takeoff site, the best chance of escape was an air hijack to a friendly country. But at Lakefront Airport, a private facility on the shore of Lake Pontchartrain, there were no long-range passenger flights. He might take over a private aircraft with range enough to reach Cuba, but that would not do. Cuba could not be depended upon to shield him. Fidel Castro was tough on hijackers, and in the face of an enraged America he might hand Fasil over. Besides, he would not have the advantage of a planeload of hostages, and no private plane would be fast enough to escape the American fighters screaming into the sky from a half-dozen coastal bases.

No, he had no desire to fall into the Gulf of Mexico in some smoke-filled cockpit, knowing it was all over as the water rushed up to smash him. That would be stupid. Fasil was fanatic enough to die gladly if it were necessary to his satisfactions, but he was not willing to die stupidly.

Even if he could slip across the city to New

Orleans International, there were no commercial flights with range enough to reach Libya without refueling, and the probabilities of making a successful refueling stop were low.

The House of War would be enraged as it had not been since Pearl Harbor. Fasil recalled the words of the Japanese admiral after the strike at Pearl: "I fear we have awakened a sleeping giant and filled him with a terrible resolve."

They would take him when he stopped to refuel—if he ever got off the ground. Very likely air traffic would be frozen within minutes of the blast.

It was clear to Fasil that his place was in Beirut, leading the new army of front-fighters who would flock to him after this triumph. It would be a disservice to the cause for him to die in New Orleans.

Now. Lander clearly had the qualifications to carry out the technical end. Having seen him, Fasil was confident that he was willing to do it. Dahlia appeared to have control of him. There simply remained the problem of last-minute muscle at the airport. If Fasil could arrange for that, then there was no need for his actual presence. He could be waiting in Beirut with a microphone in his hand. A satellite link to New York would have his picture and his statement on worldwide television in minutes. He could hold a news conference. He would be in a stroke the most formidable Arab in the world.

All that would be required at the New Orleans airport was a couple of skilled gunmen, imported at the last minute, under Dahlia's command and ignorant of their mission until just before they went into action. That could be accomplished. Fasil had made up his mind. He would see the nacelle through the final stages of its construction, would see that it got to New Orleans. Then he would leave.

To Fasil, Lander's progress with the huge bomb was maddeningly slow. Lander had asked for the maximum amount of explosives the blimp could carry, with shrapnel, under ideal conditions. He had not really expected to get as much as he asked for. Now that it was here he intended to take full advantage of it. The problem was weight and weather—the weather on January 12 in New Orleans. The blimp could fly in any conditions in which football could be played, but rain meant extra weight and New Orleans had received 77 inches of rain in the past year, far more than the national average. Even a dew covering the blimp's great skin weighed 700 pounds, detracting that much from its lifting power. Lander had calculated the lift very carefully, and he would be straining the blimp to the utmost when it rose into the sky carrying its deadly egg. On a clear day, with sunshine, he could count on some help from the "superheat" effect, added lift gained when the helium inside the bag was hotter than the outside air. But unless he was prepared, rain could ruin everything. By the time he was ready to take off, some of the ground crew would almost certainly have been shot and there could be no delay in getting airborne. The blimp must fly, and fly immediately. To allow for the possibility of rain, he had split the nacelle, so that part of it could be left behind in bad weather. It was a pity that Aldrich did not use a surplus Navy dirigible instead of the smaller blimp, Lander reflected. He had flown Navy airships when they carried six tons of ice, great sheets of it, that slid down the sides and fell away in a glittering, crashing cascade when the dirigible reached warmer air. But those long-extinct ships had been eight times the size of the Aldrich blimp.

Balance must be close to perfect with either the entire nacelle or three-quarters of it. That meant having optional mounting points on the frame. These changes had taken time, but not so much time as Lander had feared. He had a little over a month before the Super Bowl. Of that month he would lose most of the last two weeks flying football games. That left him about 17 working days. There was time for one more refinement.

He set up on his workbench a thick sheet of fiberglass five inches by seven and one-half inches in size. The sheet was reinforced with metal mesh and curved in two planes, like a section of watermelon rind. He warmed a piece of plastic explosive and rolled it into a slab of the same size, carefully increasing the thickness of the plastic from the center toward the ends.

Lander attached the slab of plastic to the convex side of the fiberglass sheet. The device now looked like a warped book with a cover on only one side. Smoothed over the plastic explosive were three layers of rubber sheeting cut from a sickroom mattress cover. On top of these went a piece of light canvas bristling with .177 caliber rifle darts. The darts sat on their flat bottoms, glued to the canvas closer together than the nails in a fakir's bed. As the dart-studded canvas was pulled tight around the convex surface of the device, the sharp tips of the darts diverged slightly. This divergence was the purpose of curving the device. It was necessary if the darts were to spread out in flight in a predetermined pattern. Lander had marked out the ballistics with great care. The shape of the darts should stabilize them in flight just like the steel flechettes used in Vietnam.

Now he attached three more layers of dart-covered canvas. In all, the four layers contained 944 darts. At a range of 60 yards, Lander calculated, they would riddle an area of 1,000 square feet, one dart striking in each 1.07 square feet with the velocity of a high-powered rifle bullet. Nothing could live in that strike zone. And this was only the small test model. The real one, the one that would hang beneath the blimp, was 317 times bigger in surface area and weight and carried an average of 3.5 darts for every one of the 80,985 persons Tulane Stadium could seat.

Fasil came into the workshop as Lander was attaching the outside cover, a sheet of fiberglass the same thickness as the skin of the nacelle.

Lander did not speak to him.

Fasil appeared to pay little attention to the object on the workbench, but he recognized what it was, and he was appalled. The Arab looked around the workshop for several minutes, careful not to touch anything. A technician himself, trained in Germany and North Vietnam, Fasil could not help admiring the neatness and economy with which the big nacelle was constructed.

"This material is hard to weld," he said, tapping the Reynolds alloy tubing. "I see no heliarc equipment, did you farm out the work?"

"I borrowed some equipment from the company over the weekend."

"The frame is stress-relieved as well. Now that, Mr. Lander, is a conceit." Fasil intended this as a joking compliment to Lander's craftsmanship. He had decided his duty lay in getting along with the American.

"If the frame warped and cracked the fiberglass shell, someone might see the darts as we rolled it out of the truck," Lander said in a monotone.

"I thought you would be packing in the plastic by now, with only a month remaining."

"Not ready yet. I have to test something first."

"Perhaps I can be of assistance."

"Do you know the explosive index of this material?"

Fasil shook his head ruefully. "It's very new."

"Have you ever seen any of it detonated?"

"No. I was instructed that it is more potent than C-4. You saw what it did to Muzi's apartment."

"I saw a hole in the wall and I can't tell enough from that. The most common mistake in making an antipersonnel device is putting the shrapnel too close to the charge, so the shrapnel loses its integrity in the explosion. Think about that, Fasil. If you don't know it you should know it. Read this field manual and you will find out all about it. I'll translate the big words for you. I don't want these darts fragmented in the blast. I am not interested in merely filling 75 institutes for the deaf. I don't know how much buffer is necessary between the darts and the plastic to protect them."

"But look at how much is in a claymore-type device—"

"That's no indication. I'm dealing with longer ranges and infinitely more explosive. Nobody has ever built one this big before. A claymore is the size of a schoolbook. This is the size of a lifeboat."

"How will the nacelle be positioned when it is detonated?"

"Over the 50-yard line at precisely 100 feet altitude, lined up lengthwise with the field. You can see how the curve of the nacelle conforms to the curve of the stadium."

"So—"

"So, Fasil, I have to also be sure that the darts will disperse in the correct arc, rather than blowing out in big lumps. I've got some leeway inside the skin. I can exaggerate the curves if I have to. I'll find out about the buffer and about the dispersal when we detonate this," Lander said, patting the device on his workbench.

"It's got at least a half-kilo of plastic in it."

"Yes."

"You can't set it off without drawing the authorities."

"Yes, I can."

"You would have no time to examine the results before the authorities came."

"Yes, I will."

"This is—" He nearly said "madness," but stopped himself in time. "This is very rash."

"Don't worry about it, A-rab."

"May I check your calculations?" Fasil hoped he could devise a way to stop the experiment.

"Help yourself. Remember, this is not a scale model of the side of the nacelle. It just contains the two compound curves used in dispersing the shrapnel."

"I'll remember, Mr. Lander."

Fasil spoke privately with Dahlia as she was carrying out the trash. "Talk to him," he said in Arabic. "We know the thing will work as it is. This business of the test is not an acceptable risk. He will lose everything."

"It might not work perfectly," she replied in English. "It must be without flaw."

"It does not have to be *that* perfect."

"For him, it does. For me too."

"For the purpose of the mission, for what we set out to do, it will work adequately the way it is."

"Comrade Fasil, pushing the button in that gondola on January 12 will be the last act of Michael Lander's life. He won't see what comes after. Neither will I, if he needs me to fly with him. We have to *know* what's coming after, do you understand that?"

"I understand that you are beginning to sound more like him than like a front-fighter."

"Then you are of limited intelligence."

"In Lebanon I would kill you for that."

"We're a long way from Lebanon, Comrade Fasil. If either of us ever sees Lebanon again, you may try at your convenience."

CHAPTER 14

Rachel Bauman, M.D., sat behind a desk at Halfway House in the South Bronx, waiting. The addict rehabilitation center held many memories for her. She looked around the bright little room with its amateurish paint job and pickup furniture and thought about some of the ravaged, desperate minds she had tried to reach, the things that she had listened to, in her volunteer work here. It was because of the memories the room evoked that she had chosen this place to meet with Eddie Stiles.

There was a light rap on the door and Stiles came in, a slight, balding man looking around with quick glances. He had shaved for the occasion. A patch of tissue was stuck to a nick on his jaw. Stiles smiled awkwardly and fiddled with his cap.

"Sit down, Eddie. You're looking well."

"Never better, Dr. Bauman."

"How's the tugboat business?"

"To tell you the truth, dull. But I like it, I like it, understand," he added quickly. "You done me a good turn getting me that job."

"I didn't get you that job, Eddie. I just asked the man to look you over."

"Yeah, well, I'd never have got it otherwise.

How's with you? You look kind of different, I mean like you feel good. What am I talking, you're the doctor." He laughed self-consciously.

Rachel could see that he had gained weight. When she met him three years ago, he had just been arrested for smuggling cigarettes up from Norfolk in a 40-foot trawler, trying to feed a $75 a day heroin habit. Eddie had spent many months at Halfway House, many hours talking to Rachel. She had worked with him when he was screaming.

"What did you want to see me about, Dr. Bauman? I mean, I'm glad to see you and all and if you was wondering if I'm clean—"

"I know you're clean, Eddie. I want to ask you for some advice." She had never before presumed on a professional relationship, and it disturbed her to do so now. Stiles noted this instantly. His native wariness warred with the respect and warmth he felt for her.

"It's got nothing to do with you," she said. "Let me lay it out for you and see what you think."

Stiles relaxed a little. He was not being asked to commit himself about anything immediately.

"I need to find a boat, Eddie. A certain boat. A funny-business boat."

His face revealed nothing. "I told you I would tugboat and that's all I do is tugboat, you know that."

"I know that. But you know a lot of people, Eddie. I don't know any people who carry on funny business in boats. I need your help."

"We level with each other, always have, right?"

"Yes."

"You never blabbed none of the stuff I told you when I was on the couch, right?"

"Nope."

"Okay, you tell me the question and who wants to know."

Rachel hesitated. The truth was the truth. Nothing else would do. She told him.

"The feds already asked me," Stiles said when she had finished. "This guy comes right on board in front of everybody to ask me, which I don't appreciate too much. I know they asked some other—guys of my acquaintance."

"And you told them zip."

Stiles smiled and reddened. "I didn't know anything to tell them, you know? To tell you the truth I didn't concentrate too hard. I guess nobody else did either, they're still asking around, I hear."

Rachel waited, she did not push him. The little man tugged at his collar, stroked his chin, deliberately put his hands back in his lap.

"You want to talk to the guy who owns this boat? I don't mean you yourself, that wouldn't be—I mean, your friends want to."

"Right."

"Just talk?"

"Just talk."

"For money? I mean, not for me, Dr. Bauman. Don't think that, for God's sake, I owe you enough already. But I mean, if I was to know some guy, very few things are free. I got a couple hundred, you're welcome, but it might—"

"Don't worry about the money," she said.

"Tell me again from where the Coast Guard first spotted the boat and who did what."

Stiles listened, nodding and asking an occasional question. "Frankly, maybe I can't help you at all, Dr. Bauman," he said finally. "But some things occur to me. I'll listen around."

"Very carefully."

"You know it."

CHAPTER 15

HARRY LOGAN drove his battered pickup along the perimeter of United Coal Company's heavy equipment compound on his hourly watchman's round, looking down the rows of bulldozers and dirt buggies. He was supposed to watch for thieves and conservation-minded saboteurs, but none ever came. Nobody was within miles of the place. All was well, he could slip away.

He turned onto a dirt track that followed the giant scar the strip mine had gouged in the Pennsylvania hills, red dust rising behind the pickup. The scar was eight miles long and two miles wide, and it was growing longer as the great earthmoving machines chewed down the hills. Twenty-four hours a day, six days a week, two of the largest earthmovers in the world slammed their maws against the hillsides like hyenas opening a belly. They stopped for nothing except the Sabbath, the president of United Coal being a very religious man.

This was Sunday, when nothing but dustdevils moved on the raw wasteland. It was the day when Harry Logan made a little extra money. He was a scavenger and he worked in the condemned area that would shortly be uprooted by the mining. Each Sunday Logan left his post at the equipment compound and drove to the small abandoned village on a hill in the path of the earthmovers.

The peeling houses stood empty, smelling of urine left by the vandals who smashed the windows. The householders had taken everything they thought was valuable when they moved out, but their eye for salable scrap was not so keen as Logan's. He was a natural scavenger. There was good lead to be found in the old-fashioned gutters and plumbing. Electrical switches could be pried from the walls and there were showerheads and copper wire. He sold these things to his son-in-law's junkyard. Logan was anxious to make a good haul on this Sunday because only an eighth of a mile of woods remained between the village and the strip mine. In two weeks the village would be devoured.

He backed his truck into the garage beside a house. It was very quiet when he turned off the motor. There was only the wind, whistling through the scattered, windowless houses. Logan was loading a stack of wallboard into his truck when he heard the airplane.

The red four-seater Cessna made two low passes over the village. Looking downhill through the trees, Logan saw it settle toward the dirt road in the strip mine. If Logan had appreciated such things, he would have enjoyed watching a superb cross-wind landing; a sideslip, a flare-out, and the little plane rolling smoothly with dust blowing off to one side.

He scratched his head and his behind. Now what could they want? Company inspectors maybe. He could say he was checking the village. The plane had rolled out of sight behind a thick grove. Logan worked his way cautiously down through the trees. When he could see the airplane again it was empty, and the wheels were chocked. He heard voices through the trees to his left and walked quietly in that direction. A big empty barn was over there with a three-acre feedlot beside it. Logan knew very well that it contained nothing worth stealing. Watching from the edge of the woods, he could see two men and a woman in the feedlot, ankle deep in bright green winter wheat.

One of the men was tall and wore sunglasses and a ski jacket. The other was darker and had a mark on his face. The men unrolled a long piece of cord and measured a distance from the side of the barn out into the feedlot. The woman set up a surveyor's transit and the tall man sighted through it while the dark one made marks on the barn wall with paint. The three gathered around a clipboard, gesturing with their arms.

Logan stepped out of the woods. The swarthy one saw him first and said something Logan couldn't hear.

"What are you folks doing out here?"

"Hello," the woman said, smiling.

"Have you got any company identification?"

"We're not with the company," the taller man said.

"This is private property. You're not allowed out here. That's what I'm out here for, to keep people off."

"We just wanted to take a few pictures," the tall man said.

"There ain't nothing to take pictures of out here," Logan said suspiciously.

"Oh yes there is," the woman said. "Me." She licked her lips.

"We're shooting a cover for what you might call a private kind of magazine, you know, a daring sort of magazine?"

"You talking about a nudie book?"

"We prefer to call it a naturist publication," the tall man said. "You can't do this sort of thing just anywhere."

"I might get arrested," the woman said, laughing. She was a looker all right.

"It's too cold for that stuff," Logan said.

"We're going to call the picture 'Goose Bumps.'"

Meanwhile, the swarthy one was unrolling a spool of wire from the tripod to the trees.

"Don't you fool with me now, I don't know anything about this. The office never said anything to me about letting anybody in here. You'd better go on back where you came from."

"Do you want to make $50 helping us? It will only take a half hour and we'll be gone," the tall man said.

Logan considered a moment. "Well, I won't take off my clothes."

"You won't have to. Is there anyone else around here?"

"No. Nobody for miles."

"We'll manage just fine then." The man was holding out $50. "Does my hand offend you?"

"No, no."

"Why are you staring at it then?" The woman shifted uncomfortably beside the tall man.

"I didn't mean to," Logan said. He could see his reflection in the man's sunglasses.

"You two get the big camera from the plane, and this gentleman and I will get things ready." The swarthy man and the woman disappeared into the woods.

"What's your name?"

"Logan."

"All right, Mr. Logan, if you'll get a couple of boards and put them down in the grass right here at the center of the barn wall for the lady to stand on."

"Do what?"

"Put some boards there, right in the middle. The ground is cold and we want her feet up out of the grass where they will show. Some people like feet."

While Logan found the boards, the tall man removed the transit and fastened a peculiar-looking curved object to the tripod. He turned and called to Logan. "No, no. One board on top of the other." He made a frame with his hands and squinted through it. "Now stand on it and let me see if it's right. Hold it right there, don't move, here they come with the viewfinder." The tall man disappeared into the trees.

Logan reached up to scratch his head. For an instant his brain registered the blinding flash, but he never heard the roar. Twenty darts shredded him and the blast slammed him back against the barn wall.

Lander, Fasil, and Dahlia came running through the smoke.

"Ground meat," Fasil said. They turned the slack body over and examined the back. Rapidly, they took pictures of the barn wall. It was bowed in and looked like a giant colander. Lander went inside the barn. Hundreds of small holes in the wall admitted points of light that freckled him as his camera clicked and clicked again.

"Very successful," Fasil said.

They dragged the body into the barn, sloshed gasoline over it and over the dry wood around it, and poured a trail of gasoline out the door for 20 yards. The fire flashed inside and lit the pools of gas with a "Whump" they felt on their faces.

Black smoke rose from the barn as the Cessna climbed out of sight.

"How did you find that place?" Fasil asked, leaning forward from the rear seat to be heard over the engine noise.

"I was hunting dynamite last summer," Lander said.

"Do you think the authorities will come soon?"

"I doubt it, they blast there all the time."

CHAPTER 16

EDDIE STILES sat by the window in the New York City Aquarium snack bar worrying. From his table he could see Rachel Bauman below him and 40 yards away at the rail of the penguin pen. It was not Rachel Bauman that disturbed him, it was the two men standing with her. Stiles did not like their looks at all. The one on her left looked like Man Mountain Dean. The other one was a little smaller, but worse. He had the easy, economical movements and the balance that Eddie had learned to fear. The predators in Eddie's world had moved that way. The expensive ones. Very different from the muscle the shylocks employed, the blocky hard guys with their weight on their heels.

Eddie did not like the way this man's eyes swept over the high places, the roof of the shark house, the fences on the dunes between the Aquarium and the Coney Island boardwalk. One slow sweep and then the man quartered the ground, going over it minutely, infantry style, from close to far, and all the time wagging his finger over an interested penguin's head.

Eddie was sorry he had chosen this place to meet. On a weekday the crowd was not big enough to give him that comfortable, anonymous feeling.

He had Dr. Bauman's word that he would not be involved. She had never lied to him. His life, the life he was trying to build, was based on what he had learned about himself with Dr. Bauman's help. If that was not true, then nothing was true. He drained his coffee cup and walked quickly down the stairs and around to the whale tank. He could hear the whale blowing before he reached the tank. It was a 40-foot female killer whale, elegant with her gleaming black and white markings. A show was underway. A young man stood on a platform over the water holding up a fish in the pale winter sunshine. The surface of the water bulged in a line across the pool as beneath the surface the whale came like a black locomotive. She cannoned vertically out of the water and her great length seemed to hang in the air as she took the fish in her triangular teeth.

Eddie heard the applause behind him as he went down the steps to the underground gallery with its big plate-glass windows. The room was dim and damp, lit by the sun shining down through the blue-green water of the whale tank. Eddie looked into the tank. The whale was moving over the light-dappled bottom, rolling over and over, chewing. Three families came down the stairs and joined him. They all had loud children.

"Daddy, I can't see."

The father hoisted the boy to his shoulders, bumping his head on the ceiling, then took him outside squalling.

"Hi, Eddie," Rachel said.

Her two companions stood on the far side of her, away from Eddie. That was good manners, Eddie thought. Goons would have come up on either side. Cops would have, too. "Hello, Dr. Bauman." His eyes flicked over her shoulder.

"Eddie, this is David and this is Robert."

"Pleased to make your acquaintance." Eddie shook their hands. The big one had a piece under his left arm, no doubt about it. Maybe the other guy had one too, but the coat fit better. This David. Enlarged knuckles on the first two fingers and the edge of his hand like a wood rasp. He didn't get that learning to yo-yo. Dr. Bauman was a very wise and understanding woman, but there were some things she did not know about, Eddie thought. "Dr. Bauman, I'd like to talk to you a second, uh, personal, if you don't mind."

At the other end of the chamber, he spoke close to her ear. Yelling children covered his voice. "Doc. I want to know, do you really know these guys? I know you think you do, but I mean *know* them? Dr. Bauman, these are some very hard guys. There are, you know, hard guys and hard guys. This is a thing I happen to know about. These are the harder type of hard guy, rather than mugs, if you follow me. These don't look like no fuzz to me. I can't see you around these type of fellows. You know, unless they were kin to you or something like that you can't do anything about."

Rachel put her hand on his arm. "Thanks, Eddie. I know what you're saying. But I've known these two for a long time. They're my friends."

A porpoise had been put in the tank with the whale to provide her company. It was busy hiding pieces of fish in the drain while the whale was distracted by the trainer. The whale slid by the underwater window, taking a full ten seconds to pass by, its small eye looking through the glass at the people talking on the other side.

"This guy I hear about, Jerry Sapp, did a job in Cuba a couple of years ago," Stiles told Kabakov. "Cuba! He ran in under the coastal radar close to Puerta Cabanas with some Cubans from Miami." Stiles looked from Kabakov to Rachel and back again. "They had some business on shore, you know, they ran in through the surf in one of these inflatables, like an Avon or a Zodiac, and they came off with this box. I don't know what the hell it was, but this guy didn't come back to Florida. He got into it with a Cuban patrol boat out of Bahia Honda and ran straight across to Yucatan. Had a big bladder tank on the foredeck."

Kabakov listened, tapping his fingers on the rail.

The whale was quiet now, resting on the surface. Her great tail arched down, dropping her flukes ten feet below the surface.

"These kids are driving me nuts," Eddie said. "Let's move."

They stood in the dark corridor of the shark house, watching the long gray shapes endlessly circling, small bright fish darting between them.

"Anyway, I had always wondered how this guy ran in close to Cuba. Since the Bay of Pigs they got radar you wouldn't believe. You said your guy slipped away from the Coast Guard radar. Same thing. So I asked around a little, you know, about this Sapp. He was in Sweeney's in Asbury Park there, about two weeks ago. But nobody's seen him since. His boat's a 38-foot sportfisherman, a Shing Lu job. They're built in Hong Kong, and I mean *built*. This one's all wood."

"Where did he keep his boat?" Kabakov asked.

"I don't know. Nobody seemed to know. I mean, you can't ask too close, you know? But look, the bartender at Sweeney's takes messages for this guy, I think he could get in touch. If it was business."

"What kind of business would he go for?"

"Depends. He has to know he's hot. If he went himself on this job you're interested in, of course he knows he's hot. If it was a contract job, if he let out the boat, then he was listening to the Coast Guard frequency the whole time. Wouldn't you?"

"Where would you run, if you were this man?"

"I would have watched the boat for a day after it was back, to make sure it wasn't staked out. Then if I had a place to work I'd paint it, put the legit registration back on and change it up—I'd put a tuna tower on it. I'd catch a string of Gold Platers running south to Florida along the ditch and I'd get right in with 'em—a string of yachts going down the Intracoastal Waterway," Eddie explained. "Those rich guys like to go in a pack."

"Give me a high-profit item away from here that would make him surface," Kabakov said. "Something that would require the boat."

"Smack," Eddie said, with a guilty glance toward Rachel. "Heroin. Out of Mexico into, say, Corpus Christi or Aransas Pass on the Texas coast. He might go for that. There would have to be some front money, though. And he would have to be approached very careful. He would spook easy."

"Think about the contact, Eddie. And thank you," Kabakov said.

"I did it for the Doc." The sharks moved silently in the lighted tank. "Look, I'm gonna split now, I don't want to look at these things anymore."

"I'll meet you back in town, David," Rachel said.

Kabakov was surprised to see a kind of distaste in her eyes when she looked at him. She and Eddie walked away together, their heads bent, talking. Her arm was around the little man's shoulders.

Kabakov would have preferred to keep Corley out of it. So far, the FBI agent knew nothing of this business of Jerry Sapp and his boat. Kabakov wanted to pursue it alone. He needed to talk to Sapp before the man wrapped himself in the Constitution.

Kabakov did not mind violating a man's rights, his dignity, or his person if the violation provided immediate benefits. The fact of doing it did not bother him, but the seed within him that was nourished by the success of these tactics made him uneasy.

He felt himself developing contemptuous attitudes toward the web of safeguards between the citizen and the expediency of investigation. He did not try to rationalize his acts with catchphrases like "the greater good," for he was not a reflective man. While Kabakov believed his measures to be necessary—knew that they worked—he feared that the mentality a man could develop in their practice was an ugly and dangerous thing, and for him it wore a face. The face of Hitler.

Kabakov recognized that the things he did marked his mind as surely as they marked his body. He wanted to think that his increasing impatience with the restraints of the law were entirely the result of his experience, that he felt anger against these obstacles just as he felt stiffness in old wounds on winter mornings.

But this was not entirely true. The seed of his attitudes was in his nature, a fact he had discovered years ago near Tiberias, in Galilee.

He was en route to inspect some positions on the Syrian border when he stopped his jeep at a well on a mountainside. A windmill, an old American Aermotor, pumped the cold water out of the rock. The windmill creaked at regular intervals as the blades slowly revolved, a lonely sound on a bright and quiet day. Leaning against his jeep, the water still cool on his face, Kabakov watched a flock of sheep grazing above him on the mountainside. A sense of aloneness pressed around him and made him aware of the shape and position of his body in these great tilted spaces. And then he saw an eagle, high, riding a thermal, wing-tip feathers splayed like fingers, slipping sideways over the mountain's face, his shadow slipping fast over the rocks. The eagle was not hunting sheep, for it was winter and there were no lambs among them, but it was above the sheep and they saw it and baaed among themselves. Kabakov became dizzy watching the bird, his horizontal reference distorted by the mountain slope. He found himself holding onto the jeep for balance.

And then he realized that he loved the eagle better than the sheep and that he always would and that, because he did, because it was in him to do it, he could never be perfect in the sight of God.

Kabakov was glad that he would never have any real power.

Now, in an apartment in a cliff face in Manhattan, Kabakov considered how the bait could be presented to Jerry Sapp. If he pursued Sapp alone, then Eddie Stiles had to make the contact. He was the only person Kabakov knew who had access to crime circles along the waterfront. Without him, Kabakov would have to use Corley's resources. Stiles would do it for Rachel.

"No," Rachel said at breakfast.

"He would do it if you asked him. We could cover him all the time—"

"He's not going to do it, so forget it."

It was hard to believe that twenty minutes before, she had been so warm and morning-rosy over him, her hair a gentle pendulum that brushed his face and chest.

"I know you don't like to use him, but God dammit—"

"I don't like me using him, I don't like you using me. I'm using you too, in a different way that I haven't figured out yet. It's okay, our using each other. We have something besides that and it's good. But no more Eddie."

She was really splendid, Kabakov thought, with the flush creeping out of the lace and up her neck.

"I can't do it. I won't do it," she said. "Would you like some orange juice?"

"Please."

Reluctantly, Kabakov went to Corley. He gave him the information on Jerry Sapp. He did not give the source.

Corley worked on the bait for two days with the Bureau of Narcotics and Dangerous Drugs. He spent an hour on the telephone to Mexico City. Then he met with Kabakov in the FBI's Manhattan office.

"Anything on the Greek?"

"Not yet," Kabakov said. "Moshevsky is still working the bars. Go on with Sapp."

"The Bureau has no record on a Jerry Sapp," Corley said. "Whoever he is, he's clean under that name. Coast Guard registration does not have him. Their files are not cross-indexed on boat type down to the detail we need. The paint we have will do for positive comparison, but tracing origin is another matter. It's not marine paint. It's a commercial brand of semi-gloss over a heavy sealer, available anywhere."

"Tell me about the dope."

"I'm getting to that. Here's the package. Did you follow the Krapf-Mendoza case in Chihuahua by any chance? Well, I didn't know the details either. From 1970 through 1973 they got 115 pounds of heroin into this country. It went to Boston. Clever method. For each shipment they used a pretext to hire an American citizen to go down to Mexico. Sometimes it was a man, sometimes a woman, but always a loner who had no close relatives. The stooge flew down on a tourist visa and after a few days unfortunately died. The body was shipped home with a belly full of heroin. They had a funeral home on this end. Your hair is growing out nicely by the way."

"Go on, go on."

"Two things we got out of it. The money man in Boston still has a good name with the mob. He helps us out because he's trying to stave off forty years mandatory in the joint. The Mexican authorities left a guy in Cozumel on the street. Better not to ask what he's trying to stave off."

"So if our man sends word down the pipeline that he is looking for a good man with a boat to run the stuff out of Cozumel into Texas, it would look reasonable because the old method was stopped," Kabakov said. "And if Sapp calls our man, he can give references in Mexico and in Boston."

"Yeah. This Sapp would check it out before he showed himself. Even getting the word to him will probably involve a couple of cutouts. This is what bothers me, if we find him we've got almost nothing on him. We might get him on some bullshit conspiracy charge involving the use of his boat, but that would take time to develop. We've got nothing to threaten him with."

Oh, yes we do, Kabakov thought to himself.

By mid-afternoon Corley had asked the U.S. District Court in Newark for permission to tap the two telephones in Sweeney's Bar & Grill in Asbury Park. By 4 P.M. the request had been denied. Corley had no evidence whatsoever of any wrongdoing at Sweeney's, and he was acting on anonymous allegations of little substance, the magistrate explained. The magistrate said that he was sorry.

At 10 A.M. on the following day a blue van pulled into the supermarket parking lot adjacent to Sweeney's. An elderly lady was at the wheel. The lot was full and she drove along slowly, apparently looking for a parking place. In a car parked beside the telephone pole 30 feet from the rear of Sweeney's Bar a man was dozing.

"He's asleep, for Christ's sake," the elderly lady said, apparently speaking to her bosom.

The dozing man in the car awoke as the radio beside him crackled angrily. With a sheepish expression, he pulled out of the parking space. The van backed into the place. A few shoppers rolled carts down the traffic aisle. The man who vacated the parking space got out of his car.

"Lady, I think you got a flat."

"Oh, yeah?"

The man walked to the rear wheel of the van, close beside the pole. Two thin wires, brown against the brown pole, led from the telephone line to the ground and terminated in a double jack. The man plugged the jack into a socket in the fender well of the van.

"No, the tire's just low. You can drive on it all right." He drove away.

In the rear of the van, Kabakov leaned back with his hands behind his head. He was wearing earphones and smoking a cigar.

"You don't have to wear them all the time," said the balding young man at the miniature switchboard. "I say you don't have to wear them all the time. When it rings or when it's picked up on this end, you'll see this light and hear the buzzer. You want some coffee? Here." He leaned close to the partition behind the cab. "Hey, mom. You want coffee?"

"No," came the voice from the front. "And you leave the bialys in the bag. You know they give you gas." Bernie Biner's mother had switched from the driver's seat to the passenger side. She was knitting an afghan. As the mother of one of the best freelance wire men in the business, it was her job to drive, look innocent, and watch for the police.

"$11.40 an hour she charges me and she's supervising my diet," Biner told Kabakov.

The buzzer sounded. Bernie's quick fingers started the tape recorder. He and Kabakov put on the earphones. They could hear the telephone ringing in the bar.

"Hello. Sweeney's."

"Freddy?" A woman's voice. "Listen, honey, I can't come in today."

"Shit, Frances, what is this, twice in two weeks?"

"Freddy, I'm sorry, I got the cramps like you wouldn't believe."

"Every week you get the cramps? You better go to the muff doctor, kid. What about Arlene?"

"I called her house already, she's not home."

"Well, you get somebody over here, I'm not waiting tables and working the bar too."

"I'll try, Freddy."

They heard the bartender hang up and a woman's laughter before the phone was replaced on the other end. Kabakov blew a smoke ring and told himself to be patient. Corley's stooge had planted an urgent message for Sapp when Sweeney's opened a half-hour ago. The stooge had given the bartender $50 to hurry it up. It was a simple message saying business was available and asking Sapp to call a number in Manhattan to talk business or to get references. The number was to be given to Sapp alone. If Sapp called, Corley would try to fool him into a meeting. Kabakov was not satisfied. That was why he had hired Biner, who already received a weekly retainer to check the Israeli mission phones for bugs. Kabakov had not consulted Corley about the matter.

A light on Biner's switchboard indicated the second telephone in the bar had been picked up. Through the earphones, they heard ten digits dialed.

Then a telephone ringing. It was not answered.

Bernie Biner ran back his tape recording of the dialing, then played it at a slower speed, counting the clicks. "Three-oh-five area code. That's Florida. Here's the number. Eight-four-four-six-oh-six-nine. Just a second." He consulted a thick table of prefixes. "It's somewhere in the West Palm Beach area."

Half an hour passed before the switchboard in the van signaled that another call was being placed from the bar. Ten digits again.

"Glamareef Lounge."

"Yeah, I'm calling for Mr. Sapp. He said I could leave him a message at this number if I needed to."

"Who is this?"

"Freddy Hodges at Sweeney's. Mr. Sapp will know."

"All right. What is it?"

"I want him to call me."

"I don't know if I can get him on the phone. You say Freddy Hodges?"

"Yeah. He knows the number. It's important, tell him. It's business."

"Uh, look, he may come in around five or six. Sometimes he comes in. I see him, I'll tell him."

"Tell him it's important. That Freddy Hodges called."

"Yeah, yeah, I'll tell him." A click.

Bernie Biner called West Palm Beach information and confirmed that the number was that of the Glamareef Lounge.

The fire on Kabakov's cigar was two inches long. He was elated. He had expected Sapp to use a telephone cutout, a person who did not know his identity, but whom he called under a code name to receive messages. Instead it was a simple message drop in a bar. Now it would not be necessary to go through the intricate process of setting up a meeting with Sapp. He could find him at the bar.

"Bernie, I want a tap until Sapp calls Sweeney's here. When that happens, let me know the second you're sure it's him."

"Where will you be?"

"In Florida. I'll give you a number when I get there." Kabakov glanced at his watch. He intended to be in the Glamareef at 5 P.M. He had six hours.

The Glamareef in West Palm Beach is a cinder-block building on a sandy lot. Like many Southern drinking places constructed after air conditioning became popular, it has no windows. Originally it was a jukebox-and-pool-table beer joint called Shangala, with a loud air conditioner and a block of ice in the urinal. Now it went after a faster crowd. Its naugahyde booths and dim bar drew people from two worlds—the paycheck playboys and the big-money yachting people who liked to slum. The Glamareef, nee Shangala, was a good place to look for young women with marital problems. It was a good place for an older, affluent woman to find a body-and-fender man who had never had it on a silk sheet.

Kabakov sat at the end of the bar drinking beer. He and Moshevsky had rented a car at the airport and their hurried drive past the four nearby marinas had been discouraging. There was a small city of boats in West Palm Beach, many of them sportfishermen. They would have to find the man first, then the boat.

He had been waiting an hour when a husky man in his middle thirties came into the bar. Kabakov ordered another beer and asked for change. He studied the new arrival in the mirrored front of the cigarette machine. He was of medium height and he had a deep suntan and heavy muscles under his polo shirt. The bartender put a drink in front of him and, with it, a note.

The husky man finished his drink in a few long swallows and went to a phone booth in the corner. Kabakov doodled on his napkin. He could see the man's mouth moving in the telephone booth.

The bar telephone rang twice before the bartender picked it up. He put his hand over the mouthpiece. "Is there a Shirley Tatum here?" he said loudly, looking around. "No, I'm sorry." He hung up.

That was Moshevsky, calling the bar from a pay phone outside, relaying the signal from Bernie Biner in Asbury Park. The man Kabakov was watching in the telephone booth was talking to Sweeney's Bar in Asbury Park with Bernie listening in. He was Jerry Sapp.

Kabakov sorted his change in a roadside telephone booth a half-hour before dark. He dialed Rachel's number.

"Hello."

"Rachel, don't wait dinner on me. I'm in Florida."

"You found the boat."

"Yes. I found Sapp first and followed him to it. I haven't examined it yet. Or talked to Sapp. Listen, tomorrow I want you to call Corley. Tell him Sapp and the boat are at the Clear Springs Marina near West Palm Beach. Have you got that? The boat is green now. Number FL 4040 AL. Call him about 10 A.M., not before."

"You're going aboard it tonight, and in the morning, if you're still alive, you're planning to call me and say you've changed your mind about telling Corley, aren't you?"

"Yes." There was a long silence. Kabakov had to break it. "It's a private marina, very exclusive. Lucky Luciano used to keep a boat here years ago. Also other arch-criminals. The man at the bait store told me. I had to buy a bucket of shrimp to find that out."

"Why don't you go in with Corley and a warrant?"

"They don't admit Jews."

"You'll take Moshevsky with you, won't you?"

"Sure. He'll be close by."

"David?"

"Yes."

"I love you, to a certain extent."

"Thank you, Rachel." He hung up.

He did not tell her that the marina was isolated, that the landward side was surrounded by a twelve-foot hurricane fence, floodlit. Or that two tall men with short shotguns manned the gate and patrolled the piers.

Kabakov drove a half-mile down the winding road through the scrub growth, the rented johnboat bouncing on its trailer behind him. He parked the car in a thicket and climbed a small knoll where Moshevsky lay with two pairs of field glasses.

"He's still aboard," the big man said. "There are fleas in this damned sand."

With his binoculars, Kabakov scanned the three long piers jutting into Lake Worth. A guard was on the farthest pier, walking slowly, his hat set back on his head. The whole marina had a sinister, fast-money look. Kabakov could imagine what would happen if a warrant were served at the gate. The alarm would be given and whatever was illegal in any of the boats would go over the side. There must be some clue aboard Sapp's boat. Or in Sapp's head. Something that would lead him to the Arabs.

"He's coming out," Moshevsky said.

Kabakov zeroed in on the green sportfisherman moored stern-to in the line of boats at the center pier. Sapp climbed up through the foredeck hatch and locked it behind him. He was dressed for dinner. He stepped down from the bow into a dinghy and pulled well away from his boat to a vacant slip, then climbed onto the pier.

"Why didn't he just walk back along the boat and get onto the pier," muttered Moshevsky, lowering his field glasses and rubbing his eyes.

"Because the damned thing is wired," Kabakov replied wearily. "Let's get our boat."

Kabakov swam slowly in the darkness under the pier, feeling ahead for the pilings. Cobwebs hanging from the planks above him brushed his face, and, from the smell, there was a dead fish nearby. He paused, hugging a piling he could not see, feet gripping the rough sea growth crusting the piling beneath the water. A little light came under the edges of the long pier, and he could see the dark, square shapes of the motor yachts moored stern-to against it.

He had counted seven on the right side. He had six to go. A foot and a half above him, the underside of the pier was studded with nail points where the planks had been nailed down. High tide would be hard on his scalp. A spider ran across his neck and he submerged to drown it. The water tasted like diesel fuel.

Kabakov heard a woman's laughter and the tinkle of ice. He shifted his equipment bag farther around on his back and swam on. This should be it. He made his way around a tangle of rusty cable and stopped just under the edge of the pier, the stern of the boat rising black above him.

Here the air was not so close, and he breathed deeply as he peered at the luminous dial of his watch. It had been 15 minutes since Moshevsky steered the outboard past the seaward end of the marina and he had slipped over the side. He hoped Sapp would linger over dessert.

The man had some kind of alarm system. Either a pressure-sensitive mat in the open cockpit at the stern or something fancier. Kabakov swam along the stern until he found the cable that carried 110-volt shore power to the craft. He unplugged the cable from the jack in the stern. If the alarm used shore power it was now inoperative. He heard footsteps and slid back under the pier. The heavy tread passed overhead, sending a trickle of grit down in his face.

No, he decided, if it were his alarm system, it would be independent of shore power. He would not go over the stern. He would go in as Sapp had come out.

Kabakov swam along the hull to the darkness under the flaring bow. Two mooring lines, slack to accommodate the tide, ran from the bow to pilings on either side of the slip. Kabakov pulled himself up, hand over hand, until he could lock his arms around the stanchion supporting the bow rail. He could see into the cabin of the yacht next door. A man and a woman were seated on a couch. The backs of their heads were visible. They were necking. The woman's head disappeared. Kabakov climbed up on the foredeck and lay against the windshield, the cabin shielding him from the dock. The windshield was dogged tightly shut. Here was the hatch.

With a screwdriver, he removed the thick plastic window in the center of it. The hole was just big enough for his arm. Reaching inside, he turned the lock and felt around the edges of the hatch until he found the contacts of the burglar alarm sensor. His mind was picturing the wiring as his fingers felt for the wires in the padded overhead. The switch was on the coaming, and it was held open by a magnet on the hatch. Take loose the magnet, then, and hold it in place on the switch. Don't drop it! Ease open the hatch. Don't ring, don't ring, don't   ring.

He dropped into the darkness of the forward cabin and closed the hatch, replacing the window and the magnet.

Kabakov felt good. Some of the sting was gone from the debacle at Muzi's house. With his flashlight he found the alarm circuit box and disconnected it from its clutch of dry-cell batteries. Sapp did neat wiring. A timer permitted him to leave without setting off the alarm, a magnet-sensitive cutout against the skin of the boat permitted him to reenter.

Now Kabakov could move around. A quick search of the forward cabin revealed nothing unusual except a full ounce of high-grade crystal cocaine and a coke spoon from which to sniff it.

He switched off his flashlight and opened the hatch leading up to the main cabin. The dock lights shining through the ports provided a little light. Suddenly Kabakov's Parabellum was out and cocked, the trigger squeezed within an ounce of firing.

Something was moving in the cabin. He saw it again, a small, repetitive movement, and again, a flicker of dark against the port. Kabakov lay down in the companionway to silhouette the movement against the light. He smiled. It was Sapp's little surprise for an intruder coming aboard from the dock, an electronic scanner of a new and expensive type. It swept the cockpit constantly, ready to sound the alarm. Kabakov came up behind it and turned off the switch.

For an hour, he searched the boat. In a concealed compartment near the wheel he found a Belgian FN automatic rifle and a revolver. But there was nothing to prove that Sapp or Sapp's boat had been involved in moving the plastic explosive.

It was in the chart bin that he found what he was looking for. A bump at the bow interrupted him. The dinghy. Sapp was coming back. Kabakov slipped into the forward cabin and squeezed into the narrow point of the bow.

Above him, the hatch opened. Feet and then legs appeared. Sapp's head was still out of the hatch when Kabakov's heel slammed into his diaphragm.

Sapp regained consciousness to find himself tied hand and foot on one of the two berths with a sock stuffed in his mouth. A lantern hanging from the ceiling gave off a yellow light and a strong odor of kerosene. Kabakov sat on the opposite bunk smoking a cigar and cleaning his fingernails with Sapp's icepick.

"Good evening, Mr. Sapp. Is your head clear or shall I throw some water on you? All right? On November twelfth, you took a load of plastic explosive from a freighter off the New Jersey Coast. I want to know who was with you and where the plastic is. I have no interest in you otherwise.

"If you tell me, you will not be harmed. If you don't, I will leave you worse than dead. I'll leave you blind, dumb, and crippled. Do I have to hurt you now to demonstrate that I'm serious? I don't think so. I'll remove this sock from your mouth now. If you scream, I'll give you something to scream about, do you understand me?"

Sapp nodded. He spat out lint. "Who the hell are you?"

"That doesn't concern you. Tell me about the plastic."

"I don't know anything about it. You got nothing on me."

"Don't think in legalistic terms, Mr. Sapp. You are not protected from me by the law. The people you worked for are not mob-connected, by the way. You don't have to protect them on that account."

Sapp said nothing.

"The FBI is looking for you on a smuggling charge. Soon they will add mass murder to the list. That's a lot of plastic, Sapp. It will kill a lot of people unless you tell me where it is. Look at me when I'm talking to you."

"Kiss my ass."

Kabakov rose and jammed the sock back in Sapp's mouth. He grabbed Sapp by the hair and forced his head back against the wooden bulkhead. The tip of the icepick rested lightly in the corner of Sapp's rolling eye. A growl rumbled from Kabakov's chest as he drew back the icepick and struck, pinning Sapp's ear to the bulkhead. The color had gone from Sapp's face and there was a foul odor in the cabin.

"You really must look at me when I'm talking to you," Kabakov said. "Are you ready to cooperate? Blink for yes. Die for no."

Sapp blinked and Kabakov removed the sock.

"I didn't go. I didn't know it was plastic."

Kabakov believed this was probably true. Sapp was shorter than the man described by the *Leticia's* first mate. "But your boat went."

"Yes. I don't know who took it out. *No!* Honestly, I don't know. Look, it's my business not to know. I didn't want to know."

"How were you contacted?"

"A man called me the last week in October. He wanted the boat ready, standing by, during the week of November eighth. He didn't say who he was and I didn't ask." Sapp grimaced with pain. "He wanted to know a few things about the boat, not much. Hours on the engines, whether it had any new electronics."

"Any *new* electronics?"

"Yeah, I told him the loran was out—for God's sake take this thing out of my ear."

"All right. You'll get it through the other one if

I catch you in a lie. This man that called, he already knew the boat?"

"Ouch!" Sapp turned his head from side to side and cut his eyes far over, as though he could see his ear. "I guess he knew the boat, he sounded like it. It was worth a thousand to him for it to be available, like a retainer. I got the thousand in the mail at Sweeney's in Asbury Park two days later."

"Do you have the envelope?"

"No, it was a plain envelope, New York City postmark."

"He called you again."

"Yeah, about November tenth. He wanted the boat for the twelfth, a Tuesday. The money was delivered to Sweeney's that night."

"How much?"

"Two thousand for the boat, sixty-five thousand deposit. All cash."

"How was it delivered?"

"A cab brought it in a picnic basket. Food was on top of it. A few minutes later the phone rang again. It was the guy. I told him where to get the boat."

"You never saw him pick it up or return it?"

"No." Sapp described the boathouse in Toms River.

Kabakov had the photo of Fasil and the composite of the woman sealed in a rubber glove in his bag. He took them out. Sapp shook his head at both pictures.

"If you still think I went out with the boat, I've got an alibi for that day. A dentist in Asbury Park fixed my teeth. I have a receipt."

"I expect you have," Kabakov said. "How long have you owned the boat?"

"A long time. Eight years."

"Any previous owners?"

"I had it built."

"How did you return the deposit?"

"I left it in the same basket in the trunk of my car by a supermarket and put the trunk key under the floor mat. Somebody picked it up."

The New Jersey coastal chart Kabakov had found in Sapp's chart bin had the course to the rendezvous marked with a neat black line, departure time and running time checks jotted beside it. The bearings for two radio direction finder fixes were penciled in. Three bearings for each fix.

Kabakov held the chart by the edges, under the lantern where Sapp could see it. "Did you mark this chart?"

"No. I didn't know it was on the boat or I would have gotten rid of it."

Kabakov took another chart from the bin, a Florida chart. "Did you plot the course on this one?"

"Yes."

He compared the two charts. Sapp's handwriting was different. He had used only two bearings for an RDF fix. Sapp's times were written in Eastern Standard. Time for the rendezvous with the *Leticia*, jotted on the New Jersey chart, was 2115. This puzzled Kabakov. He knew the Coast Guard cutter had spotted the speedboat close to the freighter at 1700 Eastern Standard. The boat must have been there for some minutes, loading the plastic, so the rendezvous was about 1615 or 1630. Yet it was marked on the chart for five hours later. Why? The departure time from Toms River and the running time checks were also marked about five hours later than they must have occurred. It didn't make sense. And then it did make sense—the man Kabakov was seeking had not used Eastern Standard time, he had used Greenwich Mean Time—Zulu time—*Pilot time*!

"What fliers do you know?" Kabakov demanded. "Professional pilots."

"I don't know any professional pilots I can think of," Sapp said.

"Think hard."

"Maybe a guy in Jamaica with a commercial license. But he's been in the jug down there ever since the feds vacuumed his luggage compartment. He's the only professional pilot I know. I'm sure of it."

"You know no pilots, you don't know who hired the boat. You know very little, Mr. Sapp."

"I don't. I can't think of any pilots. Look, you can bust me up, you probably will, but I still won't know."

Kabakov considered torturing Sapp. The idea was sickening to him, but he would do it if he thought the results would be worth it. No. Sapp was not a principal in the plot. Threatened with prosecution, fearful that he might be an accessory to a major atrocity involving the explosives, he would try to cooperate. He would try to recall any small detail that would identify the man who hired his boat. Better not to hurt him badly now.

The next step should be an intensive interrogation of Sapp about his activities and associates and a thorough lab analysis of the chart. The FBI was better equipped to do these things. Kabakov had come a long way for very little.

He called Corley from a telephone booth on the pier.

Sapp had not consciously lied to Kabakov, but he was mistaken in saying that he knew no professional pilots. It was an understandable memory lapse—it had been years since he had last seen Michael Lander or thought about the frightening, infuriating day of their first meeting.

Sapp had been on his seasonal migration northward when a floating timber mangled both his propellers off Manasquan, N.J., forcing him to stop. Sapp was strong and capable, but he could not change a jammed and twisted prop in open water with a sea running. The boat was drifting slowly toward the beach, dragging her anchor before a relentless onshore wind. He could not call the Coast Guard because they would smell the same stench that gagged him as he went below to get his storm anchor—the smell of $5,500 worth of black market alligator hides bought from a Florida poacher and bound for New York.

When Sapp returned to the deck, he saw a boat approaching.

Michael Lander, out with his family in a trim little cruiser, threw Sapp a line and towed him to a protected inlet. Sapp, not wanting to be stuck at a marina with a disabled boat loaded with hot hides, asked Lander to help him. Wearing snorkle masks and flippers, they worked beneath the boat, and their combined strength was enough to pry one of the propellers off its shaft and fit the spare. Sapp could limp home.

"Excuse the smell," Sapp said uneasily as they sat on the stern, resting. Since Lander had been below in the course of the work, he could not have helped seeing the hides.

"None of my business," Lander said.

The incident began a casual friendship that ended when Lander returned to Vietnam for his second hitch. Sapp's friendship with Margaret Lander had continued, however, for some months after that. On the rare occasions when he thought about the Landers, it was the woman Sapp recalled most clearly, not the pilot.

CHAPTER 17

On the first of December the President informed his chief of staff that he would definitely attend the Super Bowl in New Orleans, whether the Washington Redskins were playing or not.

"God dammit," said Earl Biggs, special agent in charge of the White House Secret Service detail. He said this quietly and alone. He was not surprised—the President had indicated previously that he was likely to go—but Biggs had hoped the trip would be canceled.

I should have known better than to hope, Biggs reflected. The Man's honeymoon with the nation was over and he had begun to slip a little in the polls, but he would be assured of a standing ovation in the Deep South, with the whole world watching.

Biggs dialed the number of the Secret Service's Protective Research section. "January 12. New Orleans," he said. "Get on it."

The Protective Research section has three levels of files. The largest contains every threat that has been made against a President by telephone, mail, or reported utterance in the last forty years. Persons who have made repeated threats or who are considered potentially dangerous are listed in a "live file."

The live files are reviewed every six months.

Changes in address, job status, and international travel are noted. At present, there are 840 names in the live file.

Of these, the 325 considered most serious are also listed in a geographically indexed "trip file." Before each presidential trip, the persons listed in the area involved are investigated.

With 43 days of lead time, the clerks in Protective Research and the agents in the field had plenty of time to check out New Orleans.

Lee Harvey Oswald was never listed in the Secret Service trip file. Neither was Michael Lander.

On December 3, three agents from the White House Secret Service detail were dispatched to New Orleans to take charge of security arrangements. Forty days' lead time and a three-man team have been standard procedure since 1963. On December 7, Jack Renfro, leader of the three-man detail, sent a preliminary report to Earl Biggs at the White House.

Renfro did not like Tulane Stadium. Anytime the President appeared in public, Renfro could feel the exposure crawling on his own skin. The stadium, home of Tulane's Green Wave, the Sugar Bowl Classic, and the New Orleans Saints, is the largest steel stadium in the world. It is rusty gray and tan and the area beneath the stands is a forest of girders and beams, a nightmare to search. Renfro and the other two Secret Service agents spent two days climbing through the stadium. When Renfro walked out onto the field, every one of the 80,985 seats threatened him. The glassed-in VIP booth high on the west side of the stadium at the end of the press gallery was useless. He knew the President would never consent to use it, even in the case of inclement weather. No one could see the President there. He would use the VIP box, at the front of the west stands on the 50-yard line. For hours Renfro sat in the box. He placed a member of the New Orleans police department in it for an entire day, while he and the other two agents checked the lines-of-sight from various positions in the stands.

He personally inspected the cream of the New Orleans police department's Special Events squad—the officers who would be assigned to the stadium.

He tried routes from New Orleans International Airport to the stadium via U.S. 61, state highway 3046, and U.S. 90 and a combination of Interstate 10 and the Claiborne Avenue section of U.S. 90. All routes seemed endless, especially in light of the notorious traffic problem in the stadium area.

The preliminary evaluation Renfro sent to special agent Biggs at the White House said in part:

Suggest we recommend in the strongest terms that the President be helicoptered from New Orleans International Airport to the stadium following this procedure:

1. A motorcade will be ordered to stand by at the airport, but will be used by peripheral members of traveling party.

2. No helipad will be marked at the stadium until the President's helicopter is airborne from New Orleans International. At that time a portable fabric landing marker will be deployed at the south end of the infield on the track outside the northwest corner of the stadium. (See attached diagram A-1.) The track has no overhead wires and provides a clear landing area in the infield, but has three tall light standards on each side. These standards do not appear on the New Orleans sectional and VFR terminal area chart. Their presence should be emphasized at the pilot's briefing.

3. From the landing pad to Gate 19 is 100 paces. (Note enclosed photograph A-2.) Have requested removal of the unsightly garbage container indicated beside stadium wall. Suggest agents on the ground at landing point check the bushes at the edge of the stadium at Zero minus one minute.

The landing area can be covered from the rear upper floors of five houses on Audubon Boulevard. They are numbers 49, 55, 65, 71, and 73. Preliminary check indicates they are all occupied by citizens considered zero threat. The roofs and windows should be observed during the arrival, however.

In the event a crowd remains at the ticket windows at Gate 19 when the President arrives, Gate 18 and vendor's gate 18A could be used, but these are considered less desirable, as they would necessitate a short walk under the stands.

From Gate 19, the President would be exposed to the area under the stands for 75 paces before reaching the sideline at the goal line.

The President will use Box 40, a double-size box at the 50-yard line. (See attached diagram A-3.) Note the railings allow access at front and rear. Also note the rear of the box is elevated 6 inches by a step. Tall agents seated behind the President in Box 40 would give considerable coverage from behind. Secret Service boxes will be numbers 14 and 13 in front of the Presidential Box to the right and left. At least one agent each should be in Boxes 71, 70, 69, and 68, to the rear.

The railing of box 40 is constructed of iron pipe. The ends are capped. These caps should be removed and the interior of the pipes examined immediately before the President's arrival.

The box contains one telephone terminal box. I am advising Signal Corps on details. (Memo to Signals attached.) Diagram A-4, stadium overview and seating chart, shows individual agent assignments and areas of responsibility.

Our radio frequency is clear.

Details of egress are subject to modification pending our observation of crowd flow at the Sugar Bowl game December 31.

Jack Renfro was a careful and conscientious man, skilled at his trade. He had learned the stadium by heart. But as he catalogued its dangers, he never once looked up at the sky.

CHAPTER 18

LANDER FINISHED the bomb two days after Christmas. Its sleek skin, midnight blue and bearing the bright insignia of the National Broadcasting System, reflected the harsh garage lights as it lay in its loading cradle. The clamps that would fasten it to the gondola of the blimp hung from the upper rim like open hands, and the electrical connections and backup fuse were taped in neat coils on the top. Inside the skin, the 1,316.7 pounds of plastic explosive rested in two great slabs of precise thickness, curving behind the layers of bristling darts. The detonators were packed separately, ready to be plugged into place.

Lander sat staring at the great bomb. He could see his reflection distorted on its side. He thought that he would like to sit on it now, and plug in the detonators and hold the wires like reins, touch them to the battery and ride the mighty firebloom into the face of God. Sixteen days to go.

The telephone had been ringing for some time when he answered it. Dahlia was calling from New Orleans.

"It's finished," Lander said.

"Michael, you've done a beautiful job. It's a privilege to watch you."

221

"Did you get the garage?"

"Yes. It's near the Galvez Street wharf. Twenty minutes from New Orleans Lakefront Airport. I've driven the route twice."

"You're sure it's big enough."

"It's big enough. It's a walled-off section of a warehouse. I've bought the padlocks and put them on. Now may I come home to you, Michael?"

"You're satisfied?"

"I'm satisfied."

"With the airport too?"

"Yes. I had no trouble getting in. I can make it in the truck when the time comes."

"Come home."

"I'll see you late tonight."

She did well, Lander thought as he hung up the telephone. Still, he would have preferred to make the arrangements in New Orleans himself. There had been no time. He still had to fly a National Football Conference playoff game and the Sugar Bowl in New Orleans before the Super Bowl. His time was used up.

The problem of moving the nacelle to New Orleans had worried him, and the solution he found was less than ideal. He had leased a two-and-one-half-ton truck, which now stood in his driveway, and he had engaged two bonded professional truck drivers to take it to New Orleans. They would leave tomorrow. The back of the truck would be sealed, and even if the drivers did see the device they would not know what it was.

Putting the bomb in the hands of strangers made Lander uneasy anyway. But there was no help for it. Fasil and Dahlia could not drive the truck. Lander was certain that the authorities had broadcast their descriptions in the Northeast. Fasil's forged international driving license was sure to attract attention if he were stopped by the police. Dahlia would be very conspicuous at the wheel of a big truck. She would be ogled at every step. Besides, Lander wanted Dahlia to be with him.

If he could have trusted Fasil to go to New Or-

leans, Dahlia would be here now, Lander thought
bitterly. He had no confidence in Fasil since the Arab
announced that he would not be present at the strike.
Lander had enjoyed the contempt for Fasil that flashed
in Dahlia's eyes. Supposedly Fasil was off arranging
for some muscle to be employed at the airport—Dahlia
had seen to it that he and Lander were not left in the
house together.

One item remained on Lander's checklist of materials—a tarpaulin to tie down over the nacelle. It
was 4:45 P.M. The hardware store was still open. He
just had time to make it.

Twenty minutes later, Margaret Feldman, for-
merly Margaret Lander, parked her Dart stationwagon
beside the big truck in Lander's driveway. She sat for
a moment, looking at the house.

This was the first time she had seen it since her
divorce and remarriage. Margaret felt some reservations about coming, but the bassinet and baby carriage
were rightfully hers, she would need them in a few
more months, and she intended to have them. She
had called first to make sure Michael was not at home.
She did not want him crying after her. He had been
a strong and proud man before he was broken. For
the memory of that man, she still had a great affection, in her fashion. She had tried to forget his sick
behavior at the end. She still dreamed about the kitten,
though, still heard it in her sleep.

Reflexively Margaret glanced in her compact
mirror, patting her blonde hair and checking her teeth
for lipstick before getting out of the car. It was as
much a part of her routine as turning off the ignition.
She hoped she would not get dirty loading the carriage
and bassinet into the stationwagon. Really, Roger
should have come with her. But he did not feel right
about going into Lander's house when Lander was
not there.

Roger had not always felt that way, she thought
drily. Why had Michael tried to fight? It was over
anyway.

Stooping in the thin snow on the driveway, Margaret found that the lock on the garage had been replaced with a new, stronger one. She decided to go through the house and open it from the inside. Her old key still fit the front door. She had intended to go straight through to the garage, but once inside the house her curiosity was aroused.

She looked around. There was the familiar spot on the carpet in front of the TV, residue of the children's countless Kool-Aid drippings. She had never been able to get it clean. But the living room was neat and so was the kitchen. Margaret had expected a litter of beer cans and TV dinner trays. She was a little piqued at the neatness of the house.

There is a guilty thrill in being alone in someone else's house, particularly the home of a familiar person. Much can be felt in the arrangement of a person's belongings, and the more intimate the belongings, the better. Margaret went upstairs.

Their old bedroom told her little. Lander's shoes were in a straight line in the closet, the furniture was dusted. She stood looking at the bed and smiled to herself. Roger would be angry if he knew what she was thinking about, did think about sometimes, even with him.

The bathroom. Two toothbrushes. A tiny wrinkle appeared between Margaret's eyes. A shower cap. Face creams, body lotion, bubble bath. Well, well. Now she was glad she had violated Lander's privacy. She wondered what the woman looked like. She wanted to see the rest of her things.

She tried the other bedroom, then opened the playroom door. Margaret stood wide-eyed, staring at the spirit lamp, the wall hangings, candle holders and the great bed. She walked to the bed and touched the pillow. Silk. *Well, la-de-da!* she said to herself.

"Hello, Margaret," Lander said.

She spun around with a gasp. Lander stood in the doorway, one hand on the knob, the other in his pocket. He was pale.

"I was just—"

"You're looking well." It was true. She looked splendid. He had seen her in this room before, in his mind. Crying out to him like Dahlia, touching him like Dahlia. Lander felt a hollow ache inside. He wished Dahlia were here. Looking at his ex-wife, he was trying to see Dahlia, needed to see Dahlia. He saw Margaret. She brightened the air around her.

"You seem to be all right—I mean you look well, too, Michael. I—I must say I didn't expect *this*." Her hand swept around the room.

"What *did* you expect?" Sweat was on his face. Oh, the things that he had found again in this room did not stand up to Margaret.

"Michael, I need the baby things. The bassinet and the carriage."

"I can see that Roger's knocked you up. I'm giving you the benefit of the doubt, of course."

She smiled, unthinkingly, despite the insult, trying to get past the moment, trying to get away. That smile meant to Lander that she thought infidelity was funny, a joke they could laugh about together. It pierced Lander like a red-hot poker.

"I can get the things from the garage." She moved toward the door.

"Have you looked for them yet?" *Show it to her. Show it to her and kill her.*

"No, I was about to—"

"The bassinet and the carriage aren't there. I put them in storage. The sparrows get in the garage and speckle everything. I'll have them sent over." *No! Take her in the garage and show it to her. And kill her.*

"Thank you, Michael. That would be very nice."

"How are the kids?" His own voice sounded strange to him.

"Fine. They had a good Christmas."

"Do they like Roger?"

"Yes, he's good to them. They'd like to see you sometime. They ask about you. Are you moving? I saw the big truck in the driveway and I thought—"

"Is Roger's bigger than mine?"

"What?"

He could not stop now. "You God damned slut." He moved toward her. *I must stop.*

"Goodbye, Michael." She moved sideways toward the door.

The pistol in his pocket was burning his hand. *I must stop. It will be ruined. Dahlia said it is a privilege to watch you. Dahlia said Michael you were so strong today. Dahlia said Michael I love to do it for you. I was your first time, Margaret. No. The elastic left red marks on your hips. Don't think. Dahlia will be home soon, home soon, home soon. Mustn't—. Click.*

"I'm sorry I said that, Margaret. I shouldn't have said it. It's not true, and I'm sorry."

She was still frightened. She wanted to go.

He could hold on a second longer. "Margaret, there's something I've been meaning to send you. For you and Roger. Wait, wait. I've acted badly. It's important to me that you're not angry. I'll be upset if you're angry."

"I'm not angry, Michael. I have to go. Are you seeing a doctor?"

"Yes, yes. I'm all right, it was just a shock, seeing you." His next words choked him, but he forced them out. "I've missed you and I just got disturbed. That's all. Wait one second." He walked quickly to the desk in his room, and when he came out she was going down the stairs. "Here, I want you to take these. Just take them and have a good time and don't be mad."

"All right, Michael. Goodbye now." She took the envelope.

At the door, she stopped and turned to him again. She felt like telling him. She was not sure why. He ought to know. "Michael, I was sorry to hear about your friend Jergens."

"What about Jergens?"

"He *is* the one who used to wake us up calling you in the middle of the night, isn't he?"

"What about him?"

"He killed himself. Didn't you see the paper? The first POW suicide, it said. He took some pills and pulled a plastic bag over his head," she said. "I was sorry. I remembered how you talked to him on the telephone when he couldn't sleep. Goodbye, Michael." Her eyes were like nailheads, and she felt lighter and didn't know why.

When she was three blocks away, waiting at the light, she opened the envelope Michael had given her. It contained two tickets to the Super Bowl.

As soon as Margaret left, Lander ran to the garage. The bottom was out of him. He began to work very rapidly, trying to stay above the thoughts rising like black water in his head. He eased the rented forklift forward, pushing the fork under the cradle that held the nacelle. He switched off the forklift and climbed out of the seat. He was concentrating on forklifts. He thought about all the forklifts he had seen in warehouses and on docks. He thought about the principles of hydraulic leverage. He walked outside and lowered the tailgate of the truck. He attached the sloping metal ramp to the rear of the truck. He thought about landing craft he had seen and the way their ramps were hinged. He thought desperately about loading ramps. He checked the street. Nobody was watching. It didn't matter anyway. He jumped back on the forklift and raised the nacelle off the floor. Gently now. It was a delicate job. He had to think about it. He had to be very careful. He drove the forklift slowly up the loading ramp and into the back of the truck. The truck springs creaked as they took the weight. He lowered the fork bearing the nacelle, locked the brake, chocked the wheels firmly, and secured the nacelle and forklift in place with heavy rope. He thought about knots. He knew all about knots. He could tie 12 different knots. He must remember to put a sharp knife in the back of the truck. Dahlia could cut the ropes when the time came. She would not have time to fool with knots. *Oh Dahlia. Come home, I am drowning.* He put the loading ramp and the duffle bag of small arms inside the truck and locked the tailgate. It was done.

He threw up in the garage. *Mustn't think.* He walked to the liquor cabinet and took out a bottle of vodka. His stomach heaved up the vodka. The second time it stayed down. He took the pistol from his pocket and threw it behind the kitchen stove where he could not reach it. The bottle again, and again. Half of it was gone and it was running down his shirt front, running down his neck. The bottle again, and again. His head was swimming. *I mustn't throw up. Hold it down.* He was crying. The vodka was hitting him now. He sat down on the kitchen floor. *Two more weeks and I'll be dead. Oh thank God I'll be dead. Everybody else will be too. Where it's quiet. And nothing ever is. Oh God it has been so long. Oh God it has been so long. Jergens, you were right to kill yourself. Jergens!* He was yelling now. He was up and staggering to the back door. He was yelling out the back door. Cold rain was blowing in his face as he yelled out into the yard. *Jergens, you were right!* And the back steps were coming up at him, and he rolled off into the dead grass and snow, and lay face up in the rain. A last thought, consciousness glimmering out. *Water is a good conductor of heat. Witness a million engines and my heart cold upon this ground.*

It was quite late when Dahlia set her suitcase down in the living room and called his name. She looked in the workshop and then climbed the stairs.

"Michael." The lights were on and the house was cold. She was uneasy. "Michael." She went into the kitchen.

The back door was open. She ran to it. When she saw him she thought he was dead. His face was white with a bluish tinge and his hair was plastered flat by the cold rain. She knelt beside him and felt his chest through the soggy shirt. His heart was beating. Kicking off her high-heeled shoes, she dragged him toward the door. She could feel the freezing ground through her stockings. Groaning with the effort, she dragged him up the stairs and into the kitchen. She jerked the blankets off the guest-room bed and spread them on the floor beside him, stripped the soggy clothes off him and rolled him in the blankets. She rubbed him with a rough towel, and she sat beside him in the ambulance on the way to the hospital. At daylight, his temperature was 105. He had viral pneumonia.

CHAPTER 19

THE DELTA JET approached New Orleans over Lake Pontchartrain, maintaining considerable altitude over the water, then swooped down toward New Orleans International Airport. The swoop lifted Muhammad Fasil's stomach unpleasantly, and he cursed under his breath.

Pneumonia! The woman's precious pet got drunk and fell out in the rain! The fool was half-delirious and weak as a kitten, the woman sitting beside him in the hospital, bleating expressions of pity. At least she would see to it that he kept his mouth shut about the mission. The chances of Lander being able to fly the Super Bowl in fifteen days were exactly nil, Fasil thought. When the stubborn-headed woman was finally convinced of that, when she saw that Lander could do nothing but puke in her hand, she would kill him and join Fasil in New Orleans. Fasil had her word for it.

Fasil was desperate. The truck bearing the bomb was moving toward New Orleans on schedule. Now he had a bomb and no delivery system. He must work out an alternate plan, and the place to do it was here, where the strike would be made. Hafez Najeer had erred very badly in allowing Dahlia Iyad to control this mission, Fasil told himself for the hundredth time. Well, she controlled it no longer. The new plan would be his.

The airport was jammed with the crowd arriving for the Sugar Bowl, the college invitational bowl game that would be played in Tulane Stadium in three days. Fasil called eight hotels. All were full. He had to take a room at the YMCA.

The cramped little room was quite a comedown from the Plaza in New York, where he had spent the previous night—the Plaza, with the national flags of foreign dignitaries hanging in front and a switchboard accustomed to placing international calls. The flags of Saudi Arabia, Iran, and Turkey hung among the others during the present United Nations session and calls to the Middle East were common. Fasil could have had a comfortable conversation with Beirut, arranging for the gunmen to report to New Orleans. He had finished encoding his message and was ready to make the call when he was interrupted by Dahlia on the telephone, telling him of Lander's stupid debacle. Angrily, Fasil had torn up his message to Beirut and flushed it down his elegant Plaza toilet.

Now he was stuffed in this shabby cell in New Orleans with the plan a shambles. It was time to look over the ground. Fasil had never seen Tulane Stadium. He had depended on Lander for all that. Bitterly he walked outside and flagged a taxi.

How could he make the strike? He would have the truck. He would have the bomb. He could still send for a couple of gunmen. He would have the services of Dahlia Iyad, even if her infidel was out of it. Although Fasil was an atheist, he thought of Lander as an infidel, and he spat as he muttered the name.

The taxi mounted the U.S. 90 expressway over downtown New Orleans and headed southwest into the afternoon sun. The driver kept up a steady monologue in a dialect barely intelligible to Fasil.

"These bums now don't want to work. They want something for nothing," the driver was saying. "My sister's kid used to work with me when I was plumbing, before my back went out. I never could find him half the time. You can't do any plumbing by yourself. You have to come out from under the house too many times, you don't have nobody to hand you stuff. That's why my back went out, all the time crawling under and coming back out."

Fasil wished the man would shut up. He did not shut up.

"That there's the Superdome, which I think they're never gonna finish. First they thought it would cost $168 million, now it's $200 million. Everybody says Howard Hughes bought it. What a mess. The sheet metal workers took a walk first, and then . . ."

Fasil looked at the great bulge of the domed stadium. Work was underway on it, even through the holiday. He could see tiny figures moving on it. There had been a scare in the early stages of the mission that the Superdome would be completed in time for the Super Bowl, rendering the blimp useless. But there were still big gaps visible in the roof. Not that it mattered now anyway, Fasil thought angrily.

He made a mental note to investigate the possible use of toxic gas in closed stadiums. That might be a useful technique at some future time.

The taxi shifted into the high-speed lane, the driver talking over his shoulder. "You know, they were gonna have the Super Bowl there, they thought for a while. Now they got a terrific cost overrun because the city thinks it looks bad, embarrassing you know, not to be through with it. Double time and a half they're paying to work on it through the holidays, you know. Put on a show of really hustling to finish it by spring. I wouldn't mind some of that overtime myself."

Fasil started to ask the man to be quiet. Then he changed his mind. If he were rude, the driver would remember him.

"You know what happened in Houston with the Astrodome. They got cutesy with the Oilers and now they play in Rice Stadium. These guys don't want that to happen. They got to have the Saints, you know?

They want everybody to see they're getting on with it, the NFL and all, so they work over the holidays too. You think I wouldn't work Christmas and New Year's double time and a half? Ha. The old lady could hang up the stockings by herself."

The taxi followed the curve of U.S. 90, turning northwest, and the driver adjusted his sunshade. They were nearing Tulane University now. "That's the Ursuline College on the left there. What side of the stadium you want, Willow Street?"

"Yes."

The sight of the great, shabby tan-and-gray stadium aroused Fasil. The films of Munich were running in his head.

It was big. Fasil was reminded of his first close view of an aircraft carrier. It went up and up. Fasil climbed out of the taxi, his camera banging against the door.

The southeast gate was open. Maintenance men were coming in and out in the last rush before the Sugar Bowl game. Fasil had his press card ready, and the same credentials he had brought on his flight to the Azores, but he was not stopped. He glanced at the vast, shadowy spaces under the stands, tangled with iron, then walked out into the arena.

It was so big! Its size elated him. The artificial turf was new, the numbers gleaming white against the green. He stepped on the turf and almost recoiled. It felt like flesh underfoot. Fasil walked across the field, feeling the presence of the endless tiers of seats. It is difficult to walk through the focal area of a stadium, even an empty stadium, without feeling watched. He hurried to the west side of the field and climbed the stands toward the press boxes.

High above the field, looking out at the curve of the stands, Fasil recalled the matching curves of the shaped charge and, in spite of himself, he was impressed with the genius of Michael Lander.

The stadium spread its sides open to the sky, labial, passive, waiting. The thought of those stands filled with 80,985 people, moving in their seats, the stands squirming with life, filled Fasil with an emotion that was very close to lust. This was the soft aperture to the House of War. Soon those spreading sides would be engorged with people, full and waiting.

"Quss ummak," Fasil hissed. It is an ancient Arab insult. It means "your mother's vulva."

He thought of the various possibilities. Any explosion in or close to the stadium would guarantee worldwide headlines. The gates were not really substantial. The truck possibly could plow through one of the four entrances and make it onto the field before the charge was set off. There would certainly be many casualties, but much of the explosion would be wasted in blowing a great crater in the earth. There was also the problem of traffic in the small, choked streets leading to the stadium. What if emergency vehicles were parked in the entrances? If the President was here, surely there would be armed men at the gates. What if the driver were shot before he could detonate the charge? Who would drive the truck? Not himself, certainly. Dahlia, then. She had the guts to do it, there was no question about that. Afterward, he would praise her posthumously at his news conference in Lebanon.

Perhaps an emergency vehicle, an ambulance, might have a better chance. It could be rushed onto the field, siren wailing.

But the nacelle was too big to fit inside an ordinary ambulance, and the truck that now carried it did not look anything like an emergency vehicle. But it did look like a television equipment truck. Still, an emergency vehicle was better. A big panel truck, then. He could paint it white and put a red cross on it. Whatever he did, he would have to hurry. Fourteen days remained.

The empty sky pressed on Fasil as he stood at the top of the stands, wind fluttering the collar of his coat. The open, easy sky gave perfect access, he thought bitterly. Getting the nacelle into an airplane and then hijacking it would be next to impossible. If it could be done through some ruse of carrying the nacelle as freight, he was not sure Dahlia could force a pilot to dive close enough to the stadium, even with a gun at the man's temple.

Fasil looked to the northeast at the New Orleans skyline; the Superdome two miles away, the Marriott Hotel, the International Trade Mart. Beyond that skyline, a scant eight miles away, lay New Orleans Lakefront Airport. The fat and harmless blimp would come over that skyline to the Super Bowl on January 12 while he struggled like an ant on the ground. Damn Lander and his putrid issue to the tenth generation.

Fasil was seized with a vision of what the strike might have been. The blimp shining silver, coming down, unnoticed at first by the crowd intent on the game. Then more and more of the spectators glancing up as it came lower, bigger, impossibly big, hanging over them, the long shadow darkening the field and some of them looking directly at the bright nacelle as it detonated with a flash like the sun exploding, the stands heaving, possibly collapsing, filled with 12 million pounds of ripped meat. And the roar and shock wave rolling out across the flats, deafening, blasting the windows out of homes 20 miles away, ships heeling as to a monsoon. The wind of it screaming around the towers of the House of War, screaming

Faseeeeeel!

It would have been incredibly beautiful. He had to sit down. He was shaking. He forced his mind back to the alternatives. He tried to cut his losses. When he was calm again, he felt proud of his strength of character, his forbearance in the face of misfortune. He was Fasil. He would do the best he could.

Fasil's thoughts were concerned with trucks and paint as he rode back toward downtown New Orleans. All was not lost, he told himself. It was perhaps better this way. The use of the American had always sullied the operation. Now the strike was all his. Not so spectacular perhaps, not a maximum-efficiency air burst, but he would still gain enormous prestige—and the guerrilla movement would be enhanced, he added in a quick afterthought.

There was the domed stadium, on his right this time. The sun was gleaming off the metal roof. And what was that rising behind it? A helicopter of the "skycrane" type. It was lifting something, a piece of machinery. Now it was moving over the roof. A party of workmen waited beside one of the openings in the roof. The shadow of the helicopter slid across the dome and covered them. Slowly, delicately, the helicopter lowered the heavy object into the gap on the roof. The hat of one of the workmen blew away and tumbled, a tiny dot bouncing down the dome and out into space, tumbling on the wind. The helicopter rose again, freed of its burden, and sank out of sight behind the unfinished Superdome.

Fasil no longer thought about trucks. He could always get a truck. Sweat stood out on his face. He was wondering if the helicopter worked on Sundays. He tapped the driver and told him to go to the Superdome.

Two hours later, Fasil was in the public library studying an entry in "Jane's All the World's Aircraft." From the library he went to the Monteleone Hotel, where he copied the number from a telephone in a lobby booth. He copied another number from a pay phone in the Union Passenger Terminal, then went to the Western Union office. On a cable blank, he carefully composed a message, referring frequently to a small card of coded numbers glued inside his camera case. In minutes, on the long line beneath the sea, the brief personal message flashed toward Benghazi, Libya.

Fasil was back in the passenger terminal at 9 A.M. the next day. He removed a yellow out-of-order sticker from a pay phone near the entrance and placed it on the telephone he had selected, a booth at the end of the row. He glanced at his watch. A half-hour to go. He sat down with a newspaper on a bench near the telephone.

Fasil had never before presumed on Najeer's Libyan connections. He would not dare to do it now, if Najeer were still alive. Fasil had only picked up the plastic explosive in Benghazi after Najeer's arrangements were made, but the code name "Sofia," coined by Najeer for the mission, had opened the necessary doors for Fasil in Benghazi. He had included it in his cable, and he hoped it would work again.

At 9:35 A.M., the telephone rang. Fasil picked it up on the second ring. "Hello?"

"Yes, I am trying to reach Mrs. Yusuf." Despite the scratchy connection, Fasil recognized the voice of the Libyan officer in charge of liaison with Al Fatah.

"You are calling for Sofia Yusuf, then."

"Go ahead."

Fasil spoke quickly. He knew the Libyan would not stay on the telephone long. "I need a pilot capable of flying a Sikorsky S-58 cargo helicopter. The priority is absolute. I must have him in New Orleans in six days. He must be expendable." Fasil knew he was asking something of extreme difficulty. He also knew that there were great resources available to Al Fatah in Benghazi and Tripoli. He went on quickly, before the officer could object. "It is similar to the Russian machines used on the Aswan High Dam. Take the request to the very highest level. The *very* highest level. I carry the authority of Eleven." "Eleven" was Hafez Najeer.

The voice on the other end was soft, as though the man were trying to whisper over the telephone. "There may not be such a man. This is very hard. Six days is nothing."

"If I cannot have him in that time, it will be useless. Much will be lost. I *must* have him. Call me in 24 hours at the alternate number. The priority is absolute."

"I understand," said the voice 6,000 miles away. The line went dead.

Fasil walked away from the telephone and out of the terminal at a lively pace. It was terribly dangerous to communicate directly with the Middle East, but the shortage of time demanded taking the chance. The request for a pilot was a very long shot. There were none in the fedayeen ranks. Flying a cargo helicopter with a heavy object suspended beneath it is a fine art.

Pilots capable of doing it are not common. But the Libyans had come through for Black September before. Had not Colonel Khadafy helped with the strike at Khartoum? The very weapons used to slay the American diplomats were smuggled into the country in the Libyan diplomatic pouch. Thirty million dollars a year flows to Al Fatah from the Libyan treasury. How much could a pilot be worth? Fasil had every reason to hope. If only they could find one, and soon.

The six-day time limit Fasil had stressed was not strictly true, since two weeks remained before the Super Bowl. But modifications on the bomb would be necessary to fit it to a different aircraft, and he needed lead time and the pilot's skilled help.

Fasil had weighed the odds against finding a pilot, and the risk involved in asking for one, against the splendid result if one could be located. He found the risk worth taking.

What if his cable, innocent as it appeared to be, was examined by the U.S. authorities? What if the number code for the telephones was known to the Jew Kabakov? That was hardly likely, Fasil knew, but still he was uneasy. Certainly the authorities were looking for the plastic, but they could not know the nature of the mission. There was nothing to point to New Orleans.

He wondered if Lander was delirious. Nonsense. People didn't lie around delirious with fever anymore. But crazy people sometimes rave, fever or no. If he were on the point of blabbing, Dahlia would kill him.

In Israel, at that moment, a sequence of events was underway that would have far greater bearing on Fasil's request than any influence of the late Hafez Najeer. At an airstrip near Jaffa, fourteen Israeli airmen were climbing into the cockpits of seven F-4 Phantom fighter-bombers. They taxied onto the runway, the heat distorting the air behind them like rippled glass. By twos they drove down the asphalt and leaped into the sky in a long, climbing turn that took them out over the Mediterranean and westward, toward Tobruk, Libya, at twice the speed of sound.

They were on a retaliatory raid. Still smoking at Rosh Pina was the rubble of an apartment house hit by Russian Katyusha rockets, supplied to the fedayeen by Libya. This time the reply would not be against the fedayeen bases in Lebanon and Syria. This time the supplier would suffer.

Thirty-nine minutes after takeoff, the flight leader spotted the Libyan freighter. She was exactly where the Mossad said she would be, 18 miles out of Tobruk and steaming eastward, heavily laden with armaments for the guerrillas. But they must be sure. Four Phantoms remained at altitude to provide cover from Arab aircraft. The other three went down. The lead plane, throttled back to 200 knots, passed the ship at an altitude of 60 feet. There was no mistake. Then the three of them were howling down upon her in a bomb run, and up again, pulling three and a half G's as they streaked back into the sky. There were no cries of victory in the cockpits as the ship ballooned in fire. On the way home, the Israelis watched the sky hopefully. They would feel better if the MIGs came.

Rage swept Libya's Revolutionary Command Council after the Israeli attack. Who on the Council knew of the Al Fatah strike in the United States will never be determined. But somewhere in the angry halls at Benghazi, a cog turned.

The Israelis had struck with airplanes given to them by the Americans.

The Israelis themselves had said it: "The suppliers will suffer."

So be it.

CHAPTER 20

"I TOLD HIM he could go to bed, but he said his orders are to put the box in your hands," Colonel Weisman, the military attaché, told Kabakov, as they walked toward the conference room in the Israeli embassy.

The young captain was nodding in his chair as Kabakov opened the door. He snapped to his feet.

"Major Kabakov, I'm Captain Reik. The package from Beirut, sir."

Kabakov fought down the urge to grab the box and open it. Reik had come a long way. "I remember you, Captain. You had the howitzer battery at Qana-abe." They shook hands, the younger man obviously pleased.

Kabakov turned to the fiberboard carton on the table. It was about two feet square and a foot deep and was tied with twine. Scrawled in Arabic across the lid was "Personal property of Abu Ali, 18 Rue Verdun, deceased. File 186047. Hold until February 23." There was a hole gouged through the corner of the box. A bullet hole.

"Intelligence went through it in Tel Aviv," Reik said. "There was dust in the knots. They think it hadn't been opened for some time."

Kabakov removed the lid and set the contents out

on the table. An alarm clock with the crystal smashed. Two bottles of pills. A bankbook. A clip for a Llama automatic pistol—Kabakov felt sure the pistol had been stolen—a cufflink box without the cufflinks, a pair of bent spectacles, and a few periodicals. Doubtless any items of value had been taken by the police and what was left had been carefully sifted by Al Fatah. Kabakov was bitterly disappointed. He had hoped that for once the obsessive secrecy of Black September would work against the terrorist organization, that the person assigned to "sanitize" Abu Ali's effects would not know what was harmless and what was not, and thus might miss some useful clue. He looked up at Reik. "What did this cost?"

"Yoffee got a flesh wound across the thigh. He sent you a message, sir. He—" the captain stammered.

"Go on."

"He said you owe him a bottle of Remy Martin and—and not that goat piss you passed around at Kuneitra, sir."

"I see." Kabakov grinned in spite of himself. At least the box of junk had not cost any lives.

"Yoffee went in," Reik said. "He had some funny credentials from a Saudi law firm. He had decided he would try to do it in one move, instead of bribing the clerk ahead of time—so they wouldn't have time to fool with the box and the clerk couldn't sell him a box of garbage. He gave the property clerk in the police station three Lebanese pounds and asked to see the box. The clerk brought it out, but set it behind the counter and said he would have to get clearance from the duty officer. That normally would have only meant another bribe, but Yoffee did not have great confidence in the credentials. He slugged the clerk and grabbed the box. He had a Mini-Cooper outside, and he was all right until two radio cars blocked the Mazraa in front of him at the Rue Unesco. Of course he went around them on the sidewalk, but they got a couple of rounds into the car. He had a five-block lead going down the Ramlet el Baida. Jacoby was flying the Huey, coming in to take him off. Yoffee climbed up through the sun roof of the car while it was still moving and we plucked him off. We came back at about a hundred feet in the dark. The chopper has the new terrain-following autopilot system and you just hang on."

"You were in the helicopter?"

"Yes sir. Yoffee owes me money."

Kabakov could imagine the heaving, dipping ride in the dark as the black helicopter snaked over the hills. "I'm surprised you had the range."

"We had to put down at Gesher Haziv."

"Did the Lebanese scramble any planes?"

"Yessir, finally. It took a little time for the word to get around. We were back in Israel in 24 minutes from the time the police saw the chopper."

Kabakov would not display his disappointment at the contents of the box, not after three men had risked their lives to get it. Tel Aviv must think him a fool.

"Thank you, Captain Reik, for a remarkable job. Tell Yoffee and Jacoby the same for me. Now go to bed. That's an order."

Kabakov and Weisman sat at the table with Abu Ali's effects between them. Weisman maintained a tactful silence. There were no personal papers of any kind, not even a copy of "Political and Armed Struggle," the omnipresent Fatah handbook. They had picked over Ali's belongings all right. Kabakov looked at the periodicals. Two copies of Al-Tali'ah, the Egyptian monthly. Here was something underlined in an interview. ". . . the rumor about the strength of the Israeli Intelligence Services is a myth. Israel is not particularly advanced in its Intelligence as such." Kabakov snorted. Abu Ali was mocking him from the grave.

Here were a few back issues of the Beirut newspaper Al-Hawadess. *Paris-Match.* A copy of *Sports Illustrated* dated January 21, 1974. Kabakov frowned at it. He picked it up. It was the only publication in English in the box. The cover bore a dark stain, coffee probably. He flipped through it once, then again. It was mostly concerned with football. Arabs follow soccer, but the principal article was about—Kabakov's mind was racing. Fasil. Munich. Sports. The tape had said, "Begin another year with bloodshed."

Weisman looked up quickly at the sound of Kabakov's voice. "Colonel Weisman, what do you know about this 'Super Bowl'?"

FBI Director John Baker took off his glasses and rubbed the bridge of his nose. "That's a hypothesis of considerable size, gentlemen."

Corley stirred in his chair.

Kabakov was tired of talking into Baker's blank face, tired of the caution with which Corley phrased remarks to his boss. "It's more than a hypothesis. Look at the facts—"

"I know, I know, Major. You've made it very clear. You think the target is the Super Bowl because this man—Fasil, is it?—organized the Black September attack at the Olympic Village; because the tape you captured at Beirut refers to a strike at the beginning of the year, and because the President plans to attend the game." He might have been naming the parts of speech.

"And because it would happen on live television with maximum shock value," Corley said.

"But this entire line of reasoning proceeds from the fact that this man, Ali, had a copy of *Sports Illustrated*, and you are not even positive that Ali was involved in the plot." Baker peered out the window at the gray Washington afternoon, as though he might find the answer in the street.

Baker had Corley's 302 file on his desk—the raw information on the case. Kabakov wondered why he had been called in, and then he realized that Baker, professionally paranoid, wanted to look at him. Wanted to expose the source to his own cop instincts. Kabakov could see a stubborn set in Baker's face. *He knows he will have to do something*, Kabakov thought. *But he needs for me to argue with him. He does not like to be told his business, but he wants to observe the telling. He's got to do something, now. Let him stew about it. It's his move.* "Thank you for your time, Mr. Baker," Kabakov said, rising.

"Just a moment, Major, if you don't mind. Since you have seen this kind of thing, how do you think they would go about it? Would they conceal the plastic in the stadium and then, when the crowd arrives, threaten to blow it up if certain demands are not met—freedom for Sirhan Sirhan, no more aid to Israel, that kind of thing?"

"They won't demand anything. They'll blow it up and then crow about it."

"Why do you think so?"

"What could you give them? Most of the terrorists arrested in skyjackings are already freed. Those at Munich were freed to save hostages in a subsequent skyjacking. Lelia Khaled was freed in the same way. The guerrillas who shot your own diplomats in Khartoum were turned back to their people by the Sudanese government. They're all free, Mr. Baker.

"Stop aid to Israel? Even if the promise were made, no guarantees are possible. The promise would never be made in the first place and would not be kept anyway, if it were made under duress. Besides, to use hostages you must contain them. In a stadium that could not be done. There would be panic and the crowd would rush the gates, trampling a few thousand on the way. No, they'll blow it up all right."

"How?"

"I don't know. With a half-ton of plastic they could collapse both sides of the stands, but to be sure of doing that they would have to put charges in several locations and detonate them simultaneously. That would not be easy. Fasil is no fool. There are too many radio transmissions at an event like that to use a remote electronic signal to set it off, and multiple locations increase the chance of discovery."

"We can make sure the stadium is clean," Corley said. "It will be a bitch to search, but we can do it."

"Secret Service will want to handle that themselves, I expect, but they'll ask for some manpower," Baker said.

"We can check all the personnel involved with the Super Bowl, check hot dog wagons, cold drink boxes, we can prohibit any packages being carried in," Corley continued. "We can use dogs and the electronic sniffer. There's still time to train the dogs on that piece of plastic from the ship."

"What about the sky?" Kabakov said.

"You're thinking of that pilot business with the chart, of course," the FBI director said. "I think we might shut down private aviation in New Orleans for the duration of the game. We'll check with the FAA. I'm calling in the concerned agencies this afternoon. We'll know more after that."

I doubt it, Kabakov reflected.

CHAPTER 21

THE SOUND of Abdel Awad's endless pacing was beginning to annoy the guard in the hall. The guard raised the slide in the cell door and cursed Awad through the grate. Having done that, he felt a little ashamed. The man had a right to pace. He raised the slide again and offered Awad a cigarette, cautioning him to put it out and hide it if he heard approaching footsteps.

Awad had been listening for footsteps, all right. Sometime—tonight, tomorrow, the next day—they would be coming. To cut off his hands.

A former officer in the Libyan Air Force, he had been convicted of theft and narcotics trafficking. His sentence of death had been commuted to double amputation in view of his former service to his country. This type of sentence, prescribed by the Koran, had fallen into disuse until Colonel Khadafy assumed power and reinstated it. It must be said, however, that in line with his policy of modernization, Khadafy has replaced the axe in the marketplace with a surgeon's knife and antiseptic conditions at a Benghazi hospital.

Awad had tried to write down his thoughts, had tried to write to his father apologizing for the shame he had brought on the family, but the words were difficult to find. He was afraid he would have the letter only half-finished when they came for him and he would have to mail it that way. Or finish it with the pen held between his teeth.

He wondered if the sentence permitted anesthesia.

He wondered if he could hook one leg of his trousers on the door hinge and tie the other around his neck and hang himself by sitting down. For a week since his sentencing he had entertained these considerations. It would be easier if they would tell him *when*. Perhaps not knowing was part of the sentence.

The slide flew up. "Put it out. Put it out," the guard hissed. Numbly, Awad stepped on the cigarette and kicked it under his cot. He heard the bolts sliding back. He faced the door, his hands behind him, fingernails digging into his palms.

I am a man and a good officer, Awad thought. *They could not deny that even at the trial. I will not shame myself now.*

A small man in neat civilian dress came into the cell. The man was saying something, his mouth was moving under the small mustache. ". . . Did you hear me, Lieutenant Awad? It is not yet time to—it is not yet time for your punishment. But it *is* time for a serious conversation. Speak English, please. Take the chair. I will sit on the bunk." The little man's voice was soft, and his eyes were constantly on Awad's face as he spoke.

Awad had very sensitive hands, the hands of a helicopter pilot. When he was offered a chance to keep them, to gain full reinstatement, he was quick to agree to the conditions.

Awad was removed from the Benghazi prison to the garrison at Ajdabujah, where, under tight security, he was checked out in a Russian MIL-6 helicopter, the heavy-duty model that carries the NATO code name "Hook." It is one of three owned by the Libyan armed forces. Awad was familiar with the type, though his experience was mostly in smaller craft. He handled it well. The MIL-6 was not exactly like the Sikorsky S-58, but it was close enough. At night, he pored over a Sikorsky flight manual, procured in Egypt. With a careful hand on the throttle and pitch controls and a vigilant eye on the manifold pressure, he would be all right when the time came.

The reign of President Khadafy is a strongly moralistic one, backed by terrible penalties, and as a result certain crimes have been sharply repressed in Libya. The civilized art of forgery does not flourish there, and it was necessary to contact a forger in Nicosia for the manufacture of Awad's papers.

Awad was to be thoroughly sanitized—no evidence of his origin would remain on his person. All that was necessary, really, was sufficient identification to get him into the United States. He would not be leaving, since he would be vaporized in the explosion. Awad was not aware of this last consideration. In fact, he had only been told to report to Muhammad Fasil and follow orders. He had been assured that he would get out of it all right. To preserve this illusion it was necessary to provide Awad with an escape plan and the papers to go with it.

On December 31, the day after Awad's release from prison, his Libyan passport, several recent photographs, and samples of his handwriting were delivered to a small printshop in Nicosia.

The concept of providing an entire "scene"—a set of mutually supportive papers such as passport, driving license, recent correspondence properly postmarked, and receipts—is a relatively recent development among forgers in the West, coming into wide practice only after the narcotics trade was able to pay for such elaborate service. Forgers in the Middle East have been creating "scenes" for their customers for generations.

The forger used by Al Fatah in Nicosia did marvelous work. He also supplied blank Lebanese passports to the Israelis, who filled in the details themselves. And he sold information to the Mossad.

It was an expensive job the Libyans wanted—two passports, one Italian bearing a U.S. entry stamp and one Portuguese. They did not quibble at the price. What is valuable to one party is often valuable to another, the forger thought as he put on his coat.

Within the hour, Mossad headquarters in Tel Aviv knew who Awad was and whom he would become. Awad's trial had received considerable attention in Benghazi. A Mossad agent there had only to look in the public prints to find out Awad's particular skill.

In Tel Aviv, they put it together. Awad was a helicopter pilot who was going into the United States one way and coming out another. The long line to Washington hummed for 45 minutes.

CHAPTER 22

On the afternoon of December 30, a massive search was begun at Tulane Stadium in New Orleans in preparation for the Sugar Bowl Classic to be played on New Year's Eve. Similar searches were scheduled for December 31 at stadiums in Miami, Dallas, Houston, Pasadena—every city that would host a major college bowl game on New Year's Day.

Kabakov was glad that the Americans finally had marshaled their great resources against the terrorists, but he was amused by the process that prompted them. It was typical of bureaucracy. FBI Director John Baker had called a top-level meeting of FBI, National Security Agency, and Secret Service personnel the previous afternoon, immediately after his talk with Kabakov and Corley. Kabakov, sitting in the front row, felt many pointed stares while the assembled officials emphasized the flimsiness of the evidence pointing to the target—a single magazine, unmarked, containing an article about the Super Bowl.

Each of the heavyweights from the FBI and the National Security Agency seemed determined not to let another out-skepticize him as Corley outlined the theory of an attack on the Super Bowl game in New Orleans.

Only the Secret Service representatives, Earl Biggs and Jack Renfro, remained silent. Kabakov thought the Secret Service agents were the most humorless men he had ever seen. That was understandable, he decided. They had much to be humorless about.

Kabakov knew that the men in this meeting were not stupid. Each of them would have been more receptive to an uncommon idea if the idea were presented to him in privacy. When surrounded by their peers, most men have two sets of reactions—the real ones and those designed for evaluation by their fellows. Skepticism was established as the proper attitude early in the meeting and, once established, prevailed throughout Corley's presentation.

But the herd principle also worked in the other direction. As Kabakov recounted Black September's maneuvers before the strike at Munich and the abortive attempt on the World Cup soccer matches six months ago, the seed of alarm was planted. On the face of it, was an attack on the Super Bowl less plausible than an attack on the Olympic Village? Kabakov asked.

"There's not a Jewish team playing," was an immediate rejoinder. It did not get a laugh. As the officials listened to Kabakov, dread was present in the room, subtly communicated from one listener to the next by small body movements, a certain restiveness. Hands fidgeted, hands rubbed faces. Kabakov could see the men before him changing. For as long as he could remember, Kabakov had disturbed policemen, even Israeli policemen. He attributed this to his own impatience with them, but it was more than that. There was something about him that affected policemen as a trace of musk carried on the wind sets the dogs on edge, makes them draw closer to the fire. It says that out there is something that does not love the fire; it is watching and it is not afraid.

The evidence of the magazine, supplemented by Fasil's track record, began to loom large and was extrapolated by the men in the meeting room. Once the possibility of danger was admitted, one official would not call for less stringent measures than the next. Why just the Super Bowl as a possible target? The magazine showed a packed stadium—why not any packed stadium? My God, the Sugar Bowl is New Year's Eve—day after tomorrow—and there are bowl games all over the country on New Year's Day. Search them all.

With apprehension came hostility. Suddenly Kabakov was acutely aware that he was a foreigner, and a Jew at that. Kabakov was instantly aware that a number of the men in the room were thinking about the fact that he was a Jew. He had expected that. He was not surprised when, in the minds of these men with their crisp haircuts and law school rings, he was identified with the problem rather than with the solution. The threat was from a bunch of foreigners, of which he was one. The attitude was unspoken, but it was there.

"Thank you, old buddies," Kabakov said, as he sat down. You don't know from foreigners, old buddies, he thought. But you may find out on January 12.

Kabakov did not think it reasonable that, once Black September had the capability to strike at a stadium, they would hit one that did not contain the President in preference to one that did. He stuck with the Super Bowl.

On the afternoon of December 30 he arrived in New Orleans. The search was already underway at Tulane Stadium in preparation for the Sugar Bowl. The task force at Tulane Stadium was composed of 50 men—members of the FBI and police bomb sections, police detectives, two dog handlers from the Federal Aviation Administration with dogs trained to smell explosives, and two U.S. Army technicians with an electronic "sniffer" calibrated on the Madonna recovered from the *Leticia*.

New Orleans was unique in the fact that Secret Service personnel aided in the search and in the necessity for doing the job twice—today for the Sugar

Bowl and on January 11, the eve of the Super Bowl.
The men went about their work quietly, largely
ignored by the crew of maintenance men putting the
final touches on the stadium.

The search did not interest Kabakov much. He
did not expect the searchers to find anything. What
he did was stare into the face of every employee of
Tulane Stadium. He remembered how Fasil had sent
his guerrillas to find employment in the Olympic
Village six weeks ahead of time. He knew the New
Orleans police were running background checks on
stadium employees, but still he stared into their faces
as though hoping for an instinctive, visceral reaction
if he saw a terrorist. Looking at the workers, he felt
nothing. The background check exposed one bigamist,
who was held for extradition to Coahoma County,
Mississippi.

On New Year's Eve, the Tigers of Louisiana State
University lost to Nebraska 13-7 in the Sugar Bowl
Classic. Kabakov attended.

He had never seen a football game before and he
did not see much of this one. He and Moshevsky spent
most of the time prowling under the stands and
around the gates, ignored by the numerous FBI agents
and police in the stadium. Kabakov was particularly
interested in how the gates were manned and what
access was allowed through them after the stadium was
full.

He found most public spectacles annoying, and
this one, with the pompoms and the pennants and the
massed bands, was particularly offensive. He had
always considered marching bands ridiculous. The one
pleasant moment of the afternoon was the flyover at
halftime by the Navy's Blue Angels, a neat diamond
of jets catching the sun during a beautiful slow roll
high above the droning blimp that floated around the
stadium. Kabakov knew there were other jets too—
Air Force interceptors poised on runways nearby in
the unlikely event that an unknown aircraft approached the New Orleans area while the game was
in progress.

The shadows were long across the field as the last of the crowd filtered out. Kabakov felt numbed by the hours of noise. He had difficulty understanding the English of the people he heard in conversation, and he was generally aggravated. Corley found him standing at the edge of the track outside the stadium.

"Well, no bang," Corley said.

Kabakov looked at him quickly, watching for a smirk. Corley just looked tired. Kabakov imagined that the expression "wild goose chase" was in wide use at the stadiums in other cities, where tired men were searching for explosives in preparation for the games on New Year's Day. He expected plenty was being said here, out of his hearing. He had never claimed that the target was a college bowl game, but who remembered that? It didn't matter anyway. He and Corley walked back through the stadium together, heading for the parking lot. Rachel would be waiting at the Royal Orleans.

"Major Kabakov."

He looked around for an instant before he realized the voice came from the radio in his pocket. "Kabakov, go ahead."

"Call for you in the command post."

"Right."

The FBI command post was set up in the Tulane public relations office under the stands. An agent in shirtsleeves handed Kabakov the telephone.

Weisman was calling from the Israeli embassy. Corley tried to deduce the nature of the conversation from the brief replies Kabakov made.

"Let's walk outside," Kabakov said, as he handed back the telephone. He did not like the way the agents in the office pointedly avoided looking at him after this day of extra effort.

Standing at the sideline, Kabakov looked up at the flags blowing in the wind at the top of the stadium. "They're bringing in a helicopter pilot. We don't know if it's for this job, but we know he's coming. From Libya. And they're in a hell of a hurry."

There was a brief silence as Corley digested this information.

"How much of a make have you got on him?"

"The passports, a picture, everything. The embassy is turning our file over to your office in Washington. They'll have the stuff here in a half-hour. You'll probably get a call in a minute."

"Where is he?"

"Still on the other side, we don't know where. But his papers will be picked up in Nicosia tomorrow."

"You won't interfere—"

"Of course not. We are leaving the operation strictly alone on that side. In Nicosia we're watching the place where they get the papers and the airport. That's all."

"An air strike! Here or somewhere. That's what they had in mind all the time."

"Maybe," Kabakov said. "Fasil may be running a diversion. It depends on how much he knows we know. If he is watching this stadium or any stadium, he knows we know plenty."

In the New Orleans office of the FBI, Corley and Kabakov studied the report on the pilot from Libya. Corley tapped the yellow Telex sheet. "He'll be coming in on the Portuguese passport and leaving on the Italian one with the U.S. entry stamp already on it. If he flashes that Portuguese passport at any entry point, anywhere, we'll know it within ten minutes. If he is part of this project, we've got them, David. He'll lead us to the bomb and to Fasil and the woman."

"Perhaps."

"But where were they planning to get a chopper for him? If the target is the Super Bowl, one of the people here has it set up."

"Yes. And close by. They don't have a lot of range." Kabakov ripped open a large manila envelope. It contained 100 pictures of Fasil in three-quarter profile and 100 prints of the composite drawing of the woman. Every agent in the stadium carried the pictures. "NASA did a good job on these," Kabakov said. The pictures of Fasil were remarkably clear, and a police artist had added the bullet stripe on his cheek.

"We'll get them around to the flying services, the naval station, every place that has helicopters," Corley said. "What's the matter with you?"

"Why should they get the pilot so late? It all fits very nicely except for that. A big bomb, an air strike. But why so late with the pilot? It was the chart from the boat that first suggested a pilot might be involved, but if it was a pilot who marked the chart, he was already here."

"Nautical charts are available all over the world, David. It might have been marked on the other side, in the Middle East. A safety factor. An emergency rendezvous at sea, just in case. The chart could have come over with the woman. And as it turned out, they needed the rendezvous when they thought Muzi was unreliable."

"But the last-minute rush for the papers doesn't fit. If they had known far in advance that they were going to use the Libyan, they would have had the passports ready long ago."

"The later he was brought into it, the less chance of exposure."

"No," Kabakov said, shaking his head. "Rushing around for papers is not Fasil's style. You know how far ahead he made the arrangements for Munich."

"Anyway, it's a break. I'll get the troops out to the airports with these pictures first thing tomorrow," Corley said. "A lot of the flying services will be closed over New Year's. It may take a couple of days to talk to them all."

Kabakov rode up in the elevator at the Royal Orleans Hotel with two couples, both laughing loudly, the women in elaborate beehive hairdos. He practiced understanding their speech and decided the conversation would not have made sense if he had understood it.

He found the number and knocked on the door. Hotel-room doors all look blank. They do not admit that there are people we love behind them. Rachel was there all right, and she hugged Kabakov for several seconds without saying anything.

"I'm glad the flatfeet gave you my message at the stadium. You could have invited me to meet you down here, you know."

"I was going to wait until it was over."

"You feel like a robot," she said, releasing him. "What have you got under your coat?"

"A machine gun."

"Well take it off and have a drink."

"How did you get a place like this on short notice? Corley had to go home with a local FBI agent."

"I know someone at the Plaza in New York, and the same people own this hotel. Do you like it?"

"Yes." It was a small suite, very plush.

"I'm sorry I couldn't fix Moshevsky up."

"He's right outside the door. He can sleep on the couch—no, I'm kidding. He's all right at the consulate."

"I sent for some food."

He was not listening.

"I said some food is on the way. A Chateaubriand."

"I think they're bringing in a pilot." He told her the details.

"If the pilot leads you to the rest of them, then that's it," she said.

"If we get the plastic and we can get all of them, yes."

Rachel started to ask another question and bit it off.

"How long can you stay?" Kabakov asked.

"Four or five days. Longer if I can help you. I thought I'd go back to New York and catch up on my practice and then come back on, say, the tenth or the eleventh—if you'd like me to."

"Of course I'd like you to. When this is over, let's really do New Orleans. It looks like a good town."

"Oh, David, you'll see what a town it is."

"One thing. I don't want you to come to the Super Bowl. Come to New Orleans, fine, but I don't want you around that stadium."

"If it's not safe for me, it's not safe for anybody. In that case people should be warned."

"That's what the President told the FBI and the Secret Service. If there *is* a Super Bowl, he's coming."

"It might be canceled?"

"He called in Baker and Biggs and said that if the Super Bowl crowd cannot be adequately protected, himself included, he will cancel the game and announce the reason. Baker told him the FBI could protect it."

"What did the Secret Service say?"

"Biggs doesn't make foolish promises. He's waiting to see what happens with this pilot. He isn't inviting a damned soul to the Super Bowl and neither am I. Promise me you won't come to the stadium."

"All right, David."

He smiled. "Now tell me about New Orleans."

Dinner was splendid. They ate beside the window and Kabakov relaxed for the first time in days. Outside, New Orleans glittered in the great curve of the river, and inside was Rachel, soft beyond the candles, talking about coming to New Orleans as a child with her father and how she had felt like a great lady when her father took her to Antoine's, where a waiter tactfully slipped a pillow onto her chair when he saw her coming.

She and Kabakov planned a mighty dinner at Antoine's for the night of January 12, or whenever his business was concluded. And full of Beaujolais and plans, they were happy together in the big bed. Rachel went to sleep smiling.

She awoke once after midnight and saw Kabakov propped against the headboard. When she stirred he patted her absently, and she knew he was thinking of something else.

The truck carrying the bomb entered New Orleans at 11 P.M. on December 31. The driver followed U.S. 10 past the Superdome to the intersection with U.S. 90, turned south and came to a stop near the Thalia Street wharf beneath the Mississippi River Bridge, an area deserted at that time of night.

"This is the place he said," the man at the wheel told his companion. "I'm damned if I see anybody. The whole wharf is closed."

A voice at his ear startled the driver. "Yes, this is the place," Fasil said, mounting the running board. "Here are the papers. I've signed the receipt." While the driver examined the documents with his flashlight, Fasil inspected the seals on the tailgate of the truck. They were intact.

"Buddy, could you let us have a ride to the airport? There's a late flight to Newark we're trying to catch."

"Sorry, but I can't," Fasil said. "I'll drop you where you can get a taxi."

"Christ Jesus, it'll be ten bucks to the airport."

Fasil did not want a row. He gave the man $10 and dropped the drivers off a block from a cab stand. He smiled and whistled tunelessly between his teeth as he drove toward the garage. He had been smiling all day, ever since the voice on the pay phone at the Monteleone Hotel told him the pilot was coming. His mind was alive with plans, and he had to force himself to concentrate on his driving.

First he must establish complete dominance over this man Awad. Awad must fear and respect him. That Fasil could manage. Then he must give Awad a thorough briefing and include a convincing story on how they would escape after the strike.

Fasil's plan for the strike itself was based largely on what he had learned at the Superdome. The Sikorsky S-58 helicopter that had attracted his attention was a venerable machine, sold as surplus by the West German Army. With its lift capacity of 5,000 pounds, it could not compare with the new Skycranes, but it was more than adequate for Fasil's purpose.

To make a lift requires three persons—the pilot, the "belly-man," and the loadmaster—as Fasil had learned while watching the operation at the Superdome. The pilot hovers over the cargo. He is guided by the belly-man, who lies on the floor back in the fuselage, peering straight down at the cargo and talking to the pilot via a headset.

The loadmaster is on the ground. He attaches the cargo hook to the load. The men in the aircraft cannot close the hook by remote control. It must be done on the ground. In an emergency, the pilot can drop the load instantly by pressing a red button on the control stick. Fasil learned this in conversation with the pilot during a brief break in the lifting. The pilot had been pleasant enough—a black man with clear, wide-set eyes behind his sunglasses. It was possible that this man, introduced to a fellow pilot, might allow Awad to go up with him on a lift. A fine opportunity for Awad to further familiarize himself with the cockpit. Fasil hoped Awad was personable.

On Super Bowl Sunday he would shoot the pilot immediately, and any of the ground crew that got in the way. Awad and Dahlia would man the helicopter, with Fasil on the ground as loadmaster. Dahlia would see to it that the craft was positioned correctly over the stadium and, while Awad still waited for the order to drop the nacelle, she would simply touch it off under the helicopter. Fasil had no doubt that Dahlia would go through with it.

He worried about the red drop button though. It must be rendered inoperative. If Awad, through nervousness, actually dropped the device, the effect would be ruined. It was never designed to be dropped. A lashing on the cargo hook would do it. The hook must be lashed tight at the last second before the lift, when Awad could not see what was going on beneath the helicopter. Fasil could not trust some imported front-fighter to take care of this detail. For this reason, he himself must be the loadmaster.

The risk was acceptable. He would have much more cover than he would have had at Lakefront Airport with the blimp. He would be facing unarmed construction workers rather than airport police. When the big bang came, Fasil intended to be driving toward the city limits, toward Houston and a plane to Mexico City.

Awad would believe to the last that Fasil was waiting for him in a car in Audubon Park beyond the stadium.

Here was the garage, set back from the street just as Dahlia described. Once inside with the door closed, Fasil opened the rear of the truck. All was in order. He tried the engine on the forklift. It started instantly. Well and good. As soon as Awad arrived and his arrangements were complete, it would be time to call Dahlia, tell her to kill the American and come to New Orleans.

CHAPTER 23

LANDER MOANED once and moved in the hospital bed.
Dahlia Iyad put aside the New Orleans street map
she was studying and rose stiffly. Her foot was asleep.
She hobbled to the bedside and put her hand on
Lander's forehead. The skin was hot. She sponged his
temples and cheeks with a cool cloth, and when his
breathing settled into a steady wheeze and rattle she
returned to her chair under the reading lamp.

A curious change came over Dahlia each time she
went to the bedside. Sitting in her chair with the map,
thinking about New Orleans, she could look at Lander
with the steady, cool gaze of a cat, a look in which
there were many possibilities, all determined solely by
her need. At his bedside, her face was warm and full
of concern. Both expressions were genuine. No man
ever had a kinder, deadlier nurse than Dahlia Iyad.

She had slept on a cot in the New Jersey hospital
room for four nights. She could not leave him for fear
he would rave about the mission. And he had raved,
but it was about Vietnam and persons she did not
know. And about Margaret. For one entire evening he
had repeated, "Jergens, you were right."

She did not know if his mind was gone. She knew
she had twelve days until the strike. If she could

salvage him, she would do it. If not—well, either way he would die. One way was no worse than the other.

She knew Fasil was in a hurry. But hurrying is dangerous. If Lander was unable to fly and Fasil's alternate arrangements did not suit her, she would eliminate Fasil, she decided. The bomb was too valuable to waste in a hastily contrived operation. It was far more valuable than Fasil. She would never forgive him for trying to get out of the actual operation in New Orleans. His weaseling had not been the result of a failure of nerve, as was the case with the Japanese she shot before the Lod airport strike. It was a result of personal ambition, and that was much worse.

"Try, Michael," she whispered. "Try very hard."

Early on the morning of January 1, federal agents and local police fanned out to the airports that ringed New Orleans– Houma, Thibodaux, Slidell, Hammond, Greater St. Tammany, Gulfport, Stennis International, and Bogalusa. All morning long their reports filtered in. No one had seen Fasil or the woman.

Corley, Kabakov, and Moshevsky worked New Orleans International and New Orleans Lakefront airports with no success. It was a glum drive back toward town. Corley, checking by radio, was told that all reports from Customs at entry points around the country and all reports from Interpol were negative. There had been no sign of the Libyan pilot.

"The bastard could be going anywhere," Corley said as he accelerated onto the expressway.

Kabakov stared out the window in sour silence. Only Moshevsky was unconcerned. Having attended the late-late show at the Hotsy-Totsy Club on Bourbon Street the previous evening instead of retiring, he was asleep on the back seat.

They had turned on Poydras toward the federal building when, like a great bird flushed from hiding, the helicopter rose above the surrounding buildings to hover over the Superdome, a heavy square object slung close under its belly.

"Hey. Hey. Hey, David," Corley said. He leaned

over the wheel to look up through the windshield and slammed on his brakes. The car behind them honked angrily and pulled around them on the right, the driver's mouth working behind his window.

Kabakov's heart leaped when he saw the machine, and it was still pounding. He knew it was too early for the strike, he could see now that the object hanging under the big helicopter was a piece of machinery, but the image fit the imprint in his mind too well.

The landing pad was on the east side of the Superdome. Corley parked the car a hundred yards away, beside a stack of girders.

"If Fasil is watching this place, he'd better not recognize you," Corley said. "I'll get us a couple of hardhats." He disappeared into the construction site and returned in minutes with three yellow plastic helmets with goggles.

"Take the field glasses and move up into the dome, where that opening overlooks the pad," Kabakov told Moshevsky. "Keep out of the sunlight and sweep the windows across the street, anywhere high, and the perimeter of the loading area here."

Moshevsky was moving as he spoke the last word.

The ground crew trundled another load onto the pad, and the helicopter, rocking gently, began its descent to pick it up. Kabakov went into the construction shack at the edge of the pad and watched through the window. The loadmaster was shielding his eyes from the sun with his hand and talking into a small radio as Corley approached him.

"Ask the chopper to come down, please," Corley said. He cupped his badge so only the loadmaster could see it. The loadmaster glanced at the badge and then at Corley's face.

"What is it?"

"Would you ask him to come down?"

The loadmaster spoke into the radio and yelled at the ground crew. They rolled the big refrigeration pump off the pad and turned their faces away from the blowing dust as the machine gingerly touched down. The loadmaster made a cutting motion with his hand across his wrist and beckoned. The big rotor slowed and began to droop.

The pilot swung himself out and dropped to the ground in one motion. He wore a Marine flight suit, weathered until it was almost white at the knees and elbows. "What is it, Maginty?"

"This guy wants to talk to you," the loadmaster said.

The pilot looked at Corley's ID. Kabakov could detect no expression on his dark brown face.

"Can we go in the shack? You too, Mr. Maginty," Corley said.

"Yeah," the loadmaster said. "But look, this egg-beater costs the company $500 an hour, can we sort of hurry this up?"

In the littered construction shack, Corley took out the picture of Fasil. "Have you—"

"Why don't you introduce yourselves first," the pilot said. "That's polite, and it'll only cost Maginty here $12 worth of time."

"Sam Corley."

"David Kabakov."

"I'm Lamar Jackson." He shook their hands solemnly.

"It's a matter of national security," Corley said. Kabakov thought he detected a glint of amusement in the pilot's eyes at Corley's tone. "Have you seen this man?"

Jackson's eyebrows raised as he looked at the picture. "Yeah, three or four days ago, while you were rigging the sling on that elevator hoist, Maginty. Who is he anyway?"

"He's a fugitive. We want him."

"Well, stick around. He said he was coming back."

"He did?"

"Yeah. How did you guys know to look here?"

"You've got what he wants," Corley said. "A helicopter."

"What for?"

"To hurt a lot of people with. When is he coming back?"

"He didn't say. I didn't pay too much attention to him to tell you the truth. He was kind of a creepy guy, you know, coming on friendly. What did he do? I mean you say he's bad news—"

"He is a psychopath and a killer, a political fanatic," Kabakov said. "He has committed a number of murders. He was going to kill you and take your helicopter when the time came. Tell us what happened."

"Oh, Christ," Maginty said. He mopped his face with a handkerchief. "I don't like this." He looked quickly out the door of the shack, as though he expected the maniac momentarily.

Jackson shook his head like a man making sure he is really awake, but when he spoke his voice was calm. "He was standing by the pad when I came over here for a cup of coffee. I didn't particularly notice him, because a lot of people like to watch the thing, you know. Then he started asking me about it, how you make a lift and all, what the model designation was. He asked if he could look inside. I said he could look in through the side door of the fuselage, but he shouldn't touch anything."

"And he looked?"

"Yeah, and let me see, he asked how you go back and forth from the cargo bay to the cockpit. I told him it's awkward, you have to lift one of the seats in the cockpit. I remember I thought it was a funny question. People usually ask, like, how much will it pick up and don't I get scared it will fall. Then he told me he had a brother who flies choppers and how his brother would love to see it."

"Did he ask you if you work on Sundays?"

"I was getting to that. This dude asked me three times if we were going to work through the rest of the holidays and I kept telling him yeah, yeah. I had to go back to work, and he made a point of shaking hands and all."

"He asked you your name?" Kabakov asked.

"Yes."

"And where you are from?"

"Right."

Instinctively, Kabakov liked Jackson. He looked like a man with good nerves. It would take good nerves to do Jackson's job. He also looked as though he could be very tough when he needed to be.

"You were a Marine pilot?" Kabakov asked.

"Right."

"Vietnam?"

"Thirty-eight missions. Then I got shot up a little and I was 'ree-tired' until the end of the hitch."

"Mr. Jackson, we need your help."

"To catch this guy?"

"Yes," Kabakov said. "We want to follow him when he leaves here after his next visit. He'll just come and bring his fake brother and look around. He mustn't be alarmed while he's here. We have to follow him for a little while before we take him. So we need your cooperation."

"Um-hum. Well, it so happens I need your help too. Let me see your credentials, Mr. FBI." He was looking at Kabakov, but Corley handed over his identification. The pilot picked up the telephone.

"The number is—"

"I'll get the number, Mr. Corley."

"You can ask for—"

"I can ask for the head dick in charge," Jackson said.

The New Orleans office of the FBI confirmed Corley's identity.

"Now," Jackson said, hanging up the telephone, "you wanted to know if Crazy Person asked me where I'm from. That means him locating my family if I'm not mistaken. Like to coerce me."

"It would occur to him, yes. If it was necessary," Kabakov said.

"Well, I'll tell you. You want me to help you by playing it straight when the man shows up again?"

"You'll be covered all the time. We just want to follow him when he leaves," Corley said.

"How do you know his next call won't be time for the shit to go down?"

"Because he'll bring his pilot to look at the chopper in advance. We know the day he plans to strike."

"Um-hum. I'll do that. But, in five minutes I'm going to call my wife in Orlando. I want her to tell me there is a government car parked out front containing the baddest four dudes she has *ever* seen. Do you follow me?"

"Let me use your telephone," Corley said.

The round-the-clock stakeout at the helipad stretched on for days. Corley, Kabakov, and Moshevsky were there during working hours. A three-man team of FBI agents took over when the helicopter was secured for the night. Fasil did not come.

Each day Jackson arrived cheerful and ready to go, though he complained about the pair of federal agents that stayed with him during off-duty hours. He said they cramped his style.

Once in the evening he had a drink with Kabakov and Rachel at the Royal Orleans, his two bodyguards sitting at the next table dry and glum. Jackson had been a lot of places and had seen a lot of things, and Kabakov liked him better than most of the Americans he had met.

Maginty was another matter. Kabakov wished they had avoided bringing Maginty into it. The strain was telling on the loadmaster. He was jumpy and irritable.

On the morning of January 4 rain delayed the lifting, and Jackson came into the construction shack for coffee.

"What is that piece you've got back there?" he asked Moshevsky.

"A Galil." Moshevsky had ordered the new type of automatic assault rifle from Israel at Kabakov's indulgence. He removed the clip and the round from the chamber and passed it to Jackson. Moshevsky pointed out the bottle opener built into the bipod, a feature he found of particular interest.

"We used to carry an AK-47 in the chopper in Nam," Jackson said. "Somebody took it off a Cong. I liked it better than an M-16."

Maginty came into the shack, saw the weapon, and backed out again. Kabakov decided to tell Moshevsky to keep the rifle out of sight. There was no point in spooking Maginty any further.

"But to tell you the truth, I don't like any of these things," Jackson was saying. "You know a lot of guys jerk off with guns—I don't mean *you*, that's your business—but you show me a man that just loves a piece and I'll—"

Corley's radio interrupted Jackson. "Jay Seven, Jay Seven."

"Jay Seven, go ahead."

"New York advises subject Mayfly cleared JFK customs at 0940 Eastern Standard. Has reservation on Delta 704 to New Orleans, arriving 12:30 Central Standard." Mayfly was the code name assigned Abdel Awad.

"Roger, Jay Seven out. Son of a bitch, Kabakov, he's coming! He'll lead us to Fasil and the plastic and the woman."

Kabakov gave a sigh of relief. It was the first hard evidence that he was on the right track, that the Super Bowl was the target. "I hope we can separate them from the plastic before we take them. Otherwise there will be a very loud noise."

"So today's the day," Jackson said. There was no alarm in his voice. He was steady.

"I don't know," Kabakov said. "Maybe today, maybe tomorrow. Tomorrow is Sunday. He'll want to see you working on Sunday. We'll see."

Three hours and 45 minutes later Abdel Awad got off a Delta jet at New Orleans International Airport. He was carrying a small suitcase. In the line of passengers behind him was a large, middle-aged man in a gray business suit. For an instant the eyes of the man in gray met those of Corley, who was waiting across the corridor. The big man looked briefly at Awad's back, then looked away.

Corley, carrying a suitcase, trailed the debarking passengers toward the lobby. He was not watching Awad, he was looking at the crowd waiting to greet the new arrivals. He was looking for Fasil, looking for the woman.

But Awad clearly was not looking for anyone. He went down the escalator and walked outside, where he hesitated near the line of passengers waiting for limousines.

Corley slid into the car with Kabakov and Moshevsky. Kabakov appeared to be reading a newspaper. It had been agreed that he would lie low in the event that Awad had seen his picture in a briefing.

"That's Howard, the big guy," Corley said. "Howard will stay with him if he takes the limo. If he takes a cab, Howard will finger it for the guys in the radio cars."

Awad took a taxi. Howard walked behind it and stopped to blow his nose.

It was a pleasure to watch the trailing operation. Three cars and a pickup truck were used, none staying immediately behind the taxi for more than a few minutes on the long drive into the city. When it was clear that the taxi was stopping at the Marriott Hotel, one of the chase cars shot around to the side entrance and an agent was near the registration desk before Awad came to claim his reservation.

The agent by the desk walked quickly to the elevator bank. "Six-eleven," he said as he passed the man standing under the potted palm. The agent under the tree entered the elevator. He was on the sixth floor when Awad followed the bellhop to his room.

In half an hour the FBI had the room next door and an agent at the switchboard. Awad received no calls, and he did not come down. At 8 P.M. he ordered a steak sent to his room. An agent delivered it and received a quarter tip, which he held by the edges all the way back downstairs where the coin was finger-printed. The vigil went on all night.

Sunday morning, January 5, was chill and over-cast. Moshevsky poured strong Cajun coffee and passed a cup to Kabakov, a cup to Corley. Through the thin walls of the construction shack they could hear the rotor blades of the big helicopter blatting the air as it made another lift.

It had been against Kabakov's instincts to leave the hotel where Awad was staying, but common sense told him this was the place to wait. He could not per-form close surveillance without running the risk of being seen by Awad, or by Fasil when he showed up. The surveillance at the hotel, under the direct control of the New Orleans Agent In Charge, was as good as Kabakov had ever seen. There was no question in Kabakov's mind that they would come here to the helicopter before they went to the bomb. Awad could change the load to fit the chopper, but he could not change the chopper to fit the load—he had to see the helicopter first.

This was the place of greatest peril. The Arabs would be on foot in this vast tangle of building sup-plies and they would be dealing with civilians, two of whom knew they were dangerous. At least Maginty wasn't here and that was a boon, Kabakov thought. In the six days of the stakeout, Maginty had called in sick twice and had been late on two other days.

Corley's radio growled. He fiddled with the squelch knob.

"Unit One, Unit Four." That was the team on the sixth floor of the Marriott, calling the Agent In Charge.

"Go ahead, Four."

"Mayfly left his room, heading for the elevators."

"Roger Four. Five, you got that?"

"Five standing by." A minute passed.

"Unit One, Unit Five. He's passing through the lobby now." The voice on the radio was muffled, and

Kabakov guessed the agent in the lobby was speaking into a buttonhole microphone.

Kabakov stared at the radio, a muscle in his jaw twitching. If Awad headed for another part of the city, he could join the hunt in minutes. Faintly on the radio he heard the swoosh of the revolving door, then street noises as the agent followed Awad outside the Marriott.

"One, this is Five. He's walking west on Decatur." A long pause. "One, he's going into the Bienville House."

"Three, cover the back."

"Roger."

An hour passed and Awad did not emerge. Kabakov thought about all the rooms in which he had waited. He had forgotten how sick and tired a man gets of a stakeout room. There was no conversation. Kabakov stared out the window. Corley looked at the radio. Moshevsky examined something he had removed from his ear.

"Unit One, Unit Five. He's coming out. Roach is with him." Kabakov took a deep breath and let it out slowly. "Roach" was Muhammad Fasil.

Five was still talking. "They're taking a taxi. Cab number four seven five eight. Louisiana commercial license four seven eight Juliett Lima. Mobile Twelve has—" A second message broke in.

"Unit Twelve, we've got him. He's turning west on Magazine."

"Roger Twelve."

Kabakov went to the window. He could see the ground crew adjusting a harness on the next load, one of them acting as loadmaster.

"One, Unit Twelve, he's turning north on Poydras. Looks like he's coming to you, Jay Seven."

"This is Jay Seven, Roger Twelve."

Corley remained in the construction shack while Kabakov and Moshevsky took up positions outside, Kabakov in the back of a truck, concealed by a canvas curtain, Moshevsky in a Port-O-San portable toilet with a peephole in the door. The three of them formed a triangle around the helicopter pad.

"Jay Seven, Jay Seven, Unit Twelve. Subjects are at Poydras and Rampart, proceeding north."

Corley waited until Jackson in the helicopter was clear of the roof, settling toward the ground, then spoke to him on the aircraft frequency. "You're going to have company. Take a break in about five minutes."

"Roger." Jackson's voice was calm.

"Jay Seven, this is Mobile Twelve. They're across the street from you, getting out of the taxi."

"Roger."

Kabakov had never seen Fasil before, and now he watched him through a crack in the curtain as though he were some exotic form of wildlife. The monster of Munich. Six thousand miles was a long chase.

The camera case, he thought. *That's where you have the gun. I should have gotten you in Beirut.*

Fasil and Awad stood beside a stack of crates at the side of the pad, watching the helicopter. They were closest to Moshevsky, but out of his line of vision. They were talking. Awad said something and Fasil nodded his head. Awad turned and tried the door of Moshevsky's hideout. It was hooked. He went into the next Port-O-San in the line and after a moment returned to Fasil.

The helicopter settled to the ground, and they turned their faces away from the dust. Jackson swung down from the cockpit and walked toward the ground crew's water cooler.

Kabakov was glad to see that he moved slowly and naturally. He drew a cup of water and then appeared to notice Fasil for the first time, acknowledging his presence with a casual wave.

That's good, Kabakov thought, that's good.

Fasil and Awad walked over to Jackson. Fasil was introducing Awad. They shook hands. Jackson was nodding his head. They walked toward the helicopter, talking animatedly, Awad making the hand gestures that mark all pilots' shop talk. Awad leaned into the fuselage door and looked around. He asked a question. Jackson appeared to hesitate. He looked around as though checking on the whereabouts of the boss, then nodded. Awad scrambled into the cockpit.

Kabakov was not worried about Awad trying to take the helicopter—he knew Jackson had a fuse from the ignition in his pocket. Jackson joined Awad in the cockpit. Fasil looked around the pad, alert but calm. Two minutes passed. Jackson and Awad climbed down again. Jackson was shaking his head and pointing to his watch.

It was going well, Kabakov thought. As expected, Awad had asked to go up on a lift. Jackson had told him he couldn't take him up during working hours for insurance reasons, but that later in the week, before the boss showed up for work in the morning, perhaps he could arrange it.

They were all shaking hands again. Now they would go to the plastic.

Maginty came around the corner of the construction shack, rummaging in his lunch pail. He was in the center of the pad when he saw Fasil and froze in his tracks.

Kabakov's lips moved soundlessly as he swore. *Oh, no. Get out of there, you son of a bitch.*

Maginty's face was pale, and his mouth hung open. Fasil was looking at him now. Jackson smiled broadly. *Jackson will save it. He'll save it,* Kabakov thought.

Jackson's voice was louder. Moshevsky could hear him. "Excuse me a minute, fellas. Hey, Maginty, you decided to show up, baby. It's about time."

Maginty seemed paralyzed.

"Drinking that bug juice and laying out all night, you look awful, man." Jackson was turning him around to walk him to the construction shack when Maginty said quite clearly, "Where are the police?"

Fasil barked at Awad and sprinted for the edge of the pad, his hand in the camera case.

Corley was screaming into his radio. "Bust 'em. Bust 'em, goddammit, bust 'em."

Kabakov snatched back the curtain. "Freeze, Fasil."

Fasil fired at him, the magnum knocking a fist-sized hole in the truck bed. Fasil was running hard, dodging between piles of building materials, Kabakov 20 yards behind him.

Awad started after Fasil, but Moshevsky, bursting out of his hiding place, caught him and without breaking stride slammed him to the ground with a blow at the base of his skull, then ran hard after Kabakov and Fasil. Awad tried to rise, but Jackson and Corley were on him.

Fasil ran toward the Superdome. Twice he stopped to fire at Kabakov. Kabakov felt the wind of the second one on his face as he dived for cover.

Fasil sprinted across the clear space between the stacks of materials and the yawning door of the Superdome, Kabakov laying a burst from his submachine gun in the dirt ahead of him. "Halt! *Andek!*"

Fasil did not hesitate as the grit kicked up by the bullets stung his legs. He disappeared into the Superdome.

Kabakov heard a challenge and a shot as he ran to the entrance. FBI agents were coming from the other way, through the dome. He hoped they had not killed Fasil.

Kabakov dived through the entrance and dropped behind a pallet stacked with window frames. The upper levels of the vast, shadowy chamber glowed with the lights of the construction crews. Kabakov could see the yellow helmets as the men peered down at the floor. Three pistol shots echoed through the dome. Then he heard the heavier blast of Fasil's magnum. He crawled around the end of the pallet.

There were the FBI agents, two of them, crouched behind a portable generating unit on the open floor. Thirty yards beyond them at an angle in the wall was a breast-high stack of sacked cement. One of the agents fired, and dust flew off the top tier of bags.

Running low and hard, Kabakov crossed the floor toward the agents. A flash of movement behind the breastwork, Kabakov was diving, rolling, hearing the magnum roar, and then he was behind the generator. Blood trickled down his forearm where a flying chip of concrete had stung him.

"Is he hit?" Kabakov asked.

"I don't think so," an agent replied.

Fasil was hemmed in. His breastwork of cement protected him from the front, and the angle of the bare concrete wall protected his flanks. Thirty yards of open floor separated his position from Kabakov and the agents behind the generator.

Fasil could not escape. The trick would be in taking him alive and forcing him to tell where the plastic was hidden. Taking Fasil alive would be like trying to grab a rattlesnake by the head.

The Arab fired once. The bullet slammed into the generator engine, releasing a steady trickle of water. Kabakov fired four shots to cover Moshevsky, charging across the floor to join him.

"Corley's getting gas and smoke," Moshevsky said.

The voice from behind the cement bag barricade had a weird lilt. "Why don't you come and get me, Major Kabakov? How many of you will die trying to take me alive, do you suppose? You'll never do it. Come, come, Major. I have something for you."

Peering through a space in the machine that shielded him, Kabakov studied Fasil's position. He had to work fast. He was afraid Fasil would kill himself rather than wait for the gas. There was only one feature that might be useful. A large metal fire extinguisher was clipped to the wall beside the place where Fasil was hidden. Fasil must be very near it. All right. Do it. Don't think about it anymore. He gave Moshevsky brief instructions and cut off his objection with a single shake of his head. Kabakov poised like a sprinter at the end of the generator.

Moshevsky raised his automatic rifle and laid down a terrific volume of fire across the top of Fasil's breastwork. Kabakov was running now, bent under the hail of bullets, hard for the cement bags. He crouched outside the breastwork beneath the sheet of covering fire; he tensed and, without looking back at Moshevsky, made a cutting motion with his hand. Instantly a new burst from the Galil and the fire extinguisher exploded over Fasil in a great burst of foam, Kabakov diving over the bulwark, into the spray, on top of Fasil, slick with the chemical. Fasil's face full of it, the gun going off deafeningly beside Kabakov's neck. Kabakov had the wrist of the gun hand, snapping his head from side to side to avoid a finger strike at his eyes, and with his free hand broke Fasil's collarbone on both sides. Fasil writhed out from under him, and as he tried to rise Kabakov caught him with an elbow in the diaphragm that laid him back on the ground.

Moshevsky was here now, raising Fasil's head and pulling his jaw and tongue forward to be sure his air passage was clear. The snake was taken.

Corley heard the screaming as he ran into the Superdome with a teargas gun. It was coming from behind the stack of cement, where two FBI agents stood uncertainly, Moshevsky facing them, full of menace.

Corley found Kabakov sitting on Fasil, his face an inch from the Arab's. "Where is it, Fasil? Where is it, Fasil?" He was flexing the fractures in Fasil's collarbones. Corley could hear the grating noise. "Where's the plastic?"

Corley's revolver was in his hand. He pressed the muzzle to the bridge of Kabakov's nose. "Stop it, Kabakov. God damn you, stop it."

Kabakov spoke, but not to Corley. "Don't shoot him, Moshevsky." He looked up at Corley. "This is the only chance we'll have to find it. You don't have to make a case against Fasil."

"We'll interrogate him. Take your hands off him."

Three heartbeats later: "All right. You'd better read to him from the card in your wallet."

Kabakov stood. Unsteady, splattered with fire extinguisher foam, he leaned against the rough concrete wall, and his stomach heaved. Watching him, Corley felt sick as well, but he was not angry anymore. Corley did not like the way Moshevsky was looking at him. He had his duty to do. He took a radio from one of the FBI agents. "This is Jay Seven. Get an ambulance in the east entrance of the Superdome." He looked down at Fasil, moaning on the ground. Fasil's eyes were open. "You are under arrest. You have the right to remain silent," Corley began heavily.

Fasil was held on charges of illegal entry and conspiracy to violate customs regulations. Awad was held for illegal entry. The embassy of the United Arab Republic arranged for them to be represented by a New Orleans law firm. Neither Arab said anything. Corley hammered at Fasil for hours Sunday night in the prison infirmary and received nothing but a mocking stare. Fasil's lawyer withdrew from the case when he heard the nature of the questions. He was replaced by a Legal Aid attorney. Fasil paid no attention to either lawyer. He seemed content to wait.

Corley dumped the contents of a manila envelope on a desk in the FBI office. "This is all Fasil had on him."

Kabakov poked through the pile. There was a wallet, an envelope containing $2,500 in cash, an open airline ticket to Mexico City, Fasil's fake credentials and passport, assorted change, room keys from the YMCA and the Bienville House, and two other keys.

"His room is clean," Corley said. "A few clothes. Awad's luggage is clean as a whistle. We're working on tracing Fasil's gun, but I think he brought it in with him. One of the holes in the *Leticia* was a magnum."

"He hasn't said anything?"

"No." By tacit agreement, Corley and Kabakov had not referred to their angry clash in the Superdome again, but for a moment they both thought about it.

"Have you threatened Fasil with immediate extradition to Israel to stand trial for Munich?"

"I've threatened him with everything."

"What about sodium pentathol or hallucinogens?"

"Can't do it, David. Look, I have a pretty good idea of what Dr. Bauman probably has in her purse. That's why I haven't let you in to see Fasil."

"No, you're wrong. She wouldn't do that. She wouldn't drug him."

"But I expect you asked her."

Kabakov did not reply.

"These keys are for two Master padlocks," Corley said. "There are no padlocks in Fasil's luggage or in Awad's. Fasil has locked up something. If the bomb is big, and it would have to be big if it's in a single charge or even two charges, then it's probably in a truck, or close to a truck. That means a garage, a locked garage.

"We're having 500 of these keys made. They'll be issued to patrolmen with instructions to try every padlock on their beats. When one clicks open, the patrolman is to lay back and call for us.

"I know what's bothering you. Two keys come with each new padlock, right?"

"Yes," Kabakov said. "Somebody has got the other set of keys."

CHAPTER 24

"DAHLIA? Are you here?" The room was very dark.

"Yes, Michael. Right here."

He felt her hand on his arm. "Have I been asleep?"

"You've slept for two hours. It's one A.M."

"Turn on the light. I want to see your face."

"All right. Here it is. The same old face."

He held her face in his hands, gently rubbing his thumbs in the soft hollows beneath her cheekbones. It had been three days since his fever broke. He was getting 250 milligrams of Erythromycin four times a day. It was working, but slowly.

"Let's see if I can walk."

"We should wait—"

"I want to know *now* if I can walk. Help me up." He sat on the side of the hospital bed. "Okay, here we go." He put his arm around her shoulders. She held him by the waist. He stood and took a shaky step. "Dizzy," he said. "Keep going."

She felt him trembling. "Let's go back to the bed, Michael."

"Nope. I can make the chair." He sank back in the chair and fought down a wave of nausea and dizziness. He looked at her and smiled weakly. "That's eight steps. From the bus to the cockpit won't be more than fifty-five. This is January fifth, no, the sixth, it's after midnight. We've got five and a half days. We'll make it."

"I never doubted it, Michael."

"Yes, you did. You doubt it now. You'd be a fool not to doubt it. Help me back to bed."

He slept until mid-morning, and he was able to eat breakfast. It was time to tell him.

"Michael, I'm afraid something is wrong with Fasil."

"When did you talk to him last?"

"Tuesday, the second. He called to say the truck was safe in the garage. He was scheduled to call again last night. He didn't." She had not mentioned the Libyan pilot to Lander. She never would.

"You think he's caught, don't you?"

"He wouldn't miss a call. If he hasn't called by tomorrow night, then he's taken."

"If he was caught away from the garage, what would he be carrying to give it away?"

"Nothing but his set of keys. I burned the rent receipt as soon as I got it. He never even had that. He had nothing that would identify us. If he had anything, and he was caught, the police would be here now."

"What about the hospital telephone number?"

"Only in his head. He picked pay telephones at random to call here."

"We'll go on then. Either the plastic is still there, or it's not. The loading will be harder with just the two of us, but we can do it if we're quick. Have you got the reservations?"

"Yes, at the Fairmont. I didn't ask if the blimp crew was there, I was afraid—"

"That's all right. The crew has always stayed there when we flew New Orleans. They'll do it again this time. Let's walk a little."

"I'm supposed to call the Aldrich office again this afternoon and give them your condition." She had introduced herself on the telephone as Lander's sister when she reported him ill.

"Say I've still got the flu and I'm out for at least

a week and a half. They'll keep Farley on the schedule as chief pilot and Simmons as second officer. You remember what Farley looks like? You only saw him once, when we flew the night-sign run over Shea."

"I remember."

"He's in some of the pictures at the house, if you want to look at him again."

"Tomorrow," she said. "I'll go to the house tomorrow. You must be sick of this dress." She had bought underclothing at a shop across the street from the hospital, had bathed in Lander's bathroom. Otherwise, she had not left his side. She laid her head on Lander's chest. He smiled and rubbed the back of her neck.

I can't hear him bubbling, she thought. *His chest is clear.*

CHAPTER 25

THE PRESENCE of Fasil and Awad in New Orleans left no doubt in the minds of the FBI and the Secret Service that the Arabs had planned to blow up the Super Bowl. The authorities believed that with the capture of Fasil and Awad the prime threat to the Super Bowl was blunted, but they knew they still faced a dangerous situation.

Two persons known to be at least peripherally involved in the plot—the woman and the American—were still at large. Neither had been identified, although the officers had a likeness of the woman. Worse, more than a half-ton of high explosive was cached somewhere, probably in the New Orleans area.

In the first few hours after the arrests, Corley half-expected a shattering blast somewhere in the city, or a threatening telephone call demanding Fasil's release as the price of the guerrillas not detonating the bomb in a crowded area. Neither occurred.

New Orleans' 1,300-man police force passed the duplicate padlock keys from shift to shift. The instructions to try them on warehouses and garages were repeated at every roll call. But New Orleans has a small police force for its size, and it is a city of many doors. Throughout the week the search went on, amid the

Super Bowl ballyhoo and the crowds that swelled as the big weekend approached.

The crowd coming in for the Super Bowl was different from the Sugar Bowl group that preceded them. This crowd was more diversified in origin, the clothes were smarter. The restaurants found their customers less relaxed and more demanding. Money always flows freely in New Orleans, but now there was more of it to flow. The lines outside Galatoire's and Antoine's and the Court of Two Sisters stretched for half a block, and music spilled into the streets of the French Quarter all night long.

Standing-room tickets had been sold, bringing the total expected attendance at the Super Bowl to 84,000. With the fans came the gamblers, the thieves, and the whores. The police were busy.

Kabakov went to the airport on Thursday and watched the arrival of the Washington Redskins and the Miami Dolphins. Itchy in the crowd, remembering how the Israeli athletes had died at the Munich airport, he scanned the faces of the fans and paid little attention to the players as they came off their planes, waving to the cheering crowd.

Once Kabakov went to see Muhammad Fasil.

He stood at the foot of Fasil's bed in the infirmary and stared at the Arab for five minutes. Corley and two very large FBI agents were with him.

Finally Kabakov spoke. "Fasil, if you leave American custody you are a dead man. The Americans can extradite you to Israel to stand trial for Munich, and you will hang within the week. I would be happy to see it.

"But if you tell where the plastic is hidden, they'll convict you here on a smuggling charge and you will serve some time. Five years, maybe a little more. I'm sure you believe Israel will be gone by then and will be no threat to you. It won't be gone, but I'm sure you believe it will. Consider that."

Fasil's eyes were narrowed into slits. His head jerked and a stream of spittle flew at Kabakov, speckling the front of his shirt. The effort was painful for

Fasil, strapped in his shoulder braces, and he grimaced and lay back on his pillow. Corley moved forward, but Kabakov had not stirred. The Israeli stared at Fasil a moment longer, then turned and left the room.

The expected decision came from the White House at midnight Friday. Barring further developments, the Super Bowl would be played on schedule.

On Saturday morning, January 11, Earl Biggs and Jack Renfro of the Secret Service held a final briefing at New Orleans FBI headquarters. Attending were 30 Secret Service agents, who would supplement the squad traveling with the President, 40 agents of the FBI, and Kabakov.

Renfro stood before a huge diagram of Tulane Stadium. "The stadium will be swept for explosives again beginning at 1600 today," he said. "The search will be completed by midnight, at which time the stadium will be sealed. Carson, your search team is ready." It was not a question.

"Ready."

"You will also have six men with the sniffer at the President's box for a last-minute sweep at 1340 tomorrow."

"Right. They've been briefed."

Renfro turned to the diagram on the wall behind him. "Once the possibility of concealed explosives in the stadium is eliminated, an attack could take two forms. The guerrillas could try to bring in the explosive in a vehicle, or they could settle for coming in with as much as they can conceal on their bodies.

"Vehicles first." He picked up his pointer. "Roadblocks will be prepared here at Willow Street on both sides of the stadium and at Johnson, Esther, Barret, Story, and Delord. Hickory will be blocked where it crosses Audubon. These are *positive* roadblocks that will stop a vehicle at high speed. I don't want to see anybody standing beside a sawhorse waving down traffic. The roadblocks will close tight as soon as the stadium is filled."

An agent raised his hand.

"Yeah."

"TV is bitching about the midnight setup rule. They'll have the color van set up this afternoon, but they want access throughout the night."

"Tough tit," Renfro said. "Tell them no. After midnight nobody comes in. At 10 A.M. Sunday the camera crews can take their places. Nobody carries anything. Where's the FAA?"

"Here," said a balding young man. "Considering the persons already in custody, the use of an aircraft is considered highly unlikely." He spoke as though he were reading a report. "Both airports have been checked thoroughly for hidden ordnance." The young man hesitated, choosing between "however" and "nonetheless." He decided on "however." "However. No private aircraft will take off from New Orleans International or Lakefront during the time the stadium is filled, with the exception of charter and cargo flights which have already been cleared individually by us.

"Commercial flights remain on schedule. New Orleans police will man both airports in the event someone should try to commandeer an aircraft."

"Okay," Renfro said. "The Air Force advises no unidentified aircraft will get into the New Orleans area. They're standing by as they did on December 31. Naturally, they would have to solve that kind of problem well outside the city. The perimeter they are establishing has a 150-mile radius. We'll have a chopper up to watch the crowd.

"Now, about infiltration of the stadium. We have announcements on the media requesting ticketholders to show up one and one-half hours before game time," Renfro said. "Some of them will, some won't. They will have to pass through the metal detectors provided by the airlines before they enter the stadium. That's you, Fullilove. Are your people checked out on the equipment?"

"We're ready."

"The ones who arrive late will be mad if standing in line at the metal detector makes them miss the kickoff, but that's tough. Major Kabakov, do you have any suggestions?"

"I do." Kabakov went to the front of the room. "Regarding metal detectors and personal searches: No terrorist is going to wait until he's in a metal detector with the bell going off to go for his gun. Watch the line approaching the detector. A man with a gun will be looking around for an alternate way in. He'll be looking from policeman to policeman. Maybe his head won't move, but his eyes will. If you decide someone in the line is suspect, get him from both sides suddenly. Don't give any warning. Once he knows his cover is about to be blown, he'll kill as many as he can before he goes down." Kabakov thought the officers might resent being told their business. He didn't care.

"If possible, there should be a grenade sump at every gate. A circle of sandbags will do; a hole with sandbags around it is better. A grenade rolling on the ground in a crowd is hard to get to. What's worse is to get to it and have no place to put it. The fragmentation grenades they use usually have a five-second fuse. They will be attached to the guerrilla's clothing by the pin. Don't pull a grenade off him. Kill him or control his hands first. Then take your time removing his grenades.

"If he is wounded and down, and you cannot get to him instantly and control his hands, shoot him again. In the head. He may be carrying a satchel charge, and he'll set it off if you give him time." Kabakov saw expressions of distaste on some of the faces. He did not care.

"Gunfire at one gate *must not* distract the men at another. That's the time to watch your own area of responsibility. Once it starts in one position, it will start elsewhere.

"There's one other thing. One of them is a woman, as you know." Kabakov looked down for a moment and cleared his throat. When he spoke again his voice was louder. "In Beirut once, I looked at her as a woman rather than as a guerrilla. That's one reason we are in this position today. Don't make the same mistake."

The room was very still when Kabakov sat down.

"One backup team is on each side of the stadium," Renfro said. "They will respond to any alarm. Do not leave your position. Pick up your ID tabs at this desk after the meeting. Any questions?" Renfro looked over the group. His eyes had the finish of black Teflon. "Carry on, gentlemen."

Tulane Stadium late on the eve of the Super Bowl was lit and quiet. The stadium's great spaces seemed to suck up the small noises of the search. Fog rolling off the Mississippi River a mile away swirled under the banks of floodlights.

Kabakov and Moshevsky stood at the top of the stands, their cigars glowing bright in the shadowed press box. They had been silent for half an hour.

"They could still pack it in, some of it," Moshevsky said finally. "Under their clothes. If they weren't carrying batteries or sidearms it wouldn't show on the metal detectors."

"No."

"Even if there are only two of them, it would be enough to make a big mess."

Kabakov said nothing.

"There's nothing we could do about that," Moshevsky said. Kabakov's cigar brightened in a series of angry puffs. Moshevsky decided to shut up.

"Tomorrow I want you with the backup team on the west side," Kabakov said. "I've spoken to Renfro. They'll expect you."

"Yes, sir."

"If they come with a truck, get in the back fast and get the detonators out. Each team has a man assigned to do that, but see to it yourself as well."

"If the back is canvas, it might be good to cut through the side going in. A grenade could be wired to the tailgate."

Kabakov nodded. "Mention that to the team leader as soon as you form up. Rachel is letting out the seams in a flak jacket for you. I don't like them either, but I want you to have it on. If shooting starts, you'd better look like the rest of them."

"Yes, sir."

"Corley will pick you up at 8:45. If you are in the Hotsy-Totsy Club after 1 A.M. tonight, I'll know it."

"Yes, sir."

Midnight in New Orleans, the neon lights on Bourbon Street smeared on the misty air. The Aldrich blimp hung over the Mississippi River Bridge, above the fog, Farley at the controls. Great letters rippled down the airship's sides in lights. "DON'T FORGET, HIRE THE VET."

In a room two floors above Farley's at the Fairmont Hotel, Dahlia Iyad shook down a thermometer and put it in Michael Lander's mouth. Lander had been exhausted by the trip from New Jersey. In order to avoid New Orleans International Airport, where Dahlia might be recognized, they had flown to Baton Rouge and come to New Orleans in a rented car with Lander stretched out on the back seat. Now he was pale, but his eyes were clear. She checked the thermometer. Normal.

"You'd better go see about the truck," he said.

"It's there or it's not, Michael. If you want me to check it, of course I will, but the less I'm seen on the street—"

"You're right. It's there or it's not. Is my uniform all right?"

"I hung it up. It looks fine."

She ordered hot milk from room service and gave it to Lander with a mild sedative. In half an hour, he dropped off to sleep. Dahlia Iyad did not sleep. In Lander's weakened condition, she must fly with him tomorrow on the bomb run, even if it meant leaving a section of the nacelle behind. She could help him with the elevator wheel, and she could handle the detonation. It was necessary.

Knowing that she would die tomorrow, she wept quietly for a half-hour, wept for herself. And then, deliberately, she summoned the painful memories of the refugee camp. She went through her mother's final agonies, the thin woman, old at 35, writhing in the ragged tent. Dahlia was ten, and she could do nothing but keep the flies off her mother's face. There were so many suffering. Her own life was nothing, nothing. Soon she was calm again, but she did not sleep.

At the Royal Orleans, Rachel Bauman sat at the dresser brushing her hair. Kabakov lay on the bed, smoking and watching her. He liked to watch the light shimmer on her hair as she brushed it. He liked the tiny hollows that appeared along her spine as she arched her back and shook her hair over her shoulders.

"How long will you stay after tomorrow, David?" She was watching him in the mirror.

"Until we get the plastic."

"What about the other two, the woman and the American?"

"I don't know. They'll get the woman eventually. She can't do a great deal without the plastic. When we get it, I'll have to take Fasil back to stand trial for Munich."

She wasn't looking at him anymore.

"Rachel?"

"Yes."

"Israel needs psychiatrists, you know? You'd be astounded at the number of crazy Jews. Christians, too, in the summertime. I know an Arab in Jerusalem who sells them fragments of the True Cross, which he obtains by breaking up—"

"We'll have to talk about that when you are not so distracted, and you can be more explicit."

"We'll talk about it at Antoine's tomorrow night. Now that's enough talking and hairbrushing, or shall I be more explicit?"

The lights were out in the rooms at the Royal Orleans and the Fairmont. And around them both was the old city. New Orleans has seen it all before.

CHAPTER 26

On Sunday, January 12, the red sun rising silhouetted the New Orleans skyline in fire. Michael Lander woke early. He had been dreaming of the whales, and for a moment he could not remember where he was. Then he remembered, totally and all at once. Dahlia was in a chair, her head back, watching him through half-closed eyes.

He rose carefully and went to the window. Streaks of pink and gold lay along the east-west streets. Above the ground mist he could see the lightening sky. "It's going to be clear," he said. He dialed the airport weather service. A northeast wind at 15 knots, gusting to 20. That was good. A tailwind from the Lakefront Airport to the stadium. Wide open, he could get better than 60 knots out of the blimp.

"Can you rest a little longer, Michael?"

He was pale. She knew that he did not have much strength. Perhaps he would have enough.

The blimp was always airborne at least an hour before game time to allow the TV technicians to make final adjustments and to let the fans see the airship as they arrived. Lander would have to fly that long before he came back for the bomb.

"I'll rest," he said. "The flight crew call will be

at noon. Farley flew last night, so he'll sleep in, but he'll be leaving his room well before noon to eat."

"I know, Michael. I'll take care of it."

"I'd feel better if you had a gun." They could not risk carrying firearms on the flight to Baton Rouge. The small arms were in the truck with the explosive.

"It's all right. I can do it all right. You can depend on me."

"I know it," he said. "I can depend on you."

Corley, Kabakov, and Moshevsky set out for the stadium at 9 A.M. The streets around the Royal Orleans were filled with people, pale from last night's celebrations, wandering the French Quarter with their hangovers out of some sense of duty, a grim determination to see the sights. Paper cups and bar napkins blew down Bourbon Street in the damp wind.

Corley had to drive slowly until they were clear of the Quarter. He was irritable. He had neglected to get himself a hotel reservation while the getting was good, and he had slept badly in an FBI agent's guest room. The breakfast he had been served by the agent's wife was pointedly light. Kabakov appeared to have slept and breakfasted well, adding to Corley's irritation. He was further annoyed by the smell of a cantaloupe Moshevsky was eating in the back of the car.

Kabakov shifted in his seat. He clanked against the door handle.

"What the hell was that?"

"My dentures are loose," Kabakov said.

"Very funny."

Kabakov flipped back his coat, revealing the stubby barrel of the Uzi submachine gun slung under his arm.

"What's Moshevsky carrying, a bazooka?"

"I have a cantaloupe launcher," came the voice from the back seat.

Corley shrugged his shoulders. He could not understand Moshevsky easily at the best of times and not at all when his mouth was full.

They arrived at the stadium at 9:30. The streets

that would not be used as the stadium filled were already blocked. The vehicles and barriers that would seal off the stadium when the game began were in place on the grass beside the main traffic arteries. Ten ambulances were parked close to the southeast gate. Only outbound emergency vehicles would be allowed through the blockade. Secret servicemen were already in place on the roofs along Audubon Avenue overlooking the track where the President's helicopter would land.

They were as ready as they could get.

It was curious to see sandbag emplacements beside the quiet streets. Some of the FBI agents were reminded of the Ole Miss campus in 1963.

At 9 A.M., Dahlia Iyad called room service in the Fairmont and ordered three breakfasts to be delivered to the room. While she was waiting for them, she took a pair of long scissors and a roll of friction tape from her bag. She removed the screw holding the scissors together and put a slender, three-inch bolt through the screw hole in one half of the scissors, binding it in place with the tape. Then she taped the entire handle of the scissor and slipped it up her sleeve.

The breakfasts arrived at 9:20 A.M.

"You go ahead, Michael, while it's hot," Dahlia said. "I'll be back in a minute." She took a breakfast tray to the elevator and descended two floors.

Farley's voice sounded sleepy as he answered her knock.

"Mr. Farley?"

"Yes."

"Your breakfast."

"I didn't order any breakfast."

"Compliments of the hotel. The whole crew is getting them. I'll take it away if you don't want it."

"No, I'll take it. Just a minute."

Farley, hair tousled and wearing only his trousers, let her into the room. If someone had been passing in the hall they might have heard the beginning of a scream, abruptly cut off. A minute later, Dahlia slipped outside again. She placed the "Do Not Disturb" sign on the doorknob and went back upstairs to breakfast.

There was one more piece of business to be settled. Dahlia waited until she and Lander had finished eating. They were lying on the bed together. She was holding Lander's mangled hand.

"Michael, you know I want very much to fly with you. Don't you think it would be better?"

"I can do it. There's no need."

"I want to help you. I want to be with you. I want to see it."

"You wouldn't see much. You'll hear it wherever you go from the airport."

"I'd never get out of the airport anyway, Michael. You know the weight won't make any difference now. It's 70 degrees outside and the aircraft has been standing in the sun all morning. Of course if you can't get it up—"

"I can get it up. We'll have superheat."

"May I, Michael? We've come a long way."

He rolled over and looked into her face. There were red pillow marks on his cheek. "You'll have to get the shot bags out of the back of the gondola fast. The ones beneath the back seat. We can trim it up when we're off. You can go."

She held him very close and they did not talk anymore.

At 11:30 Lander rose and Dahlia helped him dress. His cheeks were hollow, but the tanning lotion she had used on his face helped disguise the pallor. At 11:50 she took a syringe of Novacaine from her medical kit. She rolled up Lander's sleeve and deadened a small patch on his forearm. Then she took out another, smaller hypodermic syringe. It was a flexible plastic squeeze tube with a needle attached, and it was filled with a 30 milligram solution of Ritalin.

"You may feel talkative after you use this, Michael. Very up. You'll have to compensate for that. Don't use it unless you feel yourself losing strength."

"All right, just put it on."

She inserted the needle in the deadened patch on his forearm and taped the small syringe firmly in place, flat on his arm. On either side of the squeeze tube was a short length of pencil to keep the tube from being squeezed by accident. "Just feel through your sleeve and press the tube with your thumb when you need it."

"I know, I know."

She kissed him on the forehead. "If I shouldn't make it to the airport with the truck, if they are waiting for me—"

"I'll just drop the blimp into the stadium," he said. "It will mash quite a few. But don't think about the bad possibilities. We've been lucky so far, right?"

"You have been very clever so far."

"I'll see you at the airport at 2:15."

She walked him to the elevator, and then she returned to the room and sat on the bed. It was not yet time to go for the truck.

Lander spotted the blimp crew standing near the desk in the lobby. There was Simmons, Farley's co-pilot, and two network cameramen. He walked over, exerting himself to put on a brisk manner.

I'll rest in the bus, he thought.

"My God, it's Mike," Simmons said. "I thought you were out sick. Where's Farley? We called his room. We were waiting for him."

"Farley had a rough night. Some drunk girl stuck her finger in his eye."

"Jesus."

"He's all right, but he's getting it looked at. I fly today."

"When did you get in?"

"This morning. That bastard Farley called me at 4 A.M. Let's go, we're late now."

"You don't look too good, Mike."

"I look better than you do. Let's go."

At the Lakefront Airport gate, the driver could not find his vehicle pass and they all had to show their credentials. Three squad cars were parked near the tower.

The blimp, 225 feet of silver, red, and blue, rested in a grassy triangle between the runways. Unlike the airplanes squatting on the ground before the hangars, the airship gave the impression of flight even when at rest. Poised lightly on its single wheel, nose against the mooring mast, it pointed to the northeast like a giant weathervane. Near it were the big bus that transported the ground crew and the tractor-trailer that housed the mobile maintenance shop. The vehicles and the men were dwarfed by the silver airship.

Vickers, the crew chief, wiped his hands on a rag. "Glad you're back, Captain Lander. She's ready."

"Thank you." Lander began the traditional walk-around inspection. Everything was in order, as he knew it would be. The blimp was clean. He had always liked the cleanliness of the blimp. "You guys ready?" he called.

Lander and Simmons ran down the rest of the preflight checklist in the gondola.

Vickers was berating the two TV cameramen. "Captain Video, will you and your assistant kindly get your asses in that gondola so we can weigh off?"

The ground crew took hold of the handrail around the gondola and bounced the airship on its landing wheel. Vickers removed several of the 25-pound bags of shot that hung from the rail. The crew bounced the airship again.

"She's just a hair heavy. That's good." Vickers liked the blimp to take off heavy; fuel consumption would lighten it later.

"Where are the Cokes? Have we got the Cokes?" Simmons said. He thought they would be airborne for at least three hours, possibly longer. "Yeah, here they are."

"Take it, Simmons," Lander said.

"Okay." Simmons slid into the single pilot's seat on the left side of the gondola. He waved through the windshield. The crewmen at the mooring mast tripped the release, and eight men on the nose ropes pulled the blimp around. "Here we go." Simmons rolled back the elevator wheel, pushed in the throttles, and the great airship rose at a steep angle.

Lander leaned back in the passenger seat beside the pilot. The flight to the stadium, with the tailwind, took nine and a half minutes. Lander figured that, wide open, it could be done in a shade over seven minutes, if the wind held.

Beneath them, a solid stream of traffic jammed the expressway near the Tulane exit.

"Some of those people are gonna miss the kickoff," Simmons said.

"Yeah, I expect so," Lander said. They would all miss half time, he thought. It was 1:10 P.M. He had almost an hour to wait.

Dahlia Iyad got out of the taxi near the Galvez Street wharf and walked quickly down the block toward the garage. The bomb was there, or it was not. The police were waiting or they were not. She had not noticed before how cracked and tilted the sidewalk was. She looked at the cracks as she walked along. A group of small children were playing stickball in the street. The batter, no more than three and a half feet tall, whistled at her as she went by.

A police car made the players scatter and passed Dahlia at 15 miles an hour. She turned her face away from it as though she were looking for an address. The squad car turned at the next corner. She fished in her purse for the keys and walked up the alley to the garage. Here were the locks. She opened them and slipped inside, closing the door behind her. It was semi-dark in the garage. A few shafts of sunshine came in through nailholes in the walls. The truck appeared undisturbed.

She climbed into the back and switched on the dim light. There was a thin film of dust on the nacelle. It was all right. If the place were staked out, they would never have let her get to the bomb. She changed into a pair of coveralls marked with the initials of the television network and stripped the vinyl panels off the sides of the truck, revealing the network emblem in bright colors.

She found the checklist taped to the nacelle. She read it over quickly. First the detonators. She removed them from their packing and, reaching into the middle of the nacelle, she slid them into place, one in the exact center of each side of the charge. The wires from the detonators plugged into the wiring harness with its lead-in to the airship's power supply. Now the fuse and its detonator were plugged into place.

She cut all the rope lashings except two. Check the bag for Lander. One .38 caliber revolver with silencer, one pair of cable cutters, both in a paper sack. Her Schmeisser machine pistol with six extra clips and an AK-47 automatic rifle with clips were in a duffle bag.

Getting out, she laid the Schmeisser on the floor of the truck cab and covered it with a blanket. There was dust on the truck seat. She took a handkerchief from her purse and wiped it carefully. She tucked her hair into a Big Apple cap.

1:50. Time to go. She swung open the garage doors and drove outside, blinking in the sunshine, and left the truck idling as she closed the garage doors.

Driving toward the airport, she had an odd, happy feeling of falling, falling.

Kabakov watched from the command post at the stadium as the river of people poured in through the southeast gate. They were so well dressed and well fed, unaware of the trouble they were causing him.

There was some grumbling when lines formed at the metal detectors, and louder complaints when now and then a fan was asked to dump the contents of his pockets in a plastic dishpan. Standing with Kabakov were the members of the east side trouble squad, ten men in flak jackets, heavily armed. He walked outside, away from the crackle of radios, and watched the stadium fill up. Already the bands were thumping away, the music becoming less distorted as more and more bodies baffled the echoes off the stands. By 1:45 most of the spectators were in their seats. The roadblocks closed.

Eight hundred feet above the stadium, the TV crew in the blimp was conferring by radio with the director in the big television van parked behind the stands. The "NBS Sports Spectacular" was to open with a shot of the stadium from the blimp, with the network logo and the title superimposed on it. In the van, facing 12 television screens, the director was not satisfied.

"Hey, Simmons," the cameraman said, "now he wants it from the other end, the north end with Tulane in the background, can you do that?"

"You bet." The blimp wheeled majestically northward.

"Okay, that's good, that's good." The cameraman had it nicely framed, the bright green field, solidly banked with 84,000 people, the stadium wreathed with flags that snapped in the wind.

Lander could see the police helicopter darting like a dragonfly around the perimeter of the stadium.

"Tower to Nora One Zero."

Simmons picked up the microphone. "Nora One Zero, go ahead."

"Traffic in your area one mile northwest and approaching," the air controller said. "Give him plenty of room."

"Roger. I see him. Nora One Zero out."

Simmons pointed and Lander saw a military helicopter approaching at 600 feet. "It's the Prez. Take off your hat," Simmons said. He wheeled the airship away from the north end of the stadium.

Lander watched as the landing marker was deployed on the track.

"They want a shot of the arrival," the cameraman's assistant said. "Can you get us broadside to him?"

"That's fine," the cameraman said. Through his long lens, 86 million people saw the President's helicopter touch down. The President stepped out and walked quickly into the stadium and out of sight.

In the TV van, the director snapped "Take Two." Across the country and around the world, the audience saw the President striding along the sideline to his box.

Looking down, Lander could see him again now, a husky blond figure in a knot of men, his arms raised to the crowd and the crowd rising to their feet in a wave as he passed.

Kabakov heard the roar that greeted the President. He had never seen the man, and he was curious. He restrained the impulse to go and look at him. His place was here, near the command post, where he would be instantly alerted to trouble.

"I'll take it, Simmons, you watch the kickoff," Lander said. They switched places. Lander was tired already, and the elevator wheel seemed heavy under his hand.

On the field, they were "re-enacting the toss" for the benefit of the television audience. Now the teams were lined up for the kickoff.

Lander glanced at Simmons. His head was out the side window. Lander reached forward and pushed the fuel mixture lever for the port engine. He made the mixture just lean enough to make the engine overheat.

In minutes the temperature gauge was well into the red. Lander eased the fuel mixture back to normal. "Gentlemen, we've got a little problem." Lander had Simmons' instant attention. He tapped the temperature gauge.

"Now what the hell!" Simmons said. He climbed across the gondola and peered at the port engine over the shoulders of the TV crew. "She's not streaming any oil."

"What?" the cameraman said.

"Port engine's hot. Let me get past you here." He reached into the rear compartment and brought out a fire extinguisher.

"Hey, it's not burning, is it?" The cameraman and his assistant were very serious, as Lander knew they would be.

"No, hell no," Simmons said. "We have to get the extinguisher out, it's SOP."

Lander feathered the engine. He was heading away from the stadium now, to the northeast, to the airfield. "We'll let Vickers take a look at it," he said.

"Did you call him already?"

"While you were in the back." Lander had mumbled into his microphone all right, but he had not pressed the transmit button.

He was following U.S. 10, the Superdome below him on the right and the fairgrounds with its oval track on the left. Bucking the headwind on a single engine was slow going. All the better coming back, Lander thought. He was over the Pontchartrain Golf Course now, and he could see the airfield spread out in front of him. There was the truck, approaching the airport gate. Dahlia had made it.

From the cab of the truck, Dahlia could see the airship coming. She was a few seconds early. There was a policeman at the gate. She held the blue vehicle pass out the window and he waved her through. She cruised slowly along the road flanking the field.

The ground crew saw the airship now, and they stirred around the bus and the tractor-trailer. Lander wanted them to be in a hurry. At 300 feet he thumbed the button on his microphone. "All right, I'm coming in 175 heavy, give it plenty of room."

"Nora One Zero, what's up? Why didn't you say you were coming, Mike?" It was Vickers' voice.

"I did," Lander said. *Let him wonder.* The ground crew were running to their stations. "I'm coming to the mast crosswind and I want the wheel chocked. Don't let her swing to the wind, Vickers. I've got a small problem with the port engine, a *small* problem. It's nothing, but I want the port engine downwind from the ship. I *do not* want a flap. Do you understand?"

Vickers understood. Lander did not want the crash trucks howling down the field.

Dahlia Iyad waited to drive across the runway.

The tower was giving her a red light. She watched as the blimp touched down, bounced, touched again, the ground crew grabbing the ropes that trailed from the nose. They had it under control now.

The tower light flashed green. She drove across the runway and parked behind the tractor-trailer, out of sight of the crew milling around the blimp. In a second the tailgate was down, the ramp in place. She grabbed the paper bag containing the gun and the cable cutters and ran around the tractor-trailer to the blimp. The crew paid no attention to her. Vickers opened the cowling on the port engine. Dahlia passed the bag to Lander through the window of the gondola and ran back to her truck.

Lander turned to the TV crew. "Stretch your legs, it'll be a minute."

They scrambled out and he followed them.

Lander walked to the bus and immediately returned to the blimp. "Hey, Vickers, Lakehurst is on the horn for you."

"Oh, my ass—All right, Frankie, take a look in here, but don't change nothin' until I get back." He trotted toward the bus. Lander went in behind him. Vickers had just picked up the radio telephone when Lander shot him in the back of the head. Now the ground crew had no leader. As Lander stepped off the bus he heard the putt-putt of the forklift. Dahlia was in the saddle, swinging around the rear of the tractor-trailer. The crew, puzzled at the sight of the big nacelle, made room for the forklift. She eased forward, sliding the long nacelle under the gondola. She raised the fork six inches and it was in place.

"What's going on, what's this?" the man at the engine said. Dahlia ignored him. She flipped the two front clamps around the handrail. Four more to go.

"Vickers said get the shot bags off," Lander yelled.

"He said *what?*"

"Get the shot bags off. Move it!"

"What is this, Mike? I never saw this."

"Vickers will explain it. TV time costs $175,000 a minute, now get your ass in gear. The network wants this thing." Two crewmen unclipped the shot bags as Dahlia finished fastening the nacelle. She backed the forklift away. The crew was confused. Something was wrong. This big nacelle with its network markings had never been tested on the blimp.

Lander went to the port engine and looked in. Nothing had been removed. He shut the cowling.

Here came the TV cameraman. "NBS? What *is* that thing? That's not ours—"

"The director will explain it, call him from the bus." Lander climbed into his seat and started the engines. The crew skipped back, startled. Dahlia was already inside the gondola with the cable cutters. No time to unscrew anything. The TV equipment had to go before the blimp would fly.

The cameraman saw her cutting the equipment loose. "Hey! Don't do that." He scrambled into the gondola. Lander turned in his seat and shot the cameraman in the back. A startled crewman's face in the door. The men closest to the blimp were backing away now. Dahlia unclamped the camera.

"Chock and mast now!" Lander yelled.

Dahlia jumped to the ground, she had the Schmeisser out. The crewmen were backing away, some of them turning to run. She pulled the chock away from the wheel and, as the blimp swung to the wind, she ran to the mast and uncoupled it. The nose boom must come out of the socket in the mast. It must. The blimp was swinging. The men had fled the nose ropes. The wind would do it, would twist the blimp free. She heard a siren. A squad car was screaming across the runway.

The nose was free, but the blimp was still weighted with the body of the cameraman and the TV equipment. She swung into the gondola. The transmitter went first, smashing to the ground. The camera followed it.

The squad car was coming head on with the blimp, its lights flashing. Lander slammed the throttles forward and the great ship started to roll. Dahlia was struggling with the body of the cameraman. His leg was under Lander's seat. The blimp bounced once and settled again. It reared like a prehistoric animal. The squad car was 40 yards away, its doors opening. Lander dumped most of his fuel. The blimp rose heavily.

Dahlia leaned out of the gondola and fired her Schmeisser at the squad car, star fractures appearing across its windshield, the blimp rising, a policeman out of the car, blood on his shirt, drawing his gun, looking up into her face as the blimp passed over. A blast from the machine pistol cut him down, and Dahlia kicked the cameraman's body out the door to fall spread-eagled on the hood of the patrol car. The blimp surged upward. Other squad cars were coming now, growing smaller beneath them, their doors opening. She heard a "thock" against the gas bag. They were firing. She aimed a burst at the nearest police car, saw dust kick up around it. Lander had the blimp at 50 degrees, engines screaming. Up and up and out of pistol range.

The fuse and the wires! Dahlia lay on the bloody floor of the gondola, and hanging outside she could reach them.

Lander was nodding at the controls, near collapse. She reached over his shoulder and pressed the syringe beneath his sleeve. In a second his head was up again.

He checked the cabin light switch. It was off. "Hook it up."

She pried the cover off the cabin light, removed the bulb and plugged in the wires to the bomb. The fuse, to be used if the electrical system failed, must be secured around a seat bracket near the rear of the gondola. Dahlia had trouble tying the knot as the fuse became slippery with the cameraman's blood.

The airspeed indicator said 60 knots. They would be at the Super Bowl in six minutes.

Corley and Kabakov sprinted to Corley's car at the first confused report of shooting at the airfield. They were howling up Interstate 10 when the report was augmented.

"Unknown persons shooting from the Aldrich

blimp," the radio said. "Two officers down. Ground crew advises a device is attached to the aircraft."

"They got the blimp!" Corley said, pounding the seat beside him. "That's your other pilot." They could see the airship over the skyline now, growing larger by the second. Corley was on the radio to the stadium. "Get the President out!" he was yelling.

Kabakov fought the rage and frustration, the shock, the impossibility of it. He was caught, helpless, on the expressway between the stadium and the airport. He must think, must think, must think. They were passing the Superdome now. Then he was shaking Corley's shoulder. "Jackson," Kabakov said. "Lamar Jackson. The chopper. Drive this son of a bitch."

They were past the exit ramp, and Corley turned across three lanes of traffic, tires smoking, and shot the wrong way down the entrance ramp, a car was coming, big in their faces, swerving over, a rocking sideswipe and they were down into Howard Avenue beside the Superdome. A screaming turn around the huge building and they slammed to a stop. Kabakov ran to the pad, startling the stakeout team still on duty.

Jackson was descending from the roof to pick up a bundle of conduit. Kabakov ran to the loadmaster, a man he did not know.

"Get him down. Get him down."

The blimp was almost even with the Superdome now, moving fast just out of range. It was two miles from the packed stadium.

Corley came from the car. He had left the trunk open. He was carrying an M-16 automatic rifle.

The chopper settled down, Kabakov ducking as he ran in under the rotor. He scrambled up to the cockpit window. Jackson put his hand behind his ear.

"They got the Aldrich blimp," Kabakov was pointing upward. "We've got to go up. We've got to go up."

Jackson looked up at the blimp. He swallowed. There was a strange, set expression in his face. "Are you hijacking me?"

"I'm asking you. Please."

Jackson closed his eyes for a second. "Get in. Get the belly man out. I won't be responsible for him."

Kabakov and Corley pulled out the startled belly man and climbed inside the cargo bay. The helicopter leaped into the air with a great blatting of its blades. Kabakov went forward and pushed up the empty copilot's seat.

"We can—"

"Listen," Jackson said. "Are you gonna bust 'em or talk to them?"

"Bust 'em."

"All right. If we can catch them, I'll come in above them, they can't see above them in that thing. You gonna shoot the gas bag? No time for it to leak much."

Kabakov shook his head. "They might set it off on the way down. We'll try to knock out the gondola."

Jackson nodded. "I'll come in above them. When you're ready, I'll drop down beside them. This thing won't take a lot of hits and fly. You be ready. Talk to me on the headset."

The helicopter was doing 110 knots, gaining fast, but the blimp had a big lead. It would be very close.

"If we knock out the pilot, the wind will still carry it over the stadium," Jackson said.

"What about the hook? Could we hold him with the hook, pull him somewhere?"

"How could we hook on? The damn thing is slick. We can try if there's time—hey, there go the cops."

Ahead of them they could see the police helicopter rising to meet the blimp.

"Not from below," Jackson was yelling. "Don't get close—" Even as he spoke the little police helicopter staggered under a blast of gunfire and fell off to the side, its rotor flailing wildly, and plunged downward.

Jackson could see the movements of the airship's rudder as the great fin passed under him. He was over the blimp and the stadium was sliding beneath them.

Time for one pass. Kabakov and Corley braced themselves in the fuselage door.

Lander felt the rotor blast on the blimp's skin, heard the helicopter engine. He touched Dahlia and jerked his thumb upward. "Get me ten more seconds," he said.

She put a fresh clip in the Schmeisser.

Jackson's voice in Kabakov's earphones, "Hang on."

The helicopter dropped in a stomach-lifting swoop down the blimp's right side. Kabakov heard the first bullets hit the belly of the helicopter and then he and Corley were firing, hot shell casings spattering from the automatic weapons, glass flying from the gondola. Metal was ringing all around Kabakov. The helicopter lurched and rose. Corley was hit, blood spreading on his trousers at the thigh.

Jackson, his forehead slashed by the glass in his riddled cockpit, mopped away the blood that had poured into his eyes.

All the windows were out of the gondola and the instrument panel was shattered, sparks flying. Dahlia lay on the floor, she did not move.

Lander, hit in the shoulder and the leg, saw the blimp losing altitude. The airship was sinking, but they could still clear the stadium wall. It was coming, it was under him, and a floor of faces was looking up. He had his hand on the firing switch. Now. He flipped the switch. Nothing. The backup switch. Nothing. The circuits were blasted away. The fuse. He dragged himself out of the pilot's seat, his lighter in his hand, and used his good arm and leg to crawl toward the fuse at the rear of the gondola, as the blimp drifted between the solid banks of people.

The hook trailed beneath the helicopter on a 30-foot cable. Jackson dropped until the hook slipped over the blimp's slick skin. The only opening was the space between the rudder and the fin beneath the rudder hinge. Kabakov was coaching Jackson, and they got it close, close, but the hook was too thick.

They were stampeding in the stadium. Kabakov

looked around him desperately and he saw, coiled in a clip on the wall, a length of three-quarter-inch nylon rope with a snap shackle in each end. In the half second he stared at it, he knew with an awful certainty what he had to do.

From the ground, Moshevsky watched, his eyes bulging, fists clenched as the figure appeared, sliding spiderlike down the cable beneath the helicopter. He snatched the field glasses from an agent beside him, but he knew before he looked. It was Kabakov. He could see the rotor blast tearing at Kabakov as he slid down the greasy cable. A rope was tied around his waist. They were over Moshevsky now. Straining back to see, Moshevsky fell on his rear and never stopped watching.

Kabakov had his foot in the hook. Corley's face was visible in the opening in the belly of the chopper. He was talking in the headset. The hook slid down, Kabakov was beside the fin, no! The fin was rising, swinging. It hit Kabakov and knocked him away, he was swinging back, passing the length of rope between the rudder and the fin, beneath the top rudder hinge, snapping it in a loop through the hook, one arm waving, and the helicopter strained upward, the cable hardening along Kabakov's body like a steel bar.

Lander, crawling along the blood-slick floor of the gondola toward the fuse, felt the floor tilt sharply. He was sliding and scrabbled for a handhold on the floor.

The helicopter clawed the air. The tail of the blimp was up at 50 degrees now, the nose bumping against the football field. The spectators screaming, running, the exits jammed as they fought to get out. Lander could hear their cries all around him. He strained toward the fuse, lighter in hand.

The nose of the blimp dragged up the stands, the crowd scattering before it. It caught on the flagpoles at the top of the stadium, and lurched over, clear and moving over the houses toward the river, the helicopter's engine screaming. Corley, looking down, could see Kabakov standing on the fin, holding onto the cable.

"We'll make the river, we'll make the river," Jackson said over and over, as the temperature gauge climbed into the red. His thumb was poised over the red drop button.

Lander heaved himself the final foot up the slanting floor and thumbed his lighter.

Moshevsky tore his way to the top of the stands. The helicopter, the blimp, the man standing on the fin, hung over the river for one instant, fixed forever in Moshevsky's mind, and then they were gone in a blinding flash of light and a Doomsday crack that flattened him on the shuddering stands. Shrapnel slashed the trees beside the river as the blast uprooted them, and the water, whipped to foam, was blown out in a great basin that filled again with a roar of its own, the water rising in a mountainous cone into the smoke. And seconds later, far downriver, spent shrapnel pocked the water like hail and rattled off the iron hulls of ships.

Miles away, finishing a late lunch at the Top of the Mart overlooking the city, Rachel saw the flash. She rose, and then the tall building trembled, the windows shattered, and she was on her back, glass still falling and, looking up at the underside of the table, she knew. She struggled to her feet. A woman sat on the floor beside her, mouth hanging open.

Rachel looked at her. "He's dead," Rachel said.

The final casualty list totaled 512. At the stadium 14 were trampled to death in the exits, 52 suffered fractures in the struggle to escape, and the rest had cuts and bruises. Among those cut and bruised was the President of the United States. His injuries were suffered when 10 Secret Service men piled on top of him. In the town, 116 persons received minor injuries from flying glass, as windows were blasted in.

At noon on the following day, Rachel Bauman and Robert Moshevsky stood on a small pier on the north bank of the Mississippi River. They had been there for hours, watching the police boats drag the bottom. The dragging had gone on all night. In the first few hours, the grapnels had brought up a few charred pieces of metal from the helicopter. Since then, there was nothing.

The pier on which they stood was riddled and splintered with shrapnel. A large dead catfish bumped against it in the current. The fish was punched full of holes.

Moshevsky remained impassive. His eyes never left the police boats. Beside him on the pier was his canvas suitcase, for in three hours he would take Muhammad Fasil back to Israel to stand trial for the Munich massacre. The El Al jet that was coming for them also contained 14 Israeli commandos. It was felt that they would provide a suitable buffer between Moshevsky and his prisoner on the long flight home.

Rachel's face was swollen, and her eyes were red and dry. She had cried herself out on the bed in the Royal Orleans, fingers locked in a shirt of Kabakov's that reeked of his cigars.

The wind was cold off the river. Moshevsky put his jacket around Rachel. It hung below her knees.

Finally, the lead boat sounded a single long blast. The police fleet pulled in their empty grapnels and started downstream. Now there was only the river, moving in a solid piece toward the sea. Rachel heard a strange, strangled sound from Moshevsky, and he turned his face away. She pressed her cheek against his chest and reached her arms as far around him as they would go and patted him, feeling the hot tears falling in her hair. Then she took his hand and led him up the bank as she would lead a child.

ABOUT THE AUTHOR

THOMAS HARRIS was born in Tennessee, grew up in Mississippi and received his BA from Baylor University. After graduating from college, he went to work for the Waco (Texas) *Tribune-Herald*, working his way up from copy boy to police reporter. While with the paper, he began selling free-lance articles to various magazines and then moved to New York, joining the Associated Press as a reporter and deskman. While with the AP, he and fellow reporters Sam Maull and Dick Riley conceived and researched the idea for BLACK SUNDAY before Harris resigned his job to write the book.

RELAX!
SIT DOWN
and Catch Up On Your Reading!